THE BIG BOOK OF ODIA LITERATURE

THE BIG BOOK OF ODIA LITERATURE

Edited by **Manu Dash**

PENGUIN BOOKS
An imprint of Penguin Random House

PENGUIN BOOKS

Penguin Books is an imprint of the Penguin Random House group of companies whose addresses can be found at global.penguinrandomhouse.com

Published by Penguin Random House India Pvt. Ltd
4th Floor, Capital Tower 1, MG Road,
Gurugram 122 002, Haryana, India

Penguin Random House India

First published in Penguin Books by Penguin Random House India 2024

10 9 8 7 6 5 4 3 2 1

ISBN 9780143463344

Typeset in Sabon by MAP Systems, Bengaluru, India
Printed at Replika Press Pvt. Ltd, India

www.penguin.co.in

MIX
Paper | Supporting responsible forestry
FSC™ C016779

For the peace-loving and culturally rich Odia people within and outside the state,

and

for my parents, Nilamani Dash and the late Bauribandhu Dash

Contents

Section 2

Plays

Section 3

Short Stories

Editor's Note

1

The Big Book of Odia Literature showcases the richness and variety of Odia literature through a representative selection of poems, short stories, essays and plays written in various parts of the eastern Indian state of Odisha since the tenth century.

Like any other language across the globe, Odia witnessed the emergence of poetry first. Though few saint and mystic poets like Kanhupa wrote his poems in the Sandha language, for almost 600 years, it was Sarala Dasa who was identified as the first poet in Odia, for his sustained and masterly composition of epics like the Mahabharata, the Bilanka Ramayana and the Chandi Purana in the fifteenth century. The other key literary genres such as fiction, essay and play came into being only in the last quarter of the nineteenth century. Fakir Mohan Senapati published his first story, 'Rebati' in 1898, heralding the birth of fiction writing in the Odia language. 'Rebati' is considered to be the first story available in Odia literature. The first essay in Odia titled 'Mandira Manankare Kutsita Murti [Vulgar Idols Inside the Temples]' was also written by Senapati in 1873, twenty-five years before the rise of fiction in Odia. The first play, *Babaji*, was written and performed by Jagan Mohan Lal in 1877. Looking back, we find the Odia short story to be about 125 years old, the essay about 150 years old and the play nearly 146 years old. Odia poetry, mainly written by Sarala Dasa, is approximately 600 years old.

This volume curates writings culled from the above four genres that have borne witness to the journey of Odia literature from its inception to the contemporary period. It includes 105 poems, thirty short stories, twenty-three essays, one short play and one excerpt from a long play. Through these selections, the readers can glimpse the literary and sociocultural shifts that took place over these centuries.

The languages from which selections in this anthology are taken include Odia, Sambalpuri-Kosali, Sanskrit, Sandha, Santali, Kui, Oraon, Mundari, Kharia, Sadri, Kondha, Paraja and English. The anthology also includes pieces originally written in English, either by Odisha-based writers or by non-Odia writers with an interest in Odia literature and culture.

2

Odia is a language as per the Eighth Schedule of the Constitution of India. Around 35–40 million people in Odisha and adjoining areas—West Bengal, Jharkhand, Andhra Pradesh and Chhattisgarh—speak and use the Odia language, which is also one of the six classical languages of India.

The Odia language and script have evolved over a long period of time and in several stages: a) from word of mouth, b) stone and rock inscriptions, c) *pothi* or palm leaf, d) printed and e) electronic medium.

Let me start from the beginning.

Initially, the source and genesis of the Odia language was Sanskrit, which is known as an Indo-Aryan language. The latter was divided into three major categories: ancient Indo-Aryan language (1500–500 BCE), medieval Indo-Aryan language (500 BCE–1000 CE) and modern Indo-Aryan language (1000 CE onwards). The ancient Indo-Aryan language was based on Vedic Sanskrit, but the medieval Indo-Aryan language evolved from the Sanskrit spoken by the people and was again divided into three more levels. The first level was Pali (500–200 BCE), the second level was Prakrit (200 BCE–500 CE), and the third level was derived from that part of the Sanskrit language termed *Apabhramsa* (500–1000 CE).

Though it is difficult to ascertain how ancient the language really is, a broad classification can be made of the Indo-Aryan or Prakrit into four categories: Maharashtri, Shauraseni, Magadhi and Ardhamagadhi.[1]

Maharashtri Prakrit was spoken until 875 CE and was the official language of the Satavahana dynasty. Shauraseni Prakrit was the chief language used in drama in medieval northern India. The Magadhi Prakrit was an Indo–Aryan language spoken in the states of Bihar, Jharkhand and West Bengal of eastern India, and in Terai of Nepal. Ardhamagadhi Prakrit was a middle Indo-Aryan language and is spoken in modern-day Bihar and Uttar Pradesh.

Odia language is a confluence of Indo-Aryan language, Dravidian and Austric languages that had developed in the seventh century CE. A few languages emerged from Magadhi Prakrit: Purvi, Paschimi, Uttari and Dakhini. Purvi Magadhi can be further subdivided into Uttari Purvi Magadhi and Dakhini Purvi Magadhi. While Bangla and Assamese evolved from Uttari Purvi Magadhi, Odia evolved from Dakhini Purvi Magadhi.

An oral history that spans centuries was recorded in stone inscriptions written in Brahmilipi during the Ashokan period in the third century BCE, which were found at Dhauligiri and Jaugarh. Another inscription, , written in the first century BCE during the rule of Kharavela, was discovered in Udayagiri near Khandagiri. These inscriptions have evolved over the years to become the modern-day script.[2]

The Brahmi script was used in this period by the Odia people. In later stages, these Brahmi scripts evolved further and were used as the Odia script. The inscriptions during the period of Ashoka and Kharavela were written in pure Pali and Brahmi script.[3] The Hitigumpha inscription was merely a seventeen-line inscription in the Prakrit language incised in Brahmi script in a cavern called Hathigumpha in Udayagiri hills. Scholars like Suniti Kumar Chatterji and Beni Madhab Baruah have corroborated this view.[4] The inscriptions on the rocks, and the prevalence of prose and poetry written between the sixth and fifteenth century CE prove the ancientness of Odia language eloquently. We find the use of Odia language in the inscription carved during the rule of Shailodbhaba (6–8 CE), Bhaumakar (8–10 CE) and the Ganga dynasty (11–15 CE). The writing of Dharmaraj Sumandal (569 CE), the copper plate of Madhaba Varma (619 CE), Ananta Devburma's Manjusa copper plate (10 CE) and second Vajrahasta Dev's rock edict (1051 CE) are some of the examples of this. The words *kumbhar* used in Madhab Varma's and *bhitaru* used in Anant Varma's copper plates are also glaring examples of the usage of Odia language.

From the fifth century BCE, writing on palm leaves became the popular means of expression among the Odia people. The *Charyapada*, a collection of mystical poems, sourced to the Vajrayana tradition of Buddhism from the tantric tradition in Assam, Bengal, Bihar and Odisha was said to be written on palm leaves. It is said to be the oldest collection of verses written in those languages. The language of *Charyapada* is akin to the ancient Odia language.

We move quickly over the next few hundred years to a critical moment that came with the advent of the British colonial rule in the region. Along with them came the printing press.

In 1837, two missionaries, Amos Sutton (1798–1854) and Charles Lacey (1798–1852), established a printing press in

Odisha for the very first time. In 1831, *Introductory Grammar of Oriya Language* was published by Amos Sutton and it happened to be the oldest publication available in the Odia language collection to date. He published the first volume of the Odia dictionary in 1841, and the next two volumes came out by 1843. It was published by Baptist Mission Church, Calcutta, thanks to the endeavour of missionary and non-Odia administrators.[5]

This changed the trajectory of Odia to give shape to what the Odia people use today by way of script.

There are mainly four characteristics in the Odia script: top curve, loop, tail and curve. According to Prof. Khageswar Mohapatra, there is a great deal of similarity between the Tibetan and Odia script.[6]

Even though a particular language is used in any country or state, some dialects are spoken side by side by its people. We know English is used in England, but the language used by the people in Scotland or Wales is different than the one used in Oxford. Likewise, the English used in Dublin, Ireland, is markedly different from the variety in use in London. Many Hindi-speaking people do not know what exactly the form of the Hindi language is. But the language Khariboli, used around Delhi and Meerut, is considered to be the standard Hindi language, though Hindi has many dialects like Brajabhasi, Bundelkhnadi, and Awadhi.

Odia is also not confined to Odisha. Many people in Bengal, Bihar, Jharkhand, Madhya Pradesh and Andhra Pradesh speak Odia. What we call 'Odia' in Odisha is called 'Udiya' in Bengal and Bihar.

It must also be remembered that Odisha has a vast population of tribal and forest-dwelling communities who speak their languages. Most of Odisha's landmass is covered with hills and forests. People of indigenous tribes such as the Munda, Kolha, Sabar and Kondha tribes in the north and the Kui, Kondha, Sabar, Gadba, Bonda and Paraja tribes in the south speak a variety of dialects as opined by scholars.[7]

When we look into the evolution of the Odia language from its inception to the present day, we find that it has come a long way with many changes and developments. What will be its form in the centuries to come? It is believed that it shall enter the age of 'language elaboration' and it would not be so easy to use this language. Thousands of new words may enter into the lexicon of our language. Some linguists believe that currently, people in our rural areas don't use more than 10,000–15,000 words to communicate with each other. But, in the coming century, more than 2 lakh words will impinge upon Odia, which will cause a wide communication gap between the illiterate and the educated. And there won't be any dictionary available in Odia language to understand those words.[8]

3

Before 1936, Odisha was an integral part of the Bihar province. It was the first state carved out in pre-independent India based on language, namely Odia. After losing its political identity completely in 1568, following the defeat of the last king Mukunda Dev (1559–1568 CE), Odisha had to wait for nearly three centuries before it gained some measure of recompense. This came in the shape of the formation of a politically separate state on 1 April 1936, thanks to efforts spearheaded by Madhusudan Das (1846–1934 CE), the chief architect of Odia nationalism.

After seventy-eight years, in 2014, the government of India recognized Odia as the sixth classical language of India based on its ancientness, making it stand at par with other classical languages of India: Tamil, Telugu, Sanskrit, Kannada and Malayalam.

4

The 2011 census reveals that Odisha has 22.84 per cent of tribal-speaking people, which is almost one-fourth of the population of the state and the third highest in the country. It has sixty-two tribes scattered across the state, and, with the exception of Santali, the people have no script and communicate orally. Besides this, Sambalpuri-Kosali is emerging as a distinct language spoken by the majority of the people of western Odisha. It has no separate script and uses the Odia script for communication.

5

Based on form, content, tone and texture, Odia poetry can be roughly classified as follows:

a) Mystic and Tantric poetry (950–1256 CE)
b) Ancient poetry (15 CE)
c) Sacred and Spiritual poetry (16–17 CE)
d) Medieval and Musical poetry (15–16 CE)
e) Modern poetry (17–18 CE)
f) Patriotic poetry (first half of 20 CE)
g) Socialist poetry (second quarter of 20 CE)
h) Romantic poetry (mid-20 CE)
i) Postmodernism poetry (20 CE)
j) Sociocultural poetry (1969–95)

A quick and brief elaboration will be in order here.

Mystic and Tantric poetry

There were twenty-three *siddhas*, saint poets, who had written *Charyapada* over 300 years (950–1256 CE) in eastern India. Among these poets, Kanhupa, Luipa and Sarahapa were from Odisha. There was a *guru–sishya*[i] tradition among the people

[i] Teacher–disciple.

of this sect. While collecting the ancient palm leaf manuscripts in Nepal, Mahamahopadhyay Haraprasad Shastri (1853–1931), a Sanskrit scholar, archivist and historian of Bengali literature, first discovered the rare *Charyapada* in 1907. He published it in a book form in 1916 as *Boudhagan O Doha* and claimed before Bangiya Sahitya Parisad that these *dohas* or poems were part of Bengali literature.[9] But in 1920, Bijaychandra Mazumdar (1861–1942), another Bengali scholar of repute, gave a different view, claiming that most of these saint poets belonged to Odisha.[10] He wrote an article in *Bangabani* magazine to prove his claim and later, Odia scholar Pandit Binayak Mishra took the cue from Mazumdar and reiterated the claim. In 1930, Gopalchandra Praharaj (1874–1945), a major Odia litterateur and linguist, and the compiler of the *Purnachandra Odia Bhashakosha*, while giving a lecture in the sixth session of the Oriental Conference in Patna in 1930, raised this vital issue. In 1937, Praharaj observed in the first volume of his *Bhasakosa* that *Charyagitika* (the other name of *Charyapada*) is the most ancient writing in the Odia language.[11] Authors of this lyrical, enigmatic, tantric and symbolic Charyagitika were followers of the eighty-four-siddha tradition.[ii] They were also disciples of the tantric *sahajia-boudh*[iii] tradition. Many erudite scholars strongly believe that *Vajrayana* and *Sahajayana*—two important branches of Buddhism—exclusively originated from Odisha. These siddha poets were writing without any pretense or literary stylization. The wandering siddha poets—Kanhupa, Luipa, Sarahapa, who hailed from Odisha—decided for the first time to connect with people through their dohas written in mystic and spoken language, and broke free from the shackles of the regal Sanskrit language, the *deba*

[ii] Eighty-four tantric poets including Kanhupa during the tenth century.

[iii] Followers of Sahajayana sect in Buddhism.

bhasa.[iv] There were two forms of poetry written by siddha poets: *doha* and *Vajragiti.*[v]

Ancient poetry

Literary pundits unanimously regard Sarala Dasa, a fifteenth-century poet and scholar of Odia literature, as the first major ancient poet in Odia language. A poet during the reign of King Kapilendra Deva (1435–69), he was considered to be the *adikabi* or maiden poet in the Odia language. His epics, the Bilanka Ramayana and the Chandi Purana, were the first of their kind in the country. But his magnum opus, the Mahabharata was not a mere translation of the original Sanskrit text of Vyasa. Into the fabric of the Sanskrit version, Dasa had infused the history, culture, folktales and spiritual beliefs of Odisha, as if he was writing the Mahabharata of the Odia community. Though there is no evidence available so far, it is safe to assume that there existed a poetic tradition in the Odia language prior to the advent of Sarala Dasa, which facilitated the composition of such an original, outstanding and massive work.[12] Before Sarala Dasa, the use of Sanskrit language in Odisha was widely prevalent among the upper classes of society. King Kapilendra Deva, who was also a Sanskrit scholar, was not averse to the use of spoken Odia language. He was particularly fond of Sarala Dasa's epics written in spoken Odia. Common people had hardly any access to the Sanskrit language then. Hence, through Sarala's writings, which were in a colloquial form of Odia, the then establishment could be connected with common people.[13] Steering clear of the influence of the original Mahabharata (in Sanskrit language) while being inspired by it, Dasa could

[iv] Language of the gods.

[v] Songs of the Vajrajana sect.

create a separate identity of his own. Pandit Gopinath Nanda (1869–1924), a scholar in the second decade of the twentieth century, first suggested that the Sarala Mahabharata is not a mere translation of the Sanskrit version. He pointed out four aspects of Sarala Dasa's revision of the original: curtailment, elaboration, excision and insertion. He curtailed, elaborated and excised episodes from the original Sanskrit, and inserted new episodes which were not in the original text at all.[14] Not only had he played with the theme of Mahabharata, but he had also liberally used the diction of the common mass to connect with the people instantly. When no one was thinking beyond the Sanskrit language, Dasa's drastic overhauling of the original achieved nothing short of a revolutionary breakthrough.

The leading scholar of Odia literature, Chittaranjan Das, writes:

> Sarala Dasa will be remembered in Odia literature as the real creator of Odia language, who secured for the spoken language full access to written literature. He must have literally created a major part of the medium he chose when he embarked upon writing the Odia Mahabharata. Most of the *tadbhava*[vi] words that are in the Odia language today we owe to his ingenuity and courage in linguistic experimentation. If a language has anything ever to contribute to the making of a national consciousness, then we can say that it was Sarala Dasa who first created this unified national consciousness.[15]

Sacred and Spiritual Poetry

After Sarala Dasa, five saint poets named *Panchasakha* emerged in the firmament of Odia literature in the sixteenth

[vi] Derived from the Sanskrit language.

century CE. These saint poets were: Balaram Dasa (b. 1472), Jagannatha Dasa (b. 1491), Sisu Ananta Dasa (b. 1486), Achyutananda Dasa (b. 1489) and Jashobanta Dasa (b. 1489). The poetic oeuvre of these five poets, which spanned 100 years, crafted an idiom which was unprecedented. Their poems had a spiritual and mystical dimension that sprang out of Indian philosophy. Jagannatha Dasa's epic *Bhagabata* is considered a great epic among Odia readers. Their poetry was centred on the principal deity of the community, Lord Jagannath, and they were the harbingers of the Bhakti movement, which saw the confluence of three things: religion, philosophy and spiritualism. They dealt with subjects such as *guptatattwa* (theory of hidden knowledge), *sunyavad* (voidism), *sabda brahma* (word as godhead), *kundalini yoga, ida, pingala,*[vii] etc. in their poetic compositions.

These poets were also inspired by Sarala Dasa's use of earthy language in poetry. They were writing in a period of transition when Buddhism was fading and Vaishnavism was making inroads into Odisha. Deeply influenced by Buddhism, they were often described as *prachhanaboudha*.[viii] After Sarala Dasa's Mahabharata, it was Balaram Dasa's *Jagamohan Ramayana*, Jagannath Dasa's *Bhagabata*, Achyutananda Dasa's *Haribansa,* Jashobanta's *Gobindachandra*, which were hailed as milestones in Odia literature.

Medieval and Musical Poetry

The period of medieval poetry was stretched over the seventeenth and eighteenth centuries. Dinakrushna Dasa (1650–1710), Upendra Bhanja (1670–1740), Abhimanyu Samantasinghara (1760–1806), Baladeba Ratha (1789–

[vii] Tantric terms.

[viii] Buddhism in disguise.

1845), Bhakta Charan Das (1729–1813), Gopalakrusna Pattanayaka (1784–1862) and Sadananda Kabisurya Brahma (1720–90) were the major poets during that period.

Dinakrushna Dasa was known for his celebrated work, *Rasakallol,* which had thirty-four cantos and 1258 stanzas. None had attempted to write such a *kavya*,[ix] where each line of the poem begins with the alphabet 'ka'. Upendra Bhanja, the greatest poet of the medieval period, admired this innovative style and adopted it for his magnum opus *Baidehisa Bilasa*, where each line began with the alphabet 'ba', thus giving a fitting poetic tribute to Dinakrushna. Music was always the forte of medieval poetry. The poetry was more sung than read and was used as a tool to reach out to the common people, even though listeners were unable to get the full meaning of the poetry.

However, after the arrival of Upendra Bhanja in Odia poetry, things changed drastically. Instead of using colloquial or spoken language, he used the *tatsam*[x] of the Sanskrit language. He was the first poet who raised the level of the Odia language to a higher echelon at par with the Sanskrit words that were used then in the royal courts and among the upper-class people. It was also a great challenge to write several epics in the Odia language with the inflated diction and style characteristic of the classic language.

As Surendra Mohanty, an acclaimed critic and scholar, writes,

> Later, towards the beginning of the eighteenth century, poetry changed its course and complexion and became pedantic. To cater to the needs and tastes of royal patrons and the affluent elite became its sole objective. This is known as the *Riti* Age in Odia poetry. *Riti*, as

---

[ix] Poetical work.

[x] At par with Sanskrit.

> defined by Sanskrit theorists of prosody, had a distinct connotation. It referred, on one hand, to certain natural attributes which served to make poetry fascinating, and, on the other hand, to certain blemishes from which the poet was enjoined to stay away.[16]

And, as another notable critic, Mayadhar Mansinha observes,

> It has to be admitted, however, that, in spite of all artificialities and ostentation, Upendra sweeps his readers off their feet by the deep, subtle and ingenious rhythm of his lines, by his superb metrical success and, last but not least, by the enchanted world of love, beauty and youth into which he transports his readers or audience the moment his lines are sung or read. Unrivalled in the power of manipulating words most dexterously according to their own laws of beauty, unmatched in the painting of sensuous, youthful love and unique in the total grand music of his lines, Upendra Bhanja dominates Odia poetry with an influence that has been almost totalitarian for nearly two centuries. Although Upendra Bhanja abandoned his kingdom for the sake of writing poetry, he is considered the all-time emperor of Odia poetry.[17]

At the fag end of this period, a few other poets made their presence felt. Abhimanyua Samantasinghara was an accomplished poet. His *Bidagdha Chinatamani*, the magnum opus deeply linked with idioms of Odia and expressing the quintessence of earthly love, is treated as *vade mecum*[xi] of Vaishnavism followers of Odisha. It is always a delight to recite these songs that set the hearts of the listener afire with deep nostalgic emotion natural to youth, mingled with a purifying

[xi] A book for ready reference.

touch of sublimity that lifts the audience to a region of ecstasy and spiritual love. Baladeva Ratha (1789–1845), under the tutelage of Vaishnavite philosophy, wrote a good number of love songs around Radha and Krishna, a few excellent satires, and a compactly composed and well-built *Champu and Chautisa*, a slim book of thirty-four lyrics signifying thirty-four letters of the alphabets from 'ka' to 'ksha'. His songs were accepted by readers from all walks of life 'for the panorama of imagery and the dexterous manipulation of rhythmic diction'.[18] Gopalkrushna Pattanayaka's songs on the same theme seem to be full of conventional verbosity. But his songs give us the feel of the 'throbbing heart of an emotional and sensitive soul who appears to have (himself) suffered the pangs of a great love'.[19] They have a core sentiment that appeals universally. Bhakta Charan Das is another poet known in the literary map of Odisha for the spirited expression of his philosophy and wisdom, and for the outpouring of suave and elegant lines of a thinker and scholar in his *Mathuaramangala*.

Modern Poetry

Odisha's sociopolitical situation has always played a vital role in shaping its literary canon. In the last quarter of the nineteenth century, a schoolteacher called Pandit Kanti Chandra Bhattacharya from Balasore Zilla School (1872) distributed a pamphlet titled '*Odia Ekti Swatantray Bhasha Noi* [Odia is not an independent language]'. It led to a chorus of dissenting voices from Odisha, disputing this outrageous claim and arguing otherwise. This led to the Odia Bhasa Surakshya Andolan (Odia Language Protection Movement), which produced major writers such as Fakir Mohan Senapati, Radhanath Ray, Gangadhar Meher, Gourishankar Ray and many others.

Radhanath Ray, a narrative poet who belonged to that period, is treated as a flag-bearer of modernism in Odia poetry. During this period, poetry freed itself from the clutches of Sanskrit language and literature only to seek refuge in Western or European literature. It was a natural consequence of the influx of British and Eurocentric values and outlook into Odishan society during British colonial rule. The form and content of poetry, inherited from the medieval period, underwent a drastic change and a new era dawned in the literary firmament. Ray's poetry was a synthesis of Eastern and Western literary and philosophical traditions. It was obviously not an easy and seamless interaction between supporters and opponents of the new. The war of words between two literary periodicals, *Indradhanu* and *Bijuli*, bears witness to this acrimonious war. Ray's four epics—*Kedar Gouri* (Pyramus and Thisbe), *Chandrabhaga* (Apollo and Daphne), *Nandikeshari* (Scylla and Nisus), *Usha* (Atalanta Oracle)—were Odia versions of Ovid's works, and his *Parvati* was an Odia version of *Agamemnon* by Aeschylus, the Greek dramatist. In these epics, he attempted to indigenize his sources completely or partially. Though he was successful in his endeavour, taking the themes from foreign literature and transplanting them into his soil and climate was a big challenge for him. The lyrical intensity and beauty of his lines, and the recreation of an amazing environment were Ray's forte. So was his near-miraculous metamorphosis of the Eastern and Western ideas. He was inherently a devotee of nature and adept at telling brilliant stories, which he put into the casket of alluring verse.

Ray's poetry stood like a majestic rock in establishing the glamour and richness of Odia poetry, and silenced the critics who had predicted a bleak future for him.

Madhusudan Rao (1853–1912), a contemporary of Ray, was married into the religious sect, the *Brahma Samaja* when he was seventeen years old. His earlier poems in *Kabitabali* show him as being more inclined towards heavenly flights than to the soil and his poems seem to be deeply influenced by the *Rigveda*. The only sonneteer of his time, he was treated by the readers like an oracle who was speaking the language of scripture. He served the education department of Odisha for thirty-five years and his immense contribution to children's literature cannot be ignored. It would not be out of place to mention that Rao was the first modern lyrical poet in Odia.

Fakir Mohan Senapati, known as *Vyasakabi*, and generally acknowledged as the father of modern Odia literature, has been a prolific poet, and his writings in other genres have been treated as landmark contributions to Odia literature. *Puspamala, Upahara, Abasara Basare, Pujaphula* and *Dhuli* comprised his Odia poetic corpus, which were all shaped by his own life. His loneliness after the death of his wife and his passion to serve his mother tongue were clearly visible in his poetical works. Though his poems are written in simple and lucid language, they are rich with a philosophical import and satirical orientation. A deeply humane person, Senapati was a patriot and spiritual person at the same time.

Gangadhar Meher (1862–1924), an important poet from a poor weaving community in western Odisha, had little formal education but excellent knowledge of Sanskrit, Bangla, Hindi and English. Like his predecessors, the plots of his epics were not original. He was known as a sort of local Kalidas due to his habit of drawing from the bard's characters, metaphors and similes. Many of his epics including *Tapaswini* are untranslatable without destroying the original artistry. As Mansinha writes,

> The way he tackled the old meters and made them serve modern needs, the rhythmic elegance and aptness of his diction, his happy, faultless rhyming, the serene classical

> dignity that runs through his entire performance and, above all, the rare insight he displays into the mind and soul of his characters, makes him stand out among the whole galaxy of poets in Odisha.[20]

Bhima Bhoi, a Kondh poet and an iconoclast, was 'the greatest Adivasi poet of Odisha who flourished in the nineteenth century'.[21] Though unlettered and poverty-stricken, this wandering Adivasi poet was a genius who wrote poems that were full of vigour and power. Bhoi attained his spiritual vision after a long period of penance on a hill in the wilds of Keonjhar. He preached a religion called *Alekh Dharma*, a religion centred on a formless God that did not recognize the caste system or any kind of asceticism. It was a new avatar of Buddhism in Odisha. His style, expression, diction, ideas and influence were unparalleled among his peers. He was the harbinger of modernism in Odia poetry.

Patriotic poetry

Gopabandhu Das (1877–1928), Godabarish Mishra (1886–1956) and Pandit Nilakantha Dasa (1884–1967)—all from the school of Satyabadi—were prominent poets and sociopolitical activists who played a crucial role in carving out modern Odisha. During British rule, Odisha became the first province (1936) on the basis of the language spoken in the region. Besides other poems, Madhusudan Das's 'Utkal Santan' and Gopabandhu's 'Bandira Atmakatha' bore the stamp of patriotic fervour all through and touched a chord in each Odia. Dasa also had a penchant for nature and a deep sense of aesthetics. In the poetry of Pandit Nilakantha Dasa, one can see a new attitude toward the use of language, thought and rhythm. 'Konarke' happens to be his best creation, among other writings, that happily blended erudition and poetic excellence.

Romantic poetry

During the pre-independence period, Odia poetry changed its style and forms thrice. The different trends are named by the critics as Sabuja Kabita (romantic poetry), Pragatibadi Kabita (progressive poetry) and Uttar-Adhunika Kabita (postmodernist poetry).[22]

The Sabuja poets were hardly seven or eight in number and even fewer were engaged in writing. They were obsessed with Rabindranath Tagore and Pramathnath Choudhury, who initiated the romantic wave in Bangla literature. The celebration of youthful energy was a salient aspect of Bangla romanticism, but Odia poets of this era were sacrificing youthful dynamism in favour of escapism. Even though they were criticized for it, Sabuja poetry flourished. It was a big departure from the poetry of Radhanath Ray. The Sabuja poets portrayed nature differently from the poets of the Ray period and did not romanticize it. Defending the poetry of the Sabuja group, Annanda Shankar Ray said,

> The language and feeling expressed by the then-young writers may seem to be old to the present-day youngsters. What was looking like green then is now looking like pale yellow. If there was any value in those writings today, then it was the value of their dream only. Has dream no value? I consider the dream the essence of the world. A dreamless life is like insipid curry.[23]

Sabuja poets were composing a new form of poetry and were also trying out various symbols. The sun was taken as a symbol of hope, the *chakor* (dove) of love, the black cobra of mass, the red karabi flower of socialism, the iron gate of non-independence, the dawn of liberation and so on. Baikunthanath Patnaik (1904–79) used many symbols to express mysticism that were different from the words used by our ancient poets of mysticism.[24] He and Kalindi Charan Panigrahi were major contributors to this poetic tradition. Outside the Sabuja group of writers, there were two major poets whose contribution to romantic poetry was immense: Mayadhar Mansinha and Radhamohan Gadanayak. Mansinha infused a metaphysical fervour into his romanticism, and Gadanayak's lyrical ballads were a mixture of puranic myths, history, patriotism and fables.

Socialist poetry

Sachidananda Routray (1916–2004), Manmohan Mishra (1917–2000), Ananta Patnaik (1912–87) and Bhagabati Charan Panigrahi (1908–43) were known as progressive poets and authors. Of them, Routray dominated the Odia poetic scene for nearly half a century. Initially influenced by romantic poets and their metaphysical and mystic themes, he switched over to a revolutionary and socialist form of poetry in 1936 after Odisha became a separate state.

Postmodernist poetry

After World War II, Odia poetry grew more subtle. Postmodernism was an extension of modernism that shunned the old poetic tradition but not completely.

Sachidananda Routray, father of postmodernism in Odia poetry, broke away from his metaphysical moorings and revolutionary impulses, influenced by T.S. Eliot, Tagore, Mayakovski, Jibanananda Das, etc. Called the 'poet of the people', he had proved his mettle in all three phases of his poetic journey: the romantic, the progressive and the postmodernist. Later on, Guruprasad Mohanty, Binod Chandra Nayak and Bhanuji Rao (all major poets) carried forward the legacy of Routray.

Mohanty's long poem 'Kalapurusa' was greatly influenced by T.S. Eliot's 'The Wasteland'. Over the decades, many have taken cues from this poem and made humongous experiments with form and content, thus enriching Odia poetry. They include Sitakant Mahapatra, Binod Chandra Nayak, Ramakanta Rath and Soubhagya Kumar Misra. Each poet has, however, created their distinct idiom.

Sociocultural poetry (1969–95)

During the 1970s, when the little magazine movement was widespread around the country and poets were heavily inspired by Allen Ginsberg, an acclaimed poet, a movement by the name of Anam, meaning nameless, started in Odia poetry. It soon acquired the name of the Anam Poetry Movement. Kumar Mohanty (1941–95) was the flag-bearer of this movement that influenced and inspired more than fifty poets within a decade. Vocal critics of the Western influence on poetry, they were advocating for a return to their sociocultural roots, and wanted to bridge the gap between the readers and poets. Their ideas attracted the old and the young alike. All their poems bore a signature title: a black dot. These hard-hitting poems were pro-people, lyrical and anti-establishment in tone and tenor. This movement lasted for about twenty-seven years (1969–95) and started losing steam after the sudden demise of Kumar Mohanty. Narayan Prasad Singh, Chittaranjan Mishra and Uday Das were the poets who joined this movement at the initial stage, and later, Fani Mohanty, Adhyapak Biswaranjan, Netrananda Samantaray, Harihar Mishra, Subash Kar and Manu Dash made their distinctive contribution to the movement. Two names are unmissable in any stocktaking of the Anam movement—Madhu Mohanty, an editor and lawyer who gave it intellectual content, and Gokul Bihari Mohanty, his son-in-law, and a firm believer in what the movement stood for.

6

The essay in English is known as *prabandh* in the Odia language. It is also occasionally called *nibandh*. It is interesting to note that in ancient times, the term prabandh was used for only the epics and not for prose writings. Many ancient and medieval poets have called their epics prabandh. A few examples would be, Poet Jadumani Mangaraj, known for his humour, named his epic poems *Prabandh Purnachandra*; saint poet Jagannatha Dasa called his *Bhagabat Bhasa, Prabandhe Bhagabat*. Abhimanyu Samantasinghara in his epic *Bidagdha Chintamani* was also quoted as saying, *Jamakadi Chitrakabya Prabandh Prabandh*[xii] and the prominent saint poet Jayadev at the beginning of his *Gitagobinda* wrote, *sribasudev ratikeli kathasametametam karoti Jaidevkabih prabandh.*[xiii]

In the course of time, however, the term prabandh began to apply to discursive prose writings. In Odia literature, the prabandh was first written in prose in 1873 by Fakir Mohan Senapati. It is a landmark publication titled 'Mandira Manankare Kutschita Murti [Vulgar Idols inside the Temples]'.

Before delving into the arena of Odia essay-writing, it won't be out of place to look into the scenario of essay-writing in the neighbouring state, West Bengal, during the twentieth century, as Odisha and Bengal share not only proximity with each other but also commonality in sociocultural ties as well as language to great extent.

The nineteenth century witnessed many significant developments in Odisha. As mentioned earlier, the first

---

[xii] The picture poetry, i.e. poetic composition in the form of a picture pattern and figures of speech, such as alliteration of particular sounds etc. are called prabandh (category of poetic composition).

[xiii] The verse expresses that Jayadev, who is obsessed with rhythms of the Goddess of Speech (i.e. Saraswati), who sings at the lotus feet of Padma (or Lakshmi), composes this lyrical poem narrating the tales of the passionate love between Vasudeva and Sri.

printing press was established in 1836 by missionaries Charles Lacey and Amos Sutton, which was followed by the founding of the Cuttack Printing Company in 1865 by Gaurishankar Ray. Several Odia magazines were published, and many clubs and literary organizations mushroomed. The Missionary Press published *Gyanaruna* (1849), *Prabodh Chandrika* (1856) and *Arunodaya* (1861).

The second half of the nineteenth century was the period when many periodicals were published in Odia. They were *Utkal Dipika* (1866), *Baleswar Sambad Bahika* (1868), *Utkal Darpan* (1873), the first literary magazine, *Utkal Hiteisini* (1873), *Naba Sambad* (1887), *Sambalpur Hiteisini* (1889), *Utkal Prabha* (1891), *Utkal Sahitya* (1897) and *Alochana* (1900).

The flexibility of prabandh as a genre has been well-accepted over the years. An author can express his/her opinion regardless of any restraints. Though some write it off as a dry and uninteresting genre, it is very much a part of literature.

The world of the essay is sizable and can cover any subject—commerce, art, science, politics, sociology, technology, and human emotions such as love, longing and loss.

Odia literature had to wait a long time for the essay to finally emerge. With the growth of science and technology towards the end of the nineteenth century, prose became the chosen medium of expression.

Essays are broadly of two types: *bastunistha* (objective, dealing with reason, fact and knowledge) and *byaktinistha* (subjective, dealing with emotions, imagination and individual experience).

Before the development of modern literature in Odia, there was an era called *pathyapustak juga*, the vernacular era (1822–70), where there was not much prabandh or prose writing available in Odia. There is certainly little trace of the modern essay seen in Sutton's *Vernacular Reader* (1846), but the contours of the form were later discernible in

Ramabilasha (1875). 1873 is considered to be a significant year in essay writing. Fakir Mohan Senapati and Radhanath Ray wrote essays during this year followed by Madhusudan Rao whose 'Prabandhamala' (1880) is treated as a landmark achievement. Though Madhusudan Rao was well aware of *Tattwabodhini,* the magazine published in Bangla by the followers of Brahma sect, and was inspired by its language pattern, he failed to retain its mellifluous diction that came from Sanskrit. However, he was able to excel in his essays after 1890. Writing Odia essays using Sanskrit diction rather than Bangla diction, Rao raised the level of essay writing in Odia, something that nobody could have dreamed of earlier. In 1894, Chandramohan Moharana and Biswanath Kar read their essays in their first and second sessions respectively in the first edition of the newly established *Alochana Sabha*. For the next twenty-one years (1873–94), essayists continued to read their essays in various reading clubs. However, many essays that were written in recent years could not meet the standard set by Madhusudan Rao. Of course, between 1896 and 1920, essays written in Odia gained in both quantity and quality. Structurally complex and aesthetically refined, they were also vehicles of social reform and patriotic sentiments.

Biswanath Kar, though not a creator of any significant book of essays, was a flag-bearer of essay writing in Odia from 1897 to 1934. Brilliantly written speeches and exceptional editorials published in *Utkal Sahitya* bear eloquent testimony to his devotion to Odia literature. Chandramohan Moharana, Shashibhusan Ray, Gopalchandra Praharaj, Pandit Nilakantha Dasa, Mohini Mohan Senapati, Kalicharan Patnaik, Sitadevi Khadanga and Sarala Devi entertained and edified the readers with their magnificent essays during this period. Later, in the post-independent period, Bamacharan Mitra, Bhubaneswar Behera, Surendra Mohanty, Chittaranjan Das, Chandrasekhar Rath, Sarat Kumar Mohanty, Kishen Patnaik, Gopinath

Mohanty, Sitakant Mahapatra and Ganeswar Mishra took essay writing to a spectacular height. These essays were categorized into narrative, descriptive, expressive of a particular idea or ideology, expository and argumentative forms.

7

Fakir Mohan Senapati wrote 'Rebati', the first short story in Odia, in 1898 when he was fifty-six years old. Prior to this, folktales and fables dominated the scene. Of course, Senapati had confessed to having written another story before 'Rebati'.

> Going by what Fakir Mohan has revealed in his autobiography, 'Rebati' is his second story, the first being a story named 'Lachhamania', which he had published in the periodical *Bodhadayini O Baleswar Sambadbahika*. If he did so, it must have been sometime between 1868, the year in which the monthly periodical was founded, and 1871. Unfortunately, these are now untraceable. So 'Lachhamania' has remained an object of speculation and fantasy among critics and researchers.[25]

Some stories were written by Radhanath Ray ('Italiya Yuva') and Madhusudan Rao ('Pranayara Adbhuta Parinama', 'Chandra O Tara', and 'Hemamala'), but did not fall within the ambit of well-defined prose. 'Rebati' has been widely acknowledged as the first full-fledged story in Odia literature. Senapati wrote twenty-one short stories in a span of eighteen years. Dispelling the blind beliefs and hypocrisy in religion, eulogizing humanism and critiquing a hostile attitude to women's education were the mainstay in Senapati's stories.

'Rebati' has proved to be truly enduring in its penetrating insights into a world in transition, as it portrays the conflict between tradition and modernity, and its human cost poignantly and vividly. The story is also a searing study of the failed project of self-actualization of a young girl, the eponymous female protagonist. As such, it resonates with readers of every time and clime. The cult status it enjoys can be seen from the fact that almost seventy Odia authors have, over the past few decades, rewritten the story in a spirit of creative engagement with its form and content.[26] 'Rebati, the protagonist, might have lost her life in the most tragic of circumstances, bearing the unjust burden of guilt and pain, but the story makes her immortal. The story is iconic because of a cocktail of factors, among which must be counted, its compact and precise narrative delivered in the colloquial Odia idiom, its ability to sound out the key issues of the day such as superstition, poverty, illiteracy, women's education and underdevelopment that are a deterrent to progress and, above all, its ability to portray suffering in its rawest form. The story treads on that borderland between comedy and tragedy that characterizes Senapati's prose fiction. It tells a tragic tale of suffering with unflinching realism.'[27] 'Rebati' has been translated into thirty-six languages, national and international, and deserves to be part of the inheritance of every reader of fiction anywhere in the world.

The first two decades of the twentieth century (1901–20) were a crucial period for short stories in Odia. Stories published during this period were deeply reflective of contemporary sociocultural life in Odisha.

Dayanidhi Mishra, Dibyasingha Panigrahi, Bankanidhi Patnaik, Chandrasekhar Nanda, Nandakishore Bal and Chintamani Mohanty were among the prominent practitioners of the short fiction genre. They made patriotism, history, human values and social maladies the subject matter of their stories.

Chitra (1907), authored by Chandrasekhar Nanda, happens to be the first short story collection in Odia. Like other contemporary authors, Nanda explored themes like legends, history, social maladies and the evil effects of alcohol.

Between 1920–1947, Odisha was in the midst of the national movement and carving itself out as a separate state based on its language. It also keenly felt the impact of the romantic movement initiated in neighbouring Bengal by Rabindranath Tagore that resulted in the Sabuja movement on this side of the border.

Odia short stories experienced a tremendous surge during this period. Godabarish Mishra, Godabarish Mohapatra, Ananta Prasad Panda, Rajkishore Patnaik, Kanhu Charan Mohanty, Nityananda Mohapatra, Pranabandhu Kar, Gopinath Mohanty and Bhagbati Charan Panigrahi were important voices who captured the imagination of readers. They wrote about class, climate, labour and caste influenced by three great thinkers of the Western world: Charles Darwin, Karl Marx and Sigmund Freud.

Godabarish Mohapatra's (1898–1965) stories talked of matters ranging from *Naanka Durbhikshya* (the Great Famine, 1966) to the dissolution of princely states. He showed various levels of the sociopolitical life of people during the second half of the nineteenth century and the first half of the twentieth century.

The horizon of Odia stories was expanding greatly during his time. Kalindi Charan Panigrahi (1901–91) was influenced by the short stories of Rabindranath Tagore, Guy de Maupassant and Tolstoy. Like Senapati and Tagore, he delved into life in the village, its ecology and aesthetics. He wrote on child marriage, casteism and the woes of widows. He started picking up odd characters for his stories who were crazy, blind, dumb and, of course, poor. Animals like cats, dogs, and deer became the protagonists in his stories. His younger brother, Bhagawati Charan Panigrahi, was influenced by Marxism and wrote about the exploitation of the tribals. No one was as militant in Odia literature as Panigrahi's Ghinua in 'Shikaar [The Kill]'. It is treated as the first story on the theme of class war in Odia.

Major authors like Gopinath Mohanty, Surendra Mohanty, Manoj Das, Sachidananda Routray, Basanta Kumar Satapathy, Santanu Kumar Acharya, Mohapatra Nilamani Sahoo, Chandrasekhar Rath, Krushna Prasad Mishra, Akhila Mohan Patnaik, Rabi Patnaik and many others wrote a good number of stories in Odia. It was a golden period for Odia fiction writing. The 1970s witnessed the emergence of many women writers: Yashodhara Mishra, Sarojini Sahu and Puspanjali Nayak. Among male writers, Satya Misra, Jagadish Mohanty, Bijay Prasad Mohapatra, Naru Mohanty, Rajanikant Mohanty, Rabi Swain and Dash Benhur made a strong impact. The new generation of authors who took the baton from the predecessors are Paresh Patnaik, Gourhari Das, Paramita Satpathy, Bhima Prusty, Sadananda Tripathy, Manoj Kumar Panda, Sahadev Sahoo, Ajay Swain, Dipti Ranjan Pattanaik and others. Most of these authors found their own idiom and style. Nationalism, internationalism, loneliness, interpretation of myth and existentialism supplied the themes of their fictional narratives. In a way, Odia short story during this phase became more diverse and plural. Modern living and urban orientation became more vivid, and rural life along with the agrarian setting receded into the background.

The Odia short story has traversed a long road in a short span of 125 years and new talents are continuing to emerge all the time. They are reaching out beyond their language border by way of translation, which is opening a new vista in Odia literature. It is no doubt a thriving genre in Odia literature.

8

Since its advent, Odia theatre has been closely influenced by religious and spiritual issues. There were two kinds of spectators and performers associated with this genre: the first being the aristocrats and the royalty, and the second being the common masses. Both co-existed and influenced each other's taste for centuries within a slow-moving society.

From the records of the Jagannatha temple in Puri, it has been revealed that during the twelfth century, a play called *Piyushlahari* (The Wave of Nectar) by Jayadev was enacted in the Jagannatha shrine and another play in Sanskrit called *Lalita-Madhava* by Rupa Goswami was performed at Radhakant mutt, which is known as the residence of Chaitanya. Besides, Ray Ramananda's Sanskrit play *Jagannatha Vallabha Natak* was also first performed in the court of Jagannatha temple and later at the precincts of Jagannatha Vallabha monastery.

In the fifteenth century, Kapilendradev, the king of Odisha, wrote a play in the Sanskrit language called *Parasuram Bijaya*.

During the rule of the Moghuls and the Marathas, Odisha's sociocultural environment was at its lowest ebb, and playwriting was its major victim. The state and its people were in constant turmoil due to continuous invasions and counter-invasions. Though an Odia play called *Gouriharan* by an unknown author has been discovered, it was found to contain Hindi songs which were probably included to appease the then-Maratha rulers.

The British came to Odisha in 1803 and experienced Bengali officers were brought into Odisha for managing day-to-day affairs of administration. These Bengali bureaucrats staged Bengali plays at Cuttack every year during the Dussehra celebrations. Local Odia writers such as Ramashankar Ray did not accept these rhetorical performances and started writing Odia plays highlighting the glories of the Odia people.

Today, he is regarded as the father of modern Odia plays. He wrote his first play *Kanchi Kaberi* in 1880.

On 27 July 1872, students of Catholic Mission School at Cuttack staged a portion of one of Shakespeare's plays on a makeshift stage. It was the first play performed on stage in Odisha. But generally speaking, Jagan Mohan Lal's (1838–1913) *Babaji Nataka* (1877) is considered to be the first play in Odia.

'Babaji was a four-act play that anticipated Gandhi and our Constitution-in-making to make out a case for prohibition. Unfortunately, in it, ethics got the better of dramatic art, and thus this first play in Odia was a stage failure.'[28] Though *Jagannath Ballav,* published by Gourishankar Ray, was written prior to *Babaji,* it is still not regarded as the first play in Odia. Its Odia poetic stanzas were written in strict adherence to the Sanskrit grammar. Its dialogues were also written in poetic form that reminded the readers of the *Kadambari* epic in Sanskrit. However, it was clear that the modern Odia plays were staged after more than seventy years of the British Government's rule.[29] Ramashankar Ray's *Kanchi Kaberi* was the first play to be staged in Cuttack, and was patriotic in fervour and dealt with the glorious past of Odisha's history. This play influenced all Odia dramatic productions for thirty years and enjoys a high literary status to date. With an aim to include a new voice tinged with patriotism and reform, Ramashankar wrote thirty plays on diverse themes, including historical, mythological, social, comic, satirical and romantic. He adapted *The Tempest* by Shakespeare into Odia as *Banabala* (1881). Afterwards, Kamapala Mishra brought a ray of hope for Odia plays at the turn of the nineteenth century.

Banamali Pati, a countryside moneylender and a village Shylock in the district of Puri, who was also the owner of Radhakrishna Theatre in Balanga, Puri, patronized the production of his plays wholeheartedly until he was brutally murdered by a group of his victims. Radhakrishna Theatre had long run the plays *Kalapahad* (1922) and *Konarka* (1927) written by him. This repertory formed by Banamali Pati dominated the dramatic scene for almost twenty-five years until his tragic death. Ashwini Kumar Ghosh had written forty-one plays and established prose drama on the stage of Odisha. *Raghu Arakhita* (1937), *Bandhu Mahanti*, *Chandaluni* (1946) and *Sri Lokananth* (1946) were some of his masterpieces that gave historical and mythological plays a new resonance.

After the death of Pati, Radhakrishna Theatre was subsequently closed down. This time, another theatre group emerged by the name of Annapurna Theatre Group.

In the 1940s, Kalicharan Pattnaik (1897–1970) emerged as a towering personality in theatre, dance and music. Pattnaik had established his own theatre group called 'Odisha Theatres' and managed it for ten years until winding it up in 1949. He started performing *Rasalila* with his group but later on, returned to the historical and mythological plays. He then returned to Annapurna, for which he also wrote many plays where women took part in acting for the first time. Critics say that Kalicharan Patnaik's *Bhata* (Rice, 1944) ran for 100 days, which was not a mean feat during that period. He also wrote *Rakta Mati* (1945), considered the first realistic play in Odia. Though he never criticized the colonial rule directly, he portrayed the exploitation of villagers by zamindars in many of his plays.

After Kalicharan, Manoranjan Das, Gopal Chhotray, Bhanja Kishore Patnaik and Ramachandra Mishra were the prominent playwrights who highlighted social issues in their plays. The 1960s was a period in which Odia playwriting witnessed a transition, with playwrights embarking upon translating classic plays from around the world into Odia. In 1964, Srujani Natya Sanstha staged Manoranjan Das's *Sagar Manthan*, which was an adaptation of J.B. Priestley's *An Inspector Calls*. *Banahansi*, *Aranya Phasala* and *Bitarkita Aparanha* are some of the important plays written by him.

> Manoranjan Das is one such playwright whose subtle, sensitive and penetrative depiction of human action on the stage manages, unwittingly perhaps, to answer these questions more efficiently than others. He has stirred a whole generation of Odia audience to the connotations and implications of life and stimulated them to an emotional voyage to the world of both within and without. It is through his plays that they have extended the scope of their experiences and expressions.[30]

The New Theatre Movement in Odisha

In 1960, a new phase of modern Odia theatre was created by breaking the conventional style of professional theatre. The *Naba Natya Andolan* (New Theater Movement) started with modern experimentation of plays inspired by Ibsen, Brecht, Bernard Shaw and Sartre. Biswajit Das was one of the pioneers of the New Theatre Movement and started writing one-act plays in 1952. *Pratapgarhare Di Dina*, *Nija Pratinidhinka Tharu* and *Brute* are some of the plays considered milestones in Odia playwriting.

> In 1970, Das produced *Mrugaya* (The Hunt). This was an experimental play of a different taste, analyzing artistically the agony and helplessness of hypocritical human beings. Psychoanalysis of the modern mind gave this effort a touch of reality. Das is of the view that craving for happiness always ends up in agony in contemporary life. In this play, he has shown how darkness is the essence of life and the ever-increasing gap between what we aspire for and what we achieve.[31]

The following playwrights have immensely enriched the narrative of playwriting in Odia for the last four decades—Bijay Mishra (*Shababahakamane, Duiti Surya Dagdha Phula*

Ku Nei, Tata Niranjana, Jane Rajathile and *Banaprastha)*, Ramesh Prasad Panigrahi (*Mahanatak*, *Mun Ambhe, Ambhemane*), Harihar Mishra (*Nindita Gajapati*, *Adrushya Nata*), Kartika Ratha (*Mun Duhen*), Jagannath Prasad Das (*Suryasta Purbaru* and *Sabaseshaloka*), Kunja Ray (*Kalantara* and *Bidaya Bajraditya*), Rati Ranjan Mishra (*Aruna Rangara Pakshi*), Subodh Patnaik (*Ethuante*), Sankar Tripathy (*Ravanachhaya*, *Kavyapurusa*, *Gandhinka Odisha* and *Ahe Nilasaila*), Ananda Shankar Das (*Bhanumatira Khela* and *Phulachandan*), and Kamal Lochan Mohanty (*Daka Bangala* and *Ram Rahim*).

9

In this book, literary genres, selections and excerpts are arranged in the following sequence—poetry, play, short story and essay—with authors in each genre presented according to their year of birth. There may be an exception to the rule in the poetry section, especially in the presentation of the sub-categories.

While preparing this book, a sense of diffidence coupled with a strong sense of guilt kept creeping into my mind for not including some authors for whom I harbour immense love and respect. Perhaps it is an inescapable reality for any anthologist anywhere in the world—none can escape this guilt. However, I believe this book will cater to the needs of scholars, students and aficionados of the literature of this region by helping to open up before them the treasure trove of Odia literature.

***

1

Poetry

Poetry: Odia

Sarala Dasa (Fifteenth century)

'Bhima's Counsel to Yudhisthira'

(Translated 'Yudhisthiranka Prati Bhismanka Upadesha' from the Odia by Manu Dash)

Agasti spoke to Vaivasvata Manu,
Five Pandav brothers went along with Krishna.

Hereafter, said Janardana,
Go, arrange the rites of the coronation ceremony.

Listening to these words of Krishna, Yudhisthira answered:
Bhisma should be consulted before performing the rituals.

And then they, all six of them, went along to Bhisma,
Neither the soldiers nor friends accompanied them.

Bhisma was lying stretched on the bed of arrows,
There reached the king of dharma.

Bhisma was observing the rite of silence,
Seeing Yudhisthira, he lifted his eyelids.

Looking at Yudhisthira, Bhisma said,
Go and rule the country without any inhibitions.

O Dharmaraj, why did you come to me?
Yudhisthira said, Hear me, O premier of the Kuru dynasty.

For us, you abandoned the comfort of your life
Who could equal your prowess in all three universes?

Who could ever win had you been in your usual form?
You have always held us close to your heart.

You were the first who showered blessings on us before the war began,
Endorsed us to be king of Panchakatak[i] killing the enemy.

Words of the great never go in vain,
Listening to Yudhisthira, Bhisma gave a demure smile.

And said, Yudhisthira, obstacles now stand removed,
Go and rule your land merrily.

Rule the kingdom and enjoy your tenure,
No fear since Srikrishna is in your favour.

All the sons of Dhritarastra are now gone,
I had no doubt that it would at last happen.

Go and rule the kingdom and observe the rule of law,
Earth does not bear those who commit injustice for long.

Take care of subjects and ensure no one is sad,
The king who protects his people stays happy.

For serving the country well, Indra sends rain,[ii]
And the earth remains neutral when the king in peace reigns.

The king attains everything when the subjects are happy,
It's the chief duty of the king to rule the subjects well.

Adjudicating the crime, you should punish subjects,
People would then hail your judgement.

Considering all options, you should judge it legal or illegal,
Do punish him punitively who commits wrong more often.

In punishing criminals, there won't be anything wrong,
Goddess of wealth would calmly reside in your blessed kingdom.

---

[i] Five villages that the Pandavas asked Duryodhan to offer.

[ii] Agasti, Vaivasvata Manu, Pandav, Krishna, Janardana, Bhisma, Yudhisthira, Dharmaraj, Panchakatak, Dhritarastra, Indra: names of the characters in the epic Mahabharata.

You would measure twenty by your hand to make a *kathi*,
In twenty-five a *gutha*, sixteen gutha in one *mana*; in twenty *mana*, one *bati*.[iii]

If you take only a slice out of a bati for the purpose of tax,
Subjects will eternally shower blessings on you for a longer life.

Whom the subjects hail from dawn to dusk,
Yama, the king of death, can't do any harm to him.

Send your brothers to settle the problems of subjects,
Do keep a constant vigil on the administration of the country.

Appoint an honest minister picked from good people,
But do not give him the power to punish anyone.

Don't punish any farmer with a pecuniary penalty,
Forgive those who are innocent.

And give small horses to old horse riders,
Always appoint soldiers who are fifty years old.

The elephant should be seventeen years old,
A well-built mahout must decorate him.

Be vigilant about keeping horses, elephants and soldiers,
Go for a vacation looking into the state of affairs.

Listen to the *Puranas*[iv] from the mouth of Brahmins,
Do not trust women instantly at all.

Do not bathe in the shrines meant for demons,
Do not be greedy for wealth all the time.

Help people in their time of need,
Don't ever believe anyone without strolling in the dark in disguise.

Don't give up hunting completely, O king.
Do worship every day the gods and brahmins.

[iii] Kathi, guntha, mana, bati: Measures of the farming land.

[iv] Holy scriptures of Hindu religion.

Observe rites of *Ekadasi*[v] with those inclined to dharma,
Do not allow foreign messengers to enter your kingdom.

Neither covets other's wives nor their wealth,
Do live with the woman you have married.

Perform the *yagna*, rites of sacrifice, piously,
And destroy the evil-minded who appear there.

Kill the demons instantly the moment you see them,
The king would not bear any sin for this deed.

Don't take away other's wives and wealth,
Give them shelter who seek your refuge.

Give the charge of the kingdom to the faithful minister,
But don't hand him absolute power at all.

Be careful and keep in mind that the cows,
and Brahmins do not suffer in your kingdom.

O king, serve free food in different shrines,
Engage the commanders in places so required.

Offer wealth for horses and elephants and,
Leave enough space for *gochara*,[vi] lands for grazing cattle.

Pay respect to the people who deserve it,
O king, don't be miserly while dealing with the poets.

Narrating all these principles, the King Bhisma
Looked at the face of Srikrishna instantly.

***

[v] Eleventh lunar day known to be auspicious in Hindu belief.

[vi] Grazing meadows for cattle.

Balarama Dasa (1472–1556)

'Chant Ramakrishna'

(Translated 'Mukhe Bhaja Ramakrushna' from the Odia by Bidyut Bhusan Jena)

Chant Ramakrishna, O mynah, or else,
The cats of wrath will snatch you, O mynah.
The animated cow, against its own
Unfathomed nature ran helter-skelter,
And snapped the rope of three attributes,
In which I had it tethered.
The house I had erected on four columns endures,
But its spinal column stands broken now, O mynah.
The guards will gather twenty-five others to plunder the house,
Hailing from the five elements, how can the guard let go of it, O mynah.

O mynah, you didn't recognize me at the time of your birth,
I'll be entreating while being carried away by the ruthless hunter, O mynah.

Colourful are your lips, your beak slender, your teeth pomegranate seeds,

Thus speaks Balarama Dasa with ardour, who caged the mynah?

***

Jagannatha Dasa (1491–1550)

Selected Couplets from *Bhagabata*

(Translated 'Bhagabataru Nirbachita Padya' from the Odia by Manu Dash)

Whoever is born to this Earth
Will die, whether man or God.

If you cut off your own tongue
Would there be anyone to plead for you?

The body endures the pang of karma
Like the python in the forest.

Whether one's nature is good or bad
You realize only at the time of death.

You sent me here with the life of a snake
How can I then give up my nature?

What this mind thinks often
In the course of time does happen.

When God saves with His grace
What harm can a mighty ever cause him?

He who sees the presence of soul in all
Never worries about birth or death.

The human body, a rare gift
Is meant only to seek salvation.

And his breath sounded like a conch shell
Verily he saw golden images
Perched on trees.

***

Salabega (Early seventeenth century–1608)

'O Blue Mountain'

(Translated 'Ahe Nila Shaila' from the Odia by Bidyut Bhusan Jena)

O cerulean mountain, intractable, impregnable,
Trample upon on the impenetrable forest of my being, O lord.

When the mighty elephant lord remembered you in deep water,
You saved him by killing with your discus the alligator.

When in deep forest the doe writhed in pain,
You saved her from the brink of danger.

Upon hearing the entreaties of Draupadi in the Kuru court,
You protected her modesty with the gift of unending clothes.

When Ravan's brother Vibhishana sought refuge in you,
You protected him and coronated him as Lanka's king.

Prahlada's father was evil and ruthless,
You came out of the pillar and ripped him out.

Thus, says poor Salabega, Muslim by birth,
I pay obeisance unto your lotus feet.

***

Dinakrushna Dasa (1650–1710)

'No, Never Ever You Have a Lord Like Jagabandhu'

(Translated 'Jagabandhu Pari Jane Samanta, Nahin Nahin Ta' from the Odia by Kalidas Misra)

No, never you have a Lord like
Jagabandhu, the friend of this world,
He knows everything about his fourteen realms,

And he slays sorrows with his Sudarshana, his mighty wheel.
When Krishna was in Gopa, his uncle Akrura
Went there to escort him to Mathura;

While milking the cow, the plaits of his hair
Were loosened, and Ananta, the lord infinite,
Revealed himself as the four-armed God.

You befriended Sugreeba and killed Vali,
When Ravana's brother Bibhisan surrendered
You offered him the kingdom of Lanka.

When Draupadi in disgrace, prayed in the court of the Kurus,
You unfurled a million yards of cloth to cover her, and
During the Mahabharata war, you also shielded and saved a tiny lark.

Such a merciful lord is never seen in the three realms,
Who destroys the woes of the woeful, says Dinakrushna Dasa,
The humble servant, meditating on the lotus feet of Lord Srikrishna.

***

Upendra Bhanja (1670–1740)

'Salvager of Pride'

(Translated 'Mana Uddharana, Kara He Karana' from the Odia by Bidyut Bhusan Jena)

Guard my honour, O Lord
I take refuge in your lotus feet.

Father to the orphan, O cerulean mountain
you are Lord Jagannath of Nilachal.

By the ocean, under the Kalpavriksha
you have graced the grand temple.

From afar you heard the elephant lord
while in the middle of a game of dice.

In your left palm, you rescued Sage Markandeya
who was being carried away by water.

You went to Kishkindha, killed Vali and
made the bridge on the ocean.

You killed Ravana in Lanka
in the pretext of rescuing Janaki.

At the request of Yudhisthira, you went to Hastina
and ate at Vidur's place.

You assuaged Draupadi's disquiet in the
Kuru court by granting her unending clothes.

At the time of the all-consuming forest fire
You protected the children of Brij.

Thus says Upaindra, the jewel among the poets,
I take refuge at your feet.

***

Banamali Dasa (1720–93)

'O My Lord, the Master of the Universe'

(Translated 'Jagannatha Ho . . . Kichhi Magunahin Mun Tote' from the Odia by Kalidas Misra)

O my Lord, the master of the universe
I don't ask anything from you;
I don't ask for wealth, I don't ask for children.
I ask only for an arm's length of *Saradha Bali,*
The stretch of sands made holy by your divine footprints.

My eyes don't seek for anyone
Save your holy sight.

My ears don't crave to hear anything
Save the ones narrating your glory.

My tongue doesn't desire to savour
The village songs sung night and day.
Let the string of your glorious names
Be only with me as my fond companion,
Oh dear Pitabasa, my lord in yellow attire.
My sense of smell is not satisfied
With the fragrance of any other sweet offerings
I only yearn for the garland worn by you,
Your holy basil and flowers,
Your sandalwood paste and camphor.
Let the fingers of my hand only count
The holy beads of your names,

O Rama, O Krishna,
Thus says Banamali, let my feet be on a
Pilgrimage to your holy site.

***

Sadananda Kabisurya Brahma (1720–90)

'Listen to Me, O Lord!'

(Translated 'Manima Suniba Heu Gariba Daka' from the Odia by Bidyut Bhusan Jena)

Lord! Kindly listen to poor me and
keep me in your grace, O lotus-faced one.
Why did the ocean of your grace dry up for me;
though I know that my path is not righteous?

O bearer of fortitude, you hardly heed my grief,
will I be granted *darshan*[vii] at last or denied?

If this poor me dies, your honour will wither;
the glow of your glory will suffer an indelible stain.

Thus, says poor Sadananda, to this there's no cure,
since by you, my misery goes unheeded forever.

***

[vii] A glimpse.

King Birakishore (1737–93)

'Keep Me Close to Your Mighty Chest, My Lord'

(Translated 'Bhujatale Mote Rakha Mahabahu' from the Odia by Kalidas Misra)

Keep me close to your mighty chest, my Lord,
Safe in your protective embrace,
Before your expansive mighty arms, what can this minion of sorrow do?

Imagine the chariot Nandighosa,
all decked and ready, and me at your service.
Your name is Deenabandhu, a friend of the poor,
And what would the people of
The world say if you are heartless?

This huge show of mighty royalty,
This name, fame, family and wealth
Seem stale and totally useless when I am before
The world-bewitching round eyes of the Lord.

Sorrow intensifies manifold, and
I scarcely see any happiness around.
I am just drifting away from you in
This ocean of life, save me Bhabagrahi.

There in Srikshetra,
The abode of Goddess Laxmi, your consort,
You live lavishly in luxury and grandeur,
But what of me, I don't get the joy anywhere
So long as I don't climb
The twenty-two steps of your temple.

If I am deprived of your service, Lord,
Why should I hold onto this life?
Why don't you lighten the burden
From my head, my master,
The burden of this worrisome life?

I am only a worthless fallen creature.
And I have great trust in your blessed feet.
Says King Birakishore, have pity on me at this hour.

***

Gopalakrusna Pattnaik (1784–1862)

'Why Did You Wake Up So Early, My Dear?'

(Translated 'Uthilu Edebegi Kahinkire Dukhidhana' from the Odia by Kalidas Misra)

Why did you wake up so early, my precious treasure?
Won't you allow me to churn the curd?

Ever you long for my company, dear.
Won't you sleep even for a moment?
Why are you so naughty?
Better you go now and play
With your brother Rama, and when night falls,
I shall lull you to sleep with a lullaby.

How can I churn the curd,
Keep off your hand from the churning rod?
Tarry a little, you obstinate, look here,
Let me feed you this cream.

Oh, what a nuisance, don't tangle around my feet, dear,
Go call your brother Balaram.

Daily, you dabble your hand into the churning pot
And take it out, are you crazy?

Why do you dance around, licking your empty palm?
Don't you look at your shadow dance?
You shall learn the steps.
Do you expect me to hold you in
My arms, day in and day out,
Leaving all the household chores behind?

Thus spoken, she wiped his face in the
Plait of her saree and kissed him
And Gopalakrusna fondly contemplated both.

***

Madhusudan Das (1848–1934)

'The Children of Utkal'

(Translated 'Utkal Santana' from the Odia by Gopa Ranjan Mishra)

Why do you cringe in fear
When you boast of being Utkal's children
Why do you shrink to say, my dear
When your mother cries in utter pain?

Ancestors of yours had earned great fame
With their glorious heroic deeds
Why then do you shudder with fright
Before your boss to recount your plight?

From the Ganga in the north to Godavari in the south
They had conquered a great expanse of land
How do you then compare with them
Being born into the same blessed clan?

The people of England, brave and bold
Don't ever love cowardly beings
The honour the Sikhs and the Rajputs get
Is surely not there in your fate.

You think you'll raise the fame of your race
With glib-tongued artful flattering words
The sycophants, after a dog's nature
Are forever focused on leftovers.

The flatterers like swift-moving dogs
Are never easy to recognize

While licking feet with a slavish mind
They do leave deadly poison behind.

Flattery is a dark terrain
One's selfish interest hides there within
Seeing a simple folk on the way
It harms him in no time.

Can our race ever progress
If one's own interest guides his will
If a sick swollen leg gains some flesh
What good of it, do we feel?

How can he look to the interest of the race
When he is just selfish to the core
Will the corpse ever revive
If hyenas or vultures play a doctor's role?

Selfishness as its charioteer
Can the chariot Nandighosh smoothly go
If the feed is tied to its mouth
Won't the horse's gallop slow?

Selfishness with sycophancy as a daughter
And fear and lies as her son
When these do work in unison
The state surely will face rebellion?

Wake up from slumber you, Utkal's children
When will you rise, O when
The glory and bravery of the resplendent past
When will they come to your mind again?

Your mother was once a begetter of heroes
At present, look how she grovels in the dust
How do you show your wretched face
To the world with such disgrace?

In the heaven up above
Your forefathers languish, do you heed?
You do commit an unpardonable sin
When you forget their noble deed.

Shake off, folks, your self-interest
And give up that fake flattering tongue
Soon, you'll find in a free country
Your life will be like a joyous song.

***

Radhanath Ray (1848–1908)

'Adornment Welcoming Spring'

(Translated 'Basakasajja' from the Odia by Tyagraj Thakur)

A fascinating time it is
Winter has not left yet and
The time for new leaves of spring,
The king of seasons has not arrived yet.

The riverbanks look golden with
The yellow mustard flowers on both sides.
And in the middle of the braid of river, through
The evening clouds, is that a blue skyline?

The fragrance of the Babool flower
Diffused with the sheaf of harvested paddy
On the threshing field
Keeps blowing through the village, day and night.

At times, the south-breeze passes by
And kisses the earth
It feels cold in the shadow and
If you step into the sun's rays, it scorches the skin.

The summer deludes the traveller
With its shining sun
And so does delude the chirping bird
Towards the mirage till the horizons.

Fearing the fog, the lotus is unable
To rise from water, and the tender mango leaves

Are growing on the branches
For the flowers to blossom.

To wear bunches of sweet flowers
On its body
The tree is adorning tiny tender petals
On each stalk

Without the touch of a black bee
Due to dew, the flower, like a beautiful-teethed lady
Is yet to receive the glance of beauty
Yet to blossom to its fullest

The red-headed bird's song welcoming spring
Is heard from four directions
And the butterfly keeps tasting honey
Flying on marigold and porcupine flowers

As the evening steps in, in the mango grove, on the river bank
The shrikes rasp and trill together
Like housewives shrilling and
Dancing with rejoice

From the deep forest, at times, is heard
The cuckoo singing indistinctly
Is she mounting a new string
On its voice box?

Deep in the forest, at places are
Growing white tender leaves
And the atandi wild creepers as if to adorn
The beautiful forest with a paste of sandal

The wild jasmine is arranging a bunch of buds
Wishing to adore the spring
And the piyal tree is blooming in the woods
But hasn't matured yet

All are mad these days in the hope of joy
But the joy is fleeting
Who knows that the hope of joy is
More joyful than joy itself.

***

Bhima Bhoi (1850–95)

'Prayers and Reflections: Canto-XXVII'

(Translated 'Stuti Chintamanira Saptabinsha Boli' from the Odia by Siddharth Satpathy)

Relate the Lord's glory,
Light up the sacred fire'—
Thus ordained the Guru.
Having bought me as a slave,
Having led me halfway through,
He has forsaken me
In this sorry state.
Why, o, why? (1)

I have no hope,
no one to rely on.
My courage fails me.
What do I do?
O Lord,
look after this world of Yours,
carry Your own burden. (2)

The suffering of devotees
knows no bound.
Hear, o Lord,
the onus rests on You.
May You bear Your load. (3)

Fortune and misfortune,
freedom and misery—
You have created them in pairs.
Who will carry

the burden of sin and sorrow?
Let it lie at Your feet. (4)

Your devotees
are all in tears.
O venerable Guru,
kindly forgive our sins.
Kindly protect us. (6)

How can I
keep myself aloof
from limitless woe
of all living beings.
O Lord
set them free
from all misery.
In their stead,
may I suffer
in hell forever. (7)

In the saint and the sinner,
in the master and the slave,
in the worm and the insect—
You are manifest in all. (11)

People abuse
and fight each other
over loss and gain,
faults and crimes.
It hurts me deep;
I grieve and lament. (16)

A bone or two,
a drop of blood,
and a lump of flesh—
I carry such a frame
mortal and frail;

how will I then
not grieve over
the ceaseless sorrow
of all living beings! (18)

In the war of Mahabharata,
a single blow claimed
as many as ten heads.
However,
I smart in pain,
if you even
slap someone else. (19)

'If my devotion has flaws
May thunder scorch my head',
So says Bhima,
'O Lord, curse me,
and consign this body to flames'. (20)

***

Madhusudan Rao (1853–1912)

'Sound of the Conch'

(Translated 'Shankhadhwani' from the Odia by Bidyut Bhusan Jena)

1

The sun is sinking on the western horizon,
The shadow of dusk is embracing the sky.

The evening is serene, deep and gentle,
On the tranquil earth, a placid shower.

At sundown, this weary me is hurrying home.

And in a faraway village, the sound of a conch is heard
As though the entire earth is stilled by this sound.

Amazed, I heard the sonorous surge, as if in a dream!

Then in that grand awakening arose my being.
In that sound, I heard the rumblings of the boundless ocean.

The unstruck sound of the eternal salvation dwells
In the limitless expanse of the ocean conch.

2

The rhythmic chanting of the grand ocean recurrently
Chimes with the unstruck sound of the conch.

The immeasurable ocean is my majestic abode
My being reverberates with the rumblings of the infinite.

Although separated from that heavenly abode
Can I ever forget its divine music?

For a mundane existence on earth,
Have you lost your way in the maze of ignorance?

How did you forget your motherland?
Where is the note of ambrosia on your tongue?

Come with the deep chanting of the Vedas and
Awaken the earth, O offspring of immortality.

Inspired by the life eternal beyond fear,
Through your life on earth herald eternity.

***

Gangadhar Meher (1862–1924)

'Tapaswini: Canto-IV'

(Translated 'Tapaswinira Chaturtha Sarga' from the Odia by Jayanta Mahapatra and Madhusudan Pati)

With eyes of a full-blown lotus came dawn, heralding peace,[viii]
For the sight of Janaki, thirst afire in her soul.
Offering pearls of dew in the leaves of her hands,
She waited in the courtyard of the virtuous Sita.
And with the koel's voice, pleaded:
'Appear before me, noble one, for now the night is ended.'
Saffron her apparel of light, a flowery sheen manifest.
Serene of form, these arouse in the mind a belief
That some yogic goddess is here, who soothes with words sweet,
Calling out endearingly, to ease all sorrows;
As if to gift life anew
She has come from heaven, down upon the earth.

The breeze sang, the bee played on the veena,
And the morning's scents kept dancing on Dawn's orders.
The pheasant with sombre eulogy, began with notes of praise,
The drongo came as the announcer,
And with sweet elegance, said: 'Rise, O Empress
Of Chastity, for now the night is gone.'

Vedic chants of the sages rang through the green woods;
The sonorous Om rose high, piercing the skies,
Delighting the lord of Vaikuntha, into the ears

[viii] A possible variant would be 'Auspicious emerged Dawn, a full-blown lotus'.

Of the serpent Ananta,[ix] as if making the strings
Of Saraswati's veena resonate.
The forest brightened from moment to moment,
As through the power of mantra,
Life's force swelled to heights anew.

The celibate nun, Anukampa, deep-set in austerities,
Came near Janaki's daughter then, and said solemnly:
'Arise, Vaidehi! For the tender-limbed Dawn
Is here; give her the joy of your sight.
The River Tamasa too waits
For the happiness of holding you once in her lap.'

With Rama's heroic figure etched on the tablet
Of her grief-steeped mind, like the sun;
Mirrored in a drop of dew in the lotus' heart,
The chaste Janaki rose from her bed;
Then, bowing at Anukampa's feet,
Humbly offered herself at the feet of Dawn.

She praised her thus: 'O Destroyer of Darkness,
Harbinger of the sun's coming on earth,
At your tender feet he collects his light,
And with full hopes I seek succour there.
Lover of fair fragrances,
Bring good fortune to the race of Raghus.'

At night's end, with eager heart,
The nurse of the hermitage, Tamasa, clear and pure,
Threw sprays of fragrant water and flowers in the yard;
The morning star, lighting her auspicious lamp,
Her fish eyes flickering,
Waited watchfully for the chaste Sita's coming.

[ix] The mythical serpent Shesa, whose coils form a bed for Lord Vishnu as He rests upon an ocean of milk in the upper heavens of Vaikuntha.

With her wave-like hands, Tamasa fondly embraced
And caressed the virtuous form.

With a voice sweet as nectar, she said:
'My child, I had never cherished the hope
That Sita, the necklace on the royal goddess's breast,
Would renounce the world and come to me here
To play upon my bosom. Only for your sake
Will the world acclaim and call me the fortunate one.

Meandering through many forests, motionless in the lake
And canyon, overcoming numerous obstacles with a clear vision[x]
Not counting the pain of darkness, or charmed
By the joy of light, I keep to my long course
With a deep-bowed head. So I fulfil my life,
Pleasing with gifts of water all who live on my banks.

Mandakini and Godavari arc only just as able as me;
Yet are crowned in glory, having gained
Inexhaustible wealth in your footprints
And your body's scents that endow godliness—
One had always craved for that,
And without which, one had felt ever disgraced.

Because of the good deeds I had done,
And knowing my heart's desire,
Dharma[xi] in time brought you down to me.
Rare riches I have found; and now, I will be fulfilled,
Drawing you to my lap day after day;
The purity of your being
Shall wash clean the sins of my life.

---

[x] Gangadhar's words here carry a double meaning: clear water and clean life. We have substituted clear vision.

[xi] Piety, as also cosmic law.

Flocks of swans and geese, pairs of *chakrabakas*[xii] and cranes
During spirited play in my lap, shall sip the water
Made pure by the touch of your sacred form
And live by my side forever,
Singing your praise with their notes,
And these ears will be assuaged for all time.

The thought that they would be cleansed by Sita's touch
Made the flowers abandon their home of vines,
Floating, dipping, hurrying along from far to approach you;
They would be circling around
As you bathe in my waters;
Do not then, compassionate one, push them away.

Upon my banks you shall wander,
Spreading eternal splendour in the woods,
This the trees would catch and glow with light,
Acquiring strength divine, imparting peace;
Green and rose on leaf.
Forever be transparent its exquisite beauty.'

Sita said: 'The stream is clear and sweet as coconut water,
Not mere water, but truly my mother's milk;[xiii]
From the breasts of mountains, it flows as a stream of nectar
Towards Sita, who is so lifeless now.
Ah, in the garb of Tamasa,
Riven in the heart with grief,
You are indeed a mother in this land to me.

A fissure tears your back, the other side looks clear;
Still, so the daughter be pleased,
You open your loving eyes, and with adoring words
One by one, you speak solicitously, fondling me.

[xii] A kind of bird called ruddy goose or Brahmani duck.

[xiii] Sita was the daughter of the Earth.

Marvellous, O Mother, is your heart,
Full of sand to absorb my burning sorrows.

The Sita, who in the eyes of the people of Rama's kingdom,
Was held to be tainted and banished,
The same one you think, firm in her dharma of marital devotion,
Will succeed in making sacred and pure
All that moves and rests upon this earth!
A mother truly understands her daughter's pain,
And a burnt face appears lovable
Like the moon to her mother's eyes.

Your banks will surely be my permanent refuge now
And my hopes only at your peaceful lotus feet;
For one whose world is empty, it's just a mother's lap
That is the storehouse of love on this earth.
When one's mother has a womb full of gems,
Why should she yearn for other places?'

Tranquil, clear and cool were Tamasa's pure waters,
And in nature alike were all the ashram's girls;
Agile in affection, Tamasa,
Taking on the guise of their reflections,
Made herself their exact likeness;
And embracing their bodies,
In deep ardour swiftly mingled in them.

Constantly thus at Sita's side to watch her grace,
Was for her an occasion propitious;
Making herself many-eyed, the expansive one,
Gained numerous hearts, minds and forms.
The heart's delights multiply
When joined to others of similar spirit and nature.
Their bath over, they came back
And offered worship at the feet of Valmiki.

The chief sage blessed them, saying: 'May you all
Persevere, and succeed in earning the riches of wisdom'.
Then, with special warmth, addressed Sita:
'May you give birth to heroes, free of hazard.
My daughter, tend these plants of the hermitage
With labour and love, as if these be your children;
So would you naturally grow in experience and know
How precious and rare is the gem of an offspring.
Anukampa shall always be there
To attend to all your needs.'

Then, all of them left, as wished by the chief sage,
Carrying pitchers in their lotus-soft arms.
In beauty, Janaka's daughter outshone them all,
A scintillating diamond among bits of crystal;
And the forest's charm deepened with the invaluable find
When they reached the garden.

The goddess of the woods, finding the heavenly Sita
At her door, embellished herself with the rays of the sun.
Smiling with her leaf-lips, her teeth flashing
Like mahua flowers, she decked herself lovingly to steal
Sita's mind,
Offering the red salmali, and held forth
Drifts of dew on the grass to wash her feet.'

She offered a lotus-flower seat, welcoming her
Through the mynahh's melodious calls.
Made fresh lotuses to bloom in the waters of autumnal pools,
And, with the hum of bees as though greeting the she-swan,
Said: 'My night of pain is over
With the touch of your sun-bright feet.
A dream came true when I saw you by sheer luck,
And with a heart pulsing with infinite joy
Followed your life in the Chitrakuta valley,
In Dandaka, nurtured by perfect sages.
And in the asoka forests of Lanka beyond the trees;

Placed you as a model before my eyes.
And for fourteen years sculpted an icon of love.

As you flew back through the sky on the *Puspaka*,[xiv]
I kept looking up sadly with flower in hand, beseeching with peacock-cries.
And went on calling out fondly,
Till you had gone past hearing range.
Have you then come back, dear,
Recalling a friend's cries after so long a time?

Friend, unable to bear the agony of unending separation,
I became a hermit in the last resort;
Seeing my own self in the mirror of your heart, flooding it in love,
I welcomed you with deep delight;
Accept now my gratitude,
That you have fulfilled my desire with so much love.

Goodwill that ensures from the company of the good,
As the unchanging blue of the sky, never dies.
With a friend who is virtuous the heart's desire never goes in vain,
So it is why I am able to see you today;
For it is Fate which fulfils such things,
And it is my love for you, my friend,
That has made me fortunate!'
The sweet enchantment of sylvan beauties,
Like a newly risen mass of cloud.
Suddenly surfaced in Sita's mind
To cool the burning pain of the fire of separation
In the woodlands of her heart.
The daughter of Janaka muttered:
'I am your prisoner for life.'

***

[xiv] Mythical aerial vehicle.

Gopabandhu Das (1877–1928)

'Viewing Chilika from the Train'
(Translated 'Raila Upare Chilika Darshana' from the Odia by Chittaranjan Misra)

Stop, stop a while, O steaming stock!
Let me see Chilika
That comes into view as a wonderful portrait.
I feel the view to be a portrait
For the beauty of this scene is unbelievable!
Is such a picture possible in the real world?

Slowly, the blue waves move
It looks like a dream.
Flocks of birds swim
Each of them turns into a pair
With its reverse image
Mirrored in the waters.

Together when they all fly up into the air
Hundreds of their doubles
Dive into the womb of Chilika.

Before one feels the scene as real
It disappears.
The cruel steam rail carries me away
Trees and rocks come blocking the sight.
It hides now, it reveals then
Like a lovely image escaping in a dream.

Here, it's blue and lush green there
Sometimes grey and white after a moment
The scene changes, with multiple colours

Chilika! you manifest your magic.

Poet Radhanath, the seeker of beauty
The worshipper of the muse Saraswati
Roamed over most of India
Witness to diverse forms of nature
He wandered through dales and valleys
Crossed many rivers, streams and mountains
Nowhere could he quench his thirst
For pure wonder
But here, in you
He discovered the flow of
Joy, peace and love.

You are the treasure of beauty of Utkal
Through his poetic vision
He quarried from you the rare gems
Threaded them as beads
And made a garland, an offering
To the world of letters of Utkal.
The tapestry of words, his poetry
Will ever be there singing your glory
Inviting thinkers to your shore.
I'm not wise, I am witless
I know not why
My life has ever yearned for beauty
Maybe that prompted me
To come to your banks some day
And revel in your marvel.

I had kept the thought to myself
Burdened by other chores.
After ages, this opportune moment had come
But alas it slipped.

How can a man in the midst of
Worldly complications

Living with family, friends and blood relations
Act in his own way?
One is never free from worries
In the society.

Many a time I have imagined you
In silence.
I have watched the endless play of
Celestial golden rays on your blue waves.

I imagine innumerable rainbows
Dancing on your bosom
Unforgettable are those scenes.
My fancied Chilika! You fulfil me.

The memories of glories
Upset my heart in agony and ecstasy.
Your name is entwined with
The glorious heritage of Utkal.

Where has that glory gone
When the Lord Himself in human form
Arrived in the battlefield
And fought as a soldier
To protect the exalted fame of Utkal?
Where is that fortune now?
Where has that devotion gone?
This sacred land has been defiled today.
This holy Aryan land, this hallowed Nilachal
Has lost her spiritual might, her divine strength.
The serenity of her face has withered away
The godly grace has been removed from her heart.
Power and spirit once enshrined in the life of Utkal
Are lost in bewilderment.
Where have the sails of the Odias gone?
Where can one hear

The songs of the sailors?
Where are they who sailed to foreign lands
What has become of their wealth and fame?
All these have been reduced to legends
Of the sailors' wives anointing the vessels.

Your smooth coasts
Fringed by impenetrable hills
Were once home to gallant scions of Utkal.
Today the same hills, the same forests are there
The rocks are solid as before
But where is that valour today
Where has that national spirit of the Odia race gone?

***

Laxmikanta Mohapatra (1888–1953)

'Song of Life'

(Translated 'Jiban Sangita' from the Odia by Chittaranjan Misra)

Depriving me of everything
What would you gain
To keep the flag of your fame fluttering?
You have already withdrawn
What you had granted me.
What more is left to be taken away?
He who is after worldly things
Runs to you
How can you scare someone
Who has lost his trust in you?
Duped repeatedly
I have come to know your tricks
Have you planned to
Distract me from my path
In the middle of the marketplace?
To avert your trap
I have left all trades
How can you entice him
Who has cut off all ties, all bonds?
You call me, moving your hands
Tempting me to watch the drama
Are you seducing me to all this once again
To the ordeal to punish me?

***

Kuntala Kumari Sabat (1901–38)

'My Fellow Brother'

(Translated 'Suna Hey Manisa Bhai' from the Odia by Kalidas Misra)

1

Listen to me, dear fellow brother, you are not born
to pine away your grief or drown yourself in sorrow.

Dear brother, it is not man's destiny
that he would exhaust his life in sighs and disappointments endless,
in the dense darkness of despair;
that he would stay manacled, deprived and humiliated,
a victim in the prison of pain in this wide world,
This life is not for destruction, dear, for being a carrier of death;
you are immortal, dear fellow brother, a luminous being, how
can you die?

2

O, listen, my dear men and women,
this world is not the abode for anybody's luxury,
it is for cruel tyranny of the weak
and the oppressed by the bloodthirsty,
before whom he surrenders willingly
his happiness with bowed head and self-destructs,
This is not the order of destiny,
This beautiful life is not for destruction, for being a
carrier of death.

3

Listen, O people of the world, this pious realm is for work,
and you use your labour for that,
You get up quick, forsaking your shyness,
your fear, humiliation and ego,
May you be victorious in the war
between the devilish and the divine
In this world created by God, you forsake yourself.

4

Listen, O you *Arindam*, destroyer of enemies, worshipped by the six enemies, attended to by the gods,
You have your place among the cluster of stars,
With wounds innumerable and bloodstains in your body
You are not complex or fragile,
Smeared with the ink of slurs, you have not become poor or mean,
You are a great son of destiny,
You snap the century-old rope of death and hold on to the rope of life.

***

Mayadhar Mansinha (1905–73)

'Ambitions of the Young Poet'

(Translated 'Taruna Kabira Asha' from the Odia by Chittaranjan Misra)

How immense are the ambitions
Of the young poet!
They are beyond words.
I had thought of embarking on an endless journey
Charioted by a cool, gentle wind
To reach the far-off
Colourful country of spring blossoms.
I would go studded with flowers
All over my body
Wearing Ashoka buds behind my ears
My back adorned with baula[xv]
I would merge into a fragrance
Dissipating everywhere.
As a pleasant scent, I would disperse in the air
Stirring moonbeams with sparks of love
To be seduced and kissed.
I would fly away
Carrying the music of summer breeze
As free as a bird.
The cuckoo would call, 'Come on, brother'
Driving the young poet mad with excitement
The rose would say,
'You came at last, after ages.'
I had thought of easing men of their worries

[xv] A medium-sized evergreen tree known as Mimusops elengi.

Making the world a sweeter place
Following the only divine mandate
To do good to all living beings on earth.
I would fly from one country to the other
Connecting hearts of all races
Preaching love and knowledge to my fill.
I had fancied a floral bed
Under the bakul tree
I had thought of living with my beloved
A life like a dream.
I had chosen my love
The epitome of beauty, my age
Had thought of making her my darling.
I would forget the worldly loads
And worship the Radha of my heart
Play the flute
And know no separation.
Under the vast moonlit sky
I would rest on her thighs and
Forget the cycles of birth and death
As a dream.
In a hut of reeds by the quiet river
I would repose when tired
Startled I would be waking up in a moment
By the sound of your anklet bells
Knowing my beloved has come.
How eager I am

Waiting for the arrival of my love!
She would come waving her
Braided hair
Stealing a glance at me with her bewitching eyes
She would put a garland around my neck.
There would be a book by my side
Of poems about unending youth and love
She would sing one even as I would kiss her lips

To my heart's content!
Oh, how immense are the ambitions of the young poet!
They are beyond words
They create multiple earths and skies in a moment.
The young poet is grieved
Caught between fiction and truth
He searches for his Radha everywhere.
There is no Radha, no play of reeds in the wind
No dame with waving braids
Where is the time for him
To be lost in the crazy pursuit of love?
The childhood friend is not around
She has left seeking someone else
Who should he cuddle, take into his arms?
He has ceased to be a lover
Poor poet is ever
Stuck with his longing.
He is lost in the miseries of the world
Where is the time for composing verses?
What if spring is about to depart?
The young poet is sinking
Under the weight of the world
Moment by moment
The poems and dreams of love
Keep leaving him.
It's a pity
He is not even able to assuage his own pain
Let alone the sufferings of the world.
But his hopes are
To raise the earth to heaven
Words fail to describe
What he envisages
How immense are the ambitions
Of the young poet!

***

Nirmala Devi (1907–89)

'You'

(Translated 'Tume' from the Odia by Panchami Manoo Ukil)

O Colourless One!
Wherefrom do you gather this array of hues?

O Odourless One!
Wherefrom do you arrest this captivating fragrance?

O Formless One!
Whose caress is it that thrills my soul?

O Imperceptive One!
How do you excite the world with emotions?

O Shapeless Gem!
How do you enchant in myriad forms?

O Speechless One!
Why do you endure such clamour?

O Void the Great!
Why such wholeness do I witness?

I observe, O my beloved
Your inscrutable manners

Do listen, I write often for you.

***

Radhamohan Gadanayak (1911–2000)

'Uddam Singh'

(Translated from the Odia by Gopa Ranjan Mishra)

Away from the land that bore me, my friends
This is Uddam Singh, the Sikh lad
I stand captive in the prison of the far-away city of London
Before me, I see the gallows
And I am going to tell you the story of my native land.

Do hear, my friends, the tale of my crime
You might wonder why at all
I chose the hangman's noose
Around my neck in the prime of youth
Yes, with these hands of mine I've shot dead that killer of men.

You might have heard of that Dyer
That die-hard opponent of our country, our race
In the land of five rivers that day
Blood flowed in torrents
In the Jallianwala Bagh ground.

That diabolic Dyer
Who would ever call him a man?
He was indeed a beast in the garb of a man.

The impassioned mass gathered in full fury
Some said, 'These foreign rulers are big betrayers
We shed our blood for the war
We gave them all that we had with us
But our rulers didn't bother to see our plight

No more in silence shall we bear the tyrannical rule
Will show them our strength and our unbeatable will.'

The booming of guns was heard at hand
Dyer had given his cruel command
'What game do you play, you folks?' I warn
And soon there was the firing of endless bullets
The confused crowd scattered and ran pell-mell

Hundreds like winged ants dropped to the ground
The land of Jallianwala was flooded with blood
The whole of Punjab raised a protest
And the rulers then roared back
'It's not their rightful claim, it's a crime.'

Punjab turned into a fuming battlefield
And war laws were hurriedly declared by them
The army marched through the streets and lanes
The people got mercilessly outraged
It was as though tyranny was let loose
And the God of death had gone on a rampage
At last, they said they had taken some remedial measures
Would you call it a remedy after all?

Long after this barbaric act happened
I turned speechless when I heard it first
And burned and burned endless within
And yes, I am Uddam, I've sent a bullet through his chest
Whom would you hold liable
For what happened?
I have murdered a tyrant
And I'm now called a killer.

The fire that burned once
In the land of the five rivers
I had never seen that ghastly sight
Had only heard about it from others

The day I heard it first, I turned dumb
And then, the whole being of mine shaking, a storm rose within me
Someone came and blocked my pace
And a voice within me rang—rest not till you take revenge.

I rushed towards Jallianwala like someone insane
Felt an intense emotion rising in me
And saw the ground washed by many a monsoon
Yet it looked drenched to the core with fresh blood
Like one possessed, I rolled on the field
And the smouldering lava beneath it filled my veins
With the heat of the old flame.

Startled, I rose and smeared this body of mine
With the dust from the ground
The whole of me lay aflame
It was hard to bear the pain any more.

I gathered a handful of earth
And squeezed it hard in my fist
And the inside of my palm turned crimson like hibiscus
Where shall I clean this stain, this palm of mine?
Which river can wash it clean, be it Sutlej, Indus or Jhelum?

I swore as I shook with anger
'I'll never wipe clean these hands of mine
Let them lie unwashed like this'
What can calm and appease my mind
Like lightning, it struck within—'nothing but revenge'.

Inside the meeting hall
Of the Lords of this great city
Stealthily I got in and shot Dyer in his chest
In exchange for hundreds of bullets
I have shot just one
In exchange for hundreds of lives

I have taken just one.

For the honour of my dear motherland
That had been so rudely outraged
I have done this that I deemed right, befitting
But in the eyes of our ruler
I am a killer, a criminal
Before me lies the gallows
In my death, I tell you all the story of my motherland.

***

Ananta Patnaik (1912–87)

'The Destitute'

(Translated 'Sarbahara' from the Odia by Chinmoy Jena)

We gave our lifeblood to build your palaces.
We strengthen the administration while we remain destitute.
Enduring sirocco, we sowed seeds in your paddy fields
Treading mud and grime, we tortured our bodies
Mocked by the rest, we harvested paddy in winter dawn.

The power of the mighty and the dreadful engulfed us all
We looked on with skeletal bodies while
Our dues and wages were siphoned off by landlords and moneylenders.
Our children drop dead in burning ghats
While we look on in terror like figures of stone.

In an age when man flies in the air and explores the ocean bed,
We go around with bowed heads crying out for food
We beat our heads against temple doors
Unable to cope with the burden of loans with our frail bodies.

We built guns, cannons and swords for us
We also built prison walls while singing of our own imprisonment.
Enmeshed in the unyielding nets built by us,
We blocked the path of light for ages.

When our enlightened consciousness arises
We shall no more wander like mendicants carrying grief and pain
We, the class of workers shall certainly snatch our dues
We will usher in a bloody dawn by piercing the dark sky.

All the destitute, the workers and farmers
Come together, shedding fear and inaction,
Let the earth, the sky, the wind and the exploiters tremble
While our one homogeneous world cracks the mountain peak.

***

Sachidananda Routray (1916–2004)

'Konark'

(Translated from the Odia by Chittaranjan Misra)

You have seen on her stones
The forms of exquisite art,
There I have seen myriad bones of humans
A sanctuary of broken hearts.
You have seen how the pictures of golden dawn
Have blossomed on the dark screen of the parting night
How poetry has emerged from silent rocks
Through languor and dreams
Immersed in intense love.
You have tasted the springs of varied flavours
of emotion
Oozing in this temple of amazing beauty
You have drunk cupfuls of the nectar
To quench your searing thirst.
But I have returned from the Lion Gate
Unromantic and grounded as I am.
I have returned with a heavy heart, hurt
I have seen her in the eyes of a worker.
I have seen under those stones
Countless hearts of artisans
Silenced and buried.
Nobody has counted how many of them
Like donkeys have carried loads of stones
Bending their backs
Having their spines damaged.

How many of them have poured their blood, sweat and tears
Into this structure
Through their chisels, hammers and pickaxes
Executing the king's order.
So much of blood of
Carpenters, masons, smiths and workers
Have flown into the waters of the sea
Their stories have dissolved into the salty waters unnoticed.
But the world watched the great temple
Singing the glory of the king.
Wise men say
In this temple is inscribed
The identity of the nation.
The amorous watches the lovely stone statues of
Dancing women, their slim and slender waists
The patterns of lotus buds
Behind their clothes.
Someone sees a wreath dangling
Around the neck of the serpent woman
In her post-coital posture
Another perceives the pangs of
A hundred nights of separation
In the braid of a *yakshini*.[xvi]
Has anyone ever wanted to know the history of man?
Has anybody asked
How many lives have perished,
How the saws, hammers and axes
Had to embrace defeat here?
How many starving men had to bite the dust?
The artisans have no place in the palace of arts.
He leaves no footprints in this world of art
Except his work

[xvi] *Yakshini* is a female nature spirit in Hindu religious mythologies.

He has no place here.
Hail our sculpture
Laud our skills
To propagate the good name of the king!
Since the name of the king
A single name has to be immortalized
The others had to be pushed
To the graveyard of anonymity.
But this sentimental race
Still takes pride in looking at the artists' graves.
Under this shrine, the granary of art
Crores of them
Bisu Maharana and Sibei Samantara
Have slept forever.
The worker shed his blood
For building this temple
The farmer gave his golden crops
For the royal treasury.
But there is no place for their agony
In the hall of fame.
No place to house their weal and woe, their songs of harvest.
On each arch of the arcade
There are celestial creepers
Radiating heavenly beauty
Is there any space for the crops of the earth
The golden glow of paddy fields?
The lordly taste, the controls of power
Frame and mould the figures there.
There, the feet of the nude dancing girl
Move to the rhythmic beats of elegant music.
There lies a dream world of blue waves
Harvest of flowers.
At the hour of dawn
The diamond sun

While receiving her obeisance
Tells the earth—
Is a song a song
If it does not tell of wounds and insults of life?
But this epitome of elegance
This marvel of fine art
Has not said anything of man it could have.

***

Sachidananda Routray (1916–2004)

'Moon of Matiaburuja'

(Translated 'Matiaburujara Janha' from the Odia by Chittaranjan Misra)

In the grey sky of Matiaburuja
The moon has risen.
Flecks of light play waving everywhere.
The moon has risen
Let it.
Let lotus bloom in this darkness.
Within me on occasion moon rises.
Sun moves.
I too write poetry
Dream
Compose rhythms like a peacock spreading its feathers
And dance.
I imagine moving higher
With every step
The sign of my rising shines.

But when it's time for the eagle in the storm
For speeding and soaring up
Ranging from the bottom of the abyss
To the core of the sky
A frenzy of turbulence begins.
The evening star vanishes,
Night ends but morning doesn't break.
The stratagems of a dream
Never gets discussed in real terms.
The enchantment of reverie

Ever looks luminous.
The moon of Eid
Gleams through
Narrow fissures of dirty clouds.
I compare our men with ancient beasts of the ice age.
I ask:
'Are we more civilized than animals?
They may be more terrible
More wild, more cruel, darker and intensely hairy
But cleaner they are than us
Because they do not speak in terms of
Varied ideologies.
To taste freedom is their natural right.
They are neither Hindus nor Muslims
Their religion is to stay together
Or fight
For love, for food
Or anything barring the imagined religion.
The open manifesto of life
They sign, pleading for the right to life.'
This Matiaburuja
Where faces of men blur
Amid smoke from countless chimneys,
Where the shining silver rays of a thousand moons
Forget their ways in blind alleys.
On this road, there are rows of huts of tins and tiles
Where in the shady light of a flickering lantern
Too many peddle
Too many shopkeepers.
On the right of the slaughterhouse
The knife sharperner's shop is overcrowded.
Somebody gets his knife sharpened
Someone a spear
Somebody sharpens his sword

The continuous sound from the grinding stone
Pierces into the ears.
I get disturbed.
It's so overcrowded!
But everything came to a standstill.
Suddenly the place wore a deserted look.
All of a sudden
The crowded places are now without men.
Innumerable lives fell on the ground
Like broken nests in a storm.
Nobody could save
Even a single soul.
That sweat ran through blood and tears
Somebody sliced the breasts of women
Someone thrust a knife into a woman's genital

The concrete of the road was soaked in tears and blood.
No one listened to the cries from choking throats
Of infants and the old.

This ancient story
Again, was heard in this present age!

This fight is between two contraries
Under canopies and whisks of two religions,
The whole country is ablaze
By its devouring sway.
All rules splendidly worded
In the charter of the nation lapsed
Melting into thin air
Like the kite of a boy
Lost in the southern wind.
Tell me if it's already dawn?
Or it's still night, the same night of the old days
The dark python night?
I know

It's both
For these are symptoms of both.
Because night is the marker of morning
Clouds are the prelude to rain.

***

Gururprasad Mohanty (1924–2004)

'The Dove of My Eyes'

(Translated 'Akhira Kapota Mora' from the Odia by Jayanta Mahapatra)

The doves of my eyes strike against
the steel of the sky,
and repulsed, return to earth,
where, each day you wait alone
to discover the many meanings of life and death.

When the words, with their little palms,
touch the body of the motionless sands,
running through the grey heat of noons
I seek ancestral memories in your flesh.

You whisper the secrets of leaf and grass,
of cliffs and woods, moss and shell,
in forlorn nights through the tatter of clouds
the myths of the moon sailing to its death.

As you retrieve the ruined body of April
drifting helplessly in the whirlpools of sand,
it seems you love me and want me to come,
but where is your soul? and where is my body?

And when the doves of my eyes return,
ripping the sky's wrongs, it is time's river
that flows through the weariness of your flesh
and carries my dreams along.

Leaves fall, unheard, in the quiet noon,
and the sun respires in silence.

The pine forest pales like smoke in the sky.
And I don't remember when, the doves of my eyes
flew into Ujjain or Cuttack, pursuing you.

***

Bhanuji Rao (1926–2001)

'Konark'

(Translated from the Odia by Chinmoy Jena)

We all are townsfolk
Off to visit Konark.
We set out in cars
Throwing red dust up in the air
Smoking cheroots and rucksacks
Hanging from our shoulders.
We sit crammed in the car
Kurtas rubbing against blouses.

We are all gentle folks
Sporting gold buttons,
Carrying playing cards, a gramophone
And bottles of rum.

We halted far away from the limits of the city
near a solitary village,
its name unknown to us
with an acute thirst for tender coconut water.
Who is this lass approaching
With eyes as meek as a cow's?

I sit quietly
Immersed in thought.
A lady friend pointed
To a dove at the edge of a bamboo bush.
And we saw the vast expanse of paddy fields
And the groves of casuarina and cashew nuts.
White gourd on some roofs,
We saw these in daylight.

Then came the night
And moonlight glistens on the
Leaves of the mast wood tree.
And on the wide mattress of grass.
A magician in the sky
Brings forth clouds of so many shapes.
We watch all these through the dust
And the smoke of cheroots.
'Have you seen Konark?'
The girl with red lips asks.
Was the languid girl's heart
made of stone?
She smiled with pursed lips
And her smile was dear.

Then, going past many casuarine groves
And vast stretches of sand,
And while passing Gop and Nimapada
I think how huge are the
Horses and elephants of Konark!

Here we halted
And moved trudging over the sand
Dragging our feet,
We reached our destination,
Listening to the sea's distant roar.

The dog chews the chicken bones,
There are eggshells and fish bones
Strewn about everywhere
There is the dak bungalow where a *punkah*[xvii]
And a reclining chair assure
One of sound sleep.
This is sheer luxury.

[xvii] A large fan made out of jute or straw or cloth which were pulled in bungalows of the Britishers and landlords.

While lying there I contemplate,
Forgetting what lies ahead
And what has gone by.
The same girl asks me again
Raising her eyelids and
Arching her eyebrows
'Have you seen Konark?'

***

Rabi Singh (1931–2020)

'Life'

(Translated 'Jiban Bidiru Nian Nivilani' from the Odia by Gopa Ranjan Mishra)

From the umbrella of my life
The ribs snapped in the midday
At the peak of summer
Now, it's all fire burning along the path of life.

From the fence of my life
A split bamboo broke
The cattle rushed in, all deceitful
The straw flew off the thatched roof
And I'm deprived of living a life.

From the stairs of life
The feet slipped
And I am disabled
What a bother
Life's vessel has a hole in it now
The throat lies parched for a drop of water.

Life's bitch swaggered about for a while
And kicked the bucket at last
There you see that resting place for pilgrims
Before that only, it breathed its end.

In the marshy land at life's edge
Just see how that pale brown cobra
Flicks its tongue, with its hood raised
Why, that's no tongue—that's the banner of death.

The sweet-toned blackbird of my life
Flew away in a flash
I wasn't able to see it
The astrologer said, 'The Saturn's wrath on you.'
I heard it dumbfounded, feeling cheated.

From my life's aviary
The pigeons have flown away
Shedding their feathers
Let's go then like them
As kites in the open sky.

From the bidi of my life
The fire has dimmed, my dear
There is no fire here in this land
And one can only hear the darkness yawning.

Let's go walking in the dark
Carrying our own flame along the way
It's not possible to sustain life here any longer
The poor man's wife is the butt of everyone's banter.

Our path is hard and thorny
But dear, we have to keep walking
Pushing with our feet our own funeral pyre
With death ringing in our ears

Life is just unbearable here
Anger and wailing rises in the heart
Life's charm wears off
And hot tears roll down one's face.

But once we cross this land
We'll come to a new country
Where no one exploits another
Where a brother doesn't poison a brother
There we shall dwell

And celebrate life.

We'll leave behind our footprints
In the course of our journey
In hills, woods and along the banks of streams
In cities, villages and in the country.

The travellers who walk in this terrain
After us may wonder,
'Who are the discontented folks
That trod upon this path
And left behind them the flame of wrath?'

Delay not, my beloved
Come along
We'll tear through the hills and forests
And the rough, uneven path
And the dense impenetrable darkness.

Soon we'll see in the east–
In obstructed rage–
The sun rising on the horizon
The night will dawn at last
At the end of the journey.

***

Ramakanta Rath (b. 1934)

'Arithmetic'

(Translated 'Ganita' from the Odia by Bidyut Bhusan Jena)

If I gave you all my sleepless nights and
you mixed them up with your soporific ones;
and after all the addition, what if it came
to be the years I had waited for you?
Now, tell me how many nights I have given you.

Does the woman who would finally turn into space,[xviii]
still exist after subtracting her tears from the smiles
undulating on her pulsating lips? What of you would still
endure after the one persisting in you for ages departs?

With what one needs to multiply the final sighs
to attain the elation of the first meeting?
Whose curses need to be divided with how much
of repentance to not be left with any quotient?

Since when did someone like me so adept at failing
in arithmetic learn to answer such questions!
One would even forget the notebook after the bell and
if it were to be opened, it would appear that one wouldn't
even return to answer any of the questions.

***

[xviii] Out of five elements, where the souls mingle after death, Vyoma or Sky is one of them. Space is other name of Vyoma.

Jagannath Prasad Das (b. 1936)

'The Mask'

(Translated 'Mukha' from the Odia by Jayanta Mahapatra)

I treasure many masks: for day and night
and evening; for a moment of happiness;
for the last act of the tragedy;
for guest and fellow traveller, one-time lover
and her husband, emperor, soldier and whore;
for the sorcerer and the funeral procession;
for the exiled sky and startled dawn;
for love and for deceiving; for defense.
Holding different masks over my face,
I change disguises for every phase of life.

I sought a mask in the scant blue of whose eyes
maidens would fall under my spell;
sensing the slight firmness of my lips
enemies would acknowledge defeat;
at one glance, every bird in the sky
would fly into my cage;
I'd call for night and the sun would drop.

That mask was never found; all masks of mine
are only small surprises, trivial smiles,
morbid pleasure and sullen arrogance,
feeble cries, impotent anger; my masks are merely
a little love and parting's common grief.
Under these masks, I know, I honour guests,
recite mantras, make love to my wife and mistress,

speak with the skies, watch the stars,
and lose myself easily in a throng of people.

And my age increases from one mask to the other,
from one deceit to another.
From the depths of disguise, some try
to recognize me, while others
who know me behave as strangers;
if at times I lose my identity,
I try to find myself, I look at the walls:
masks lined up row after row,
and bits of scattered broken glass—
It is meaningless to question a mirror.

***

Sitakant Mahapatra (b. 1937)

'Artist'

(Translated 'Chitrakar' from the Odia by Jayanta Mahapatra)

From the pores of his skin
innumerable yogic suns
wipe the entire sky
with darkening cloth
and fly off somewhere
under the weight of wonder's meaning
the breathless hills
hint of forgotten distances,
the rivers turn and look behind.

Colour is merely the unitary mode
          between dream and death,
which breaks into bits the clean breeze
          in mindless abandon.

Quite common the random handiwork of moonlight
strewn over the entire landscape,
the torments striving to dance
to the slow strains of the melody
after having removed their masks in the light.
The streets and lanes of the peaks of fire
meet in the meadow of darkness,
dream and death become one,
whatever binds each to each in intimacy:
time to possibility
and shape with the voiceless leaf.

***

Bibek Jena (1937–85)

'Autobiographical'

(Translated 'Atibyaktika' from the Odia by Jayanta Mahapatra)

Down the steps of this room, I return
now from your closed door.

Here, to break open this door
the terrible cry across my blood
as my closed eyes experience
the establishment of desire
in the excited flesh.

The darkness here is thick.
in its embrace
you would be lying unconscious
and crowded in your breath
the body and the scents of desire
and the uncovered fatigue of your heart

Even though I return from the barred door
you hold my being on the edge
tied to your blood and fibre.
But today I return
from your closed door.
In the dark.

***

Sourindra Barik (1938–2016)

'Now, I Am'

(Translated 'Mun, Ebe' from the Odia by Manu Dash)

Now, I am in transit.
I have been relieved from my old post,
But I am yet to join in my new place.
A charade is going on to bid me farewell.
A tea party somewhere
And a plan for dinner elsewhere
It is really distressing to bid adieu this way;
With this is attached many a thing
Some bonds feel severed
Some people are simply snatched away
Building relation with someone is such a bond
That no one wants to snap.
Freedom from this bond is such anguish.
But putting all that behind me
I am moving to my new station.
I know nothing about that place
No one here knows anything either.
Some say it's a wonderful place,
Others think it's terrible
And too tough to manage.
Come what may
I've to move to that place;
I have to build new relations.
Someone reveals
There's nothing new or old there.

Only great attachment, great relationship and
Great deliverance
Yes, great deliverance
Here there is neither bonding nor liberation on deliverance
Neither any location nor any identity whatsoever
Nothing endures there;
Even emptiness doesn't even exist.
Only an endless void.
Now, I am in transit.

***

Banshidhar Sarangi (b. 1940)

'Nothing Exists Outside'
(Translated 'Bahare Nathaye' from the Odia by Bidyut Bhusan Jena)

Let's be in our own places—
I in mine, you in yours, for
nothing exists outside
everything finds an abode within,
but light can enter every space.

The gecko can move effortlessly
on the wall, but not us.
Perhaps, not all terrains are easy
to tread, but who can really
hinder the recalcitrant wind!

Sand-bubblers can
tunnel through the sand.
Can we really do so, for
not everything is
possible for everyone.

One day you'll return to orbit
of the words of the poems you had
once pushed away as unwanted.
Meaning and not its absence
will bring you back to itself.

Your look is too piercing to
face and so ruthlessly
entangled that it's not easy

to measure its form.

While speaking to someone,
one thinks that one exists outside.
But in fact, he lives somewhere inside.
Is he then I after all?!

***

Kumar Mohanty (1941–95)

●[xix]

(Translated poem, whose first line, ‘Ki Katha Kahibi Kaha’, from the Odia by Chinmoy Jena)

Tell me,
which tale do I narrate before the other?
I have unending tales—
that do not let me live in peace,
trying to tell them would be the death of me.

I am guiltless and infirm,
bludgeoned needlessly—
Look at the blood streaming from my wound,
and they accuse me of staining the soil?
To which realm does such justice belong?
I have unending tales like this to narrate.

The police here are imposters,
bootlickers even—
them saluting power
instead of people like you or me.
They have dug their own graves—
designed by Lord Jagannath,
for them.
Kalia made me his watchman,
helped cleanse my conscience—
but I have many tales to narrate still.

[xix] ‘Dot’ signifies the title of each Anam poem. All Anam poems begin with a ‘dot’ as their title.

I neither believe in kings,
or the subjects of those kings—
no caste for me either.
I am a vanquished soul,
the *Garuda Stambha*, my life's oar.
I have to ascend the *Baisipahacha*,[xx]
but my feet are in chains—
and there are many more tales that I have to narrate.

Odias are handicapped today—
selling their self-respect,
with a begging bowl in place
before alms are offered.
Like the nest-dwelling bird,
what is life when the soul is sold—
There is not enough time,
just not enough time—
and I have many more tales to go.

The bird, while within the nest,
looks for a nest—
just as, he who lives by the river
thirsts for a home by the river.
While we who inhabit beautiful homes,
seek shelter in whorehouses.
The blind leads the blind here—
But saying so,
Will earn their wrath.
And I have unending tales to tell.

There are victims here
who serve as a beacon of light,
and those who provide refuge intuitively—

[xx] Baisipahacha are the steps within the temple premises, which lead from the main gate (Singha Dwar) to the sanctum of Lord Jagannath.

Then why this greed?
The cage that you flew away from—
return there Kumara,
For I have unending tales to tell.

***

Soubhagya Kumar Misra (b. 1941)

'Odisha'

(Translated from the Odia by the poet)

Whatever I couldn't learn
from clusters of mango blossoms,
from the full moon of *Kumara Purnima*,[xxi]
from the anxious hooves of the cattle
fleeing from the rising storm,
I just couldn't. What then, what!

I failed the exam.
I put the ring on the wrong nose,
On the wrong toes.
I pressed the feet of insolent lords
to earn an estate.
I kissed the biting horse on the mouth.

In the darkness of all my mistakes
the only star, you,
I don't know why I fell for you.
I don't know who the god was
who then in a good mood
made my inside redolent
with the fragrance of your body.
The sun of my morning
rose in the Mahanadi
and set in the dazzling sands

[xxi] Kumar Purnima is a religious festival celebrated on the full moon day of the Hindu lunar month of Ashvin, marking the end of the monsoon season.

of the Rushikulya.[xxii]

I couldn't get to know
what to be in love is. Well,
why this dream then, why,
that at the time of my return,
wherever I arrive
you will be standing with the sacred plate
to greet me!
Why again this notion
that you're the end of the road
I am destined to take,
you're the supreme mistake
my hands can ever commit,
you are the lotus-coloured fire
in the depths of the air I breathe?

***

[xxii] A river in South Odisha.

Pratibha Satpathy (b. 1945)

'Because I Am Surviving'

(Translated 'Banchirahichi Boli' from the Odia by Nikhilesh Mishra)

Forgive me, Earth,
I haven't been attentive to you.
Again and again
My ego has lost its way
And without the address on me,
I have roamed for entire days
Looking for my home.

Sometimes I have slept, careless,
My head curled on the bare chest
Of a mother under harsh rains,
And sometimes I have poked
My own wounds, getting blood all over.

Are you a ray of sunlight or some
Intimacy that has come to find me,
That has fallen onto my bed?
Do you really care
If I cuddle you close or not?

I have been avoiding you, Truth,
On a regular basis now, making
Some excuse or the other,
But please don't mind my mistakes,
See, see how shameless
My utterances are
When the axe of words falls!

How pitiful is this existence
When one has nothing
In one's hands to give!
Please forgive my pale face, Little Flower,
I need reasons to even smile.

Don't get me wrong, World,
I haven't been able to preserve you,
Bear with my stupidity, Warmth of Setting Sun!
Bear with my dreams.

All Pervasive Hunger! Forgive
My meagre plate of rice, spare it
The heartless sighs.
Would you care to know
How I have survived!

***

Hrushikesh Mallick (b. 1955)

'The India Grandfather Hasn't Seen'

(Translated 'Jeje Dekhinathiba Bharat' from the Odia by Jayanta Mahapatra)

Back from his tour, our grandson asked:
Did you attend the rally last time
in Bhubaneswar, grandfather?

Grandfather answered: Yes, I did.
Where did you stay?
Grandfather said: In the MLA's house.
Our grandson prodded him: Had your meal there?
Grandfather said: Rice, you know the dwarf kind,
a prawn goulash and a chutney
made from home-grown tomatoes.

Our grandson asked him again: Well,
How did you go there and come back?
Grandfather replied excitedly: Stupid, aren't you?
In Tuku Babu's truck!
Which Tuku Babu?
Don't you know Tuku, the son of Chema, the oil dealer?
And is he the same old Tuku now?
From the days plain *Saga*[xxiii] used to stick
to the gaps in his teeth, he's the owner now
of truck after truck, bus after bus . . .

[xxiii] Fried leaves, a poor man's accompaniment with rice.

At his door, any BDO,[xxiv] minister or bureaucrat
would call out: Oh Tuku Babu! Are you in?
Where else did you go, grandfather?
And what did you see? asked our grandson.
We visited Konark, watched Kumkum Mohanty
dancing Odissi; then went off to Puri, where
we saw the huge granite block that had fallen.
And what a crowd was there in the canteen square!
Leaders everywhere, unending speeches,
What a crowd in the canteen square!

Our grandson leaned back on his pillow.
took a deep breath,
like God, old at the end of the *Dwapara* era,[xxv]
lying exhausted
among the creepers for an hour!
He then asked:
Did you chance to see at Konark
a teetering Dharama[xxvi] drunk with charas?
The one who tore open
the red shorts of a girl yesterday afternoon?

Grandfather, did you notice too
That bony ashram owner of Puri
Who's been absconding on a number of counts?
Did you see in Mancheswar
a line of whiskey-laden trucks
crossing the boundary of the cola company

[xxiv] Block Development Officer.

[xxv] According to Hinduism, it is the third yuga (era) among the four during the period of Lord Krishna.

[xxvi] The legendary youth who was instrumental in finishing construction of the Sun temple of Konark.

as they swayed like the idols
carried aloft in their ornamental thrones during Holi?
And did you notice also
under the mattress
the printed Gandhi heads, the stolen guns??

***

Ratnamala Swain (b. 1967)

'Dhauli, the Hillock'

(Translated 'Dhauli Pahad' from the Odia by Panchami Manoo Ukil)

Whenever I visit Dhauli
Find Buddha always in a deep slumber
Outside the premises
A cacophony of groundnut sellers, photographers
Visiting tourists and troop of monkeys
Fail to awaken him.

In the incessant crying wolf of the soil
Chandashoka turns into *Dharmashoka.*[xxvii]
Red river of blood transforms again into the Dayanadi[xxviii]
Adding a new sheaf to the pages of history;
Mute witness is Dhauli hillock
To the newly built monument of peace.

More than Dhauli, its path oft beckons me
Unaware of all great souls who have trodden this holy path
But never returned.
I don't want to be Buddha
Let this mundane world be my grazing field.

In fact, I too have few queries for Buddha

[xxvii] Prior to the Kalinga war, emperor Ashoka was known for his cruelty (Chandashoka).The legend says, he turned to be a king of righteousness (Dharmashoka) after witnessing the Daya river full of blood after the war and wedded Buddhism.

[xxviii] Daya river.

For that alone I visit Dhauli, the timeless monument, time and again
And return sans an answer
Though I know Buddha will never arise from his deep slumber
Or maybe he would, when this world
Lapses into eternal sleep.

***

Akhila Naik (1970–2021)

'Scripture of the Farmland' (Translated 'Khetapurana' from the Odia by Tyagraj Thakur)

You were born on *Raebar*, Sunday
So you were named Raebaru.
Your father had not acquired the wit to name you
Harekrushna or Bijayananda or Janakiballhaba
for he hadn't read Ramayana or Mahabharata.
Battling the forest, chopping wood
he set up a village
Battling stones, digging earth
he created fertile land
With spades and shovels he wrote
many poems and songs
of paddy, greengram, little millet and ragi
The farmland was his manuscript, scripture, his Bhagabata.

Handing over the scripture of the land to your custody
your father became an ancestor
resting in the bushes by the spring
to guard the moth bean farm and the palm trees.
After him, you became the chief of the village
Became Raebaru Naik
Shouldered the loss and gain of kith and kin
on a carrying pole of thick bamboo.
You befriended the forest, hills and spring
buddied up with wind, rocks and sky
These friends and buddies of yours stood with you,
shoulder to shoulder, through thick and thin

Sent you a bagful of presents
before you extended your palms asking for them.

Some sent marking nut, tamarind and mahua
Some sent sorghum, maize and horse gram
Some sent fire, some water, some light
Some sent semel shoot, red ant, fish, crab, and boar meat
Some sent ebony fruit, gooseberry, char berry,
mango, custard apple and jackfruit.
Drunken bachelors and maidens, old men and women
fuddled with palm toddy, made merry, celebrated
the mango seed fest, the *Pausa*[xxix] fest of winter,
swirled and danced in ecstasy
to the beats of *dhumsa, tamak* and *dhap*[xxx]
The naughty wind came from behind on tiptoes
towards the trees lost in watching the dance and tickled them
And the giggling sky rolled down to the dusty road.

Your everyday world was as straight as the wild sal tree
Like a flowing spring piercing the rocks
A clean flow of water was your life and livelihood
Only you, your goddess Darni or your god Bhima knew
if you were in pleasure or pain.
But an intellectual falcon from the capital city
who never touched food in the morning without first reading the Gita
shook the sky crying aloud, that
Raebaru Naik of Kendudangri is trapped
In deep sorrow in the dense forest
In acute darkness of utter ignorance
Spending suffocated sleepless nights
In the clutch of the Duma-witches, the devil spirits

[xxix] December to January in Odia.

[xxx] Musical instruments played during tribal dance.

He is in need of, badly in need of, instantly in need of
The illuminating light of wisdom.

Then a jasmine white stork flew in to your village from somewhere
From its nose scattered hatred
From its tongue dipped drops of greed
Fiery ego burned in its eyes
But from its lips dripped verses filled with compassion
It opened before you, your children and your clan
A bag of wisdom:
God's wife was trapped by a demon
for she crossed the three forbidden lines
The elephant pleaded and invoked God
from millions of miles away
And the God with the spinning discus
destroyed the crocodile to save the elephant
Wicked Duryodhan suffered the consequences of deceiving in dice
Golden Lanka perished to ashes for too much arrogance.
Hail to Hanuman, hail to the son of wind!

Your eyelids started to close
with the smoke of the opiate wisdom
You got into deep slumber and dreamt how
Flying like the jasmine white stork, you reached
A sparkling kingdom with a house, a spring and trees, all of light
Who is this smiling sparkling God before you
with the posture of granting a boon?
As you bent to touch his gold-like feet
Your hands got burnt
Screaming, 'Oh! I'm dead, save me, save me'
you woke up all of a sudden, returned to your senses.

Untying yourself with great difficulty
When you look around—
Oh, what's this!
Where are your kith and kin, your friends and family?

Where is the sorghum, maize, moth bean, horse gram and the farmland?
Where is the sal, teak, mango, jackfruit, gooseberry, mahua forest?
Where are your friends, buddies?
Where are the hares, deer, boars, tigers, sambars?
Where is the giggling spring?
Where are the fishes, crabs, toads, snakes, mongooses?
Where are the temples of goddess Darni and god Bhima?
Wherever one looks one sees heaps of bones, heaps of skulls
On the mound of bones stands a colossal temple
And at the top of the temple flies a shameless flag.
Where did the jasmine white stork go?
Wherever one looks, one only sees
Kettles of falcons and vultures and packs of dogs

Whose temple, hotel, sacrificial altar, farmhouse are these
There where your father had set up a village,
battling the forest, chopping wood?
Whose cashew orchard, coffee garden, eucalyptus and oak garden are these
There where your father had created a fertile land
battling stones, digging earth?
Who are these kettles of falcons and vultures and packs of dogs
Ask Raebaru, ask; you won't get the answer unless you ask.
Who ordered you to sweep the temple floor,
to pluck the beans in the coffee garden?
Why? Ask.
Collecting leftover bones, fish bones,
shards of glass, why will you bleed, so profusely? Ask.
Where is the village Kendudangari now? Ask.
Where did the chief of the village go? Ask your own self.
Where is his dagger, axe, spear, bow, and arrow? Ask.

***

Bharat Majhi (b. 1972)

'Fire'

(Translated 'Nian' from the Odia by Jayanta Mahapatra)

For the past few days
I've been dreaming only of fires.

When I chance to see a mountain
There are fires raging on its peak
When I see a forest, it's on fire,
Buildings, houses, whatever
I happen to see is ablaze—
Fire in the Secretariat,
In the legislative assembly,
In books, notebooks, pen and paper
Even in rivers and the sea.

For the past few days
I've been dreaming only of fires,
Such flames
That have both hands and feet.
I've not asked anyone else but myself
As to how fire grew hands and feet,
I simply realize
That if I ask anyone,
They will think me to be a lunatic.

You would say
I have a leaning in the future
Towards the fear of fire,
Behind success and failure

Is this fall through fire,
To be annihilated
Through sacred suffering
Or an apt planetary ring.

But would you confess
That you know the art
Of tying up fire's hands and feet
And throwing it away,
An effortless thing
For a six-centimeter-long happening
On the newspaper's page three.

Still, why can't I admit
That of the fires
Emerging out of dreams all are not red,
Some are green, some pale
And some yellow.

Maybe
To narrate half of my dreams
Is just my fate!

***

Gayatribala Panda (b. 1977)

'The Hand'

(Translated 'Hata' from the Odia by Jayanta Mahapatra)

Often, in my dreams
a hand stretches out towards me.

Neither face nor body
or feet can be seen,
simply a hand
whose hand could it be?

Row after row of lepers
sitting in front of the temple
The mad old woman roaming
in the bus stand
A weeping ten-year-old
with a baby cradled to her waist
The tender boy washing plates
at a roadside eatery
And the woman burning in a fire:
Among these, whose hand could it be?

Begging for alms
Begging for rice
Begging for sleep
Begging for safety
Begging for answers
I can see that hand even in the dark
So much so that even when
I close my eyes, I see that hand.

It seems to me it's not just a hand
but a sharp adze dripping blood
from the inhumanities of man.

No one has ever seen
its reach from generation to generation,
from history to the future,
and so there's been no thought
or discussions about it.

I would gladly place that hand
among all those drumming hands,
and the universe would resound
with the enormity of sound;
when the men playing cards
at the crossroads would suddenly leave,
the man locked inside
the closed door of his house
would open it wide,
and the king seated upon his throne
would discard all his finery.

That very day the hand
would free itself from its piteous fate.

***

Kamadev Moharana (b. 1979)

●

(Translated poem, whose first line is 'Kichhiloka Telamari Shikhara Chhuinle' from the Odia by Manu Dash)

Some people attained the peak
By virtue of sycophancy,
Some people stumbled down from the platform
By virtue of groveling,
Some people acquired the hillock
By selling the oil,
Some people lost their life
By carrying the weight of oil tins on their back.

For the sake of oil
Some people globetrotted,
Some got angry seeing oil
Some people looked oily after applying oil on skin
Some looked dry-haired without the oil.

Some people became oil in bullock cart axle
Some doused the oil on the lips of the wick
Some people cursed the oil as they turned dregs,
Some got burnt seeing fair-skinned face.

Some people ascended to the throne by sheer sycophancy
But, sans oil, *Anam*[xxxi] turned a beating drum.

***

---

xxxi Anam is a poetry movement in Odia literature that started in 1969 in Puri. Here, it stands for nameless common people.

Akshaya Bahibala (b. 1980)

'The War'

(Translated 'Yudh' from the Odia by Chandrahas Choudhury)

For a thousand years now
I have tried my best to love
to understand what life means
but it always ends in war. Only war.

In me is hunger's war
In me is love's war
In me the body's war
In me the wars of caste and creed.

In me a war to search for the truth
and then, when I came to know too much
another war to damp it down.

Tyranny, brutality, humiliation
all the wars to destroy these
I had to fight in the war.

Just to be accepted as a human being—a war.
This world is an endless war of chalking out lines
lines of good and evil, truth and lies.
The war is in me and in everything I do.

***

Nikhilesh Mishra (b. 1996)

'The Newspaper'

(Translated 'Khabarkagaj' from the Odia by the poet)

The newspaper usually comes
Early in the morning,
Everyday.

In my childhood though,
It used to be the evening when
The newspaper finally arrived,
Jeje[xxxii] used to wait
Eagerly,
'As if you have plans to join politics!'
Jejema[xxxiii] used to make faces.

The old hawker guy who brought
A newspaper to my place everyday,
A truck hit him yesterday near the crossing.
Today, the newspaper hasn't come.
No way to know
If the old man has made it
To the newspaper or
Not.

I have sold all the old newspapers
To the *kabaadiwala*[xxxiv] yesterday,

[xxxii] Grandfather in Odia.

[xxxiii] Grandmother in Odia.

[xxxiv] The man who goes door to door and collects junk.

Sold the already stale 2G Spectrum,
Dadri and IPL, sold
The smile of the baby with that diaper,
All the fairness of the girl
Who attained it
In just three weeks using that cream,
Colourful promises to
Bring back the missing pleasure
With *that* capsule,
Sexy look of *that* item girl,
Sold everything
At one fixed rate,
Five rupees per kilo.

There's not a single piece of newspaper
In my house anymore.
I am about to leave for the hospital.
I will look for the bed
Of that old hawker guy
And bring my copy of the newspaper
From him.

***

Poetry: Sambalpuri-Kosali

Satyanarayan Bohidar (1913–80)

'Don't Care'

(Translated 'Parbaae Ledu' from the Sambalpuri-Kosali by Bhagirathi Mishra)

No use to stress oneself,
Whatever happens or doesn't happen
Accept it as it is.
Do you carry your legs on your shoulder?

Everyone worries for oneself.
But there is only One
Who worries for all
And fulfils at the appropriate moment.

Worries slowly eat your body
Like the salt eating the earthen pot.
Leave aside everything,
Don't care.

***

Mangalucharan Biswal (1935–2022)

'Days to Come'

(Translated 'Aaebaa Din' from the Sambalpuri-Kosali by Bhagirathi Mishra)

Let's go away from this place, oh my son's father!
The evil landlord causes sorrows to us.
Even after our hard labour day and night
We don't get a fistful to sustain ourselves,
It is like a little hay for a herd of cows.
None to blame for our misfortune.

Oh my daughter's mother!
How can we live here if you think like this?
Let's be here and wait for the days to come.
Everything would be fine.
This soil, our mother,
Makes our arms strong as iron.
You will see one day
All these cheats will suffer.
We, the labourers shall happily grow more
And the story of our struggle for life and living
Shall remain forever.

***

Prafulla Kumar Tripathy (b. 1945)

'Let Us Be Quiet'

(Translated 'Tun Padun Ame' from the Sambalpuri-Kosali by the poet)

Let us be quiet,
A baby is asleep and dreaming
In the side room.

Let us wait till he wakes.

We shall surround him and ask
What dream entered
Into his sleep.

Let us stop our
Urge to talk
Let us learn to listen.

***

Haldhar Nag (b. 1950)

'River Ghensali'[xxxv]

(Translated 'Ghensali' from the Sambalpuri-Kosali by Surendranath)

Listen O Ghensali, wait a while;
Where do you go rushing by?

Roaring, churning as if in anger,
You run down in Kali's figure.

Sleeping you had been peacefully,
In the Baisi Khalsa[xxxvi] valley.

Startled, you run single-minded
Across mounds, ditches, corners and bends

Forsaking joy and love of mother's house
Where will you enter as a live-in spouse?

You want to meet friends of yours,
Ang, Ib, Tel, Jira, Koel rivers.[xxxvii]

Your heart is excited and mind flitting,
Like a young girl to elope is waiting.

Bear in mind matters future and past.
The further you run, more you'll be slashed.

Let me say a word, listen, Ghensali,

[xxxv] A river that originates from a spot close to village Ghens—the poet's village.

[xxxvi] A pair of hills between which the river commences/originates.

[xxxvii] Names of rivers of the same network as Ghensali.

One trait of yours with mine does tally.

Over low and highlands you cross,
I too surmount my joys and sorrows.

You are heading to the deep seas,
I too am heading to rest in peace.

***

Poetry: Sanskrit

Sri Jayadeva (Twelfth century)

'Lotus-Eyed Krishna with Desire'

(Translated 'Pancham Sarga, Gita Govindam' from the Sanskrit by Mani Rao)

1.

I'll stay here, you go
to Radha, cajole her
with my words
and fetch her

Thus directed
by Madhu's enemy,
the friend returned in person
to Radha, and said this:

2.

When the wind flows
from Malaya mountains
off sandalwood slopes
gathers mad love

When flower clusters bloom
Ripping lovelorn hearts

Friend, he who wears
wildflower garlands
wilts

from pangs of separation
'Radha-O-Radha'
he raves

3.

When cool moon rays scorch
he's tagging death

When Love's arrows fall
        flowers
he moans, frantic

Friend, he who wears
wildflower garlands
droops

from pangs of separation
'Radha-O-Radha'
        he raves

4.

When bee swarms buzz
he covers his ears

Night after night his
pained, lovelorn heart
breaks

Friend, he who wears
wildflower garlands
aches

from pangs of separation
'Radha-O-Radha'
        he raves

5.

He lives in a dense forest
forsaking luxuries

Tosses and turns
on mud his bed

Repeatedly cries
your name

Friend, he who wears
wildflower garlands
suffers

from pangs of separation
'Radha-O-Radha'
he raves

6.

When poet Jayadeva
sings

of separation's
love-play

in passionate intensity

May Krishna dawn
in worthy hearts

Friend, he who wears
wildflower garlands
pines

from pangs of separation
'Radha-O-Radha'
he raves

***

Poetry: Sandha

Kanhupa (Tenth century)

'Your House Is Outskirts of the City, Dombi!'

(Translated 'Nagara Bahire Re Dombi Tohori Kudia' from the Sandha by Manu Dash)

Your hut is on the city outskirts, o Dombi!
You quickly touch the lustful tonsured brahmin
and slip away
O Dombi, I'll befriend you
This Kanhu is a brazen indifferent *kapali*, a *yogi*.[xxxviii]
Mounting on this lotus with sixty-four petals
Dances poor Dombi.

O, dear Dombi, let me ask you gently
On whose boat do you sail to and fro the petals? You please quit selling baskets
made of bamboo skin for livelihood
I have also left my puppetry box
for your sake.

Oh dear, you are untouchable
And I am a kapali, an outcaste
For your sake
I donned a garland of bones
Dancing and jumping in the pond

---

xxxviii It derives from the Sanskrit term meaning 'skull-man'. This in tradition was a Tantric, non-Puranic form of Shaivism which originated in Medieval India between the seventh and eighth century CE.

You eat tender lotus stem
Accept me dear Dombi, or else
I'll kill myself, take my life away.

***

Poetry: Santali

Pandit Raghunath Murmu (1905–82)

'No Matter How Poor a Mother Is'

(Translated 'Janam Ayo doy Rengej Rehon Unige Duhlalay' from the Santali by Anpa Marndi and Ajit Kumar Kullu)

No matter how poor a mother is
She brings up the child with love and care
No matter how neglected a mother's tongue is
Her sweet utterances are companions forever.
Through the mother tongue
Other tongues can be conquered.
It is a must to learn to be counted
Among the wise and civilized.

***

Arjun Charan Hembram (b. 1952)

'The Slanting Sal Tree'

(Translated 'Lade Sarjom' from the Santali by Naku Hansdah and Ajit Kumar Kullu)

I am a slant sal tree
Neglected
But firmly rooted to the ground.
If you dig, you won't reach my depth.
If you try to uproot me, I won't come out.
I might break, I might die
Many of me will sprout up from me.
I can't be finished
I don't have an end.
I have roots in the juicy soil
And in my flesh, blood and bones
Spread from top to toe,
From the sole to the crown
From the skull to the entire brain.
I am like a dry tree enshrined
In the middle of the field.
The cuts all over the body
Ooze and dry again.
Perspiration burns
Rashes and all dermatitis
And it also heals the diseases.
A trampled down,
Neglected Sal tree I am.
The herdsmen lead their cattle around

To cut and play with my body.
The widow handles her saree around her waist
And pulls down the dry branches
With the help of a long bamboo stick.
The timid blacksmith
Dares not go into the forest
And pulls out from my chest
The thick ribs to make charcoal.
Thunderstorms hit me from above
And barge into my heart.
Tears flow down from my eyes
Like in the eyes of a girl
Going to her in-laws' house.
What to say of the goat kids
Who are just learning to walk
They wriggle all over me
Like a girl walking on a tightrope
Until they are hungry
For their mother's milk.
Kerketta bird in the morning
Defecates and dirties
My colourful silk saree
Bought for the *Makara*[xxxix] festival.
I won't be finished
I cannot be erased,
Wait and watch
One day I will stand up straight
If not like eucalyptus, at least like the teak
For the travellers to rest under my shade

[xxxix] A festival that marks the transition of the sun from the zodiac of Sagittarius to Capricorn. It falls on 14 January every year.

In the fragrance of the *phagun* month[xl]
Spreading from Tokyo to California
Farther away beyond Greenland
Up to distant Antarctica.

***

[xl] Linked with the month of spring.

Damayanti Beshra (b. 1962)

'March On'

(Translated 'Lahag Me' from the Santali by Naku Hansdah and Ajit Kumar Kullu)

You dare say that your rights be honoured
But while working for them, you flee.
Why arrogantly stand here,
Why not pick up a pen instead?

When together, you are full of enthusiasm, and
Left alone, you are so very calm.
You give a battle cry from behind the back
How on earth will you march on thus?

There aren't any wars these days,
There are no arrows to shoot, wound or kill,
How will they know
That you are a true *Kheruwal*?[xli]

You don't envy others,
You don't even hurry up to take your shares.
When will you be vigilant,
And lift up your race and religion?

You don't use the given chances coming your way
When you do, you are so uncertain
Days pass but your arguments don't.
When will you learn to sort out your thoughts?

Many have become rich by robbing you.
Many are wise through education,

[xli] A race from the Austro-Asiatic family.

When will you know the rules of looting?
And when will you learn your lessons?

You are educated and wise
But you know not your clan and creed,
You identify yourself as a Hindu
But Sarna[xlii] is your religion that you never say.

Have faith in your Sarna.
Hesitate not to declare it your religion,
Lest you be labelled an infidel
And get your tongue speared.

When are you going to wake up, you slacker?
Why do you pretend to be ignorant?
Why don't you plan your future?
And learn, so that you become mature?

***

xlii A distinct religion of the indigenous peoples of Chhota Nagpur plateau.

Jadumani Beshra (1964–2022)

'The Forest Fire'

(Translated 'Bir Sengal' from the Santali by Anpa Marndi and Ajit Kumar Kullu)

Someone has unstrapped
The tall red horse.
It has been frightfully jumping
From hill to hill
Big and small
From Dhinkia to Ukam
From Ukam to Similipal.

The soft breeze of the phagun
And the clouds move away at its sight.
The buds of flowers wail
And shed streams of tears
The tender twigs turn and twist
The courtyard cries
In the inextinguishable flames.

The birds and insects
Run for life helter-skelter
The death has arrived unannounced
It is at the door knocking
The hill was once green
Now it is gone.
Wherever the eyes go
There are burnt houses and trees
One after another.

With the blunt and bent axes
People chop the wood
Like the vultures
That snatch the dead cow.

The remains of the burnt forest
Its ashes spread all over
Deep inside my heart.

***

Purna Chandra Hembram (b. 1964)

'As the Country Is Free'

(Translated 'Phurgal Jakhan Disom' from the Santali by the poet)

As the country is free, the desire becomes upbeat,
Hold the pen like others, waste not time to follow development
Some become aware, enjoy the world's fine fruit
Left out next, have very meagre wealth in the nest.

Mind is like a spinning top, spins as well as jumps a lot
Collage of the future, it takes the onus to create
Happy zippy mind tells, has reached his own target
This life will defeat odds and roam with contentment.

Mind has fascination for power, it feels sometime near or distant
When it is recharged with power, settles after getting its right
Unease, argue, untidy, many varieties make belief difficult
One is perturbed by mere words, better use tends to unite.

Fear in the mind while reaping, makes life low when late
Despite being told intensely, repeatedly continue to forget
Language in eighth schedule, paves the path for advancement
Adoption of one script sprouts solidarity, resilience unity and agreement.

***

Naku Hansdah (b. 1969)

'Village'

(Translated 'Aatu' from the Santali by Naku Hasadah and Ajit Kumar Kullu)

(I)
When one ponders over the work of the creator,
About where lies the origin and where the end
One wonders,
Up there a blue cover, with the planets and stars,
And here below a lot of water and earth
Everything is so full of marvels.
All tales of creation
So difficult to fathom.
The hills, rivers, forests, reptiles and animals
But the best of all is humankind.
They live in clusters
Known as villages.
They erect the best structures where one is born
And there are the temples
Where the presiding deities are the ancestors.

(II)
This village is our first country,
Our land is given to us by God.
And each village here has its own story
Its legends—
Of an old man nesting here somewhere
Or the auspicious arrow hitting the target
Here somewhere nearby.

Apart from this, there are stories
Of the ancestors living
Near the streams or the rivers,
This is how in the ancient times
The villages were named.
Some names later on changed
In *diku*[xliii] tongues,
And in mispronunciations.
Human life then was just and true.
Mandal[xliv] resounded in each *dharam akhada*[xlv]
To its beats,
There were dances
According to the seasons.
The joy overflowed from the folks
And rose to the gods.
Even today, there are talks of the dance of the gods
In dharam akhada, they came in human forms and danced.
When the rains poured the gods became happy
In the company of the people.
There were grain-rich people in the village
That was the heavenly abode for all.
In the village that was far away
From the filth-filled market and city,
People were clean like the stream.
Majhi[xlvi] and *Majhiari*[xlvii] ruled the village
Where the villagers were with their children.
In death and birth, in weal or woe
They stood by each other.

[xliii] Outsiders.

[xliv] Tribal musical instrument.

[xlv] The commonplace of a village.

[xlvi] Village head.

[xlvii] Female village head/wife of the village head.

As the saying goes, the village kills, the village keeps
One was there for the other.
The purity of the village began to fade.
Contagious quarrels
Began to infect and spread.
People from the village went to the city
And to the market
Where they worked and earned
Money, discord and disease
And carried them back to the village.
They became lazy in farming,
They gave up faith in gods and deities
And their dance and songs began to fade.
The village *chatsala*[xlviii] became history
The Baruas disappeared.
The people who could know the pulse
The ones who could dispel the evil eye
Dwindled with the days.
The mantras of healing and protection
The chants and prayers to gods
From the villages began to vanish.

(III)
There is still time.
A day will come
The glorious era will return.
This zahira tree is a witness
That will testify the truth.
Once again
The Gods and Goddesses
Will be worshipped
There will be joy in farming.

[xlviii] A kind of educational space where mantras and medicines were taught to students.

If we do not go to the city markets
We will not get lost.
If we go
The Marangburu[xlix] will lead us from the front
In the transition of the ages
JaherAayo[l] will guide us from the back.

***

xlix The great God.

l The presiding deities of the Santals.

Anpa Marndi (b. 1981)

'Samay Soren Knows the Snake by Its Colour'

(Translated 'Rang Njelet Binje Chinhau Kawa Samay Soren' from the Santali by Anpa Marndi and Ajit Kumar Kullu)

Samay Soren has already drunk
Seventy-two summers
With the *handia*[li]
And a side dish of rat-snake-meat
Hemmed in leaves
And roasted on the embers.

Solid Samay Soren
Who lives down the Similipal hill
Guards the forest and the mountain
He plays the mandal and the flute
And dances to the tunes of Lagne.[lii]

Samay Soren is not a snake charmer
Yet, by the colour of the snake
He can say its nature.
He is not a reptile-handler
But by the skin, it sheds
He can say its type.
He can break the lethal fangs
Make the snake dance

[li] Rice beer/wine/alcoholic drink made out of rice and other roots.

[lii] A form of Santal dance.

And if it becomes unruly
He can shoot it with his arrow.

This old man suddenly looks
Towards the Adivasi village
Where the Maranguru and Jaher Aayo live
He sees a pariah serpent
Heading towards the sal orchard.

Fatally poisonous
But looks like non-poisonous
There is a trident on its hood
Its colour is the same as the clothes
The devotees wear.

Samay Soren very well recognizes
This is a polymorphic snake
Of shape-shifting breed
And venomous.

The snake knows not
That before it coils
In the divine abode,[liii]
Samay Soren would have chopped
And separated its head from the body.

***

[liii] Worship place of Maranguru and JaherAayo.

Poetry: Kui

Sarangadhar Pradhan (1922–2012)

'Prayer'

(Translated 'Prarthana' from the Kui by Anuja Mohan Pradhan)

With great love, You created us,
O Bura God, You are the greatest of all,
Salutations to You, from afar.

You reside in our souls,
You are omnipresent on this earth,
Your creation has no parallel,
You are the beginning and the end,
You are the saviour, O great Lord.

Shed our sufferings,
For You, it is just a whisk to repel,
Remit our burden of sin,
Lend us Your hand of kindness,
O kind heart!

You are filled in all three worlds,
All that moves is Your wish,
You are the success of all penance,
You bestow all, O epitome of kindness,
Relieve us from the pain of death.

You are almighty,
You are the reason for everything,
You alone can bless,
The living beings get salvation,
Keep us away from the wrong path.

We are your children,

We are the ignorant people,
Forgetting Your name,
We indulge in ill and sin,
Forgive us O abode of kindness.
I am Sarangdhar, the Kondh,
Born in Jhimangia hamlet,
Salutations to You, O great God,
Submit myself to Your holy feet,
Recite Your name, pray for salvation.

The sages and the learned,
Do penance with fast,
Meditate for years and eons,
Reciting and remembering Your name,
With Your blessings beget salvation.

***

Umacharan Digal (1942–2013)

'Prayer'

(Translated 'Prarthana' from the Kui by Anuja Mohan Pradhan)

O God of Heaven,
You do not heed to my prayers,
If you do not listen,
Then to whom shall I appeal?

Nothing in this vast earth,
Goes unnoticed to you,
If you do not listen,
Then to whom shall I appeal?

I sacrificed fowl, goat,
Offered you the blood,
If it is not enough,
I shall bring you more,
If you do not listen,
Then to whom shall I appeal?

You need not give me riches,
Let my mind be in connection,
Says Uma Charan,
With flowing tears,
If you do not listen,
Then to whom shall I appeal?

***

Anuja Mohan Pradhan (b. 1969)

'Lycanthrope'[liv]

(Translated 'Mliba Kadadi' from the Kui by the poet)

No more hares hop and
Deer leap in the forest,
Tiger strolls in full moon neither,[lv]
Beware all my people,
A new tiger prowls in the streets,
A Lycanthrope.

Beware, entering the forest for a pole for your house,
Walk cautiously while going to sell charcoal,
Keep mum, if a thief steals from your house,
For the new tiger has tasted human blood.

It comes closer when you shout,
Smiles when you try to scare,
Says, you are in my row, no way out,
Present me flakes of nickel and silver,
Then see, whatever you want in favour,
Pension, certificate or finance,
Can produce with a wag of my tail,
I am the state's pet, the big cat,
The bureaucrat.

***

[liv] The word comes from two Greek words, Lycos and Anthropos meaning a man transformed into a hyena. The magic of changing someone into a werewolf. In the present context of the poem, into a tiger.

[lv] It is believed that the tiger passes through a particular route in the full moon night.

Poetry: Oraon

Anonymous

(Four oral poems from the Oraon collected and translated by Chonhen Ekka and Ajit Kumar Kullu)

'The Time'

The old age
And all of the time will pass
But the sun and moon won't.
Youth is passing
Childhood has vanished
It won't return
But the sun and moon will.

'This Life Is like a Long Walk'

This life is like a long walk.
As I move, I am maddened.
It is like a shelter in this world
My life suffers as I live through it.
As I see the strength to go on
is slowly waning.

'Who Will Wash My Floral Clothes?'

My floral clothes are full of dirt
Who will wash it clean?
My father has passed away
And my mother too.

Who will wash my stained dress?
I have no uncle,
I don't have an aunt
Who will clean my muddy clothes?
I have neither a brother
Nor a sister-in-law.
Who will wash my floral cloth clean?

'We Won't Stay, Father, in This House'

We won't stay, father
In this mud house.

The wooden wall
And the bamboo door
Someday will fall,
That's not our home.

It's made of weak Erandi wood
And the roof of limp Sanai reeds
Someday it will be ruined
That's not our home.

We won't stay, father
In this house of mud.

***

Poetry: Mundari

Anonymous

(Four oral poems from the Mundari collected and translated by Anita Resma Guria and Ajit Kumar Kullu)

'Glory Unto You, O God Who Created the Sky and the Earth'

Glory unto you, O God who created the sky and the earth.
You planted rice in our fields,
Provided it with sun and shower
And made it bear fruit.
Blessed be your strength, O God.

We harvested, we gathered
We piled on the threshing floor
With grains, we filled our houses
Thank you, God, for this precious gift.

'Paddy Planting Song'

(These songs are sung during the plantation of paddy in the field.)

Hello brother
Dear sister
Let us come to the field.
On this earth
God has given us strength.
From the heavens
He has given us the rains.
Let us go out joyfully
To plant paddy
In the muddy fields,

And to make the earth green
Through the strength
We have received.

'Bless the Man and the Wife'

(This song is to bless the newly married couple.)

O sacred king
You are the source of everything.
Come and bless
The man and his wife.
When they are scared,
Protect them and
Satisfy all their needs.
Keep them both
Through thick and thin.

'I Do Not Want to Live Any Longer In This World'

(This is a song on the death of an individual.)

I do not want to live
In this world
I want to go
To the world I belong to.
O sacred father
Have mercy on me
And open my eyes
Here there is suffering,
But when I go there
I will find
Endless delight.

***

Poetry: Kisan

Anonymous

(Three oral poems from the Kisan collected and translated by Birendra Kujur and Ajit Kumar Kullu)

'When Will You Return'

(This song is sung during the visit by the relatives of the would-be bride to the house of the would-be groom after the engagement.)

When will you return
My brother?
You who carries water in a *tumba*[lvi]
When will you return?

Give me some hot rice
Also, some rice gruel.
The stick is broken, and
My lungi is also torn.
I have no idea if I will win or lose.
If I win, I'll come back
Be with my siblings and family members.
If I lose, I'll visit the seven oceans.

'The Hen of the House'

(This song is sung when the parents and relatives bid farewell to the bride, and the groom and his relatives are about to take the bride to their house after the rituals in the bride's house.)

O Dear father
O Dear mother

[lvi] A water carrier made of dried and processed bottle gourd.

The white hen of the house
Had laid twelve eggs.

From the eggs, the chicks came out.
Along the fence
The mother and chicks
Searched for food.

As they were taking food along the fence
From nowhere swooped down a kite,
Picked up a chick
And flew away into the sky again.

'A Spotted Bird Flew Down'

(This song is sung during the engagement. The groom is the hunter and the bird is the bride in the song.)

A spotted dove
Dropped into the thicket
And began to feed on grains.

A hunter arrived
With a gilded bow
And his dazzling arrows.

As the bird picked food with its beak
The hunter sneaked about
And cautiously spied on it.

He raised his bow and
pulled the string
before the bird could fly, and
He shot at it
Before the bird could cry.

As the arrow hit the bird
The spotted dove began to swoon
And thus, the hunter won.

***

Poetry: Kharia/Khadia

Anonymous

(Three oral poems from the Kharia/Khadia collected and translated by Ajit Kumar Kullu)

The Kharia/Khadia tribe belongs to the Austro–asiatic ethnic group. They also speak a language known as Kharia/Khadia. Three Kharias/Khadias exist: Pahari, also known as Hill, Delki and Dudh. Odisha, Jharkhand, Chhattisgarh, Madhya Pradesh, Bihar, West Bengal, as well as Assam and the Andaman and Nicobar Islands, are where they are most commonly found. The state of Odisha, particularly the Sundargarh and undivided Sambalpur districts, is home to half of the nation's Khadia population. The Similipal area of the Mayurbhanj district is where the majority of Hill Kharias reside. The Dudh Khadia tradition is represented here through the songs that have been translated.

'From across the River'

(The song deals with the loss and grief of a son who is mourning his deceased father. He longs to go and hear his father who has left this world and entered into a life beyond life.)

From across the river
My father calls out to me.
God knows how I will cross over
To listen to my beloved father?

The Koel is full to the brim, and
The Sankh overflows;
The ore is broken,
And my boat has drowned.

How am I to go to him
How am I to cross over to him
How will I go near him
How will I go and hear him?

You fisher boy,
You are my only hope.
It's up to you to help me cross over
Or drown me in the middle of the flow.

'Amko Simko Massacre'

(The song is about the shooting that happened on 25 April 1939, in a location between the villages of Amko and Simko. The tribes kept a chronicle of the entire episode through this song.)

When Queen Janaki reigned over the land
In Amko–Simko hamlets,
The Adivasis were gathered for a meeting.
On the queen's orders,
A troup of soldiers rushed in
And gunned down the Adivasis.

The bullets mowed them down, and
There flowed a bloodstream from the site.
The dead bodies piled up.
They carried the dead on carts
To Panposh via Raiboga
And brought them back to Raipura.

In a mango orchard at Bahmanmara
They prepared a pit and buried the bodies,
One over the other, and filled them with sand and soil.
The half-dead bodies were carried
And dumped to die in the limestone quarry at Raipura.
Life ceased to be with cries and moans.
Life got drowned in whines and whimpers.

'Under the Kadamba Tree'

(This song is usually sung during the engagement ceremonies.)

There beyond the river,
Under the Kadamba tree,
Love plays the flute
Toot tootle . . . tootle-too . . .
He plays the flute
Toot tootle . . . tootle-too . . .

With one of her hands
She scrubs the dishes, and
With another, she wipes her tears
As she hears him play the flute
Toot tootle . . . tootle-too . . .

***

Poetry: Sadri

Anonymous

(Two oral poems: 'Give Me Some Water' and 'Bitter Neem' from the Sadri collected and translated by Ajit Kumar Kullu)

Sadri is a language which was initially spoken by the Sadans. This gradually became the lingua franca of the tribes, mostly among the Kharias, Mundas, Oraons and Kisans, residing in Sundargarh and the undivided district of Sambalpur. Today, most people in the districts of western Odisha speak this language. It is quite interesting to note that the tribes have found this language as an alternative to their tribal tongues, and therefore, all their rituals and cultural practices these days can be found in Sadri.

'Give Me Some Water'

(When the guests arrive at the prospective bride's house for the matchmaking, they generally sing this song. The song can also be sung when individuals go to other people's homes, particularly as guests.)

Give me some water
Dear girl, I come from a faraway land.
My throat is parched and dry with thirst.
Give me some water
Dear girl, I am your guest here.

The rope used to draw water from the well
Has snapped, and the bucket is broken,
Come baba, I will take you
To drink from the spring

Come baba, I will guide you there
To drink from the clear stream.

'Bitter Neem'

(It is a song that discusses a woman's relationship with her husband and in-laws.)

Neem is bitter, Karanj is more bitter
But the most bitter of all
Are the words spoken by the parents-in-law

Jaggery is sweet, sugar is sweeter than that
But the sweetest of all
Are the words uttered by my man.

***

Poetry: Kondh

Anonymous

(Four oral love poems from the Kondh translated by Sitakant Mahapatra)

1

Why then did you leave?
The dance in the grove is yet to end,
The cock yet to crow;
Dancing to the tune,
How gracefully you were floating along,
Sweet as a song;
And the jingling of your bangles
Had the soft melody of hailstones
Falling in the dark,
But in a moment,
What illusive mist or dark clouds,
What lunacy swallowed you?
You quietly left.

Didn't you proclaim unending love?
Our intimacy that is
Anklet to the feet, ring to the ear,
Why, why, then did you leave?

2

Beloved.
How fickle, how impatient you are!
Only the flash of a face,
A streak of lightning—
In a moment you fade in the dark;
The distant firefly,
Coming near no more,

Not in the armpit of leaves nor on the branches.
Like the jungle fowl!
The esi bird of the dense grove.

Always you peer at me
From behind,
And never come before,
My eyes do not see you.
From your lonely verandah
You have the crab's all-seeing silent stare.

How fickle, how impatient,
Lost in your dream-world.
A child you are.
Like an overflowing basket of vegetables,
Thinning to emptiness in the weekly market.
Like articles sold out on the way,
Nothing remains.
What drives you mad?
Whose call rings in your ears?
Or is it of shame you die?
The crowded big bustee overawes you?
Or with milling flow of the sap of youth,
Like the siali creeper you surge forward?

3

The barbet is weeping,
The peacock cries,
My dear slender Solamali,
I am your friend, your beloved,
You are my uncle's daughter,
I have a right to claim your love.
How many affectionate names
Have I given you?
Nilas, Talas, Lembar, Dumber . . .
And how intense is my love for you!

Our togetherness is like
Anklets to the feet,
Rings to the ears.
So do not jump hedges,
Come to me, we will play.
Life is fleeting.
Old age exhausts everything.
As crops do not thrive well
On lands once cultivated
And again dug up,
In an old man's life
Joy withers;
So as long as life lasts
And hearts beat
Come, let us enjoy,
Let us play.

4

Dhangda[lvii]

You are the rich sahukar
Living in a palace,
Brick and lime,
Particles of lime floating,
And you never bother,
Never care for me,
Not a word for me on your lips.
And I go on calling you,
Pining for you,
Nilas, Talas, Ambar. Lomber . . .

Dhangdi[lviii] replies:

[lvii] Young bachelor.

[lviii] Young unmarried girl.

You are the rich sahukar,
You have stored so much turmeric
That turmeric powder rains everywhere
In your house.
You are rich,
I am poor.

***

Poems: Paraja

Anonymous

(Twenty-one oral love poems from the Paraja and other tribal languages translated by Sitakant Mahapatra)

1

My song
Of three measures of *mandia*[lix]
Four measures of the soft
And delicate kosla millet;
Come, my dear, let us play,
Come running,
Come and entwine me,
Delicate pumpkin creeper,
Let us frolic.
And now look!
There comes my Kajodi,[lx]
My hefty Kajodi,
Let us play.
Take my song's meaning,
The pulp inside the rind,
Come running, come tumbling,
We will play.

2

Such is my song.
Of paddy and ragi,
O my dear girl, get up and come to me.
We are of this Sodabisi area,

[lix] A type of millet.

[lx] Name of the beloved.

Come waving your cascading locks,
We will enjoy ourselves.
The Sundhi money lenders of Lalla village
Charge interest on borrowings,
But my plain song has no claim to make.
No interest to charge,
My words have no horizon,
Nor do I know
Other songs, other stories.
My song does not smell,
Of tobacco or ganja smoke.
Come away to my land,
There, others cannot reach us.
Only you and me
Will enjoy and enjoy ourselves.

3

Linking in words
The roasted maize
And the boiled maize
I am weaving this song for you

My dear, dear girl,
How beautiful is the golden *phasi*[lxi]
Down the bridge of your nose.
Pining for that face.
The brass string of my *dunga*[lxii] weeps

How sweetly
It rings out the agony.

4

The bare-naked voice of grief,
And I cry,

[lxi] Nose ring.

[lxii] A tribal musical instrument.

Helpless, forlorn,
Like the little girl
Whose widowed mother
Walks away with a stranger
To a new house.

My dear, dear girl,
With your name Jili-Jili
Quivering on my lips
I die.

5

I know you will come.
Silently sweet and fragrant
Like the mallika[lxiii] on the stalk.
Flower-bedecked,
With jai flowers sparkling
In your dense dark locks.
You are eternal
As death.
The fear of death
And your love
As intimate neighbours
They inhabit my dream.
And so I play with life.
Every day;
And so I know you will come.
Your dark locks mingling
With the ink-black clouds and lightning.
My dear, dear girl,
Now the rains are here.
Their trampling feet
Echo in the death-like dark.
And lightning-streaks join the hill-top

---

lxiii Name of a flower.

To the singing deep stream below.
Streams come cascading down the hill.
The refrain of thunder
Echoes in the forest.
In the dark cold
The moon is wiped out,
Stars are no more,
Sky and Earth encased
In the primeval dark;
Shivering cold, the rains.
Rains sing down from the rooftops,
And then flow away,
In nameless water torrents.
In ecstasy, the kadamba listens

6

To the splashing streams and the frogs music,
Your coming in the rains;
The new bride washes
The feet of elders.
You are the rain, the new bride,
The rain drops are you,
They fill me up.

7

The night seeks farewell.
Fields, trees, hills
are now being disgorged
from its dark womb.
The time for parting has come.

I am so angry
at this dawn!
Why could not it wait,
sleep on a little more?

Without you
the home will not be a home;
Without you
the village will not be
a village.

Our enemy the dawn
has come.

8

Her body
The flame
Of an earthen or brass lamp:
My heart bids me touch;
The flute sings on
Tiri-riri tiri-riri.

What work is there in the field
To serve as pretext
For going out;
In-laws swarm in the house
And the flute sings on
Tiri-riri tiri-riri.

9

Speak no cruel words to me
Dear girl
How my heart beats for you
Dear girl.
You a maiden
And I a bachelor
We are made for each other
The pitcher to sit firm
On its stand.

Speak no cruel words to me
Dear girl

My heart pines for you
Dear girl.

10

Dear friend, in such heat
In the glittering sun
You are collecting lettuce at Kesaribeda,
Dear friend, in this head-breaking sun
The bright green creepers are breaking as waves
on the fences
From the shrub jungles, the girl emerges
Cut twigs and branches on her head in a bundle.

Let us heed the almanac of sal leaves
The almanac of mahul flowers
What a beautiful coiffure
What wild flowers on her coiffure
I have seen wild flowers in the jungle
I remember the wild flowers in the jungle.

11

When you were a little girl
I saw you playing in the dust
On our village street
When I obstructed your path
You claimed your right of way.

Now when I have grown up
I only want to have a word with you
But nonchalantly you reply
You are asking for a word from me
A song from me
Come back then with fifteen rupees

12

He plays his flute on the hill
As I fill my pitcher in the spring

How do I go there leaving my pitcher
How do I withstand the insistence of the flute's call?

13

In the village street, the dance has ended
The flowers have withered on the trees
The stars are setting in the west
Allow me to go home
Allow me to go back and dream of you

14

In the tank, the blue deep waters
The lotus flowers blossom
The lotus flowers look at the sky
Swim across and collect them
And kiss them with your lips

15

The koel sings in the mango grove at the end of the road
Dear friend, summer is already here
The kusum and the palas have set the forest on fire
And where have you vanished, my beloved?

16

All my girl companions have gone to their husband's houses
All my boy-friends now have wives
The flowers have withered on the trees
The leaves have fallen
And have been blown away by the restless wind
And now I sit alone.

17

Dhangda

Where were you going?
And why do you stay here?

No hearth.
No home.
Why in the open, in the sun.
Like this?
Nothing here, no sound of water.
Are you going to the market?
And why do you stay here?
Here, there is no hearth and home.
No market, no road.
Why here?
Here there is no firewood, no leave,
No water-pit, nothing, nothing.
Nothing here.
For nothing you have come.

Dhangdi
Brass utensils we have sent earlier,
And then come:
To the house, those were sent,
To our relatives, our friends,
Not for nothing have we come.
It is after giving all
We have come.
I have brought tassels for my hair.
Rings for my fingers.
We have come noticing
The water-pit,
We liked, felt drawn,
And have come.
We have seen the beautiful home.
The dense mango grove.
And so we have come.

18

The old heart still beats.
And we are alive

Here in this ancient village
Of dead ancestors;
And so today we join
In this great jubilation.
This overflowing joy.
Short-lived is the dance of an old man.
Meagre the meat of the barking deer.
So as life lasts
We make merry
My dear, dear sweetheart.
My bride-to-be.
I will have fun with you;
My maternal uncle's daughter.
You are the first charge to me.
And here I call you as the groom.

19

O Sagar Godi, O Bandhar Pani[lxiv]
Are you feeling coy
In this teeming village of ours?
But we have no shame.
No bangles on our hands
Endless is our misery.
As the bamboo tree dies
Swaying in the wind
The poor Paraja dies
Driven to the grave by ceaseless labour
Here on Earth.
You alone are happiness.
And so the youngsters give you love-names
Dembar, Lembar, Gajuli, Denjuri
I ask you only one thing—

[lxiv] Sagar Godi, Bandhar Pani, Nilas, Talas, Lembar, Dembar, etc. are love names given by young bachelors to their sweethearts.

I have brought you a bunch of banana
And some yams.
Your voice dragged me here
An old man, my mouth waters for you,
I have come to your house.
As you are my uncle's daughter
So even if ashamed,
Do come near me.
They are calling you Nilas, Talas
With great affection, I have come to you;
Summons from Yama have been received,
Futile is my joy.

The pumpkin plant's tragedy is from the day
Two leaves shoot forth from the seed
Men pluck them out.
Man's tragedy is alike
From childhood
Useless iron is thrown into corners.
The poor man enters the forest,
Crowbar on shoulders.
Basket on heat,
And life, only a tragic song.

20

Your feet, they make
a tiny little arch;
Your waist
Thin as a banana tree;
Your belly a *ghumra*[lxv] drum;
Your breasts
Two flaps of a door.

[lxv] Round-shaped.

We tie mango leaves
on your hands.
Your ears are siali leaves
and the nose a nest for hornets
the nostrils its two doors
And your eyes
they are stars
in a dark night.

21

O uncle moon
Today you have come anew in the sky
From the full moon you went on
Reducing yourself to a thin grass-blade

Today you have arisen afresh
In the western sky:
Make us like you
When we are old
We would again come back to childhood

We can worship you
And be happy
Only if we are alive!

Poetry: English

Jayanta Mahapatra (1928–2023)

'Hunger'

It was hard to believe the flesh was heavy on my back.
The fisherman said: Will you have her, carelessly,
trailing his nets and his nerves, as though his words
sanctified the purpose with which he faced himself.
I saw his white bone thrash his eyes.

I followed him across the sprawling sands,
my mind thumping in the flesh's sling.
Hope lay perhaps in burning the house I lived in.
Silence gripped my sleeves; his body clawed at the froth
his old nets had only dragged up from the seas.

In the flickering dark, his hut opened like a wound.
The wind was I, and the days and nights before.
Palm fronds scratched my skin. Inside the shack
an oil lamp splayed the hours bunched to those walls.
Over and over the sticky soot crossed the space of my mind.

I heard him say: My daughter, she's just turned fifteen . . .
Feel her. I'll be back soon, your bus leaves at nine.
The sky fell on me, and a father's exhausted wile.
Long and lean, her years were cold as rubber.
She opened her wormy legs wide. I felt the hunger there,
the other one, the fish slithering, turning inside.

***

Niranjan Mohanty (1953–2008)

'A Temple in Ruins'

It really hurts your eyes
like the blood of woe
oozing out of some familiar face.

Its mossy odour
slaps on your sleek cheek
teasingly warning you

the sudden breakdown
of this machine; of the sky
being oppressed by sodden solitude.

It's a quiet sob
Breaking into your bones
with an ununderstood thud.

An arc of fear
is drawn somewhere
in the corner of your mind.

Yet its mystery
flutters in the reasonless wind
of your faith.

From its ruins
a lamp of belief beacons
the sinking ships of desire in the blood.

***

Satya Mohanty (b. 1957)

'No Earthly Colour Will Change'

No earthly colour will change
She is dead, her voice silenced forever,
The grass is limp with damp,
Nothing can hurt her anymore.

No colour changed,
Her tongue was slit
Even the hasty incineration can't hide
The bleeding silence of the time.

No colour changed
When fingers dug into the flesh
She hated her mouth sealed by mouths
Hands pinioned, body still like carcass.

No colour changed,
When the clear tears hung like melons
No fantasies but a muffled outcry
Of violation fraying her apart.

No earthly colour will change
They didn't need a hideout, vastness was an ally
Karma was hidden with countless collaborators
Justice drowned in traffic; a quicksand of forgetfulness,
It was a past buried in future.

***

Satya Dash (b. 1991)

'A Body Becomes a Story'

a boy's head inscribed on a coin flipped
soon takes shape of the torso of the angel
who cared about tails so much he ran
out of luck on bets against tsunamis and viruses
because he fell sick while earnestly trying
we loved remembering him while sneezing
when tragedy strikes the possibilities of humility
grow manifold an orthogonal line of sweat
on the temple cools the boy's body down
the green fire he was born with is now a garden
of strictly afternoon sounds little brambling
supernovas the boy stomached over years
constellations grunting at a daily construction
site all sentience is intestinal delight accumulated
over seasons bred low by reason in a corner
the boy under his bedsheets spurts to groggy life
five sevenths of unknown is known his marshes
a rorschach print of graying gels when his eyes fall
on a bare shoulder he thinks of an ocean then wants
to kiss it his throat dries up a pressure builds
for an abdominal release this miracle impossible
to touch while it's happening like the noiseless sear
of fever against an underarm tattoo the boy grows
to love his wetland ghosts they meet him at the holy
spot between two mango trees that speak

the vernacular of salted summer winds when the boy
is mugged in broad daylight the thugs find no notes
in his denim wallet they spit in disgust then rub
their palms on his saccharine crotch the murder
of pleasure is vengeance for some on the way back
the boy eats noodles of light curled from his tears
masculinity creamed blue like a rock of
butter tongued
from a cactus blade the boy pirouettes on floors
of jealousy absorbing the difficulties of grace
while ceaselessly slipping the boy
is a girl the boy is you the boy loves
the lover of the boy he loves the boy
who is a hue who is no longer me

***

2
Plays

Jagan Mohan Lal (1838–1913)

The Monk

(A Selection from the Play)

(Translated *Babaji* from the Odia by Manu Dash)

Act I

Babu Subal Patnaik's drawing room
(The monk enters)

Monk: Victory to you, Babu.

Babu: I pay my salutation to you, *Maharaj*.[i]
(Babu prostrates before the monk)

Monk: God be with you and make you happy always.

Babu: Please take a seat. Here's a chair for you. What is the reason for your gracious presence here?

Monk: Just came to meet you.

Babu: Where's your *mutt*?[ii]

Monk: We don't have any mutt, son! What work do we have in mutt after abandoning home? Both home and mutt are the same. We do not stay for long at any place and go moving around places. We have been staying for the last two days on the banks of the river. Came here since no food was available there.

---

[i] A kind of address for a respected saint or person.

[ii] An abode of the followers of Vaishnavism sect.

Babu *(Offers two paisa)*: Please have it, Maharaj.

Monk: Money! We don't take money as alms, son! It would take the whole day if we go begging for money from door to door. Then where shall we get time to pray and meditate? Money breeds greed. What's the need for money for monks? A square meal is needed. If you wish, you could give me a square meal, or else I shall look for another benefactor. I do not have any worries, I will get it anyway by the grace of God.

Babu: Well, Maharaj. I shall offer you a plain meal. Whom shall I offer if not to you? I have not seen a monk as simple and wise as you are.

Monk: No, dear son. What sort of a monk am I? What knowledge do I have? I am worse than a worm; not worth being called a monk.

Babu: You may say so, but I haven't come across anyone like you earlier!

(Calls out for the house help) Rama, O Rama. Where are you?

Rama *(Shouts from offstage)*: Yes, sir.

(Rama enters)

Babu: *Arre,*[iii] bring some *siddha*[iv] for the monk.

(Rama leaves the stage)

Babu: Maharaj, take some weed.

(Hands over the chillum[v] *to the monk)* Do you need the grass?

Monk: I do not take weed. What shall I do with grass? Keep the chillum with you. I don't crave any weed, grass or bhang.

[iii] An expletive used to express oneself while directing a subordinate.

[iv] Uncooked food items.

[v] A small pipe used for smoking cannabis.

I need food, without which I can't sustain my life. What's the use of any intoxicant? It doesn't keep the mind in order.

Babu: It doesn't keep the mind in order? How then do the holy men take these intoxicants? There's a saying, that 'the monk takes intoxicant for concentrating on his meditation and to take the name of the Lord.'

Monk: Yes, the saying is there. But this aphorism is invented by potheads; it is not there in any scripture. Any intoxicant is bad—it should not be touched.

Babu: I beg to differ, Maharaj. Intoxicants have both good and bad effects. Taking too much of it is bad, but it is not bad if taken occasionally in moderate quantity. Rather, it has a good effect. The mind remains focused, one forgets all sorrows and suffering, and the heart fills with pleasure.

Monk: Of course, there is pleasure. But, what's the use of that pleasure for me? For intoxicants, I need money and for money, I have to go begging from door to door. All my time will be consumed in this process and when will I get the scope to pray and meditate? Rich people search for pleasure from the intoxicants first, but later it causes displeasure. All pleasure lies in the meditation of the Lord. However, there is no crime in using intoxicants to cure diseases.

(Rama enters with siddha)

Babu: Please receive the siddha, Maharaj.

Monk: I am very pleased, son. But it is too tough for me to cook and organize cooking accessories. I had a disciple whom I had trained to cook, but he is no longer with me.

Babu: Why did you leave him? You must be facing lots of difficulties.

Monk: What is pain? Everything is managed by the Almighty. No association with any human is everlasting. Religion gives us permanent company. Please keep this siddha with you. If possible, I would prefer a square meal and thereafter, I shall go for prayer and meditation.

Babu: We have all already taken our meal. But we shall cook the food for you. *(Calls Rama)* Take this siddha to the pujari and tell him to prepare food.

Rama: He's taking a midday siesta. The moment I ask, he shall shout and pounce on me.

Babu: Let me call him then. Pujari . . . pujari!

(Enters Anada Panda, the cook)

Take this siddha and cook near the worship room for the Monk. Do it fast. Maharaj will have his meal.

(Taking the siddha, Anada Panda exits)

Maharaj, it will take some time to prepare food. In the meantime, please chant some devotional songs. Let our ears be blessed.

Monk: That's fine! *(Sings devotional song)*

('Raag Jhinjhit', 'Taal Ektaal')

I have none other than the friend of the poor
He is eternal, omnipotent, abinashi[vi]
Father and mother of the universe
He fathoms the feelings of His devotees
He resurrects the life of the downtrodden
Who worship Him.

Babu: Wah, you sing so well! Had there been instruments, it would have been amazing. Well, I am inviting a gentleman who will play an instrument and you will sing. *(to Rama)* Rama! Go and call Jashu Babu. Ask him to come immediately.

(Rama exits and Jashu Bhattacharya enters)

[vi] Indestructible.

Babu: Welcome, Bhattacharya Babu! Please come.

Jashu: Good day! What was this urgent call at midday for?

Babu: Here's the monk who sings devotional songs very well. His lunch is being prepared. During this time, he will continue singing and you shall be playing the instrument. *(Calls out)* Rama, bring the tobacco and the tabla.

(Rama enters and gives tobacco and tabla)

Please take the tobacco first. Every Sunday, we play a game of dice. This Sunday, let's have this entertainment.

Jashu: What's enjoyment without alcohol? Where were you yesterday? We had great fun indeed. You ruined our Saturday night.

Babu: It was not ruined completely. We had also fun to some extent. Some friends make loud noises after boozing which invites a bad name for us. It's wise to do such things behind closed doors. But now, how can we do this? This fellow is present.

Jashu: Let him be here. What does he know? Tell him it's pomegranate sherbet.

Babu: Good idea. *(to the monk)* Maharaj, this gentleman has come in blistering sun. Let me serve some pomegranate sherbet for him. Rama *(winks at him)*, get some sherbet and glasses. Secure the door latch.

(Rama keeps the bottle and glasses and Babu pours the drink)

Take this sherbet, Mr Bhattacharya. You shall need two more doses after this one.

Jashu *(drinks)*: No more, please. Last evening's hangover is still there. I cannot play the instrument if I take any more.

Babu: Then, will I have to consume the whole bottle? *(Feels his stomach)* See, my stomach is also bloated. What shall I do?

Jashu: Take a little more sherbet and it shall be fine soon.

Babu: How? I shall take it if it makes me fine. *(Babu drinks again and again)*

Jashu *(takes the tabla)*: Maharaj, please begin the song.

(The monk sings the devotional song)

('Raag Jangla', 'Taal Thumri')

O redeemer of the downtrodden,
May this evildoer behold your feet?
Those feet, like ambrosia,
thaw the evils and woes of millions
My heart is immersed in worldly bonds,
I am entangled in mundane spheres.
There is no alternative than You,
Save me, O redeemer of the downtrodden!
Do punish me the way you wish and dispel my sins
Accept me as Your servant
Do fulfil my request
Please listen to my prayer.

(Babu loses self-control and starts dancing)

Jashu: Dance to your heart's content. Let me play the tabla.

Babu: Okay, I am dancing.

(Babu dances like a professional, makes a lot of gestures and drops down on the floor)

Monk *(To himself)*: My words are still fresh on my lips! What a sad fall of a man of such stature!

Jashu: Maharaj, Babu is down for a short nap. I will take leave of you. Please have your meal. I am instructing the cook. Pujari . . . pujari.

(Pujari enters)

Pujari, I am leaving. Serve the monk his food. Rama, keep a watch on Babu.

Pujari: Please come to the verandah of the puja room for the meal.

(Exits)

Act-II

Babu's balcony near the worship room

Pujari: Maharaj, please sit here *(points out to the side of the verandah and moves forward while Dama, a house help enters from the other side)*. *(To Dama)* Dama, I am supposed to feed this monk a sumptuous meal.

Our Babu is always ready to help whenever someone is in need of it, but he grumbles when it is a question of our salary. One has to run to him twenty times to get our payment, but for the monk, he is so generous. How absurd is this? He who flatters him gets the benefit and we turn into dumb onlookers? Whatever it may be, where did this fellow appear from? I had just had a midday siesta after working hard since the morning and this fellow has become a thorn in my flesh. Wait and watch, I shall make his life miserable.

Dama: There is a saying, 'There is no ladder to heaven and no answer to the bigshots.' Do you have any idea what will happen if you do not cook and feed the monk? I guess you are fated to be scolded today.

Pujari: Babu is not here. He is dead drunk. So, I don't care.

Dama: Try to understand. The monk has come hungry—he will curse you if you don't feed him.

Pujari: Huh! I have seen many monks like him. And I have taught them many lessons. How can the curse of a Vaishnav fall on a Brahmin? You know, he disturbed my sleep. Will not my curse fall upon him? Wait, let me play some pranks on him.

Dama: Okay. Do whatever you wish. You are capable of teaching lessons to Babu! We are petty, insignificant fellows.

Pujari: Maharaj, there is cooked rice but no curry. What will you eat with it? Will shukhua[vii] do?

Monk: Whatever's there, dried or wet, please give, son!

Pujari: I am talking of shukhua.

Monk: What is shukhua? I have never eaten it.

Pujari: What do you know then if you do not know about shukhua. It is a dish prepared out of fish. Everyone eats it. Nowadays, Vaishnavs are also eating it secretly.

Monk: What? Vaishnavs eat shukhua? I have never heard of it.

Pujari: Will you then take saguati?[viii]

Monk: Yes, that would do; that's more than enough.

Pujari (To Dama): *Lo*,[ix] he doesn't take shukhua but saguati.

Dama: It seems he did not get you.

Pujari: It's better he didn't follow. He shall be responsible for the wrong committed by him.

(Pujari places the leaf-plate before the monk and exits with Dama)

Monk: Pujari baba, where have you vanished placing the empty plate before me? Tell me if there is no food. I will go back.

(Pujari enters with a covered earthen pot)

[vii] Dried fish.

[viii] Goat meat

[ix] See.

Pujari: Just arrived, Maharaj. *(He places the earthen pot near the leaf-plate)* Here's the delicious prasad, Maharaj. Please serve yourself.

Maharaj: Okay, son. *(A rooster comes out of the pot the moment the monk takes off the cover, startling him.)* What the hell is this?

Pujari: Maharaj, you agreed to take saguati meat, so I prepared a full-roasted kebab. Our Babu also often takes this dish. What's my offence if it got back its life with your touch? Maharaj, you are bestowed with supernatural power. I had cooked the rooster, but it returned to a live chicken. Oh, I have never had such an experience earlier.

(Enters Raghu Singh, another house help)

Monk: You told me of leafy vegetable curry, but I find you serving a live chicken? Speaking so inappropriately and ridiculing me? You are a discourteous person and are ill-treating a hungry man.

Raghu: Really, what rubbish are you doing, Pujari? Does a man behave like this? You are ill-treating a hungry monk. You are so impolite! Are you not a Brahmin? Are you a Brahmin by merely putting a sacred thread on your shoulder or by performing your duties? What happened to these Brahmins in this *Kalyug*?[x] No trace of care or respect for religion, rituals or dignity. These people are inviting trouble for themselves. From where did you bring a rooster to the verandah of the worship room? Could you retain your caste? Will God reside here anymore?

Pujari: Babu gives me the rooster for cooking. I am only guilty of touching it. Don't you know, the rooster needs to be cooked?

---

[x] Kalyug is the fourth, shortest and worst of the four yugas in a Yuga cycle in Hinduism. It is believed to be the present age, which is full of conflict and sin.

Raghu *(fuming)*: What did you say? Babu eats chicken? Don't I know Babu? He observes so many rites and rituals, and is such a giver and believer! He's praised by Brahmins and Vaishnavs alike. You have the cheek to slander him? He's not an English-educated Babu. Nowadays, even some of these Babus in Calcutta have stopped drinking alcohol and eating meat. They have become learned and pious. Never was a person of your stupidity and ignorance seen before. Tell me in what way do you compare with our Babu? Even if he has strayed or erred once or twice, would you do the same thing? Listen, Maharaj, he has wronged you so much and now he is training his guns on Babu. Let us go and report to him.

Monk: No, son. We won't inform him. Babu will be angry at him or terminate him from the job. The poor fellow will die. They are simpletons. When they see any shortcomings of the employer, instead of covering them up, they blame him and propagate them everywhere. We shall advise him to refrain from doing such a thing in future. What would happen if we informed Babu? Did you get me, Pujari? It's a great evil and sin to ill-treat the hungry, blame your master and tell a lie. You will be punished on your next birth. Please do not repeat such evil in future. Keep in mind to observe what you pledged during your sacred thread ceremony, 'Don't tell a lie.' Unless you observe the ten vows said at that time, you cannot be a real Brahmin.

Raghu *(with brimming tears)*: What a kind and wise person! Pujari, do you realize what bad behaviour you showed to this monk? You will meet an untimely death. *(To monk)* Maharaj, if you come to my residence, I will arrange your food immediately.

Monk: No, son. It's not possible to go for food. I shall leave for my mutt and have the meal there. Don't feel otherwise. Stay happy and blessed.

Pujari Baba, take my advice seriously as an elder. Let me go. God bless you.

(The monk leaves)

Raghu: Did you observe, Pujari? No trace of anger or ego. He left blessing you.

Pujari: Yes. Such an amazing monk—godlike. I tortured him. He left the plate without touching anything. I committed a serious crime. I feel very bad now. I don't see anything good coming out of this.

(He slaps himself and weeps)

***

Biswajit Das (1936–2004)

Chief Guest

(Translated from the Odia by Samanjasa Das)

The only library-cum-office-cum-conference hall of the Friends' Cultural Club. It is evening. The furniture in the room is not plentiful but quite distinct. There are a couple of wooden almirahs with labels like 'Novel', 'Politics', 'Health Science', 'History', 'Detective' etc. There is a broken table with a few old newspapers on it and three or four rickety wooden chairs. The room has two doors but no windows. The calendars of the last two to three years are hanging on the wall in chronological order. Apart from these, there are a few cardboard posters inscribed with inspirational quotes: 'If you aspire to be great, make your mother tongue richer' and 'Nobody is permanent, all will depart after playing their roles.'

Noted literary figure and poet Bholanath Choudhary is seated on a chair. There is nothing extraordinary about his appearance—just a shawl around his neck and a garland in his hand. A young man is busy fanning him with a handheld fan while another is holding a plate with some laddus and bananas on it. Bholanath Babu is around forty years old and appears to be a man of amiable nature. The youth on his right is Jatindra (Jati), who seems to be from a well-to-do family. The healthy young man on his left is Bhimacharan, whose appearance is somewhat rough and brash.

Bhimacharan *(in a soft voice)*: Sir, at least this laddu . . .

Bholanath *(smiling politely)*: I don't eat laddus. Has the crowd assembled for the meeting?

Bhimacharan *(tries to explain)*: People are coming . . . Sir, laddu is a speciality of this area . . . Not made from vegetable oil. Nothing like that ever happens in a function of the Friends' Cultural Club.

Bholanath *(to Jatindra, with a friendly smile)*: Let it be. Why are you taking all this unnecessary trouble? Do you think I don't like laddus? I do. However, it should be avoided by a diabetic patient like myself.

Bhimacharan *(to Jati, irritatingly)*: This is what happens if you place the order with Kali Sahu. He could have prepared some fried stuff.

Bholanath: Aha, the same thing again. Actually, I am not hungry at all after my morning meal. *(To Jati)* Didn't I ask you to stop fanning? It is not very hot. I can manage.

Jatindra *(politely)*: No, sir. These mosquitoes are enemy number one. They will not let you sit without a fan even for a moment.

Bholanath: No, no, that is not what I meant. What I wanted to tell you is that if the meeting can somehow commence, you don't have to unnecessarily take all these troubles.

Bhimacharan *(irritatingly to Jati)*: Something is wrong with the publicity. *(Courteously to Bholanath)* Not much longer, sir. The vice president and secretary of the club have gone towards the cinema house. As soon as the movie is over, the crowd will assemble here.

Bholanath *(Looking at his wristwatch—slightly irritable)*: As soon as the movie is over! Isn't the show over yet?

Bhimacharan: The audience should assemble here as soon as the movie is over, sir.

Bholanath *(in a mild voice)*: But if I miss the last train . . .

Bhimacharan: Yes, the last train is indeed an issue. You may conclude your speech as the chief guest a little early.

Bholanath *(laughing)*: Haha, do you think I don't know that? But how can the speech be over if the meeting does not start? *(Looking at his watch)* It is already 9.30 p.m. . . .

Bhimacharan: The vice president and secretary must be returning with the crowd.

Bholanath: I know they will come. But after watching a movie, who will be in the mood to attend a literary function?

Bhimacharan *(puts down the plate of snacks on the table)*: Sir, leave that to us. I have managed several functions of the Friends' Cultural Club. Let the vice president and secretary return.

Bholanath *(to Bhima)*: What is your name? I can't exactly remember.

Bhimacharan: Sir, Bhima . . . Bhimacharan Satpathy.

Bholanath: Yes, yes. Bhimacharan babu, what I wanted to ask you is that with a speaker like Jameshwara babu around, why have you chosen an ordinary literary figure like me?

Bhimacharan: Ordinary! You are an ordinary literary figure? *(Ordering Jati)* Fan properly. *(Smilingly)* Who does not know Bholanath Choudhary, sir? After studying your creations from junior class to matriculation, our children know your name by heart.

Bholanath: I know all that. But with Jameshwara babu around . . .

Bhimacharan: Leave aside Jameshwara babu. He is a local person. Besides, after writing *Jatras* and *palas*,[xi] his manner of speaking has also become like the jatra.

[xi] Jatra and Pala are traditional indigenous Lokanatya.

Bholanath: Where is Jameshwara babu? I don't see him.

Bhimacharan: Rehearsing his speech, sir. He is a little nervous. Will reach anytime now.

Bholanath: I am sure he will. But if I fail to catch the last train . . .

Bhimacharan: You will not miss the train, sir. That is our responsibility.

Bholanath: Even then, if we can conclude the function a little early.

Bhimacharan: It will get over in time, sir. It will. We are taking that responsibility.

Bholanath: I can understand. But if we wait for the movie to get over . . .

Bhimacharan: The publicity has failed and we have no other option. Otherwise, the pandal would have been packed with people by now.

Bholanath *(sighing deeply)*: I have plenty of work in Cuttack. There will be a lot of difficulty if I don't return tonight.

Bhimacharan: You will definitely return tonight, sir. Having invited you to this cultural function, it is our duty to ensure that you return.

Bholanath: I understand, but the way it is getting delayed . . .

Bhimacharan: There is no delay—we are just waiting for the cinema show to get over.

(An old and apparently busy Jameshwara Pradhan enters the room with some papers in his hand)

Jameshwara: Nothing will happen unless I do it myself.

Bholanath: Please come, Jameshwara babu. Have a seat.

Jameshwara *(without paying attention to Bholanath)*: Please don't ask me to sit. How much work can one person do? I will write the speech, distribute the invitation cards and go from door to door to arrange wooden cots for the pandal. There is a limit to human endurance. *(To Bhima)* Where is the tabla?

Bhimacharan: What tabla?

Jameshwara: Whose duty was it to bring the *dubi* and tabla[xii] from Jadu babu's house?

Bhimacharan: Whose duty was it?

Jameshwara: You can't remember, right? How can you? Now, take out the duty list—every detail is there.

Bhimacharan: You have the list.

Jameshwara *(feeling around in his pocket)*: I have the list? Where is it then? Yes, I got it. *(Takes out the list and reads it)* Here it is. Two garlands—Shri Jatindranath Panda. Refreshments for the chief guest—Shri Bhimacharan Satpathy.

Bhimacharan: Refreshment is ready, read on.

Jameshwara: Harmonium—Shri Chaitanya Sahu. Tabla—yes, yes, it is here. One dubi and one tabla—Shri, Shri *(He stops)*

Bhimacharan: Why did you stop? Please read on.

Jameshwara *(uncomfortably)*: My name is written here. I will arrange the tabla?

Bhimacharan: You have prepared the list yourself.

Jameshwara: In the capacity of the club's president, I had to write the speech, distribute the invitation cards and arrange the cots for the pandal. The tabla also has to be arranged by me?

[xii] Dubi and Tabla are percussion musical instruments.

Bholanath *(coughing slightly but politely)*: Excuse me, Jameshwara babu. Tabla, Harmonium . . . What are all these for?

Jameshwara: What are you saying? Opening and closing songs. Without these, I mean . . .

Bholanath: I understand that. But if the meeting does not start, who will listen to the opening and closing songs?

Jameshwara: What can I do alone? On top of all that, even a tabla has to be arranged by me. I am the president of the club!

Bholanath *(fidgeting)*: Please do something.

Jameshwara: I certainly will. I will arrange a dubi and tabla—no matter from where. I will not have the function without the opening and closing songs.

Bholanath: You did not get me. I have no objection to the opening and closing songs—they should be there. But who will listen to them? Where is the audience? On the other hand, it is also time to catch my train.

Jameshwara: You are right—you have to catch the last train. *(Irritatingly to Bhima)* Bhima, instead of wasting your time here, you should supervise the arrangements there.

Bhimacharan: Do you think I was having fun here? The chief guest will sit alone and all the members of the club will be wandering here and there!

Jameshwara: Speak for yourself. What were you doing here?

Bhimacharan *(agitatedly brings the plate of snacks from the table and gives it to Jameshwara)*: Why did you give me the refreshment charge then? From the beginning, I wanted to be in charge of pandal decoration.

Jameshwara *(looking at the plate of snacks)*: Who are these snacks for? Did I not circulate the message that the refreshments for the members would follow the meeting?

Bhimacharan: Who cares about your refreshments? This plate was for the chief guest.

Jameshwara: Then, why did the chief guest not have it?

Bhimacharan: You can ask the chief guest himself—he is sitting right across from you. You can verify whether I am telling the truth or not.

Bholanath *(intolerantly trying to stop the altercation)*: Oh, I can see you all have started a problem. There is no sign of any meeting. Yet, so many arguments over refreshments!

Jameshwara: But according to our programme, the chief guest's refreshment is before the meeting.

Bholanath: Who is disputing that? Where is the question of refreshment after the programme? It will be difficult to catch the train.

Jameshwara: Why have you not eaten then?

Bholanath *(with a wry smile)*: You tell me, how can I eat? I am diabetic. On top of that, this is too much food.

Jameshwara *(taking the plate into his own hands)*: Now I understand. Kali Sahu has given whatever he wanted to. No, I will not let you eat these other sweets. These are from Kali Sahu's shop and will lead to dysentery immediately. Rather, these two laddus . . .

Bholanath *(intervenes)*: Excuse me, Jameshwara babu. I can't eat these laddus.

Jameshwara *(pleading with Bholanath)*: Please don't say that. You must be angry with us. I will not let you go if you don't have these two laddus.

Bholanath *(failing at his attempt to smile)*: What do you mean—you will not let me go? How strange! *(To Bhima)* Bhimakanta babu!

Bhimacharan: Bhimacharan, sir.

Bholanath: Yes, Bhimacharan babu! Did I not tell you about my difficulty with these laddus?

Bhimacharan: What can I do, sir? Please explain it to the president.

Jameshwara *(to Bhimacharan)*: I told you to quickly go and supervise the arrangements there.

Bhimacharan: There is no clarity in what duty you have assigned to me. In the list, it is refreshments for the chief guest. Now you are telling me.

Jameshwara: Oh! It is an emergency. Refreshment duty does not mean that you will not do anything else. *(Ordering Bhim)* Go and stand near the roundabout of the Atmashanti Hotel. Keep a watch and divert everyone you see to the meeting.

Bhimacharan: But Sadabhai and Jagannath babu are keeping a watch near the cinema house!

Jameshwara: I can't rely on those two. Otherwise, I would not have to arrange for the tabla. Hmm, vice president and secretary . . .

Bhimacharan *(was leaving but stops)*: But what about the tabla?

Jameshwara: Oh yes, the tabla. Well, I am arranging that. Perhaps Chaitanya Sahu will arrive soon. You go quickly. *(Bhima is ready to go)* Do you remember? The Atmashanti Hotel roundabout . . . Don't leave anybody. *(Trying to explain to Bholanath)* Don't ask about the people. They don't understand anything about literature. No enthusiasm to attend a literary meeting either. That is the root cause of the sorry state of Odia literature.

Bholanath *(thoughtfully)*: Not only Odia literature but all.

Jameshwara: You are right. Otherwise, the president of the club would not have to arrange for the tabla.

Bholanath: You will arrange the tabla. What shall I do?

Jameshwara: That is why I was asking you to have the laddus.

Bholanath *(irritably)*: What do you mean? Do you mean to say that I took all this trouble to eat laddus?

Jameshwara *(sadly)*: What can we do? Mofussil[xiii] area—it is a misnomer to call this place a town. Where can we get rasgullas from?

Bholanath *(caught off guard)*: That's not what I am saying. I like laddus; I don't hate them.

Jameshwara *(grinning from ear to ear)*: Then, I shan't listen to anything. You must have these laddus.

Bholanath *(anticipating a problem)*: I told you, I am diabetic. I can't eat laddus.

Jameshwara: All of us will feel bad if you don't have it. You are an established literary figure of Odisha. How can I not offer you something to eat?

Bholanath: Oh, what a problem! I am telling you that I will not have any laddus. *(Looking at the watch)* I can see that you all will make me miss my train. How much longer will it take for the meeting to begin?

[xiii] Rural area/countryside.

Jameshwara *(puts down the plate on the table)*: No more delay. Please don't worry at all. We have shortened the programme. *(Takes out a paper from his pocket and starts reading)* First garlanding, then opening song, *(recites)* Our Guest, heartfelt welcome, immediately after that, your speech. Then my speech followed by a vote of thanks. Then comes the closing song—*(recites)* Heart bleeds, separation pangs . . .

Bholanath: Then what? Will the train wait for the closing song?

Jameshwara *(thoughtfully)*: That is also correct. But if all of us try . . .

Bholanath: If we try, the closing song may get over in time. But the train will not wait.

(Chaitanya Sahu enters—the only singer of the locality—well-dressed, he is holding a book of songs. Behind him, another young man enters carrying a harmonium on his shoulder)

Jameshwara: Why have you all come here?

Chaitanya *(irritably)*: It cannot be done. While the opening song can be managed without a tabla, it is necessary for the closing song. To add to that, there has not been any rehearsal.

Jameshwara: You could not arrange a tabla from somewhere?

Chaitanya: Who will arrange a tabla? Shall I rehearse or arrange a tabla? *(To his companion)* Put down the harmonium on the table. Let me rehearse once.

Jameshwara: Who will go to fetch the tabla then?

Chaitanya: What shall I do? It is not fair to harass the artists like this.

Jameshwara: Oh! You are an artist! Fine. *(To Jati)* Jati, go running to get the tabla from Jadu uncle's house. Give me the fan.

(Jatindra gives the fan to Jameshwara and leaves hurriedly. Bholanath gets up worriedly)

Bholanath *(holding Jameshwara's hands)*: What are you doing? Are you going to fan me?

Jameshwara: It's no bother. As the president of the club, I too have a duty towards the chief guest.

Bholanath: No, no. I don't approve of all this. Instead, would you ensure that the meeting starts as soon as possible?

Jameshwara *(starts fanning forcibly)*: The meeting will start. Our members are watching everywhere—from the cinema hall to the Atmashanti Hotel.

Chaitanya *(sits down on the table and tells his companion)*: Raju, what are you looking at? Play the harmonium. The closing song is completely messed up. There is no time in hand. *(Chooses a song from his songbook. Raju starts playing the harmonium. Chaitanya clears his throat to tune the harmonium.)*

Raju *(expresses dissatisfaction)*: Completely out of tune.

(Chaitanya again starts to match the tune with a high-pitched tone)

Raju *(stops playing the harmonium)*: No, it does not match the scale.

Chaitanya *(feeling offended)*: Something is wrong with the scale.

Raju: The scale is fine. *You* are out of tune.

Chaitanya *(angrily)*: Raju, speak properly. You are teaching me scale?

Raju: Fine. You show me the scale you can tune with.

Chaitanya: Are you challenging me? Ok.

(Chaitanya starts playing the harmonium and tries to tune with the scale)

Bholanath *(after a few moments, with consternation)*: What is going on?

Jameshwara: It's the closing song,

Bholanath: I can understand that. But I will miss my train.

Jameshwara: The meeting is about to begin *(gravely to Chaitanya and Raju)* You two are hopeless. The closing song is not ready yet. I think I shall have to sing it myself.

Chaitanya: I can't rehearse if you create such a disturbance.

Jameshwara: I am disturbing? *(To Bholanath)* See, they accuse me of creating disturbance.

Chaitanya: I had asked for a tabla so many days ago. Why did it not come?

Jameshwara: You are out of tune from the beginning. Why are you putting the blame on the tabla?

Chaitanya *(angrily)*: Out of tune? What do you know about scale to say that I am out of tune? *(To Raju)* Play B sharp. I will see how it is out of tune.

(Raju starts playing the harmonium loudly. Chaitanya tries to match his tone with the scale. In the meantime, Jagannath babu, the secretary of the club, enters very quietly. His face is grim.)

Jameshwara: Here comes the secretary. *(To Jagannath)* Where has the vice president gone?

Jagannath *(unsure of himself)*: To the hospital.

Jameshwara *(taken aback)*: The hospital? Why?

Jagannath: For bandages. He has been seriously wounded from falling off his bicycle.

Jameshwara: Where is the audience for the meeting? Where have the people gone?

Jagannath: They are coming. Many people are coming. Because of the cycle accident, many people have gathered and I have not spared anyone.

Jameshwara: But weren't the two of you watching for people near the cinema hall?

Jagannath: Don't ask. After coming out of the cinema hall, nobody was prepared to listen. Everyone was heading home. That is why the cycle accident had to happen.

Jameshwara: What are you saying? You knowingly had the cycle accident?

Jagannath: What else could I do? After all, we needed an audience for the meeting.

Jameshwara *(to Chaitanya and Raju)*: Why have you stopped? Keep rehearsing. There's not much delay. People are coming, didn't you hear?

(Chaitanya and Raju start singing with renewed enthusiasm: Heart is breaking, separation pang etc.)

Jameshwara *(out of irritation)*: It's not done. Your voice is not clear.

Chaitanya *(angrily)*: What did you say?

Jameshwara: The tone is not clear. I mean, the lyrics are not clear.

Chaitanya: What do you mean by saying that it is not clear? I am singing with so much emotion.

Jameshwara: The emotion is there. But that does not mean that the words will not be clear.

Chaitanya: How clear?

Jameshwara: It should be absolutely clear, word by word. I mean, 'heart is breaking, separation pang'. Do you understand?

Chaitanya: I have tried my best. It can't be clearer than this.

Jameshwara: What do you mean—it can't be clearer? For the sake of the reputation of the club, the closing song must be crystal clear.

Chaitanya *(pushes the harmonium towards Jameshwara)*: Take it. You make it clear.

Jameshwara: I? I will do it?

Chaitanya: Who else? Easier said than done.

Jameshwara: Everything has a limit. What do you think of yourself? I have managed so many closing songs myself.

Chaitanya: You manage then. Who is stopping you?

Jameshwara: I must deliver a speech as the president. Otherwise, I would have managed the closing song myself.

Jagannath: Why do you argue so much? Just direct them a little. The meeting will start in a while.

Jameshwara: Jagannath, I don't know what to do. If I knew that being the president of the club would entail so many problems . . .

Jagannath: Not only the president. Being the secretary is also no less difficult. Otherwise, there would not be any need to cause an accident to assemble a crowd for the meeting.

Jamshwara: But even after so many efforts over the past seven days, these fellows could not prepare the closing song.

Chaitanya: Don't say that. Everything is just fine. If you don't like it, show us how it should be done.

Jagannath *(to Jameshwara)*: It's ok. Just show them a little and be done with it.

Jameshwara *(looking at everybody and heading towards the harmonium, starts singing)*: Heart is breaking . . .

Chaitanya *(faintly smiling)*: Out of rhythm . . .

Raju: Out of tune.

(Jameshwara stops for a while and looks at Chaitanya and Raju. He resumes singing with renewed efforts.)

Chaitanya *(covering both the ears with his hands)*: Totally out of rhythm.

Raju *(covering both his ears)*: Completely out of tune.

Jameshwara *(shouting angrily)*: Shut up! How dare kids like you criticize my song as 'out of rhythm' and 'out of tune'?

Chaitanya: Of course, I will.

Jameshwara *(shouting)*: Shut up! How dare you talk over me? Do you know who I am?

Chaitanya: Jameshwara Pradhan. In short, Yamraj.[xiv]

Jameshwara *(trembling in anger)*: What did you just say? I am Yamraj? Yamraj? Yes, I am. *(To Bholanath)* Did you hear them? You are a noted figure of Odia literature. You are the witness—this tiny fellow has the audacity to call me Yamraj.

Chaitanya: I am warning you. Don't you call me a tiny fellow.

Jameshwara: Again, you are showing me your red eyes![xv]

---

xiv God of death.

xv A way of displaying one's anger.

Jagannath *(runs and tries to stop Jameshwara from getting into a fight with Chaitanya)*: What is happening?

Chaitanya: President, my foot. He is a tout.[xvi]

Jameshwara: What, I am a tout? You called me a tout? Jagannath, leave me. I will teach this fellow a lesson.

Chaitanya: Take a walk. What can you do? I have seen many presidents like you.

Jagannath: Raju, what are you looking at? Stop Chaitanya.

Raju: Oh, Chaitanya *bhai*.[xvii] Please stop this *(tries to stop Chaitanya)*.

Chaitanya *(tries to free himself)*: Leave me. This fellow does not know Chaitanya Sahu. I will break his skull.

Jameshwara: Your father and fourteen generations cannot even touch me.

Chaitanya: Again? Again, you uttered the names of my father and grandfather? *(To Bholanath)* Sir, you are the witness. Nobody can protect him now. Raju, let me go.

Jameshwara: Let go of me, Jagannath.

Chaitanya: I will break your head.

Jameshwara: I will break your teeth.

(A scared Bholanath stands up. Without knowing what to do, he slowly heads towards the door. At this point, Bhimacharan and Jatindra, with a tabla in hand, enter the room. Bholanath stops. Realizing the situation, Bhimacharan shouts.)

Bhimacharan: It is over, over. It is a disaster.

[xvi] A tout is one who solicits business in a brazen manner.

[xvii] Brother.

(Everyone looks at the door.)

Bhimacharan *(In a distraught voice)*: The chief guest is about to leave.

Jagannath *(runs towards Bholanath)*: Sir, where will you go?

Bholanath: Please let me go.

Jagannath: How can that be, sir? People are going to reach here any moment now.

Bholanath: I am a family man. My children must be waiting for me to return home.

Bhimacharan: But what about literature? Don't you have any duty towards the growth of Odia literature? You are such a great literary figure!

Bholanath: I will stop practising literature.

Bhimacharan: What are you saying, sir? If you take leave of literature, who will be the chief guest in our cultural function?

Bholanath: I don't care who, but it will not be me. Let me go.

Bhimacharan: What about our meeting? Who will be the chief guest in our meeting? The meeting is about to start. Another five minutes.

Bholanath: Five minutes?

Bhimacharan: Yes, yes. Don't worry. In the meantime, you should have your refreshments.

Jagannath: Bhima is right. Where is the plate? *(Picks up the plate from the table himself)*

Bholanath *(Looking at the plate, almost shouts)*: Oh, laddu again?

Jagannath: Yes, laddu. Sir, please don't say no. Eat it quietly.

Bhimacharan: Please eat it.

Jagannath: We will not let you go if you don't eat the laddus.

Bhimacharan: Perhaps sir is feeling embarrassed.

Jagannath: Why do you feel embarrassed, sir? Please eat the laddus. *(Forcefully tries to put the laddu in Bholanath's mouth. A helpless Bholanath starts eating the laddus)*

Bhimacharan: Is the closing song ready?

Chaitanya: Absolutely ready. Raju, play B sharp.
(Chaitanya starts singing loudly—'Heart is breaking . . .')

Lights out. Curtain falls.

3

Short Stories

Fakir Mohan Senapati (1843–1918)

'Ananta, the Widow's Son'

(Translated 'Randipua Ananta' from the Odia by Jayanta Mahapatra)

Subal Singh had been handed down a herd of buffaloes from his father. Singh spent his days tending to the herd in the jungles of Harispur. He rarely came home. Instead, he built a small hut for himself in the jungle without a fence. As he lay inside it at night, Singh could easily keep a lookout for any tigers that happened to stray into the fold.

The buffaloes slept out in the open. Only towards the last quarter of the night would they move off to graze in the jungle. Singh lay awake since then, for that was the hour when a tiger usually carried away a calf. Singh's bamboo staff lay beside him. A single snort from the buffaloes warned him that a tiger was somewhere close by. He would then bawl so loudly that even the largest tiger made its escape!

Singh looked after his herd with great care. He never complained, so happy he was with his herd. Around noon every day, his wife brought him 5 kilos of coarse rice and a packet of tobacco leaves from the village. In addition, 5 kilos of pure buffalo milk made up his food for the day.

Suddenly one year, a bout of smallpox attacked the herd and within a week, the entire herd of fifty-five buffaloes disappeared! Singh was beside himself with grief. His wife did all she could to console him.

Singh sold the remaining three calves that were still alive and took over as the chief cowherd for the landlord. He became known as the Setha. It was such an important job for Singh!

His wife was highly flattered. She would fight with anyone in the village who did not address her as the Setha's wife!

Winter set in. The sahib of police came on a visit to Makrampur. A mile away lay the salt marsh, which was teeming with duck, geese and various waterfowl. The sahib was taken aback at the sight of so much game. With his shotgun on his shoulder, he strode towards the lake. A dozen constables and *chowkidars*[i] followed him. As soon as he reached the marsh, he aimed his gun and fired.

Two of the waterfowl were hit in the wings and legs. But they could still fly and plunged into the middle of the marsh. Nobody moved to recover the birds. The sahib looked helplessly at his men. The water was quite deep in the middle, and people talked of two man-eating crocodiles. No one present there had the courage to go into the water. At that moment, Singh happened to pass by. Without a word, he stepped in. In no time, he was back with the birds which he placed before the sahib.

The sahib was greatly pleased. He looked carefully at Singh. His eyes took in the tall figure, the broad chest and square jaw, the thighs built solidly like tree trunks. He barked out an order to Singh: 'Meet me tomorrow morning.'

Subal Singh became the sahib's orderly. The sahib was very fond of hunting and Singh became his constant companion. Three months later, the sahib of police and the magistrate sahib went hunting in the jungles of Dompara. The magistrate shot at a tiger, wounding the animal. It entered a bush and started roaring. Two elephants and almost a hundred men accompanied the sahibs, but nobody dared to approach it! After all, what difference was there between death and a wounded tiger? The sahib looked at Singh. At once, he strode into the jungle. He still carried his old staff with him. Four times he struck at the tiger's head and then, dragged the beast

[i] Village watchmen.

by the tail before the sahibs. Singh was paid 20 rupees for his bravery and promoted to the rank of *jemadar*.[ii]

But fate seemed to be against Singh. When he came home on leave in the month of November, he was struck by pneumonia, and within three days, he was gone.

But Singh's wife did not lack in strength or courage, much like her late husband.

She could fearlessly face any danger. Tall as her husband, her belly bulged out like a paddy boiling pot. She was very fond of jewellery. The day after her husband's funeral rites were over, she covered herself with heavy bangles of brass. A gold ring adorned her nose. A long chain linked to eighty silver coins reached down to her navel. Afraid of nobody, she lived alone with her child at one end of the village. Knowing she had enough money, three robbers entered her house on a dark night. But she easily overcame the men. Two of them fled for their lives while she caught the third and gave him a severe thrashing.

Ananta was four years old at the time of his father's death. As the son was born late, the parents thought a lot of him. His mother would caress him, singing softly:

The moon moves across the sky
where a million stars abound,
Ananta rocks in Mother's lap
enjoying the milk he's found.
Father is away with the buffalo-herd
and Mother will do the milking,
Elephants at the Raja's palace
for Ananta to go a-riding.

Days went by. At the age of ten, Ananta looked like a rugged youth of twenty. His mother placed 3 kilos of cold watered

[ii] A minor official or junior officer.

rice before him every day. Like his father, he never needed any curry to take with the rice. He finished his meal with about 2 kilos of milk.

Singh's wife was beginning to worry about her son. Villagers complained that Ananta never left a vegetable or fruit behind in their gardens. Annoyed by constant complaints, she approached the village schoolmaster Baishnab Mahanti and placed Ananta under his care.

The master taught the children at the foot of the Boul tree. He wrote out the first two letters of the alphabet for Ananta. The whole time Ananta's hand kept moving over the letters, his eyes searched for ripe fruit in the tree overhead. He would then climb up the tree nimbly as a monkey, stuff the fruit into his mouth and be back at his place, all in a matter of seconds. The master lost his patience. The moment his back was turned, Ananta was up to some mischief. Finding no other way to control him, the master used his cane, but even the beating had little effect. Ananta would simply look around the tree when he was being caned. And he would forget his punishment as soon as he left school.

Five months passed by and Ananta was still at the second letter of the alphabet. Many a cane had been broken. In the end, the master could not bear it any longer. Throwing away his cane, he got hold of some branches of poison ivy and thrashed Ananta. Ananta was badly hurt. Yet there were no tears in his eyes. He boasted to his schoolmates that he would get even with the master.

The next day, Ananta was seen writing quietly, his eyes on his work. As he observed him, the master thought, 'What an upright boy he's become! Alas! Why couldn't I think of this before?'

Around noon, the master wanted to go out to the paddy fields to relieve himself. He called, 'Boys! Fetch me my tobacco leaves and my lota! And a little fire!' At his bidding, a few boys ran and kept things ready for him.

The master rolled a *pika* from the tobacco leaves and looked at Ananta. Ananta was silently doing his work. The master felt pity for the boy and called him gently, 'Son Ananta! Will you get me some water in the lota?' Down went Ananta to the pond at once. The master sat and waited, smoking. But Ananta wasn't to be seen. At last, the master rose and walked towards the pond. Hidden below the bank, Ananta had been observing the master's movements. When he saw the master approach, he meekly handed over the lota of water. Puffing at his pika, the master walked towards the fields.

Not even twenty minutes would have passed by when the master came running with six-foot leaps in the air, yelling at the top of his voice! His lota had fallen somewhere. His dhoti would also have fallen off; only he held onto it as he kept screaming, 'The murderer! That Ananta! He's killed me!' When he reached the school, he picked up his cane and shouted, 'Ananta! Where is Ananta?' But who could find Ananta? Ananta had vanished!

The master lay rolling on the ground and pleaded for water. A boy brought him a bowl of water from the kitchen. As soon as he washed himself with it, he flung the vessel away. He began to groan in pain. He couldn't shout any more. His face had swollen. The villagers crowded around him. They tossed the master into the pond. In the evening, he began to shiver from the cold. They pulled him out and massaged sesame oil over his body. The master managed to speak a few words. His face was still puffed up. He muttered, 'Very hungry.' The villagers gave him sips of hot milk. Slowly, his body cooled and he could sit.

The village elders inquired into the matter. Evidence was taken. In the end, it became clear that it was the work of the widow's son, Ananta. Ananta had not forgotten the thrashing he'd got with the stalks of poison ivy. He had plucked the poison fruit which grew beside the pond and scraped off the rough skin of the fruit. Half of these he'd put inside the *lota* and had hidden the rest. When the master went out to the fields, Ananta had also mixed the fruit with the water in the kitchen.

The master picked up his cane and rushed towards Ananta's house. Rage had no sense of time and place. From a distance, he kept shouting, 'You milkwoman! Where is that widow's son Ananta?' The Singh woman had heard everything by then and had hidden her son inside. Hearing the master's shouts, she brought out her husband's staff and leapt at him. Her head was bare. Her hair blew wildly in the wind. She yelled, 'How dare you call me a milkwoman! My husband was jemadar to the sahib, don't you remember? Wait till I get my hands on you!'

Her screams made the master turn cold with fright. He took off in a panic. The Singh woman ran behind him, the staff on her shoulder. Her huge belly gave out a loud thump as she ran. The jingle of her brass bangles could be heard from a distance. The village shook with her screams. Soon, the master merged into the darkness in the middle of the village. Only the woman's shouts could be heard: 'You slave Mahanti! Tomorrow I'll crush your head with these bangles'.

The schoolmaster was never seen in the village again.

Six more years went by. Most of the villagers were annoyed with Ananta. Not a single fruit or vegetable was left in their fields. But Ananta never cast a glance at any gold or silver lying around their houses. Heaven save the one who made him angry! For he would break down the door of his enemy's house! Yet, if you pleaded gently with him, he'd do anything—even wash your dirty clothes!

It was the month of October, the time for *Durga Puja*[iii]. Villagers who worked in distant places had all come home. Festivities swept the entire village. Food and drinks were in plenty. Music and dancing stretched far into the night. The sixth day of the Puja came. In the morning, a small cloud was

[iii] An annual festival that reveres and pays homage to the Hindu goddess Durga, and is also celebrated because of Durga's victory over Mahishasura.

seen in the north. The sun came up and soon hid behind the clouds. In a short while, the sky was covered with dark masses of clouds. Gusts of wind blew and large drops of rain began to fall. Once the rain started, it did not stop. It rained through the sixth, seventh and eighth day of Puja. The fury of the rain did not lessen till the evening of the ninth. People were stranded. The walls of many houses in the village collapsed. Wind and rain lashed the village day and night.

On the dawn of the tenth day, the village rang with cries of 'Lost! Our village is gone!' People could not stay inside their houses any longer. With baskets and shovels, they ran to the riverbank. Both young and old worked together to stop the flooding waters. The southern part of the river was one unending stretch of water with the floods rising to the top of the embankment. People piled up load after load of earth at the breaches. The base of the embankment had hollowed out. Meanwhile, a few miles down, the floodwater gushed through a breach and began lapping at the foot of the village. Low-lying areas turned into seas of water. It became evident that even if the water did not flow over the bank, its spreading lower down would submerge the village. Each moment the floodwater rose higher. Women began blowing conches while some wept with infants in their arms.

The sun began to set. Water entered the village through the bathing ghat. In minutes, the water stood 7 feet high! It swept through the village. Shouts of 'Help! Save us! We're lost!' echoed everywhere. Loads of earth were piled up to check the flow through the breach, but all was washed away in the savage torrent.

Meanwhile, Ananta had been roaming around the village, gathering the fruit that floated in the floodwater. Hearing shouts coming from the ghat, he ran to see what the fun was about. There, he noticed the fierce stream of water rushing into the village. He overheard that the entire village would soon be swept away. The entrance door of the Binod Behari Temple caught his eye. Wrenching out the huge door, he placed it over his head and ran. He suddenly remembered that a heavy paddy husker was lurking around. He pushed the door upright into the breach and rammed the husker against it. With all his strength, he thrust his shoulder to the door and called out loudly, 'Earth! More earth!' Loads of earth began piling up on either side of the door. His shouts to throw earth went on. The fallen earth came up to his chest. Without a thought for himself, he urged the villagers on. As the earth reached his mouth, he cried out, 'Oh God! Earth! More earth!'

Ananta's cries could be heard no more. The earth went on piling up. The breach began to close. The people stopped to breathe. And then they thought of Ananta. Where was Ananta? But Ananta? 3 feet of earth lay above his head. The village began to resound with shouts of 'Praise to Ananta, the widow's son!' Old men and young women all joined together to sing praises. As fate would have it, the rain ceased. The level of the river came down.

Ananta's mother was sitting on the verandah of her house. Hearing joyous cries, she said to herself, 'Let me see what has happened. That son of mine hasn't come back as yet; let me call him home.' She placed her husband's staff on her shoulder and stepped out. As she passed through the village, she heard each one say, 'Praise to Ananta. Glory to Your son!'

The Singh woman walked straight to the ghat. She did not utter a word. It was already quite dark. She walked over the embankment. She stood and stared at the ghat, her back towards the river. Unaware that 15 feet of water lay below her, she turned around. Suddenly, the sound of a loud splash was heard. Villagers ran with flares to see what had happened. 7 feet from the bank in a dip in the water, a lump of foam was spinning around and 15 feet away, a bamboo staff floated by.

* * *

Nandakishore Bal (1875–1928)

'Lakshmi'

(Translated from the Odia by Bikram K. Das)

She was truly Lakshmi, the Goddess of Wealth—why else would her father have been offered 700 rupees for her on the eve of her marriage? She was already fourteen by then; how long could a girl of her age remain unmarried in a Brahmin family? She was her father's only daughter. Sahu, her father, whom the villagers addressed as 'Sahu-ey' as a token of respect, had brought up his daughter with the utmost care, making sure she had the choicest food and the finest clothes. He had also arranged for her to get her hair tied and decorated in the traditional Odia style by the women of the village, and they followed his instructions meticulously. Other girls were in the habit of making their faces and bodies look grotesque by applying turmeric and lamp-black but following her father's orders, Lakshmi had taken lessons from the mistress who visited the girls' school in the village to instruct them in the arts of dressing. Seeing how graceful she looked, none of the other girls wanted to return to their former untutored state; consequently, the wild malati flower blossoming in the forest was being nurtured by the disciplined hand of nature.

All Brahmins belonging to the Balaram *gotra*[iv] are well-to-do. There were very few unhappy souls in Anantapur village. Among these people, the more mature and pretty a girl was, the higher the price she commanded. That was why Lakshmi's marriage had been delayed longer than usual. Her father had demanded 1400 rupees for her, basing his calculation on her

[iv] Lineage.

age. Many were scared away when they heard his demand. Some raised their bids to 300, others to 400. Sahu-ey attached no importance to beauty, family reputation or feminine accomplishment; Lakshmi would be given away to the highest bidder. Sahu-ey seemed to have moderated his demands since then, seeing that no bidder seemed keen. To himself, he said: 'How long can I go on feeding her? What if she dies while she is in my custody? I shall have lost both principal and interest!'

Narayan was growing older by the day. To date, he had remained as solitary and unattached as a goblin. He wouldn't be able to find a wife like Lakshmi now. That was why he agreed to pay 700 rupees. However, making the actual payment proved to be difficult. Where was he to find so much money? He made arrangements to pay up almost the entire amount and only 30 rupees remained to be paid. A bullock was sold and he was able to arrange the rest of the money by pledging his house to the *mahajan*.[v] Neither the attraction of ancestral property nor the soil which had nurtured him could restrain him—all inducements were sacrificed to the beauty of Lakshmi's face.

Everyone said Lakshmi's bridegroom, Narayan, was highly educated. But he was incurably eccentric. It was said in his village that too much learning had made him mad. On top of that, he was all alone at home, with no one to keep him company. Narayan had lost both parents when he was a child. He had been attached for a time to a babu and served him as his cook. They had travelled abroad together, garnered great wisdom from books, including a knowledge of English and Devanagari, and visited many exotic lands. But suddenly, the idea of starting a business instead of taking up a job occurred to him. He started by setting up a small godown to store jute. It was while he was going from village to village, looking for

[v] Moneylender.

jute, that he saw Lakshmi and decided he wanted to marry her. Lakshmi's father learnt of his interest, checked upon his credentials and decided he would marry off Lakshmi to Narayan for a price of 1400 rupees. Sahu-ey seemed reluctant to hand Lakshmi over to Narayan, but this was only a pretence. He would not have hesitated to give her away to a ghost if he could get a good price. Narayan was a gem of a bridegroom, of whom even Lord Brahma, the god of matrimony, would approve. Lakshmi's father proposed that Narayan should pay him a sum of 1400 rupees over fourteen years, but Narayan agreed to pay only 700. This was all the money that he could muster. If he sacrificed his entire life's savings, the dream of the little godown which he had contemplated would have to be abandoned. He might have to incur a debt, and that was a hazard best avoided. Debts tend to keep mounting and no one knows just where the indebtedness will end. Besides, why should Narayan agree to pay such a high price for Lakshmi? She was getting on in age—yes, she was well-equipped to take over the management of a house, but that wasn't everything. Didn't Narayan have a widowed aunt who could manage a house just as well? The real reason was different. The fact was, Narayan had taken one look at Lakshmi's moon-like face and had been unable to take his eyes off her since then. There was no one else he could think of now. Before the radiance of her face could brighten the courtyard of his house, it had already filled his life with effulgence. What beauty there was in that face! What brightness! 700 rupees seemed a paltry amount to pay. Narayan was prepared to sacrifice everything for her, including life itself. That was not all. He had not only admired her for her beauty; he had seen the nobility of her character reflected in her face as well. He had met her often and spoken to her without restraint while roaming from village to village. Her father had offered no objection. That was because he knew well—each gesture of the demon of poverty would have to be attended to. Poor Lakshmi was a simple girl; she could not have known that hidden inside Narayan was a tiger, a snake—in short, a husband-to-be. Why should she feel shy in his presence? She behaved with the 'jute babu' as she would have behaved with anyone else. Lakshmi's family had grown some *nalita*[vi] in their backyard. Narayan found an excuse to visit their home and went there to collect jute for his godown. He was able to observe how adroitly Lakshmi performed her household chores, how deftly and gracefully she folded the leaves of paan into triangular delicacies redolent with spices that were offered to visitors. One day, while returning from a long and tiring journey, he was offered some refreshments in the house of Lakshmi's next-door neighbour, Anand Mishra. The food was lovingly served by Lakshmi herself: puris, kakra-pitha and chhunchi-patra pitha—delicacies that only nubile Odia girls could produce. He could never forget the affection that had been blended into the sweets. He agreed to pay Sahu-ey the 700 rupees that had been demanded and to accept Lakshmi. In less than no time, the *sweekaar*[vii] was sent and the response was received. Sahu-ey's aunt performed the ritual of stylized wailing that signals that the bride-to-be is ready to depart from her father's house. But Lakshmi did not weep much. As expected, this gave rise to a great deal of gossip among the women of the village.

First woman: What sort of girl is she? Who has seen such a thing before? A girl who has grown as tall as a palm tree, without a tear in her eyes or a word of regret on her lips. We are truly in the 'kali' age!

Second: Well, that's how she has always been! She refuses even to veil her face. The edge of her sari is always a hand's width above her forehead.

[vi] Unprocessed jute fibre.

[vii] The formal acceptance of a ritual marriage proposal.

Third: It's her father that is to blame! Children should be kept restrained but he only pampers her. He wants everyone to admire his daughter's beauty—that's how she has been spoilt. You know what people say: 'A daughter should be a credit to both families: her father's as well her in-laws, or she will only spread bitterness.'

Second: Why should she cry? The 'jute babu' is an old friend of hers. She has been seen serving him food!

First: Tell me, couldn't he have found another girl? Why should he have paid 700 rupees for her hand? What superlative feminine qualities does she possess?

Second: Well, it's Prajapati (Brahma), the god of marriage, who decides these things. Marriages are pre-arranged in heaven! They say drums and trumpets can be heard a mile away but the sound from a garrulous tongue can travel over a thousand miles. Narayan heard all the gossip. He heard of Lakshmi's simplicity, her spontaneity and naturalness, her attachment to him and her keenness to join him in his house, and was overjoyed. There are girls who can fake grief and pretend to shed tears when departing from the parental home; one can only marvel at their cunning. To him, Lakshmi was a goddess from heaven. He recited the following lines to her, which he had composed for the occasion:

Two unknown people meeting, oh heavenly beauty—
I had seen your divine grace and quenched my eyes;
Like a streak of lightning among the dark clouds,
I imagined your radiance;
Like the moon's incandescence spreading through autumnal skies;
We two had been roaming unconcerned through distant horizons;
Before we experienced
The fragrance of the cool south wind;
What happy chance was it that brought

This bird, redolent of spring
To fulfil my dreams?

But today, joy is mixed with sorrow. A Hindu wedding is always a trial—a plunder, not a celebration. As the proverb says, 'A *baha-ghara* [wedding] is really a *buha–ghara* [a burden to be carried on one's back].' A celebration of this kind becomes an occasion for unrestrained gossip by garrulous women. Women are the garbage of the world. A woman participating in a wedding feast will eat until her nose is drowning in food. Commotion and confusion, giving and receiving, feasting until you are overflowing—that's all she understands. This is particularly true of Narayan's home, where there are no women in the family. Everything is left to outsiders to manage. That's why, if one woman does something to help, there is always another waiting to find fault with her. You will often hear such lines:

'Do you suppose that if you pour milk mixed with molasses at the foot of a neem tree, the tree will turn sweet?' The women mean to say to Narayan: 'Poor man! There are so many people here waiting to rob you of your money, and only me to protect your interests!' Naturally, these statements aggravate others, and it takes a great deal of appeasement and reconciliation to restore peace again.

Narayan had assumed that peace would prevail in his house as soon as Lakshmi set foot in it. It would be lit up at once with the effulgence of divine light; the gods would shower them with the fragrance of flower petals. All their labour, sacrifice and pain would be rewarded. The *chakor*[viii] and its beloved, the moon, would be reunited. But alas! When God is not on your side, what happiness can you expect? The women

[viii] The *chakor* is the mythical bird which is so madly in love with the moon that it will die rather than quench its thirst from any source other than the dew from the constellation of the *swati nakshatra* (the fifteenth nakshatra in Hindu astrology, associated with independence, leadership and communication).

who had come to escort the new bride to her husband's home left after giving her a cynical and meaningful smile. While leaving, they exchanged significant glances among themselves, gesturing with their eyes to the bride's unnatural gait and her bulging body. Many meaningful and sarcastic proverbs were exchanged. Unable to understand the implication of what he saw or heard, Narayan summoned a distant female relative to his side and asked her, 'What is going on here?'

'What is going on?' she repeated his words. 'You don't understand anything, do you? My head! You have paid a pile of money and what have you got in return? Nothing but disrepute!' She went home.

The house was empty. Narayan felt as if he had been struck by a thunderbolt. The loneliness was stifling. Lakshmi! How could you do this to me? I had taken you to be a goddess, but you turned out to be a demoness! Who could have guessed it by looking at your face?

'Which evil spirit could have done me this harm? How could the Earth have allowed this crime?'

Meanwhile, Lakshmi had grown restless inside the house. She felt it would be a mistake on her part to behave in a manner that might raise doubts in her husband's mind. But what was she to do? Nothing could be done before the house was free of the wedding guests. When everyone left, Lakshmi shook the ornaments on her body, causing them to rattle, signalling to her husband that she wanted to speak to him alone inside the house. Narayan was in a bitter and cynical frame of mind, feeling inclined to renounce the world and become an ascetic. Then he had another thought. Whoever it was that had turned Lakshmi into a demoness and a sinner deserved to be punished, even killed. He would commit the deed himself, even if he had to hang for this crime. But why should he take the blame for a sin that he had not committed? He wanted to sacrifice his own life so that the blot which had tarnished his life could be removed. But what about Lakshmi?

At this moment, she had been abandoned by society and left unprotected. She needed his protection.

Hardening his heart and giving up all hope of happiness in his marital life, he went to Lakshmi. He had gone only a little way when he felt mentally agitated. Unable to walk further, he threw himself on the ground. Lakshmi was trying to draw his attention with a gesture of her hand. Seeing that gesture, he almost gave up his noble intention to come to her rescue. Feelings of hatred, anger and shame pierced him. He told himself: 'Be patient, oh heart!' Lakshmi was shaken when she saw the determined look on his face. But in a situation such as this, the patience and forbearance of a woman outstrips that of any man, or else, no woman could have transformed herself into a Durga or a Kali.[ix] Men like to indulge themselves with false self-praise, but it is really the woman's flag of victory that flies high.

Lakshmi reminded herself of all the brave and spirited women of lore whose names are mentioned before those of their consorts: Sita-Ram; Lakshmi-Narayan; Savitri-Satyavan. The victorious women. Lakshmi looked at her husband once again with appealing eyes and gestured to him with her hand. When Narayan came closer to her, Lakshmi loosened the waistband of her sari and took out a brass thali that had been concealed inside the folds of the sari. It contained 700 rupees, tied into a bundle. It was the money that Narayan had paid her father for the privilege of marrying her. She bent down, bowed low and placed the thali at his feet, saying 'This money belongs to you. Please accept it.' Having said these words, she relapsed into the usual Lakshmi that she had been—humble, bowed with sorrow and obeisance.

All doubts vanished from Narayan's mind. The next day, Lakshmi's father, unable to find the thali full of money, asked everyone if they had seen it. Champa, Lakshmi's friend, said,

[ix] Names of female goddesses.

'Yes, Lakshmi has taken it. She asked me to tell everyone that she had taken the money, in case anyone inquired.' Immediately, Lakshmi's father rushed to Lakshmi and asked her if she had taken the money. 'Yes,' she said. 'The money has been returned to its rightful owner. Shame on you, Father! If you had sold me for 700 rupees and taken the money, what a sin that would have been! You have no son—I am both son and daughter to you. I shall take care of you for all the time to come. When you go on a fast, I shall feed you. You have enough money, Father; please give up your greed and do not thirst for more.'

She fell at his feet, draped them with the edge of her sari and bathed them with her tears. Her father, realizing his own error, returned to the house.

Lakshmi knew that her father was hurt. But in time, she said to herself, he would forget his pain.

* * *

Narayan's home had been brightened once again by Lakshmi's presence. All their troubles had ended. There was no trace of pain or suffering and Narayan's heart was overflowing with joy.

Narayan asked Lakshmi: Do you love me, Lakshmi?

Lakshmi: What do you think?

Narayan: I don't know for sure but I feel you do.

Lakshmi: Why is there doubt in your mind then?

Narayan: Your love is perhaps so precious that I cannot be sure I still have it.

Lakshmi: Perhaps?

Narayan: The look in your eyes, your gesture, your walk—everything makes me feel that the love is real.

Lakshmi: Haven't you heard of beautiful ogresses?[x]

---

[x] She-demons.

Narayan: I have, but I do not believe that you could be one of them. If it proved to be true, my life would not be worth living.

Lakshmi: In that case, why don't you believe that which makes you feel happy? Why the questions in your mind?

Narayan: I want to hear the words from your lips.

Lakshmi: And you will believe me if I say the words?

Narayan: Yes. But I want to hear the words again and again.

Lakshmi: Should I say 'no' then?

Narayan: If you do, I shall take it as a joke. The romantics have said that many a time, a woman's 'no' means 'yes'. If you do say 'no', I shall be pained, but I shall not lose hope—for you might have said 'no' without thinking whether that is the answer your mind really wants to give. Besides, do I really deserve to receive your entire love? A drop from the ocean should be enough. You are pure like a 'sati', like Lakshmi. A grain of pity from you will sweeten my life. In time, my dedication and devotion will win your love completely.

Lakshmi: Do you think our love will become stronger with the passage of time instead of weaker?

Narayan: Lakshmi, no one can read a woman's mind. But you are a Hindu wife, to whom her husband is her god. I can give up my life for you. My eyes are fixed steadily on you, like those of a *chatak*[xi] on the moon. You are my whole world. Have pity on me and give me your love. I know that there can be no love where there is pity. But tell me, would it be fair to deprive me of your love after you have married me?

Lakshmi: Pardon me, but what if I said to you—for the sake of argument—that since you have bought me with your money, you are entitled to ownership of my body? But when did you give me your love? You and I have hardly even spoken to each other.

[xi] Jacobi cuckoo.

Narayan: I am unable to think further. Your lack of love is agonizing to me. I would like to conquer your heart and mind together with your body. My heart tells me that you love me. You could not have turned against your father if you did not love me.

Lakshmi: Do you have reason to think that I am really so noble? On the contrary, I have been guilty of ingratitude. It was only the sense of justice that made me return your money to you—nothing else.

Narayan: It was not *my* money. I was bound by my promise.

Lakshmi: A marriage is based on mutual sacrifice—on giving and receiving. I have read somewhere that it is wrong for a bride to allow herself to be sold for money. It was also what my teacher taught me in school.

Narayan: But that is only a stray, superficial thought. If you think deeply into the matter, you will realize that unless love is freely given, the feeling of loyalty is only a convention that one must bow to.

Lakshmi: But if you had bought me for money, you would have hated me.

Narayan: What harm is there in hatred if there is no love?

Lakshmi: What would the people in our village have said? People's opinions matter, don't they?

Narayan: You are contradicting yourself now. You never showed the money to anyone. Rather, you risked criticism by giving me the money secretly.

Lakshmi: That may have been done only to mislead you. You had said all women are cunning and treacherous, helping others only out of pity. My father has no heirs. Who will inherit his wealth? Someone wicked and undeserving. Meanwhile, you would be in agony. So I must have taken pity on you, which is the enemy of love, in your opinion.

Narayan: Your keen intellect has surprised and defeated me. But of what use is one's intellect? What matters is a loving heart. Is this hope to remain unfulfilled? Am I to die of thirst though sitting so close to the river's bank?

The sight of her husband's mournful face was too much for Lakshmi. Her mind and body were anxious to be united with those of her beloved. Like a river rushing to merge into the ocean, Lakshmi buried her face in her husband's bosom and bathed him with her tears. All of Narayan's doubts were removed. The sight of her beautiful face filled him with joy. Thus were two bodies and souls reunited.

* * *

Reba Ray (1876–1957)

'The Monk'

(Translated 'Sanyasi' from the Odia by Manu Dash)

1

A poor woman and her six-year-old daughter had been residing in the house of Nityananda Patnaik (of Jajpur) for a few days. She was the wife of his friend, who had been a zamindar of the same caste. The girl, Parasmani, was her daughter.

Three years ago, reduced to a pauper in a legal battle, her husband had passed away, leaving her in a dire situation. The years following the death of her husband were difficult. Taking pity on her plight, Nityananda babu had given her shelter in his home.

Nityananda babu had retired to the life of a pensioner after serving many years at the treasury office in Cuttack. He had separately inherited a small bit of land and zamindari, which amply provided for his family of three—himself, his son Shibaprasad and his wife Ushabati. When Shibaprasad turned thirteen, he was sent to Cuttack to stay with a friend to receive a suitable education.

Unlike his wife, Ushabati, who was arrogant, impolite and rude, Nityananda babu was simple and easygoing.

From the day Parasmani's mother had arrived at their house, she had taken up all the household chores. Since she could not satisfy Ushabati, she often faced her wrath. Parasmani was not spared either and had to tolerate thrashings.

Praise the lord for bestowing them the patience to put up with such behaviour. Or else, who knew what the consequences would have been?

Parasmani's mother had to bear the brunt of all these humiliations. However, Nityananda babu was unaware of the situation. Moreover, it is doubtful if he could have averted the situation even if he were aware.

Shibaprasad was happy to have Parasmani around during the Dussehra[xii] vacation. It broke the loneliness he used to feel otherwise, and they became instant friends.

One day, Parasmani was seated by Shibaparasad while he was reading a book.

On an impulse, she blurted out, 'I also have an urge to learn how to read.'

Shibaprasad brought out his textbook *Barna Bodhak* and began teaching her.

From that day till he left for Cuttack, Shibaprasad sat down with the *Barna Bodhak* each afternoon with her. He even gave her a chalk so she could trace her alphabet.

In merely twenty days, the intelligent Parasmani had learnt the first half of *Barna Bodhak* by heart. But her learning ceased soon after Shibaprasad left for Cuttack.

Six or seven months passed by. When Shibaprasad returned home for the summer vacation, Parasmani resumed her studies. After *Barna Bodhak*, she began reading the *Bodhadayak*. But when Shibaprasad's mother caught him teaching her, she chided them severely so that Parasmani would not go to Shibaprasad any more and choose to study alone.

Calm and well-mannered, Parasmani was as pretty as a picture. Although Nityananda babu always cared for her and loved her, she had never succeeded in capturing Ushabati's heart.

[xii] Holiday marking the triumph of Rama, an avatar of Vishnu, over the ten-headed demon king Ravana, who abducted Rama's wife, Sita.

2

Five years of joy and sorrow went by.

These five years dragged so many human souls from the pit of sorrow towards blinding light, hauled numerous people from the nectar of happiness towards a bottomless ocean of sorrow, whisked away so many people towards the citadel of eternal peace, and brought out countless babies, as fresh as marigold flowers, from the land of the god, and showered the nectar of blessings on the dark heart of this mundane world.

Be it fortune or misfortune, nothing much changed in Nityananda babu's family except the good news that Shibaprasad had cleared his intermediate examinations and returned home.

Ushabati wanted to get her son married soon. Every now and then, she nagged her husband about this.

One day, Nityananda babu called his wife and said, 'Place your palm on my head and make a pledge that you will keep my request.'

Ushabati did not agree with her husband in the first instance but consented after his persistence.

Nityananda said, 'When Parasmani was two years old, I had been to meet with her father. When I saw the child, I swore that I would get her married to Shibaprasad. The wish was so strong that I confessed to her father and we pledged to make this happen irrespective of death or misfortune.'

Ushabati was furious.

'You made me swear to this? What will people say if we choose Parasmani as our daughter-in-law? Can't you find any good-looking girl? How could I bring this penniless girl into my home as a daughter-in-law? How could I get my son married to a girl whose mother works as a maid in my house?'

She went on protesting with a litany of complaints.

Giving her a patient listen, Nityananda babu said, 'I can't take back my words. If you don't agree with my proposal, you may marry your son off to anyone you like.'

The husband and wife didn't talk to each other for several days after this. Ushabati let off steam by yelling at Parasmani and her mother, but finding no alternative, she finally consented to the proposal offered by Nityananda babu.

On the auspicious day, the marriage ceremony was held with pomp and ceremony.

Nityananda babu was happy to be able to keep his promise and Parasmani's mother felt lucky that her daughter found a good life partner.

The only disappointed person was Ushabati.

3

After the marriage ceremony, Nityananda babu did not agree to Shibaprasad going back to Cuttack for his studies, though this was what he craved to do.

He attempted twice or thrice to pursue his studies further but gave up as his father was not in favour. Only Nityananda babu knew why he wanted his son to stay at home.

By nature, Ushabati was short-tempered, and to add insult to injury, Parasmani had become her daughter-in-law against her wishes. This intensified her anger and she picked on the girl for trivial matters. She also continued to beat the girl.

Parasmani's mother witnessed the plight of her daughter but kept mum.

With her mother's affection and husband's love, Parasmani was inclined to forget her mother-in-law's unkindness.

When the fourteen-year-old Parasmani came to sleep at night after doing the daily chores, she felt blessed when she heard her husband's soft, caring words.

Shibaprasad recognized his mother's ill behaviour and said, 'I am aware how hurt you are with the behaviour of my mother, but I earnestly beseech you not to take it to heart.'

Hearing these words, Parasmani replied, 'Why would I be in anguish if I have a loving husband like you? She reprimands me because I make mistakes.'

One day, Parasmani fell ill. When the fever did not break for five or six days, Nityananda babu called in a *baidya*, a country physician, who gave her a *panchana*, an herbal prescription.

Ushabati did not even care to ask once about her daughter-in-law's health.

Parasmani's mother visited her intermittently during the day and gave her fried flat rice, ginger, salt and puffed rice.

Without his mother's knowledge, Shibaprasad also went to see Parasmani on three or four occasions.

After Parasmani's recovery from fever, one day Ushabati casually confided in her son that she had observed something when she went to the ailing Parasmani, which Shibaprasad was utterly surprised to hear.

After five or six days, Shibaprasad requested his father to permit him to visit Cuttack since he had not been there for quite a long time.

Nityananda babu agreed at last, and his visit was scheduled for the auspicious hours between the ensuing Tuesday night and dawn on Wednesday.

On Tuesday night, Shibaprasad counselled Parasmani to take care of her health as she was expecting a child. That night, husband and wife shed tears silently.

After the day dawned, Shibaprasad said goodbye to his parents and headed for Cuttack.

Shibaprasad stayed at a friend's house in Cuttack and wrote a letter with good news.

After fifteen days in Cuttack, Shibaprasad got an offer letter with a salary of Rs 50 per month—his job gave him the opportunity to avoid going home.

Four months after he left, Parasmani gave birth to a baby boy. A delighted Nityananda babu sent a message to his son, but this joyous moment did not last long.

While in *entudisala*, the labour room, the child passed away, leaving Nityananda babu's family devastated. Besides this, Parasmani came down with a fever for fifteen long days without any reprieve.

Shibaprasad was unable to come home because his leave was not sanctioned. Nityananda babu called in a string of doctors and baidyas for treatment, but to no avail.

In the meantime, Parasmani secretly wrote a letter to Shibaprasad.

My love,

Your beloved craves to see you at her last moment. Could you fulfil the last wish of this servant by taking the dust from your feet on her head?

Yours forever,
Parasmani

After writing this letter and putting it in an envelope with a postage stamp on it, she asked her mother to post it through a reliable woman.

Receiving Parasmani's letter, Shibaprasad was deeply worried and hastened home.

On his arrival, Shibaprasad met his wife first. Witnessing Shibaprasad's arrival, Parasmani's ill-fated mother burst into tears.

Once Shibaprasad sat down, Parasmani drew his right hand onto her chest and said, 'How I had longed to put your child on your lap when you come home but my desire will never be fulfilled. This is my last meeting with you in this life. I invoke God to grant you as my husband in the next life.'

Parasmani uttered these few words with immense difficulty. Silent tears rolled down from Shibaprasad's eyes and drenched Parasmani's hands.

Her mother moaned inconsolably.

Hearing their cries, Nityananda babu and Ushabati came running.

Parasmani begged them to bless her with the dust of their feet.

She then looked wistfully at her husband and breathed her last.

Two months passed, during which the family saw more bereavement.

After the death of her only child, Parasmani's heartbroken mother also departed for her heavenly abode.

Were these preordained by the Almighty? Does anyone have the strength to alter their destiny?

Shibaprasad did not go back to Cuttack. He withdrew to himself and spent all his time alone.

Nityananda and Ushabati couldn't bear to see their son so lonely and made arrangements for him to get married a second time. This time, Ushabati got her wish; Shibaprasad was marrying the daughter of a rich man. The wedding was a month away, but it disturbed Shibaprasad greatly. He felt he could never be the husband of another woman.

He missed Parasmani, her smile, her love, and her presence. Knowing about his parents' plans, Shibaprasad went to his mother and said to her, without hesitation, 'I won't marry again. Don't get a bee on your bonnet about my wedding.'

His mother was stunned. 'My boy, older men are marrying twice or more and you are so young, yet you don't want to marry?'

Shibaprasad refused. The matter was placed before Nityananda babu. He presumed that the refusal was what was being said on the surface but his son's heart wanted something else. Also, that Shibaprasad would accept the marriage once the wedding was over.

Eventually, the marriage day arrived. It was eight in the morning, but Shibaprasad had not yet gotten out of bed. A servant entered his room to call him but could not find him there.

He searched for him in every nook and cranny but in vain. Nityananda babu got the information and worried, he sent people outside to search for him. Tears of angst rolled down from the eyes of Ushabati. However, her son was nowhere to be found.

The celebratory mood was absolutely ruined.

Nityananda babu and Ushabati cried and berated themselves, and fell silent. Their house had been plunged into abysmal darkness.

Since Shibaprasad had been sure his parents would ignore his choice and marry him off, he ran away from his home with a few clothes and a little money after his parents retired to bed, the night before his wedding.

He left for Cuttack and then further still to Kolkata. But he remained worried about getting caught.

A month passed by. He had exhausted the money he had.

He had not yet made any friends in Kolkata either, who would lend him Rs 5 or Rs 10.

Deeply worried and resting his neck in the cup of his palm, Shibaprasad was brooding in his room. Suddenly, he overheard someone singing a folksong from the adjacent room.

He went next door and sat beside the singer, requesting him to continue. The song, one of deep thought and detachment, left him spellbound. It moved him so deeply that it changed his perspective on life.

The next day, Shibaprasad dressed up like a monk, took on a new name, and set out on a new journey to preach across the country and beyond.

It is not essential to make the readers realize what happiness and peace Shibaprasad attained by preaching and clutching the Almighty's name in his heart, under whose feet he found shelter. Before this, the immeasurable wealth of the world seemed like a grain of sand.

Postscript

Finally, I don't have any desire to hurt the reader by describing the miserable state of Nityananda babu and Ushabati.

If any reader is desperate to know, I can tell you this. A few days after the disappearance of Shibaprasad, Ushabati passed away.

Nityananda babu kept some of his land and donated a major portion of it to the Lord Jagannath endowment service and took shelter in Puri.

However, this was not for long and he left for his heavenly abode soon after.

* * *

Laxmikanta Mohapatra (1888–1953)

'The Old Maker of Bangles'

(Translated 'Budha Sankhari' from the Odia by Bikram K. Das)

The month of Phagun (March–April) was about to end. A sixty-year-old man who had lost all his teeth was walking through the village in the blazing hot sun. The thinning hair on his head and chest had turned white as snow. He carried a large basket on his head and his knees were heavily covered with dust. The sweat from his entire body was pouring down his legs in streams.

There was only one house at the end of the village. The front verandah had been neatly plastered with cement; the straw-thatched roof rose in tiers and the front door had heavy double panels. The old man put down his basket and slumped on the verandah. After some time, a maid who knew the old man walked out of the house.

She asked him, '*Sankhari*,[xiii] have you brought some *sankhas*[xiv] today?' 'Yes,' the old man replied, adding 'Daughter, could you bring me a drop of water to drink? My throat is parched.' The maid went inside to get some water for the old man and returned with a brass lota full of water, which she placed in front of him. The old man raised the lota high above his head, opened his mouth wide and poured out a thin stream of water, which he drank in thirsty gulps—about half a lota full. His lips never came in contact with the lota. Having drunk the water, he drew in a deep breath and

---

[xiii] Maker of bangles.

[xiv] Bangles made of shellac.

said to the maid, 'Daughter, you have earned a lot of dharma today.' She replied, 'Well, all right—if you say so!' Then she said, 'Come with me now; the *santaani*[xv] is waiting to see what kind of sankhas you have brought today.' The old man picked up his basket and rose slowly to his feet. Once past the heavy main door, he came to the cemented courtyard; in front of him was the raised platform, the *chowpadhi,* where members of the family rested in the evenings. There was another door inside, to the left of the main door, leading to the inner room. A young lady stood near the door, with the end of her sari drawn across her face, forming an *odhana*.[xvi] She appeared to be the mistress of the house, although she had made her entry into the family not long ago as a *bohu*.[xvii] The old man put his basket down and stood next to it.

The bohu said in a soft voice to the maid, 'Ask the old man what kind of sankhas he has brought.' The maid, who seemed to be an old retainer in the family, was inclined to be blunt and outspoken in her speech. 'For shame!' she said. 'Do you have to be so shy and guarded when you are speaking to this old man? Why don't you come and pick what you like from his basket?' The bohu seemed to like the suggestion. She pushed the odhana away from her face and came out onto the verandah smiling faintly. Her round face was visible now and her skin glowed like a champaka flower. She wore a hand-woven *mayur-kanthi*[xviii] sari, shimmering with the dancing rainbow colours of the peacock's tail in bright sunlight, stretched right down to her heels. Through the delicate translucent fabric, one could catch a glimpse of the glowing body, like freshly beaten gold, perfectly shaped, as

---

[xv] Mistress.

[xvi] Veil.

[xvii] Daughter-in-law.

[xviii] The colour of a peacock's throat; dark green.

though carved out of a single grain of rice. The old man's eyes felt fulfilled. He had never seen such beauty in a human being anywhere. He could not turn his eyes away and kept looking fixedly at the bohu. He wanted to say something but no words came. After a while, he said, 'Ma, choose the sankha you want!' The moment he uttered the word 'ma', his chest puffed with affectionate pride. The bohu said, discarding her shyness, 'Do you have the kind of sankha called *aasmaan-tara*[xix]?' Oh, what sweetness in a human voice! Who speaks so sweetly nowadays? The tone reverberated in his ears repeatedly. The old man said, 'No, ma. I have many other designs and colours—*raha-jhili*, *baula-phulia*, *bichcha-malia*, *chuna-tipi*—take what you like from those. I shall bring you some aasmaan-tara sankhas as soon as they are ready.'

The bohu went through the collection of sankhas and picked out the ones she liked. But would they fit her wrists? The old man said, 'Ma, give me your hand, I shall select the ones that fit.' How could the bohu extend her hand to him suddenly? She hesitated. The old man then said, 'Ma, why do you feel so shy in giving me your hand? I am your son! Does any mother feel shy with her own son?'

The maid, who had been watching the scene, roared with laughter. 'Bohu Santaani, what a son you have found! Just your luck!'

'Go away!' the bohu said to her, laughing.

She extended her hand to the sankhari. What dainty hands! How beautifully shaped! The fingers were like champaka buds. Soft, velvety palms. How beautiful the sankhas would look on her hand! Can this be a human hand? Or is it the image of a goddess carved by a master craftsman? The old sankhari dared not touch her hands with his dirty, rough hands. He put out his left hand gingerly and touched

---

[xix] Star of the night sky.

her lightly to slide the sankha across her wrist. What if he scratched her or cut her wrist? What if he drew blood? He paused, slowly brought out another sankha from his basket and carefully slid it across her wrist. What happiness he experienced as his fingers moved gently across her hand! It felt as though this was the supreme moment in his life, the fulfilment of all his joys, all his hopes. But then he had to let go of the hand. *If only I could put a sankha around her wrist every day*, he thought!

Just then, the supreme mistress of the house—the *bada*[xx] santaani—arrived. When the bohu saw her mother-in-law, she hurriedly pulled her odhana back across her face, covering it up completely. The bada santaani asked the maid, 'Have you been buying *sankhas*?'

'Yes,' the maid replied. 'The bohu santaani has selected this lot to buy.'

'How much do they cost?' the bada santaani asked.

To this, the old sankhari said, 'Just a handful of sankhas, Ma—what price could they have?'

'But how much should I pay you?' the bada santaani asked.

'What price can I ask my Ma to pay?' he said.

A little mystified, the bada santaani turned to the maid and asked, 'What's this that he is saying about his Ma?'

Laughing, the maid said, 'He has adopted her as his ma!'

The bada santaani laughed and said, 'You can accept payment this time and give us the sankhas for free next time. You are a poor man.'

'No, no santaani,' the old man said. 'What I have given to my mother has no price. I can't sink back into poverty just for the sake of a few sankhas.'

He put the handful of sankhas on the floor, picked up his basket, turned around and walked away. They called him but he did not listen. The maid ran after him but he did not return.

[xx] Elder.

From that day, the sankhari seemed to have made a habit of returning to the villages in the neighbourhood regularly after an interval of three or four days. But nothing came out of these visits. A sankha is not something that one needs to buy regularly; it's only on festive occasions such as a *punei*[xxi] that one is reminded of the need for them. The old man would go round every village from door to door carrying his basket and return empty-handed. But selling sankhas was not the objective; he came only to catch a glimpse of his Ma. Whenever he came to this house, he would walk up to the front door without saying a word to anyone. He made no attempt to put his basket down and instead would shout: 'Do you want new sankhas, Ma?' Sometimes, but not always, the bohu would hear his shout, and come and stand awhile behind the door. The old man would look at her and his heart would fill with happiness. The old sankhari always hoped that she would want to buy something; then he would get a chance to put a sankha round her wrists, which were like champaka buds. But she always shook her head no. The old man would then go back.

On some days, there was a slight delay in her coming to the door and then the old maid would remind her, 'Bohu santaani, your son is here!' If the old man called out three or four times, the bohu would come and stand behind the door. 'Ma, some new sankhas for you?' he would ask. This drama was repeated each time he came. As he went back he would tell himself: 'My Ma's mind is fixed on aasmaan-tara sankhas; I must get her some. Finally, he decided, 'Next Raja Sankranti,[xxii] I must get a pack of aasmaan-tara sankhas for my Ma somehow. She will hold out her wrists and I shall put the sankhas around them. How happy she will be!'

[xxi] A full moon night.

[xxii] A local festival in coastal Odisha that falls invariably on 14 June.

The month of Baisakh arrived. The old man, trudging from door to door in the heat, drinking water from different wells in the village to cool his body, couldn't take the abuse any more. He came down with a great fever, his body burning for several days, hands and feet swollen. But he was unconcerned about his own health; he was only unhappy at missing his opportunity to visit his Ma.

Raja Sankranti arrived without anyone noticing. The old man had not been to see his Ma for two months. If he had been able to walk, you couldn't have stopped him. He would *have* to get a fistful of the aasmaan-tara shankhas for his Ma. With a great deal of difficulty, he got up and started making a sankha with his own hands. They would *have* to be made by him, or she wouldn't approve of them. Into that sankha, he put in all the skill and expertise that he had gathered over sixty years. It didn't matter if one day's work took him four days now, the sankha had to be perfect. Two days before Raja, he was able to finish the work. It was the state of his mind that decided the results. Had he ever made such a flawless set of sankha with his own hands before? He couldn't remember. The longer he looked at the sankha, the happier he felt. How beautiful these sankhas would look on his Ma's wrists!

The day before the Rajaa Sankranti was *pahili raja.*[xxiii] This was the day when young daughters and bohus in each family would put on their new saris. The old man got up early in the morning and thought to himself, *I can't even walk; what will I be able to do today? No one else can deliver these sankhas for me. I must do this myself. How long it has been since I saw my Ma! Will I be able to recover from this illness? This may be the last time! Let me go and have a look at her. I'll put the sankhas on her wrist with my own hands.* Just thinking about her made him feel stronger. He swallowed a

[xxiii] The opening day of the festival.

couple of handfuls of rice, tied up some of the new sankhas he had made in a *gamuchcha*[xxiv] and set out. Each step was an effort. He had 5 *kosas* (10 miles) to walk. It was almost evening when he arrived.

He went and stood in the usual place on the verandah where he always stood and called out, 'Do you want any sankhas Ma?' What joy, what excitement he felt! He called out again, 'Any sankhas for you today, Ma?' No one seemed to have heard him. Again, he called, 'Don't you need some sankhas?' Still no response—no one came out to meet him. He called out once again and started growing impatient. Usually, his Ma appeared at the door as soon as she heard his first call. Once again he called out, 'Ma, I've brought the sankhas for you. This time the bada santaani came out; behind her was the old maid. Seeing the bada santaani, he said, 'Where is my Ma? I've brought some aasmaan-taara sankhas for her to wear on Raja.'

On any other day, the old maid would have raised a storm by this time, but today she was silent. It was the santaani who told him quietly, 'No, we don't require any sankhas today.'

'I made these sankhas specially for her,' he said. 'With great affection.'

'No,' the santaani told him again. 'No one wants any sankhas today. Go.'

'Very well, santaani,' he said. 'It's all right if you won't buy any sankhas today. But could you please let my Ma know I am here? I would like to see her once. I haven't seen her for a long time.'

The santaani said, 'You can't see her.'

It felt like a lightning strike. 'I can't see her?' he repeated. 'I can't see my Ma even once?' His eyes brimmed with tears.

[xxiv] A towel made of coarse cotton.

'I want to see her just once. I am not going to live very long,' he said.

The bada santaani told the maid, 'Go and call the bohu.' The maid went. After a few minutes, the bohu came and stood behind the door. That was where she always stood. She would stand there and look at the old man for a few minutes. The old man's mind would surge with happiness when he saw her smile. Today, she came and stood there in silence. The red sari with the four-fingers wide border wasn't there, nor was the South Indian *pata*[xxv] silk sari with the *kumbha*[xxvi] border. Her feet were bare. On her body was a white *thana* sari.[xxvii] The old man's body quivered, his head reeled, and he couldn't keep his eyes open. When he opened his eyes again, they fell on her wrists. The old man said, 'My Ma—why did I come here to see you? I should have died instead!' He was unable to speak further. Inside his gamuchcha, knotted with great care, was the pack of sankhas. He picked them up and dashed them to the ground, shattering them into bits.

He turned around and walked away.

* * *

[xxv] Costly sari with quality yarn.

[xxvi] Temple.

[xxvii] A piece of white cloth fresh off the loom with no border or ornamentation.

Godabarish Mohapatra (1898–1965)

'Nila, the School Teacher'

(Translated 'Nila Mastrani' from the Odia by Sudeshna Mohanty)

It may be a tale of three villages, but it was a familiar story in the neighbouring ten, or even twenty-five villages. The crow of this village flew across the skies as soon as day broke, scouring for food, and settled in the rafters of the other villages with scant regard for right and wrong—the notes that it cawed here were the same as the ones it cawed in the next village. The herd of cattle uninhibitedly went looking for fresh pastures in the other village. Stray dogs went foraging for food in the neighbouring villages. But no one mentioned the tale to the crows, the dogs or the cattle; it was only when people from this village walked across to the next to reach the village common in the third village, or when people from the other village came to this one or when people from the three villages met, that they gossiped. One said what happened was the fault of education, another said it was the fault of society, and a third person said that neither education nor society was to blame, it was the fault of Nila mastrani.

In the three villages around Nimapada, such gossip is commonplace.

Who is Nila mastrani? Who is Nila, the school teacher?

It is a hot summer night. The sky is smouldering. The ineffective moonlight only casts dark shadows all around and doesn't mitigate the heat. It is long past midnight. In a small hut in one of the three villages, a twenty-two-year-old girl is lost in thought as she lies with her head buried in the bundles of dirty clothes that surround her. It seems as if the young girl is resting on the clothes after a hard day's work. As she restlessly tosses and turns, it appears as if physical labour has drained her of all her strength. But no, her fatigue is more mental than physical. In the past three years, she has been sapped of all mental strength.

She lies with her eyes closed among the dirty bundles, but sleep eludes her. Her life story unfolds before her closed eyes. She sees a fragmented, shattered world. There are no pathways in this world, no banks or islands, no place to shelter oneself. Her mind goes back ten to twelve years in time. Beautiful images appear in her mind's eye.

She sees a solitary cottage in which lives a Brahmin family. A father with his two young children. It's been two years since the mother died. The father misses his wife more than the children miss their mother. He gets up before daybreak every morning, collects a handful of flowers from the premises of the temple at the edge of the pond and sets out. The children sit on the front verandah waiting for his return and greet him with much joy when he comes back. As the father gathers them close to his chest, he stealthily wipes away his tears. Then he sweeps the house, lights the fire, cooks a meal and settles down at the altar at home to pray to the gods. He has so much to say to the gods; the children do not understand a word!

The young woman turns on her side. She opens her eyes and finds herself staring at nothingness. The house is empty—there is no one at home. She closes them again and the images from the past continue to haunt her.

The youngest of the motherless children is a boy while the older one is an eight–ten-year-old girl. The siblings study at the *chatasali*, the thatched primary school, in the village. They return tired and weary, with their books and slates, to their motherless home where the father's love envelopes them. But they are happy.

The girl turns over again as the images flit in her mind.

The little girl grows older and the father finds her a suitable groom. She sits on the wedding platform in new clothes, and as the *purohit*[xxviii] chants mantras, she is given away in marriage to become someone's wife. The half-supine girl trembles as the image of the *panigrahana,* the wedding, flashes in her mind's eye. Her skin prickles with goosebumps. She tries to sit up but crumples and falls on the bundles of dirty clothes.

And then disaster strikes. Barely six months after the wedding, the elegant arms of this motherless girl are shorn of ornaments, like the night jasmine flowers that fall from the tree at night and lie scattered around it in the morning. Who would pick up these wilted flowers and weave a crown for the gods with them? Society would baulk at it. That was not the way of the world.

Drops of tears trickle from the girl's eyes and are lost among the dirty bundles. A pitiful cry escapes her lips—*Bou lo*! Oh, my mother!

Her mother is nowhere around. She has been gone long since; so too has her father.

The unadorned girl had been taken back home by her father. The father began educating his daughter. She learned needlework, how to read books, how to write and how to keep accounts. Her father helped her ride the crest of the wave of the women's empowerment movement that was sweeping the village at that time. He enrolled her as a teacher in the village primary school and she was known as Nila mastrani—Nila, the school teacher.

The young woman lifts her head from the clothes and sees that the image of Nila mastrani too has faded. Her father has

---

[xxviii] A holy man who conducts the wedding in Hinduism.

gone away to the land from where no one returns; her brother doesn't live with her any more.

But where is Nila mastrani? In the village that was in the middle of the three villages, Nila mastrani was a teacher. Old men censured her, the young applauded her and the students revered her. Nila mastrani taught in one village and went back to her orphaned hut in the other village where she devoted herself to bringing up her young brother.

As the young woman tosses and turns restlessly, images of many hues play out before her.

A *jatra*[xxix] troupe comprising of young men emerged in the village where Nila mastrani taught. They taught themselves stories from the epics and enacted the *Ramaleela, Krishnaleela and Bharataleela*[xxx]. And with these stories, a new chapter in the life of Nila mastrani played itself out. Sebayat Madana Sethi, who played the role of Arjuna in Bharataleela, lived in the third village. The arrow that Madana aimed to hit the eye of the fish in Draupadi's *swayambara*[xxxi], furtively pierced the heart of Nila mastrani and blinded her.

This image tortures the young woman and she buries her head deeper in the dirty clothes.

Nila mastrani stepped into Draupadi's mantle and followed Madana with tightly shut eyes, blind to the consequences of her actions. And with that one step, she turned her back on her education, her sibling and the ties that bound her to society. She didn't care about social censure and paid little heed to what the people of the village would say. She walked out of the hut, renouncing all that was dear to her as she followed Madana wherever he led.

[xxix] Folk theatre.

[xxx] Indian epics.

[xxxi] The practice of a woman choosing a husband from a group of suitors.

Nila mastrani lived happily as Madan's bride for only two months.

Ah! What a pitiful sight! Nila mastrani in dire straits. The troupe fell apart. Arjun did not rain arrows and Madana hit the bottle. She tried to stop him. Then came quarrels and poverty. Finally, shouldering the bundle of dirty clothes, Nila mastrani made her way to the washing ghat. Shame and disgrace so weighed her down that she stooped and walked with a drooping head and sagging shoulders even when she was not carrying her load of dirty clothes.

At this point, the young woman raises her head from the bundle of clothes and looks around her for comfort. *She* was the Nila mastrani of yesteryear. *She* was the motherless child of the other village who has walked so far away from her childhood.

The night progresses as Nila, the school teacher, also Nila the washerwoman, reminiscences about the past.

As the night advances, she hears raised voices from the hut next door. Like a woman possessed, Nila the washerwoman barges into the neighbour's house and says, 'Come, share with me what you have brought back from the Brahmin boy's wedding feast! It's my brother's wedding feast, don't you know? Had I been there, wouldn't I be doling out the food? Won't you share something with me?'

And the women thought, *Hasn't Nila, the school teacher morphed completely into Nila, the washerwoman yet?*

The next day, Nila the school teacher is so absorbed in thoughts of her brother's wedding and the wedding feast that she doesn't go to the washing ghat. The daughter-in-law of the hut next door had brought back with her Nila's brother's wife's, her *bhauja's baulapata,* her bridal sari, to wash. A distraught Nila mastrani implored, 'Give that to me, *lo*! Let me wash it! That's my bhauja's baulapata, shouldn't I be washing it?'

They gave it to her. Nila mastrani washed the baulapata, but did not take it back to the neighbour. Summons came from the next village demanding the baulapata. The baulapata was auspicious; it would enhance the good fortune of the household. But who would return it? It was with Nila mastrani! And she claimed that she would return it only if her brother came to ask for it!

Would the brother come? Would the Brahmin boy come to the washerwoman's door and address his sister as *nani*? It created a sensation in three villages—the village in which she had been born, the village in which she had been a teacher and the village in which she washed dirty clothes as a washerwoman. And the brother, closeted in his house wondered, *Should I or shouldn't I go to her door? Why shouldn't I go? She is, after all, my nani*! *But to the washermen's colony?* His mind in a whirl, he found himself at his sister's door.

In the dead of night, a knock sounded on the door.

'nani!' he called.

Nila came to the door in a distressed state. Dishevelled hair and a sad, tearful face, she came with the baulapata neatly folded in her hand. Clasping her brother tightly to her chest, she mumbled, 'Did you have to come too? Just because I had walked away? What will people say? Will you too cast a slur on the family and tarnish its image? Go back, my brother! Do return!'

As the brother walked back, he noticed that his palms were moist with someone's tears. A sister's loving touch had unsettled him, and her repentance had churned his insides.

The villagers were struck dumb when they saw the baulapata in the brother's hands!

* * *

Kalindi Charan Panigrahi (1901–91)

'Bewailing Flesh'

(Translated 'Mansara Bilapa' from the Odia by Asima Ranjan Parhi)

Jolly and Dora had been the closest of friends from their childhood. Both dreaded separation. Once, when Jolly was unwell, Dora spent the entire day by her side trying to comfort her. All attempts to send him away were futile. Finally, arrangements had to be made to bring his food to the place where Jolly lay ailing. One day, Dora suffered an injury to his leg. Jolly knew well that Dora possessed limitless strength but was unable to understand why he had to remain stuck to one place for long. She caressed Dora's foot and tried to find out where the pain was.

Dora was an English greyhound while Jolly was a black buck born in the jungles of Gadjat.[xxxii] Dora had been brought to India from the famous city of London while Jolly's birthplace was in some unknown wilderness. Dora was exclusively a flesh eater while Jolly lived only on herbs and grass. But their friendship had grown strong since childhood.

Jolly continued taking care of her childhood friend and helped him heal. Finally, Dora grew a little stronger and was able to walk with slow steps. When spring arrived and the south winds blew with fragrant flowers, the two friends got involved in merrymaking and boisterous play, as though they had come in search of the lost source from which the fountain of joy had flowed towards them and were determined to rediscover it. There was unique grace and elegance in the style

---

[xxxii] A kingdom ruled by a native prince under the British Raj.

of running which each adopted. When Dora ran, he seemed to be tethered to the earth and it was not possible for anyone to distinguish his mouth, ears and feet from each other. Jolly's style of running was different. She seemed to be the very embodiment of a Parisian ballet dancer. Her feet seemed not to touch the earth at all; she was dancing in the air.

Jolly and Dora were the pets of the zamindar, who was very fond of them. Dora had been given an English name because of his English origin and Jolly had received hers in the same language because of her friendship with Dora. When, at the end of a long and tiring day, the zamindar went for a walk in the evening across the enormous meadow in front of his *kacheri*,[xxxiii] the refreshing, playful antics of the two friends put his mind at ease. Jolly walked alongside, licking his hands and rubbing against his feet with her entire body. If Dora was occasionally left behind, he would come running and roll on his back on the ground in front of him with his front legs joined together, as though offering a namaskar in apology. Sometimes the two friends would creep between the zamindar's legs and slow down his walk. If another dog intruded the scene or looked at Jolly, she looked at the zamindar appealingly as though seeking his help to drive the intruder away. But Dora would have anticipated this before and his mere appearance on the scene was enough to do the job.

The zamindar had received his education at Raipur. A person of refined taste, he was soft-spoken and courteous. He dressed as per company; with Indians, he wore dhoti–kurta and with the British, he chose to dress like an English sahib.

At leisure, British officials would visit the zamindar and be his guest. Elaborate arrangements would be made at his guest house for the entertainment of the guests. Jolly and Dora were not his only pets—many other animals of different

[xxxiii] Courthouse.

species: birds, monkeys and fish of different kinds were being reared in the palace. In other words, his palace was quite like a menagerie.

But Dora and Jolly were never far from him. His only daughter, who was about ten years old, was just as great a friend of the two animals. All her leisure hours were spent with them. When she plucked tender tufts of grass in the garden to feed Jolly under the watchful eyes of her *dhai-ma*,[xxxiv] Jolly would instinctively come to know about it and perform many amusing antics to show her pleasure. The zamindar, relaxed in his easy chair on the lawns, would watch indulgently.

It would not be true to say that the zamindar's hospitality was extended only to English guests and not to the rest of his countrymen. All respectable guests, regardless of their nationality, were equally welcome at his home. Despite his hospitality, the public opinion was often against him, and the elders in his village accused him of being corrupt and immoral in his habits. There was perhaps a grain of truth in these charges.

This year, he was preparing to receive an important guest whom he had not entertained before. The DIG (deputy inspector general) of police had written to him from Calcutta expressing his desire to visit the estate during winter holidays with his wife and daughter. The guest house was getting cleaned and decorated in anticipation of the visit. No one had any respite for a moment, and everyone cursed the zamindar for burdening them with additional chores. The DIG was an old friend and had expressed his desire to spend some time in the estate's jungle with the zamindar. Elaborate tents were being set up for the shikar of deer and birds.

The zamindar also went to great lengths to receive his guests. The tents had been set up about 12–14 miles away from the zamindar's palace and the shikar company would have to travel through dense jungle to get to the location. Two hunting dogs would accompany the convoy. Dora and Jolly would sit

[xxxiv] Housemaid.

with the zamindar in his motor car. Jolly was not a suitable animal for this trip, but could not be separated from Dora and had to be taken along. The zamindar's servants went into the jungle on foot in advance of the hunting party, carrying the necessary utensils for a sumptuous feast after the hunt was over.

There was much merrymaking in the lonely jungle. After lunch, the zamindar and sahib left for their hunting expedition. The women didn't accompany them this time, being very tired.

It was getting late. The sun was about to set behind the distant hill. The reddened sky in the west looked amazing but didn't attract the notice of the hunters who were instead looking for the red blood of an animal. The eastern side of the sky was full of clouds about to burst. But the two hunters were glued to the ground. Why would they look at the sky? The servants started searching for the two who had vanished.

Suddenly, both friends had a feel of the cool wind and decided to return in the face of heavy rain. It was difficult to get back to the tent in the rain. So they had a flag march with gunshots that drove away the deer and others while they walked under the rain, their drenched clothes getting wetter and heavier. It was 8 p.m. by the time they were back.

There was no arrangement for dinner as nothing was killed in the hunting in the evening. The palace was 22 km away from this place and in this rainy night, there was no way one could go and arrange for food. The zamindar had been about to send some people in the afternoon for meat but the sahib's insistence of getting an animal by hunting had made him stop that plan. Now, he was unnecessarily scolding the servants. Observing this, the sahib suggested that he could devise some means for dinner. The zamindar looked at him with curiosity. The DIG asked if he would spare his deer for a sumptuous dinner, and later replace him with many such Jolly's from the jungle. The zamindar, lost in thought, nodded and appreciated the idea though his heartbeat stopped for a while. He was so fond of this animal. He remembered how, in order to impress one of his British friends, he had once shot Jolly's mother during one such hunting spree, while Jolly was sucking milk from her. The little animal stood quiet, being under the impression that her mother was still alive and near her to protect. The zamindar developed a filial attraction towards her.

He had never thought that one day, she would be killed to eat her meat. He was concerned and felt gloomy but didn't want to disappoint his friend. Getting his consent, the British officer swiftly got ready to kill it by his knife. It was heard that he didn't feel satisfied unless he killed an animal during the hunting exercise. He had the good reputation of killing many in war and used to kill a pet hen if he didn't find any prey. That made him calm. His wife even said that once he was about to slit his own throat after failing in one such shikar.

The two friends Dora and Jolly were lying curled up in each other's lap. No unknown person would have dared to approach Jolly at a time like this when she was being guarded by Dora. It was only Madhia, the zamindar's trusted servant, who could be brave enough to get close to the two animals and persuade Jolly to come out from her secluded place near Dora. When Dora heard the sound of Madhia's footsteps, he sprang up and began to bark loudly. Madhia spoke softly to calm him down. However, when Madhia took hold of Jolly's chain and started to lead her away, Dora started barking ferociously once again. He would not permit Jolly to be led away. Jolly remained calm throughout the exercise, looking at Dora frequently through her large, limpid eyes and towards the zamindar, who was involved in conversation with his friend's wife and daughter trying to conceal his inner restless spirit. Eventually, Dora allowed Madhia to lead Jolly away.

Dora started doubting the intention seeing the knife in the Britisher's hand. He had seen many animals being killed there for food. Jolly looked at her master pleadingly but he avoided her eyes. Dora sensed Jolly's fate in the hands of the cruel knife, and jumped and bit Madhia, who was holding Jolly. The zamindar scolded Madhia and apologized before his friend, though he was feeling guilty in his heart. Madhia held Dora back and tied him securely to a tree. The cruel officer teased Dora flaunting his knife towards him. Jolly looked like she wanted to say something. When the zamindar heard Dora's cry, it choked him and burned his soul. Removing the cloth from his face, he found that it was all over. His heart didn't allow him to eat Jolly's flesh. He only gave company to his friend while an inexplicable and inexpressible pain gripped him all through. Madhia came and informed him that Dora hadn't touched the food or meat given to him.

Sleep evaded him. He went on thinking, he was in the jungle, it was dark and rainy, the killed mother and her innocent child, its unsuspecting eyes in surrender, then their return, the Englishman's knife and cruel act and then a question from somewhere, 'Didn't I trust and take sheltr in you leaving my mother?' He got up. 'Oh it was a dream.' But again, he saw the same scene, the pleading eyes and the utter truth, followed by sleeplessness.

In the morning, arrangements were made for departure. All his attempts at laughing in the company of his friend proved futile on the way. Later, his friend and his family left for the city.

When Madhia brought Dora with a lot of difficulty, he said that Dora had been forcing the servant to leave him in that place all alone. The master was in deep thought with guilt, self-humiliation and hurt. He wanted to go on his knees before this carnivorous dog and seek forgiveness. He thought, *Is this world governed by the mighty and powerful who would keep the weak under them and devour all, take all benefits? Man has been trying to own the universe, to control it and to destroy it. Is he really the most intelligent one and conscientious in his act?* The zamindar developed bitterness, and a sense of detachment engulfed him. He felt that if the tongue that tasted Jolly's flesh and throat and devoured her heart would be cut and choked, he might get some relief.

Suddenly, someone called from the back, 'Where is Jolly? He looked back—it was his four-year-old daughter. He rose and held her close in an embrace and said, 'She is here, my dear, she is here'. She didn't hear it and said in a choked voice with teary eyes, 'Lies, all lies, Madhia said that sahib has killed her. I will kill that sahib.' The zamindar's eyes were flooded with tears. He gave her to the governess and cried like a child, burying his head in the bed. His heart was echoing his daughter's words, 'Where is Jolly?' As he looked at his own body parts, he heard the bewailing voice of the small black buck in every artery and corner of his body. Her lament flowed like lightning through his veins and he became ill with fever. When he recovered, he had changed. The guest house in his premises made for the British guests was converted to a residence for the poor. Non-vegetarian food was banned in his palace and an order was passed by him to stop the hunting or killing of deer or such animals in his zamindari.

Dora didn't eat and lay dull on the floor. On the first day of the master's illness, he freed himself and left. Madhia found him smelling and cajoling the place where Jolly was slaughtered. He had lost his childhood friend here and thought he might somehow find her there. He was searching for her everywhere and lamenting. Madhia brought him back but he vanished again one day. All attempts of searching for him proved futile. Nobody has seen him after that. Some say he has gone in the direction of the place where the tents were set. The woodcutters from the jungle say they have heard a distressful, bewailing sound from the choked voice of an animal in the deep forest. But whose voice is this? Of Jolly or Dora?

* * *

Bhagabati Charan Panigrahi (1908–43)

'The Kill'

(Translated 'Shikar' from the Odia by Jayanta Mahapatra)

Ghinua's name was quite well known in those parts as an excellent huntsman. He didn't know how to use a gun. His principal weapon was a bow he had made with his own hands. He stretched himself flat on the ground when he used it. His left foot resting against the bow, he would pull the arrow way back till it touched his ear and then release it. He could take aim from as far as a mile and still hit his target. Deer, sambar, boar and bear; many of these animals he had killed with his bow, and some cheetahs too. But he had only been able to bag two Royal Bengal tigers. He had been favoured with adequate rewards from the deputy commissioner for killing the tigers. Early that morning, carrying a bizarre kill with him, there he was, at the bungalow of the deputy commissioner. His bow rested on one shoulder. In his hand were two or three arrows, from the other shoulder slung his axe. The orderly at the door took one look at Ghinua and asked:

'What game have you brought this morning?'

Ghinua was an old acquaintance of his. Often, he had shared the other's *bukshish*.[xxxv] In answer, Ghinua merely showed two rows of dirty, stained teeth. It was impossible to tell whether it was a smile or a grimace. Nobody had ever seen what could be called a real smile on Ghinua. At times, he simply laid bare his teeth clear and empty; neither a grin nor an expression of sorrow—just a plain display of teeth.

[xxxv] Reward.

The orderly said, 'Speak up, man! What is it you've brought today?'

Ghinua merely pointed at the bundle tied up in his flimsy shoulder-cloth and said that it was a formidable creature he had killed and brought this time.

'Tiger?' the orderly enquired.

Ghinua shook his head and answered in the negative. 'Then what is it . . . cheetah, bear or boar?' Ghinua simply shook his head in reply. 'Then what is it, fellow?'

The sahib heard the commotion and came outside. Ghinua bowed low before the sahib and showed his teeth, as was his habit. When the sahib indicated his curiosity to see the nature of the kill, Ghinua untied the cloth and laid a freshly severed human head at the sahib's feet.

Startled, the sahib fell back two steps. Ghinua stretched his hand forward and pleaded, 'Sahib, bukshish'. A few moments later, the sahib pulled himself together and gestured to Ghinua to wait for his bukshish. Then he went inside and telephoned for a team of armed police. There was no other way to subdue Ghinua otherwise. He had the strength of a demon in his body, and his bow, arrow and axe were very much visible in his hands.

Ghinua was puzzled when shackles were placed on his wrists and feet, and he was placed in lock-up. What was the idea behind such a detention? He made up his mind to ask someone about this when the opportunity arose. One said that he would be hanged and another that he would be sent away to the Andamans. Why, what great crime had he committed? Unable to understand what was happening to him, he never believed their words. One day, the deputy commissioner came to inspect the prison. Ghinua enquired of him what the whole matter was. He was told that on previous occasions, he got his bukshish at once after he had killed a tiger or a bear. But now he had killed a human being. What reward he would get for this, had, after all, to be decided upon by a committee of five persons. The explanation seemed fairly sensible to Ghinua and he felt certain that he would receive his reward on the day of his judgment. Excited, he went on babbling about the entire incident before the judge: 'It wasn't easy work to axe Gobinda Sardar to death. So many people had tried to kill him, but nobody could. For Gobinda Sardar invariably travelled by car! He had amassed all his wealth robbing and fleeing others, and was the greatest of rogues. How many he had killed, how many lives he had ruined, and how many women he had molested—who could tell? He had even usurped my entire paddyland. The other evening, he was on the verge of raping my wife. The nerve of him! When he caught sight of me, he tried to escape in his car. I shot an arrow at the wheels and wrecked it. Then I lopped off his head with the axe and ran through the forest all night. I covered thirty miles without stopping to rest until I reached the bungalow of the deputy commissioner.'

Gobinda Sardar had been no ordinary man and always carried a gun. People were afraid of him more than they were of the denizens of the jungle. And he caused much greater harm to people then tigers or bears. Ghinua had exercised no mean daring and shrewdness to kill him.

Some years back, Dora[xxxvi] had been rewarded with 500 rupees for cutting off the ringleader Jhapat Singh's head. Jhapat Singh was, in a way, a better person. He had neither assaulted women nor had he appropriated other people's property. He had merely looted the government treasury and killed a few policemen. Gobinda Sardar, however, was a heinous person. Ghinua deserved a greater bukshish for killing him.

[xxxvi] Dora was also a murderer, like Ghinua, for ringleader Jhapat Singh.

Ghinua's reasoning made everyone in the court roar with laughter. The judge smiled and said, 'Yes, a befitting bukshish will be given.' The government lawyer reassured him, 'Yes, you've been brought here only to be given a reward!'

Ghinua, without thinking that it was a joke, took this in earnest. Pranks or sarcasm were unknown to him and he had a totally humourless nature.

In the end, the sentence was pronounced to be death.

Ghinua could not comprehend its meaning. As he was being led back to prison, he was told that the day was not far off when he would get his longed-for bukshish.

Ghinua was still unaware that he was a criminal and had been sentenced to death. How could he realize that killing Jhapat Singh and killing Gobinda Sardar wasn't the same thing? He failed to understand that one was a deed of glory, the other a crime. Had he the sense to go into the gossamer web of the law? He was just a wild *santal*.[xxxvii]

He would think over and over that because Dora had got 500 rupees for killing Jhapat Singh, if he wasn't given more than that, why should he accept it? He would return the entire amount and say, 'Then don't give me anything at all, sahib, but it's my due to get more than Dora.'

In the dark and lonely cave of the prison cell, so many thoughts would come to him. He did not see anyone to whom he could talk; there was no desire in him to converse. He grew restless only to receive his bukshish and go back home.

At last, the day of his execution came. When asked about his last wish, he answered simply, 'My bukshish'.

They said, 'All right, come for your bukshish' and took him along. A sheath of black cloth was pulled over his head. Ghinua thought that maybe they had blindfolded him just to fill his hands with gold and silver. The government had its

---

[xxxvii] A member of the Scheduled Tribe known as santal.

own ways of doing things, its own manoeuvres and devices. Would any bukshish be given away, just like that, into his outstretched palm? How delighted his wife would be when he returned home and showed off everything to her! He'd build a better house, till his land and live happily. Was Gobinda Sardar there any more that he would loot all Ghinua had?

Suddenly he felt something go round his neck.

* * *

Gopinath Mohanty (1914–91)

'Hidden Ganga'

(Translated 'Gupta Ganga' from the Odia by Sudeshna Mohanty)

The same old story. The husband has taken another woman and doesn't want to have anything to do with her. She lives in her father's house, earns a living by engaging herself as a labourer; the son is six years old, and the daughter is three. She is here not to ask for a poultice for her emotions; blows, insults and neglect culminating in rejection—she has borne them all. What she asks for is money to buy food—for herself and her young children—at least Rs 50 a month, and the man has the means to give it to her. That is the decree she wants.

She has got this written down in legal terms. The primal story of human existence is reduced to a number—legal proceedings to be initiated under Sec 488.

And the narrator of this story—that woman crouching in the corner of the courtroom with a bowed head and downcast eyes, clad in a not-too-wide, coarse, red-bordered sari. She exudes a sort of wilted charm, the charm of a full-bodied beauty, fading prematurely after bearing years of oppression. Tiny neem sticks in her pierced nose and ears. Cheap bangles on her wrists. A huge eight-anna-sized vermilion dot on her forehead. The lawyer who represents her stands beside her in a black coat.

The other story is familiar too. She had no respect for the family she married into. She spoke rudely with her husband, father-in-law and mother-in-law. She insulted visiting friends and family, and always went away to her father's house.

And to cap it all, indulged in extramarital relationships. This child is not mine, *huzoor*.[xxxviii] She is the product of her illicit relationship with another man. Despite this, I took her back. I repeatedly ask her to come back. She is a wanton woman who wants to enjoy herself, but why should my earnings fund her promiscuousness? I can't afford to give her any money. All my land has been taken away by the tenant farmers. Who will go to court against them? I don't even have enough money to buy food.

This was the claim of the tall, slim young man. His lawyer too wore a black coat. The tall, slim youth garnered a fair amount of sympathy. A shock of curly hair, neatly parted at the centre; wide-set eyes that looked even more ponderous from under his glasses; impatient, thin lips; a round face; the nose neither too wide nor too sharp and the forehead slanted backwards.

No, he did not appear cruel. Weak? Maybe. Wearing a wide billowy dhoti and a loose white kurta, he had a slight tremor in his leg as he walked. He appeared to be someone who appreciated the fragrance of cheap perfumes. He probably put up calendars in his house—couple calendars, where the woman lovingly bent over the man from behind and playfully blindfolded him with her cupped palms, or maybe a calendar of a single woman, who, while posing for an advertisement herself became the product she was modelling for. Maybe he enjoyed music and sang a few sentimental songs himself in a strong nasal voice—songs that had no special style and therefore passed off as modern songs; songs in which one only sighed and moaned over a woman lost.

He did not look like the defendant before him, the one who took pleasure in tying his wife's hand and foot to the bedpost, and sadistically thrashing her black and blue. The woman

---

[xxxviii] Milord.

had bared her back in the open court to exhibit the deep welts on her back—love bites given to her by her husband.

Instead, here was a gentleman who did not physically abuse his wife, but could, without batting an eyelid, call her a whore in an open court and label his own child illegitimate.

The judge looked from one side to the other, from one face to the next. Both parties had approached the court with their grievances. A simple case to be settled in three sittings. And then?

It flashed across his mind that here only relevant legal steps were to be followed. The statements of the witnesses recorded on paper were all that mattered—nothing else was to be taken into account. But the human element of the story that was being enacted before him could not be overlooked—whether the story fit into the framework of the law or not was immaterial. He found himself recreating in his mind's eye the early life of this couple. On the wedding altar, both of them with *mukutas*[xxxix] on their heads and feet decorated with lac-dye. So many curious eyes on them. A shy, demure bride. So much affection between them then, so many desires, so many dreams. Just eight years ago. He might have sprayed jasmine-scented attar on her. They would have gazed together at the full moon from the window of their dark house. He would have stolen a glance at his wife and said to himself, 'My wife is so beautiful!' He would have thought so many times that her body was a poem, an inspiration. Would have thought that she was a fragrant garland of flowers or a tasty morsel of food.

The middle-aged judge looked straight ahead, neither to the right nor to the left.

He can see in the distance, a row of old, tiled houses. A little to the side were two tall neem trees. The goalpost on the playground of the school. A wide playground. Patches

[xxxix] The tiara made of sholapith worn by an Odia bride and groom.

of grass. Three cows grazing on the grass. A footpath has opened up from one end of the field to the other. People walking across. The blazing sun beats down.

This is life. Everything is clean and crystal clear. Sometimes, dark clouds cast their shadows, storms arise, and everything is churned and turned upside down. And sometimes, everything turns to venom and is scorched. Life becomes discordant and turbulent.

The judge looks for solutions. His thoughts unwittingly stray to his own marital life. Although not separated, the bond between them has weakened over time. But why? He has done his duty—raised a family, taken care of their needs to the best of his ability, paid for the children's tutors, provided for servants and cooks, and taken care of medical expenses. He has done all this ungrudgingly. His wife too, has done her duty without complaints. The countless nights that she has stayed awake for the children or the chores of the household, she has done them all with her nose to the grindstone. She has carried on her shoulders the weight of her responsibilities as the lady of the house. She has sacrificed her own interests in the larger interest of the family. Yes, both have done their duty. But maybe gritting one's teeth to do one's duty uncomplainingly has in itself been a mistake. Because both of them have held up the list of their chores as a silent reproach against the other.

He is forty-five. The body has become heavy. A rotundness has crept into his face. He is bald and his fair complexion has dulled. When he peers from behind his blue bifocal glasses from his high seat of justice, he looks serious and stable, his mind used to balancing itself on the tightrope of justice. There is no vacillation in his mind, and he harbours a strong faith in his instinct for what is good and bad, right and wrong.

From his demeanour, one can guess his nature. He won't play with children or run joyfully. He won't easily forget what is due to him. He will have no qualms about bluntly refusing alms to a beggar in front of people. He is polite, respectable and grave.

His household revolves around similar principles. His wife is just like him. She is forty to his forty-five. She hasn't balded but her hair is streaked with grey. A round face, exuding unmindful, greying solemnity. Sagging cheeks. A thick neck. The stout body reflects the prosperity of the family. She moves slowly, like a chariot. Devoted to her husband and unfailing in her duties to her children. The one-rupee-coin-sized vermilion dot on her forehead reflects her pride in her marital status.

From time to time, the judge's thoughts go back to this image of his wife. He absentmindedly nods his head and emits deep-throated grunts which presumably mean 'Hmm!' Sometimes, he doodles on the paper in front of him. The lawyers from both sides have presented their cases. The judge is nodding his head and looking at everyone coldly. But his mind is elsewhere. He was thinking that his wife's looks of bygone days were lost forever. Her laughter, her curiosity and her desire for physical intimacy have been dead for long. As for him, for years he has suppressed his desire and not been able to resuscitate his youth.

They have presumed that this is the way of the world, and that desire vanishes as one gets immersed in the business of living. There is no place for poetry, passion, stolen glances, anticipation or ecstasy in the mundane routine of life. *Putrarthe kriyate bharya*—one should marry just to have a son. Nowadays, a son can be begotten artificially through a rented womb, making intimacy between man and woman unnecessary. The relationship between a man and a woman has become mechanical, even commercial. The man will earn money, and the woman will count it and hoard it. The man gives judgment in court, and the woman lords over the household, berating the servants.

He did not feel connected with his wife. On the contrary, he feels that over the years, they have become estranged. He may have wanted to stray further, but what held him back was the age-old *sanskar*[xl] and a fear of social censure. What if someone saw him with another woman? Many a time, another woman's company has given him pleasure or another woman's beauty and grace has attracted him. He has wanted to rest for a while, and share his joys and sorrows under the shade of a spreading tree so many times. And many a time, the memory of some woman he has met has taken over his mind and possessed him for a few days. But on the outside, he is a mild, calm, serious gentleman—a learned magistrate.

He rationalizes with himself. This life is meant for action. Desire is only to beget progeny. It is madness to unbridle desire. If one lived one's life as a disciplined schoolboy, walking on the trodden path, one would live happily. But there occasionally rises in the mind this blazing fire of revolt, the urge to pierce through the veneer of respectability and let loose the basic instincts. A deep frustration gnaws the entrails. There are various roads leading to enjoyment but these paths are closed to him. And he is getting on in years. He realizes that these urges originate in the level of the physical and like defecation, urination or sweat, excrete from the body, take the form of thoughts and just melt away.

He examines these thoughts that arise in his mind before the ordinary Sec. 488 cases. What he hasn't been able to do, this young man has done. He hasn't cared for respectability. He has walked off the beaten track and gone wherever he fancied. He has rejected the old and welcomed the new. What the judge had dismissed as distorted and anti-social impulses originating in the dark recesses of his mind, this young man has embraced. Birds and beasts did just this. The young

[xl] Moral values.

man's biggest offence is that he has done what the judge himself could not do. Jealousy raises its head. Jealousy that gives rise to a slow, simmering rage. All sympathy for the wronged woman. He wants to talk to her kindly, offer her some solace; then again, he wants to console her, revive in her by his compassionate touch all that has dried up due to cruel negligence. Here is a woman wounded by injustice and torture. All the justice of the universe could not compensate for even a fraction of the sorrow and insult that has been heaped upon her.

With eyes spewing fire, the judge looks at the defendant. And the cross-examination begins.

Taramani is the first witness to be summoned. She neither weeps nor rants. She answers the lawyer's questions quietly. Her voice is heavy with hopelessness. A crowded courtroom, but pin-drop silence. She is giving evidence in the court, and her sorrowful, understated gestures are more eloquent than what she expresses in words. It is as if darkness has descended at noon. All around, people let out deep sighs. The story of her life unfolds before everyone's eyes like the unfurling of the petals of a flower as she speaks in her low, tired voice. Then, like a gust of hot air, enters the other woman. She is childless, pretty, young and healthy. The husband says that he finds her very desirable. Her voice trembles as she speaks as if her heart is being pierced with a hot knife. She grits her teeth and hisses the words. Her life story shrivels and wilts. The same old story. One person's tenure ended, and another's began. Added to that is the narrative of poverty, hunger, starvation and neglect. The courtroom is filled with sympathetic clicks of the tongue. She is everyone's daughter, the daughter of the nation.

The defendant's lawyer contests what she said. The cross-examination starts. Who else does the man know? Who else visits him? Does he enquire about your welfare? Were there quarrels at home? If you claim that the husband started it, what words does he use to abuse you? What faults does he accuse you of? How do you reply to his allegations? Have you ever asked the panchayat to settle your disputes? Has anyone from the village stepped in to settle your quarrels? The questions pour in like a deluge, overwhelming the poor woman.

She realizes through the web of questions that this stranger—the man who is her husband's lawyer—is trying to ensnare her and malign her character. She forgets that she is in a crowded courtroom. Forgets that people are jostling each other and craning their necks to look at her. In a voice quaking with anger, she points an accusing finger at her husband and shouts, 'How dare you! Is there no dharma in the universe? Why doesn't your tongue shrivel up before it can utter another word? The universe will not bear the insult that you are piling on yourself, your race and your ancestors with a hired tongue. Look me in the eye and tell me, is what the lawyer accusing me of, true? Am I an adultress? Are these two children illegitimate? Why don't you answer?'

The blazing eyes of a person possessed. An extraordinary restlessness in the body. As if the spark of life struggles within her, attempting to fly away. Flared nostrils, a tear-stained face and fading youth. Anger and insult rage within her. The turmoil within her mind continues to rise rapidly. The scene in the courtroom has changed. As if there are no walls and no ceiling, a dark overcast sky rains down torrential downpours. Thunder, lightning, storm. No sun. As if the creator is enraged and wants to avenge this insult to all women. And man with folded hands and bowed head begged for deliverance.

Her lawyer tries to soothe her. 'Listen, listen, Ma! Calm down. This is a courtroom. Answer the questions. Don't get upset.'

The defendant's lawyer addresses the judge and says, 'I can't cross-examine her when she is in this state. Let her be charged with contempt of court.'

She is like a woman possessed. 'Why do you think I came here? To experience the pride of victory? Not at all! I came here for the sake of these two children. To ask for what is due to them. To keep them alive. You are enjoying yourself in the arms of a young wife. Pouring money like water from a running tap, while your children battle hunger and starvation. You don't care about their welfare! You, their father! Shame on you! You are our tormenter! I'm here because someone told me if I came here, my troubles would be resolved!'

She has the sympathy of the entire courtroom. Many comments are heard. 'What a pity! A wronged woman's tears destroyed Lanka, and this man is but a dandy!' And from the doorway, where the spectators had formed a human wall came, 'Give him a blow! Hold him by the neck and give him two tight whacks. That will set him right, the Casanova!' Milling crowds were joined by others who came asking 'What's happening?' The magistrate raises his voice and orders, 'Silence! All remain quiet!'

All eyes are on the magistrate. An unusual solemnity on his face. A sentient human face and not a face of brick and stone. The chaos subsided.

But then, it so happens that the defendant's counsel loses all interest in the case. He asks a few stray questions and rests the case. The six other witnesses for the petitioner are summoned one by one and their statements duly recorded.

There is a crowd of people the next morning. The defendant's witnesses will be cross-examined. But the cross-examination is lifeless. Five of the eight witnesses are not even summoned. The three who are, are dismissed after some curt questioning. Under the gaze of so many eyes, the defendant retreats into himself. As if he didn't have the courage to hold his head up. As if he just wanted to get done with the case. After a brief exchange of legal pedagogy between the two lawyers, the verdict is pronounced. Exactly what the people expected. The defendant has to pay Rs 40 per month for the upkeep of the children and their mother. 'You are dismissed,' is the magistrate's final verdict.

The woman neither smiles nor says a word. She melts like a shadow into the crowd from where she had come—a woman so used to experiencing sorrow that she has lost the power to experience joy. The judge appraises her in his mind for a moment. And buries himself in his books again.

Ten months passed. Many cases came up. Many verdicts were passed. The statements of many people were taken and passed into the annals of court records. The history of so many blows, so many raised fists, so many killings and stabbings. How can one man pick up a machete to hit another? The wonder is that even though the body is cut into pieces and bathed in blood, the person still lives. Also records of thefts and burglaries—a variety of cases. So many that make headline news. Many cases under Sec. 488, many verdicts given. So many women came to the court asking for justice. The story of this particular woman was buried in a remote corner of the magistrate's mind.

And then the woman appealed to the courts again and asked for Rs 40 per month for the ten months that had passed. The magistrate marvelled at how swiftly time had flown. It seemed it was only yesterday that he had passed a verdict in her favour. And now almost a year has elapsed. In this one year, how had she managed to make both ends meet? How had she fed the children and kept them alive? The circles under her eyes have become darker. She has aged by five years. Her face has withered and she looks frail. Every pore of her being reflects her neglect towards herself. Worry and anxiety writ large on her face. A date is fixed for the next hearing. The man asks for an adjournment. The request is denied. It is then decreed that in fifteen days, he should give her her due. But the woman does not express joy or excitement. The magistrate looks at the woman in astonishment. She remains unmoved, unaffected and stoic.

Another date. The two sides face each other again. The man was disrespectful, irritated, and nonchalantly chewing a paan. Another application for adjournment. A pitiful appeal from the woman's lawyer. 'My lord! One full year has elapsed after the verdict that he should give money to my client. He did not give her a single paisa before the decree, he hasn't given her anything after the decree. He will keep asking for adjournments and he will keep depriving my client of her due.'

At that point, the magistrate's eye catches the careless snigger with which the defendant reacts to the lawyer's passionate plea. Incensed, he immediately decrees that for non-payment of the stipulated Rs 480, the defendant be sentenced to four months in jail.

Jail!

It takes some time for the verdict to sink in. As if the verdict is not final yet. And then it slowly penetrates. The mouth is agape. The eyes open wide. The long hair, slickly combed back, the long fingers adorned with rings, the clean freshly ironed clothes, all these external trappings of gentlemanship—his physical asylum—are being stripped away.

Two armed sentries converge on him from both sides, hustle him and say, 'Move! Move!' All his arrogance melts into drops of tears that trickle from his eyes. And in a choking voice, he screams, 'Jail! Jail! No, huzoor, don't send me to jail!

The magistrate purses his lips even tighter. This is a familiar stance, of stifling a smile. Just as a doctor is familiar with the grunts of a patient suffering from a terminal disease, similarly, the magistrate, with his experience of twenty-five years, is well acquainted with this reaction of an accused when he hears an unpleasant verdict. He feels no pity. On the contrary, a sense of satisfaction comes over him—a satisfaction that comes from having done one's duty. It is precisely at this moment, when he sees the plight of the condemned man that he feels that the law, which empowers him to punish people is not man-made. It is prescribed by the divine, and he is only his representative in the disbursement of justice. He is the incarnation of justice.

'No! No! Don't send me to jail, huzoor, I am a gentleman, I haven't committed any offence!'

The magistrate gives him a piercing glance and orders, 'Take him away! Quick!' Following the magistrate's instructions, the two sentries grab hold of him and forcefully pull him away.

And exactly at that moment, waiving all fear of consequences, and all regard for laws and verdicts, enters the woman who has been fighting this case for almost a year.

Like a lunatic, oblivious of everyone and everything, she stands below the judge's bench and says, 'Huzoor! I will give whatever statement you want me to submit. Don't send my husband to jail!' Through the tears that stream down her cheeks and trickle into her mouth, she piteously pleads, 'Don't send him to jail! Don't send him to jail! I don't need any wealth! I will forgo my due. I would rather die of starvation, but I can't bear this sorrow! I say I have received my due. Wretch that I am, what have I done! I've sent my own husband to jail! Could I ever do anything worse than this!'

The sentries forget that they have been ordered to take the man away.

The magistrate, court officials, lawyers, spectators—all of them have forgotten that the final decree has been delivered. In the midst of the mundane day-to-day activities of the court, a great performance is being enacted. The woman continues to silently shed copious tears. In a fraction of a second, the atmosphere of the courthouse has changed. It was as if nothing had physical form. Everything was a play of emotions—nothing else.

The newspaper hawker forgets to announce the headlines. He cranes his neck and strains his eyes to look. The tall peddler, who was loudly advertising his wares, pauses to stare agape. So too the seller of pamphlets, almanacks and flutes. And the seller of shoes and slippers, with a garland of footwear round his neck. A short man with sandalwood paste on his forehead, a calm smiling face happily chewing a paan, a stubble that looked like a kadamba flower on his unshaven face, wearing a coat that was left unbuttoned, a bundle of papers tucked under his arm—he must be the village pundit. Even the tout who has divided the village into two camps and ignited numerous legal cases and is living in a rented house near the court—even he is surprised and stands gazing awestruck.

All of them stand dumbfounded. In a moment, the woman signs a receipt saying she has received the total amount that was due to her. 'You are acquitted!' was the magistrate's final verdict. The sentries set him free. Through eyes brimming with tears of gratitude, the man looks for his wife, as if he is seeing her for the first time. But the woman has melted into the shadows. She did not pause to hear whatever kind words her husband had to say. She is gone.

* * *

Pranabandhu Kar (1914–98)

'A Leaf in the Stream'

(Translated 'Sua Munhare Patar' from the Odia by Jatindra Kumar Nayak)

Aparti was ploughing his plot of land. Sweat poured down his shiny, black and sinewy body. As he tilled his land, many thoughts crossed his mind. Whenever his grip on the handle of the plough slackened, the oxen would slow down. Prodding his oxen with a stick, he would shout, 'Sons of a bitch! Why do you stand still, you don't want to move or what?'

When the oxen began pulling the plough, Aparti would again get lost in thought. Many thoughts kept crowding his mind today. It seemed as if the events that had taken place eight or nine years ago had happened only yesterday. They passed before his eyes like pictures. Life was so simple then. People lived happily on rice and saag.

Then this horrible war broke out and everything turned upside down. The British government fell out with Germany or some such country and fought against it. But I don't understand, why should that matter to us at all?

We were told that the Japanese were marching into our land, and would conquer and occupy it; so we should get ready to do battle with them.

Now tell me, how does it matter if the Japanese or the British rule us? The fact is whoever rules us loots us.

The war came to an end some three or four years ago, but the prices show no signs of falling.

Aparti was confused by it all. This war in some far-off place leads to prices soaring here.

Aparti and thousands of farmers like him could never find an answer to this question. When the war was on and fighter planes flew in the sky, they would scare Aparti out of his wits. He would rush to the bushes growing near the ridges and hide himself behind them. His oxen would get frightened and run away carrying the yoke tied to their necks.

However, in a few days, he overcame his fear and got used to the sight. In fact, he felt excitedly happy whenever he saw five or six planes fly over his field. It seemed to him as if a war was taking place somewhere near his village, and he and the people of his village had also joined it.

Fighting this imaginary war filled him with great joy and enthusiasm. But the war continued for years and showed no signs of coming to an end. As its outcome was not visible, the thrill of pleasure it had aroused in Aparti waned.

It no longer mattered where the war was taking place. A gloomy weariness came over Aparti. Everything—kerosene, rice and clothes—now cost more and more. Rice sold at two seers a rupee and to make matters worse, it looked like horse feed. A thick layer of dust covered the bottom of kerosene lamps as not a drop of kerosene was available. Aparti could move about in the dark at night without the help of a lamp, but he was worried about his old mother, who couldn't see well even during the day. Sometimes, she had a fall when she stepped out of the house after dark. He often rubbed oil on her limbs to lessen the pain. His mother's plight distressed Aparti and he begged Dhani Sahu, the shopkeeper, to give him a little kerosene but Dhani Sahu refused to oblige him. One day, his mother slipped and fell in the dark and breathed her last.

Aparti's heart overflowed with rebellious thoughts as he tried to soothe his anguish by shedding copious tears. He deeply resented the fact that the moneylender took away whatever he grew on his land every year and left nothing for him to satiate his hunger.

Everyone in the village advised Aparti to get married. This thought had also crossed Aparti's mind, for after his mother's death, there was no one in his house to cook a meal for him.

Everything had become so costly during the war, so whenever anyone asked him to get married, he would say, 'Let's wait for this war to come to an end. I now find it difficult to feed myself, marrying now would be like bringing an elephant home and finding food for it.'

Although he averted these discussions, deep in the recesses of his heart, the face of Gurei filled him with restless longings. Every day, early in the morning, when carrying his plough he led his oxen to his field, Gurei would walk past him after having taken her bath in the young zamindar's pond, bearing a pitcher of water on her head and holding another in her hand.

Aparti's unruly glance would pierce her sari. The water spilling from the pitcher she carried drenched her sari and made it cling to her waist. Aparti couldn't help turning round and staring at her.

This didn't escape Gurei's notice. But rather than scold him, she would give him a smile and raise his hopes.

Aparti couldn't bear his loneliness any longer and one day, stopped Gurei when she was returning from the pond after taking a bath, and asked her if she would marry him.

Gurei happily accepted his proposal. They got married at a time when the war was raging, the Japanese army was marching menacingly towards India, and finding food to eat and clothes to cover one's body was becoming difficult.

The early excitement of the newly-weds waned as their poverty made them experience deprivation more and more keenly. A few days later, Aparti noticed that his wife's khadi sari was torn in many places. But he could never find the money to buy her a new one.

Dhani Sahu, the shopkeeper, had gotten a pukka house constructed with the money he made in the black market that flourished during the war. Even when Aparti offered him a fair price for a sari, Dhani Sahu wouldn't sell it to him. No matter how much he tried, he couldn't buy it at an inflated black-market price. Aparti often felt like burning Dhani Sahu's shop to the ground but would restrain himself.

One day, word reached the village that the government had won the war. Government officials toured villages to announce this good news. The air was rent with loudspeakers celebrating the news of the victory.

All this made everyone feel happy. Aparti also thought that his miseries would now come to an end. Prices of things would come down and his beloved Gurei would no longer have to wear a tattered sari. A thick layer of dirt had settled on her sari. If she would try to wash it, it would fall apart.

The government announced that clothes would be distributed free of charge to the poor to celebrate its victory in the war.

Aparti asked Gurei, 'My dear, would you like to go there and get a sari?'

Despite all the hardships she had endured after her marriage, she replied without bitterness, 'No! How could I step out of the house wearing this tattered sari? I would die of embarrassment in such a huge crowd.'

Aparti could understand her reluctance. He went there alone and received a dhoti for himself. He came back home, gave it to Gurei and said, 'Had you accompanied me, you would have got a sari. Anyway, you put it on. I will manage.'

The war ended. Aparti, while ploughing the moneylender's land, could no longer hear or see planes flying overhead. Days wore on but the prices of rice, clothes and kerosene did not come down.

Not getting enough to eat, Gurei was losing her youthful charm. The dhoti Aparti had given her one and a half years ago, was now worn out.

After a few days, Aparti went to Dhani Sahu's shop. Dhani Sahu said, 'Go away. You think you can buy a sari paying me only three rupees!'

Aparti said, humbly, 'You have turned me away so many times. My wife doesn't have decent clothes to wear. She can't even step out of the house to fetch a pitcher of water!'

Hearing this, Dhani Sahu made fun of him and turned him away.

Wild rage made Aparti's veins bulge and eyes glow. *Money has turned the head of Dhani Sahu, who, before the war, used to go from door to door in villages and sell needles, threads, etc. He now thinks the world of himself.* Gnashing his teeth, Aparti went home.

Freedom fighters went round villages telling people that they should spin threads and get their clothes woven from these. They also asked them not to depend on anyone and become self-reliant. Unless they did so, they would never break the shackles of slavery.

Many farmers' and wage labourers' meetings were held. While some said that they should stop paying land revenue to zamindars, others suggested that a strike should be organized.

Aparti listened to everyone but no one offered a solution to his problem of mere survival. The doctrines that were preached by political parties didn't make any sense to him.

The sight of Gurei's emaciated body pained Aparti deeply. She could step out of the house only after dark to go to the field and fetch a pot of water from the pond.

Aparti tilled his moneylender's land like a machine. He would overhear people telling each other that the country would become independent, but this meant nothing to him. All that he gathered from talking to a few people was that in a few days' time, all white people would leave the country. Our country would be run by our own people. There would be no black marketing and corruption and the prices of common necessities like kerosene, rice and clothes would come down. One would never have to pay bribes.

Aparti would feel happy hearing all this. He would come and tell Gurei, 'My dear, things will now get better for us! From now on, we will be ruled by our own people. The whites will depart for their own country, bag and baggage.'

Aparti eagerly waited for that day to come.

Then came the 15th of August 1947. Every house celebrated it joyously. The tricolour, symbolizing liberty and fraternity, fluttered in the wind. Aparti, for his part, unfurled a tricolour on the roof of his own house. He looked unblinkingly at it with a smile on his face. In it, he saw his wife wearing a fine sari and smiling radiantly at him. He could also see the black marketeer Dhani Sahu arrested and handcuffed.

Days went by. People started forgetting Gandhi and his noble ideals. The weather-beaten tricolour began losing its sheen. Aparti was utterly confused and began wondering if the country had really changed. He could see no change in the condition of his village! His wife wore the same worn-out, tattered sari, and ate curries made of leaves of kanasiri plants and stems of lilies. How had things changed? Sometimes, Aparti would stop ploughing the field, sit on a ridge and think to himself, *I can't notice any change anywhere! Dhani Sahu continues to sell goods on the black market and the ponds in the village remain choked with water hyacinths.*

But one thing had certainly changed—people who came to the village once or twice every month and promised to the villagers that the dream of *Ramrajya*[xli] would come true, were now nowhere to be seen. A freedom fighter, wearing simple clothes, who frequently came to their village to talk to the villagers about the ideals of Gandhi and his simple and austere lifestyle, was one day seen by Aparti, riding a big car through

[xli] A society built on the teachings of the Ramayana.

the village. This sight filled Aparti's heart with unbearable anguish and despair.

The sight of Gurei's pale face and half-naked body would fill his eyes with tears. Aparti would say, 'O Gurei, you suffered so much only because you married me!' Gurei would cry disconsolately on hearing Aparti say this in a voice full of such helpless agony. However, in the midst of such misery and deprivation, his wife's sympathy would give Aparti a strange kind of consolation.

Yet, Aparti blamed himself for deceiving a simple-hearted Gurei, painting pictures of a bright future for her and raising hopes for a better life in her heart. He wanted to take revenge on someone for his misery, but on whom?

He now resolved that he must do something to end his suffering. One day, in the pitch darkness of the night, he headed for Dhani Sahu's shop. A little later, Gurei roused from sleep, rubbed her eyes and saw Aparti sitting by her side with two new Khadi saris in his hand. Utterly confused, she asked, 'Where did you get these from?'

Aparti replied, smiling, 'Don't you worry about where I got these from. Take a bath quickly and put on one of these. It breaks my heart to see you wearing a tattered sari.'

Giving him a suspicious look, Gurei asked, 'Tell me the truth, where did you get these from? They certainly didn't fall through a hole in the roof at night!' Aparti tried to evade the questions, but in the end told her, 'I stole these from Dhani Sahu's shop.'

Startled, Gurei exclaimed, 'What! Stole these?'

'Yes, I did. So what. Who is not a thief? Dhani Sahu charges five rupees for something that actually costs only one rupee. Isn't he a thief? Are the babus who overlook his crime honest people? Isn't the moneylender who pitilessly extorts land revenue from us a thief? How does it matter if someone like me who doesn't get enough to eat and find clothes to cover his body steals what he desperately needs?' said Aparti.

Gurei said, in a quivering voice, 'What if you get caught?'

Aparti said defiantly, 'I don't care if I get caught. At least I will have the satisfaction of seeing you wear a decent sari. Throw your worn-out clothes in the courtyard and hide this new sari in the ash heap in the backyard.'

At noon, the police arrived and searched Aparti's house. Wearing her new sari, Gurei stood before the policemen, looking awkward and bashful. Pointing at her sari, a policeman asked Aparti, 'Where did you get this sari from?'

Showing no signs of nervousness, Aparti replied, 'I bought it.'

The policeman asked, 'From where?'

Aparti said, 'From Dhani Sahu, who has come with you to my house.'

Turning to Dhani Sahu, the policeman asked, 'Did you sell it to him?'

His eyes growing wide, Dhani Sahu exclaimed, 'No, sir, he is lying. You can take a look at my sales register. You won't find his signature in it!'

Aparti replied in a sarcastic tone, 'How could anyone find my signature in your register, Sahu? Like a thief, you sold me this sari at a black-market price at midnight in your backyard! For this sari, which actually costs two rupees and a half, you made me pay five rupees and four annas. How dare you, who do your business under the cover of darkness, accuse me of theft!'

Turning to the policemen, Aparti said, 'Please ask people in the village if I am a thief. You can also find out from them if Dhani Sahu sells clothes at black-market prices. Some of them must have bought clothes from him at such prices.

The police asked Dhani Sahu, 'How many items of clothing have got stolen from your shop?'

He began to stutter and say, 'I think 10–15.'

The sub-inspector of police asked him in a threatening tone, 'How come you can't tell us the exact number of items you say have been stolen? You run a control shop!'

Dhani Sahu now looked helpless and miserable. They found nothing after conducting a thorough search of Aparti's house and told Dhani Sahu, 'So, you claim that you have been robbed, but you yourself are engaged in black marketing in your shop! Come, we will now go and search your control shop. You seem to be a devious person.'

The police now headed for his shop and Dhani Sahu, shaking with fear, walked behind them like a culprit with folded hands. Aparti cast a glance at Gurei, a triumphant smile playing on his face.

Thoroughly shocked, Gurei asked Aparti, 'How could you tell so many black lies with a straight face? My heart was pounding when I heard you utter them!'

Aparti replied, 'There is nothing wrong with stealing something if you know how to do the job deftly!'

Deeply upset, Gurei said, 'No matter if we die of starvation, don't you ever steal anything from anyone. My heart is going to burst out of my chest.'

Aparti said nothing and sat quietly for some time. Then he said, his eyes brimming with tears, 'Gurei, my dear, do you think I stole the sari to have fun? The rich are stealing thousands of rupees to amuse themselves and we poor people can't even find money to buy clothes to cover our bodies. Can't we steal even a few pieces of clothing? Everyone told us that when our country would win independence, our miseries would come to an end; but did this really happen?'

Gurei placed her hand on his shoulder and said, 'Swear on me that you will never do such a terrible thing again, no matter what happens. Not all days are the same. One day, things will change for the better.'

Aparti said, 'My darling, good people always suffer!'

Gurei replied, 'Let's suffer, then!'

* * *

Faturanand (1915–95)

'Birth Anniversary of Meher at a Medical College'

(Translated 'Medical Collegere Meher Jayanti' from the Odia by Aditya Nayak)

Once every year, Odisha celebrates Gangadhar Meher's birth anniversary. Lovers of literature look upon it as a festival. Many seminars and meetings are organized to mark the occasion. Young orators start desperately scanning Meher's collected works to find suitable subjects to speak on. They remind one of the fishermen sifting through the mud to catch eels. On the appointed day, the young orators spew the knowledge thus gathered from the collected works just like the fishermen pour out the eels from a basket. Worn-out, old speakers stir their brains to present Meher in a new light to the audience like someone churning milk to produce butter. Inquisitive and sentimental students pray to Saraswati the goddess of learning, to help them become someone like Meher in the future. In short, the prospect of the celebration of Meher's birth anniversary fills people's hearts with anticipated pleasure. Everyone enthusiastically welcomed the birth anniversary of the great poet.

That year, students and staff of the medical college became accidentally aware of the poet's birth anniversary. As the saying goes, goats are a real nuisance to a gardener. True, the doctors and medical students got a little unsettled when they first encountered the anniversary, but they soon rose to the occasion. A birth anniversary could not unnerve people like them who take death in their stride! So, they decided that they would celebrate the anniversary with great pomp and ceremony.

They wanted to convincingly demonstrate to the lovers of literature that they too could pay proper tribute to the great poet. The doctors and medical students decided to invite a renowned author from outside, but no eminent writer would agree to address a meet held at a medical college. Someone remarked, 'If we invite an author who suffers from gastric problems, he/she would eagerly accept our invitation. We don't have to exert ourselves to look for such a writer, as most writers suffer from gastritis.' Two medical students set out to find a writer who would grace the occasion.

Time was running out; the hall had to be decked up. Two skeletons were placed on either side of the gate leading into the lecture hall. The palms of the skeletons were tied up so that they would appear as if they were greeting visitors with folded hands. A skull was placed above two thigh bones arranged in a cross. 'Welcome' was written below this.

Some people whispered to each other, 'These strange fellows are welcoming people into the abode of Yama, the God of death. Only fools will enter it willingly.' Their voices did not reach anyone. The interior of the hall had to be decorated! The walls were covered with huge pictures of blood cells. The cells formed patterns of red and blue, which looked very beautiful. A table where a portrait of Gangadhar Meher would be kept was needed. So, a squeaky-clean table was promptly brought from the operation theatre. A length of gauze was spread over it and Meher's portrait was kept in position by a pair of bones. For the president of the meeting, a dentist's chair was brought in. In place of flower vases, a few jars, in which embryos were preserved, were arranged on the table.

Soon after the preparations for holding the meeting were over, two medical students ushered a writer whose face was contorted with pain as he clutched his belly, into the hall.

The students had found the writer with such ease because they had seen him enter the gates of the medical college in a rickshaw, pressing his belly desperately with his hands. So, they didn't have to go into the town looking to look for a celebrated author. When fortune smiles on you, fish jumps into your basket on its own. The writer had arrived at the medical college to find relief from colic when the two students found him and told him that they were actually going to his house to invite him. He accepted their invitation to preside over the function for he thought he would get better treatment if he did so.

As he entered the hall, the sight of skulls and bones greeting him deeply repelled the author. He thought, *I have seen evil early in the morning*. But he suppressed his feeling of unease and dutifully entered the meeting hall. The sight of the dentist's chair unnerved him since he had once been made to sit on it. In spite of himself, he felt all his teeth with the tip of his tongue to make sure they were in good shape and sat on it out of courtesy.

The author was agonized to see jars full of embryos in the place of flower vases. A medical student offered him a bottle of hot water and two tablets under the impression that his colic had grown worse. When his stomach ache eased a little bit, he sat more comfortably. The meeting began after the usual rituals were performed.

A doctor addressed the gathering:

> Dear brothers and sisters, today we are celebrating the birth anniversary of a person who is known in every nook and corner of Odisha. There might be places in our state where there may not be any doctor, but I am sure that there is no place where the late Gangadhar Meher might be unknown. Gangadhar Meher was born one year one month and forty days after the great soul Henry Grey, father of the science of anatomy, breathed his last. The

district of Sambalpur, which experiences oppressively high temperatures and in which the famous Professor of Anatomy Sanatan Pujari was born, was blessed to have been the birthplace of Gangadhar Meher. He looked emaciated as he did not get proper nutritious food in his childhood days. He suffered from an acute deficiency of Vitamin D. It is possible that he also suffered from a calcium deficiency. When he was a child, he once had a bad fall and his wrist bone cracked. There is no doubt that this must have been caused by calcium deficiency. By the time he became a young man, he grew healthy and fit as he followed nature. His spine grew slightly bent because he used to work at the loom for long hours every day. Once his finger was pierced by a spindle, it led to sepsis—

One medical student stood up and asked, 'Why wasn't he given a penicillin injection or sulphonamide?'

The speaker replied, 'At that time, these two famous drugs had not been invented. Anyway, he survived, thanks to his natural immunity and a few nostrums he took. Once his house caught fire and while trying to put out the fire, he suffered burn injuries.'

That student again stood up and asked, 'Why didn't he apply tanic acid gel to the affected parts of his body?'

The speaker answered, 'You are right, tanic acid gel was there, but in those days, nobody knew that it could be applied to burn injuries. However, his wounds healed when he rubbed coconut oil on them. The suffering he went through then deeply distressed his father Chaitan Dev and mother Sevati Devi. In the year 1900, *Utkala Sahitya* published his essay titled 'Is the Sound Emitted by Earth'. He wrote this because he mistook the sound in his ears for the sound made by the earth. The sound in his ears would have been caused by nervous debility. His body continued its struggle against all manner of odds until 14 April 1924. On that day, the people of Odisha learnt that the poet, whom they had adored, was no more.'

A murmur rose from the audience, 'What happened to him! What caused his death?'

The speaker went on, 'This is where history remains mute. In those days, our country was ruled by the British. These white people cared nothing for our great men and women. Had a doctor been sent to attend to him on time, he would have easily lived for another ten years. The rustic uneducated quacks or *vaidyas* were responsible for his untimely death as they could not diagnose what ailed him. The kind of treatment he received from them can be easily imagined.'

Members of the audience shouted, 'Shame! Shame!' Someone exclaimed, 'Had this happened in our time, the quacks would have been hung from the nearest lamp post. Fie on those who ruled the country then.'

In the middle of this bustle, the speaker sat down and a member of the audience said, 'Just as the vapours of chloroform spread rapidly through the air, the sweet smell of Gangadhar Meher's poetry has pervaded the whole of Odisha. Like chloroform, the beauty of his poems has left everyone stunned. If one puts a drop of saccharine on the tip of one's tongue, a taste of sweetness lingers for the entire day; similarly, the joy one gets from reading Meher's poems lasts for a very long time. His poem 'Pranayavallavi' (the creeper of love) has the taste of opium—one gets addicted to it and wants to savour it again and again. The scene describing the meeting between Shakuntala and King Dushyant, on whom a curse was laid, has the sweetness of Vinum Galicia. You all know that when you drink Vinum Galicia, at first you feel elated but then a mood of melancholy grips you. Doesn't the scene mentioned above remind you of a similar experience? Do not you think Shakuntala's companions, Priyamvadha and Anasuya, remind you of two nurses standing beside a gynaecologist? Everything except one thing in this poem is excellent. The poem abounds in descriptions of forests; however, one finds in them no mention of medicinal herbs such as patalagaruda, sinkona, kochila, chatiana, shatamuli or sonamukhi. These precious herbs grow plentifully in our forests. This is the only shortcoming I can find in Meher as a poet.'

Before the speaker could sit down, another rose and began delivering a speech, 'Meher's poem 'Tapashwini'[xlii] fills one's heart with extreme distress and has the effect of bromide on one's mind. If you read it repeatedly, you may suffer from melancholia. One is enthralled by his poem 'Bharati Bhabana'.[xliii] The British rulers found it bitter like quinine pills, but fortunately for him, as this poem was an allegory, he narrowly escaped being punished by the British. The poet thus cleverly deceived the British. The poems he wrote on grains such as paddy, moong, wheat and betel leaves bear testimony to his deep love for plants. However, it is a pity that he has never written about any medicinal plants. He should have at least mentioned mutha grass, something with which farmers are intimately familiar. Mutha grass has high medicinal values.'

While the meeting was in progress, the writer thought to himself, *May God, save the poet from the surgical knives wielded by these doctors*. Then he rose to address the audience, 'I am glad that you have shone light on the unexplored aspects of literature. I am sure, in the future, if literature gets wounded, you doctors will apply lotion and dress it with bandage. Now I request you to do something about the pain

[xlii] Tapashwini means 'hermitess'.

[xliii] Bhabana means 'thoughts'.

in my stomach, which is now making it difficult for me to deliver a speech.'

The meeting came to an end, after the writer was carried off into a college ward on a stretcher.

* * *

Sachidananda Routray (1916–2004)

'The Burning-Ground Flower'

(Translated 'Mashanira Phula' from the Odia by Jayanta Mahapatra)

Jagu Tiadi of Podabasanta village spends his time singing devotional hymns, praying to the *mrudanga*[xliv] and smoking ganja as he goes on burning the dead for a living. He's well-known throughout the countryside as one who can efficiently burn dead bodies to ash.

When the corpse makes a hissing sound on the pyre, a leg springs up with a sudden jerk in the heat, or when the ooze from the body's innards doesn't catch fire, everyone present at the cremation casts inquiring glances at Jagu Tiadi for his advice.

Even if he were dozing off some distance away at that time, high on his ganja, Jagu would promptly pull himself together and stand up, pull out a 5-feet-long bamboo from the flaming pyre, heft it and bring it down hard on the corpse a few times, all the while shouting '*Maar! Maar!*' Maybe the corpse's head would shatter to smithereens or the brain matter would burst open dousing a strip of flame. The unruly leg, severed at the knee by the fierce blow, would sway somewhat between the logs of wood. The belly of the corpse would split apart in two and the lolling tongue of fire would play around the intestines. In moments, body and all would be burnt to ash.

A knee-high pile of ash, brooms, shards of earthen pots and tatters of burnt clothing make up the swampy burning ground. Hair and nails, bits of bone, ugly heaps of debris!

[xliv] A percussion instrument.

Jagu Tiadi comes home pleased with himself. Down the steps of the pond's bathing-ghat, he rubs oil all over his body, slaps his thighs excitedly and mutters to himself, 'Thank god, everything went well!'

In a time of cholera, when the Goddess's wrath falls over the village and corpses pile up everywhere, Jagu Tiadi's services are much in demand. Everyone's there to cajole him. While someone will have tears in his eyes, someone will be taking out the money tucked into his waist, and someone will touch Jagu's lips with a finger and coax him by saying, 'Jagu dear! You're my own!'. Jagu Tiadi will listen to their entreaties with a grave look on his face but never utter a word.

'The corpse lying inside the house is giving off a foul smell.'

'Lying dead for the last two days.'

'The newly married bride is rotting in a corner . . .'

Many such grievances reach Jagu's ears.

Jagu is very particular about his dues. Nothing less than 10 grams of ganja, a pellet of opium and a four-anna coin as a small advance will be the incentive to make him budge from his place. Besides these, he had to have fried rice, a new bath-cloth and about ten invitations from relatives of the dead.

If the body is that of a married woman, Jagu has more to gain. If she belonged to a well-to-do family, he'd get both her earrings and the nose ring; if she was not, he'd be given the silver rings adorning her toes. Before he places the corpse onto the pyre, he goes over every inch of the body with an unrelenting eye, lest a piece of jewellery be left behind. At times when a nose ring or an earring fails to come off from the dead woman's limbs, Jagu becomes irritated, grinds his teeth and uses brute force to prise them free. The earlobes might split open, the nose bone might come apart or a watery-blue blood may seep over the face—still, Jagu Tiadi never gives it a thought. It was his regular routine—the practice had hardened him to stone. If the corpse happens to be that of a pregnant woman, he will never lend a shoulder to the bier unless he has had his due. Anything less than the customary amount, and he'll threaten that the body will be cremated only on the following day, dissuading his corpse-bearer-friends from laying their hands on the corpse at the same time.

On those rare occasions when he gets a rupee, in a spurt of delight, Jagu Tiadi keeps stride with the drum-beaters right down the middle of the village road with shouts of '*Ram Nam Satya Hai.*'[xlv] The white sacred thread crossing his granite-coloured body will be clearly visible, shining in the distance.

The entire village will resound with his noisy cries. Men and women will crowd the main square while the children will run into their houses in fear.

When the village washerwoman cuts open the belly of the pregnant woman with a nail scalpel and scoops out the dead baby, Jagu Tiadi hollows out two spaces for both mother and child and lays them on the pyre. When the space isn't enough for both, he'll use the bamboo pole to lever the body around as though it were a mound of flesh and shove it in between the mother's legs.

And so, Jagu Tiadi manages in this way to earn a little for himself, for the expenses of his household, and for the time-to-time payments he has to make for marriages and ritual occasions. All this along with the few measures of paddy he is gifted at harvest time.

No one ever dared to say anything to him. For there was no one else, no other experienced Brahmin corpse-bearer in the village besides Jagu.

Jagu puts forth his arguments that his demands were in no way excessive for the exacting work he performed. And to show off his worth, he would go over reciting his past actions, to prove that there was none other like him who'd cremate a corpse as perfectly as he did.

[xlv] May the name of Ram stand for truth!

That he was able to burn the corpse of Narsinga Misra's wife in torrential rain and on his return had stumbled upon a headless ghost at the far end of the seven-tree grove; and how two full pitchers of water had burst out from the swollen belly of Natha Brahma as he was being cremated that wintry night, so Jagu had to tactfully stoke the fire to burn this impossible giant of a corpse—he was quite adept at narrating these tales over and over again.

Anyone who engaged in small talk with Jagu Tiadi for some time could assess his deep expertise in cremating the dead.

In the assembly room at the village's end, he'd sit down every evening and recount his experiences to those gathered there; through the unending drizzle of the rain, the listeners would eagerly lap up his words. Jaggu would breathe in deeply from his pipe at first and clears his throat. Everyone would become aware that his stories were about to begin.

Returning from the burning ground once after the cremation of a pregnant woman at Muktajhara, he narrated how he came across the spirit of a woman sitting astride a branch of a forked mango tree, warming her body in the flames of her burning intestines—a tale he related with unrestrained relish. Hearing this, his listeners shifted uneasily and snuggled close to each other.

In this manner, Jagu Tiadi went on with his life in that small Brahmin settlement.

A rainy night in the month of June. It had been cloudy all evening. Possibly Jagu was having a severe headache, for he had smeared some shell-lime paste on his temples, wound a cloth tightly on his forehead, and was listening to the recitation of *Harivamsa* on the raised platform in his front yard.

A long wail suddenly swept through the village. Someone was on his way back from the adjoining village shop with paan leaves and nuts. From him, people got to know that the daughter-in-law of old Jatia Ma had died.

News spread like wildfire throughout the village and Jagu felt a quiver of joy run through him at the prospect of earning something.

Villagers gathered, making various kinds of remarks. Women slandered the dead woman in low whispers. Someone said, 'She was carrying someone else's child.' Another, that 'She had taken drugs to abort the baby, but the poison spread and proved fatal.'

Jagu Tiadi listened to everyone with a straight face and then turned away. He gave up all hopes of earning a fair sum for fear of being ostracized by members of his caste.

No one else made up the world of the old Jatia Ma—there were just the two of them. She and her daughter-in-law. Her son had left for Calcutta a month after marriage so he could clear his debts with his earnings. Three years had passed, but there was no news of him. A few letters had come at first, but those had ended as well. Some Brahmin cooks returning to the village from Calcutta said that he lived with a woman in Matia Buruj. Just the young bride lived at home in the village. *And now that she's gone*, thought Jatia Ma, *the burden of indignities has fallen on my head*. Her despondent hand had always been there on the forehead of the old Brahmin woman.

Such was her state on that day that the public ire would not end; it was the work of a few village elders who managed at last to thwart it all. A few aged among them, after having berated Jatia Ma for not keeping her daughter-in-law in check, decided finally to cremate the corpse as soon as they could. Or else, if this news leaked to the Chhatia Police Station, the entire Brahmin settlement would get a bad name. After all, each one of them had families who led seemingly upright lives.

A straw between her decaying teeth, Jatia Ma prostrated herself before everyone present. She was deeply grateful to them for saving her from a harrowing disgrace.

About four athletic young men stepped forward to shoulder the bier. Straw was twisted into ropes and the bier was readied. A winnowing fan, a broom and staff, and shards of earthen pots were brought in. The corpse was wrapped up head to foot in a cloth, hefted and placed on the bier. Still, a competent corpse bearer for the cremation was needed. If the corpse wasn't disposed of in about half-an-hour, the village would be at risk—the police would arrive and arrest the villagers. There was no dearth of informers in the village.

The elders shouted, 'Bring in Tiadi. This work can't be done smoothly without Tiadi!'

The message was conveyed to Jagu Tiadi but he was unwilling. He stuck stubbornly to his decision and declared, 'She died for her own sin. Why will I touch the corpse? Will I carry this unchaste woman on my shoulder?'

All present concurred. And Jagu waited, unmoving and unshaken.

After many appeals by the village elders, Jagu relented and agreed to carry the bier. But only if he was paid 5 rupees. When the hidden little pit beneath Jatia Ma's floor was dug out, the little money inside wasn't enough for the wood, kerosene and the washerman's dues. Finally, it was decided that Jagu Tiadi would be given the gold stud on the daughter-in-law's nose.

Elated, Jagu Tiadi cried out, 'Ram Nam Satya Hai'.

The burning ground, swampy and foul; earthen pots, charred logs, skulls, winnowing fans, piles of ash amid burnt-out embers. A repulsive filthy odour floated around the surrounding area.

The first rites over, Jagu Tiadi hollowed out a large space for the fire. Then he laid the corpse flat on its back on the logs of wood and whisked open the cloth off its face.

Gold almost a quarter of a rupee in weight. Jagu noticed how the nose stud shimmered on the corpse in the lantern light.

The clouds had given way to a softening of the moonlight. On the alabaster face of the corpse was a blur of shadows from the light.

Jagu's companions observed, 'Get the work over with, fast! If the police are here, we've had it.'

Jagu stretched out his hand to rip the stud off. He could make out how the pale face of the young daughter-in-law appeared like a half-wilted lily in the moonlight. Her face was covered on all sides by a jungle of dark masses of hair, just as dense shadows of dark cloud lodge behind the moon in the sky.

The loneliness of wilting blossoms swam over the face of the woman on the pyre. Waves of moonlight swept over her dishevelled hair, broke down and rolled away.

Jagu withdrew his hand.

He looked up at the ashen moon in the sky.

So many times Jagu had cremated corpses as this one, but he had never faced such a storm in his heart. His hands couldn't overcome the aversion he felt to pull apart the stud from such an innocently exquisite face. The stud shone bright on the girl's nose, a thing of beauty in his eyes. There was so much to think about and so many things about her that kept playing on his mind.

In a few more days, had she lived, she'd have become a mother! And maybe gone on to other greater things, but she couldn't any more. Who was to blame?

On the naked breast of a lonely burning ground, in the middle of an endless ocean of mottled moonlight, lay a half-blossomed woman, all alone. How lonesome! Jagu Tiadi was unable to take his eyes off her. In his own rural, unlettered tongue, Jagu ruminated: *Truly how alone was she! Not just as she lay there, but she had been friendless and forlorn throughout her life! She had sought a change from her day-to-day cloistered existence, trying for a different life and had come to such a fate!* Life's many hungers were visible to Jagu in her pale supine face.

Jagu's companions were getting irritated at his seeming delay. A few of them threatened him, saying, 'Delay more, and we'll dump the corpse here and leave! Who'll be responsible if the police come? Take your stud soon or else we'll set fire to the corpse. A little while ago, you were dying for her nose stud. Why don't your hands move now?'

Jagu Tiadi's dreaming snapped. He felt quite ashamed. Still then, he stifled his weakness and blurted out, 'How can I? Can I keep this corpse's nose stud in my home? She was with child. In sin.'

His friends pressed him. 'Then you won't have it? We're setting fire to the body.'

As though unconcerned, Jagu Tiadi answered, 'Yes. Do set fire to the corpse. Burn it all thoroughly to ash!'

The flames leapt high. In a trice, the tongues of fire would lick the pyre clean. The fair fleshy body of the girl soon turned a sullen black in the heat; blisters began to form and layers of skin were shredded away.

Stunned, Jagu Tiadi kept staring unflinchingly at the burning body.

On a faraway kochila tree, owls, vultures and night birds crowded together. At that moment from somewhere beyond the distant paddy fields, floated in the cold-blooded wail of a male jackal.

Filth, darkness, bone, ashes, embers. A rotting smell surfaced from the pyre and scattered in the wind. Someone said, 'You've done the right thing, Jagu, by not removing the jewellery of that loose woman. It would have been inauspicious. What agony she must have gone through when she ended her life? And when she wanted to kill her own living child, wasn't it right that she killed herself? Where has dharma gone?'

Somewhat annoyed, Jagu kept on looking into the burning ash. He said roughly, 'That's enough! Don't judge others. Can one ever truly understand another?'

* * *

Rajkishore Patnaik (1917–97)

'Grass'

(Translated 'Ghasa' from the Odia by Manu Dash)

It was the third day after Kumar Purnima.[xlvi]

Around two *ghadi*, or 8 p.m., I was walking back alone from the Mangalabag outpost in Cuttack. There was hardly anyone to be seen on the road except the occasional pedestrian or cyclist.

After covering some distance, I noticed a boy waiting at a road crossing. Around 3 feet in height, he wore a dusty vest and a short dhoti. As soon as I passed the crossing, he started following me.

As he walked, his hands swung up and down continuously, like people walk during winter mornings to beat the cold.

The legs of the boy were puny and he had to walk briskly to keep up with me.

Like a person in the habit of consuming titbits every now and then, I could not resist chatting with him. I enquired, 'Where are you going, boy?'

I am going towards Nima Sahi,' he responded.

Gathering courage, he continued with a slightly raised voice, 'Would you also go up to Nima Sahi?'

He seemed to be rather desperate.

I asked, 'Are you scared?'

He seemed startled and came closer to me. 'Yeah, I feel scared.'

xlvi The full moon night in the months of October–November.

His small eyes were writ large with fear. I held out my hand to provide some succour and comfort him.

He instantly caught hold of my outstretched hand, and I could see that he was nervous.

To boost his courage, I asked him, 'You belong to Cuttack, yet you are so scared?'

Unnerved, he answered, 'You don't know, sir. We have just left behind the Muslim cemetery. There is someone there who often pelts stones at people.'

Patting him on the back, I said, 'Nothing like that. I use this road frequently but there never has been any untoward incident.'

He protested and replied, 'No, sir, he targets children only. Once, while I was passing through this road and a stone hit my leg. Since then, I don't walk alone on this road. I cross that cemetery with the help of passersby.'

I felt it wasn't possible to uproot the fear ingrained in him. Fear had made a firm citadel in his heart the way superstition mingles in the blood of the people.

Patting his back, I asked, 'What's your name?'

'I am Linga,' he said. 'You must know my father, Jogi Moharana?'

I was really surprised.

'My father is an expert in singing the *chhanda*[xlvii]. He does not go for any work; always busy in practicing the songs. Bana Pahilman, the wrestler, invites him to his home. No one can surpass my father in singing chhanda; he has brought home many cups as accolades also.'

I asked him, 'Arre, how much does your father earn in a day?'

'Earn? He hasn't worked for six months,' said Linga. 'I have been earning seven paisa per day for a fortnight. The walls of our house have caved in because we failed to thatch the roof this year.'

[xlvii] Rhythmical songs.

I found his behaviour oddly poetic.

I thought to myself that no poet or artist should keep their talent hidden. I could also understand that this poor family had been torn by the whims of Jogi Moharana.

I asked him, 'Why have you hoarded those cups and shields at home? Why don't you sell those?'

Linga answered, 'Bana Pahilman would reprimand us! After all, that's the only treasure we have! Those are made of silver. We don't know how much price those would fetch.'

Engrossed in the theme, he continued, 'We have kept those things now in our *petara*.[xlviii] They were good when kept out of the cane basket, but termites attacked its wooden stand. My father has replaced them recently with new stands.'

His conversation displayed his poverty and simplicity.

I asked him, 'When did you have food today?'

'I had torani[xlix] this morning and nothing else the whole day. Let me go home and find out if there is anything left to eat!'

He had not eaten anything throughout the day and wasn't sure if there would be any food in that unthatched house. Yet he was full of life.

I was almost a foot taller than him. While walking, he had crossed his hands on his chest to beat the cold.

I felt guilty as I walked beside him fully wrapped and wearing a warm *Panjabi*.[l]

This world seems so puny in our yearning and greed, but we have no peace in our mind. Whereas a boy with hardly any clothes was returning home with seven paisa after toiling for eight hours without eating any food to feed his parents.

There was a half-burnt cigarette between my fingers. I tossed it away.

[xlviii] Cane basket.

[xlix] Rice water.

[l] A long shirt.

How mean and petty are our college educated babudom in front of this poor boy's heart! I reached into my rear pocket; there were nine paisa and a rupee.

At first, I thought of giving him a rupee, but my heart did not agree. Out of the nine paisa, I took out an *anna,* four paisa, and gave them to him saying, 'Take it and eat some puffed rice.'

He took it but gave me a skeptical look.

Nima Sahi was only a stone's throw away. The Muslim cemetery had already been left behind. The road was now quite crowded. Linga's fear disappeared. He was conversing and walking along with me.

I thought of his father not going for any work for the sake of pursuing his art.

On the other hand, our college-going babus burn their blood for the purpose of reading good books.

I craved to meet Jogi Maharana, but his son was reluctant to take me. He thought that maybe I would reveal to his father that I had given him four paisa and his father would snatch that money from him.

He tried to put me off by saying, 'Our home is quite far from this street; my father will not be home now. I won't go home right now.'

Giving up, I gave Linga five paisa again and told him to give it to his father.

He stared at me in disbelief. Someone might have watched him take the money. I could easily grasp that he would not give the money to his father.

His house was much nearer now. He suddenly said to me, 'Babu, our house is located here on this street.'

And saying so, he suddenly shouted, 'O Haria!' and ran away.

I walked all alone.

A cow was busy grazing on a patch of grass. So many times, this tender grass had been consumed by the cows, but always grew back again. It could not be destroyed though it was on the roadside and had come into contact with so many people and cattle.

Then why would this little boy be defeated by poverty? He has been walking on the path of hope. That should not come as a surprise.

All these thoughts were tangled in my mind. Could it happen the same way with humans as it happened with the grass?

* * *

Surendra Mohanty (1922–90)

'Nayanpur Express'

(Translated 'Nayanpur Express' from the Odia by Bikram K. Das)

The gathering darkness of approaching clouds had gripped the sky like some prehistoric monster. Even the usual swarm of stray dogs was not to be seen on the road leading to the station—each one had sought shelter in a different place. Vivid flashes of lightning streaked across the sky like gigantic serpents' tongues.

Narendra narrowly escaped banging his head against a telegraph pole at the side of the road. He had strayed off the road in the darkness.

Ohh! Half the distance still to be covered. The rain again, in drops as large as plums, Narendra thought.

The time is 12.45 on his watch. The No. 5-down Express is due at 2.57 am. Another three hours to go. Where might the train have reached by this time? Madhupur? Sankrail? Kamarghati? His stride grew longer in his excitement.

It was too early for him to return to the 'cell'. This would be a memorable night among the countless nights that he had spent on the road. The rain had increased in intensity and the storm with it. There was an ongoing duet between the rain and the wind, with the thunder providing the accompaniment. The battle cry of an enfeebled, battered and limping society trying to revolt.

Once again, the lightning. If he turned left into the narrow lane, he would enter the labour colony. Those working in the 2'o clock shift, sensing the approaching storm, had left for the mill some time ago. *Ish*! The cigarettes in his chest-pocket had gotten soaked in the rain and turned to mud long ago. What nonsense!

He could hear the sound of an approaching train in the distance. Narendra was shocked. A train? Up or Down? Up, surely. It was just beginning to cross the bridge across the Maina river. Must be a goods train. There were no passenger trains scheduled at this time. The 5-down would come only at 2.57—The Nayanpur Express.

A new Canadian locomotive, capable of 80 miles per hour, was rushing across the dark world like an iron monster.

His feet came to a halt. The milestone by the side of the railway track indicated 472 miles from Howrah and then the Megha bridge.

Narendra felt his head reeling. He couldn't think of what would follow. Agonized screams in female voices, infants howling, old men crying aloud, the death-agonies of old women and the laughter of death.

The early morning editions of newspapers would print in large letters: 'Nayanpur Express Meets Fatal Accident'

This is murder. The murder of women. Children. Yes, what else but murder! An old man could be dozing on his bench, wrapped in his blanket. Eyes deep in sleep would still be lost in dreams of tomorrow's rainbow-coloured headlines: 'A third-class bogey was telescoped into an inter-class bogey.' An eyewitness account by our special correspondent.'

Murder—cruel, beastly, merciless. However, what would you find if you turned over the pages of history? The more cruel the murder, the louder would be the anthems of victory! Page after page of triumphant shouting. Alexander, Ashok, Kharavel, Shivaji, Napoleon, Hitler . . .

A dim, smoky lantern was burning away feebly in a labourer's hut . . . Someone was sitting at the door of the hut with a foul-smelling *pinka*[li] between his lips. The tip of the pinka was smouldering away. Who was it? Waiting for whom?

'Who is it?' Narendra called out.

'It's me, Babu,' the man replied in the Chhattisgarhi language. Kamala's mother is due to return from the mill in half an hour. I don't how she'll manage in this storm. I am waiting for her.'

Narendra had been soaked all over in the rain. He got off the muddy road and entered the hut. 'Does Bindia have some bidis stored somewhere?' he asked.

Bindia had felt dismayed when she saw Narendra at such a time and in such a condition. But she was familiar with the habits of these *babus*. Nothing mattered to them—neither day nor night, neither wind nor rain. Saying nothing, she reached into a corner of the hut and found a few bidis, which she handed over to Narendra. The floor was damp. Bindia's two daughters, Kamala and Bimla, were huddled together under the sheet. The space previously occupied by Kamala's mother was vacant.

Narendra used the flame of the lantern to light a bidi. There must be a female passenger in the Nayanpur Express in some compartment or other with a small child. Her intended destination might have been Masudgarh. The Nayanpur Express must have arrived at 2.57. The child must be sleeping without a care in the world, in one corner of the berth. But sleep wouldn't come to his wife. She had pulled down the shutter of the window and was staring aimlessly into the dark. The Nayanpur Express was travelling at its usual speed of 80 miles an hour.

Her husband must be labouring away night and day, far away from his home. So that the world could go on. Would he have come to the station on this stormy night? Yes, surely!

[li] Rolled tobacco leaves.

He had written that he had found a rented shed with great difficulty. There was a tiny garden facing the shed. Sunu could play there in the morning and evening. It would be nice if he could plant a few flowers there, as well; tiny flowering plants to tie her hair with, if not flowers. The garden facing the temple in Nayanpur was alive with flowers. Here comes the Megha bridge! The passengers who had been unable to make any arrangements to snatch a little sleep, were looking out of the window with curiosity at the Megha bridge. Masudgarh was the next station. Many passengers got off there. All the compartments were suddenly bustling with activity. The woman passenger must be trying to wake up her sleeping child. Wake up Sunu—your father has come!

Next? Next was the milepost by the track with the inscription '472 miles.'

The fish plates[lii] had been removed. The Nayanpur Express . . . Narendra rushed out of the hut like a storm!

In the middle of the basti was a shed with the tin roof. This was the 'cell'.

Narendra shook the chain that fastened the door with his fingers. Shymal had gone to sleep without fastening the door. The rain had not lessened in intensity. The wind was still howling fiercely. Narendra's throat felt dry with thirst. He picked up the pitcher of water from a corner of the hut. There was no water in it. Furiously, Narendra hurled the pitcher down and threw the fragments out of the window.

Narendra had been wandering aimlessly from one spot to another for the last seven days, ever since he had been assigned the responsibility for removing the fish plates from the milepost of the Megha bridge bearing the inscription '472'. Today was the day when he was returning with his responsibility discharged. But what a brute Shymal was! He

[lii] The function of fish plates is to hold the two rails together in horizontal as well as in vertical planes.

hadn't kept even a drop of water in the pitcher! The rascal! Narendra suddenly remembered his own wife. He had driven the poor woman out one day!

'Manju,' he had said, 'what I want is a co-worker, not a companion for the night.' She had sobbed through her tears. 'Pardon me but I cannot do these things! My chest quakes when I see your pistol, bullets and the bombs.'

Narendra had replied roughly, 'Your treachery against the revolution that is coming is more than I can tolerate. You have to join the underground movement. Otherwise, you have no place here.'

What followed was much condemnation, all of which Manju tolerated quietly, being as tolerant as the earth. Finally, Narendra had turned her out.

That day, Narendra had returned home just before dawn, having spent the night somewhere. Manju had taken him to task for not maintaining a regular routine and neglecting his health. He had treated her in a barbaric manner. He felt ashamed now when he remembered his uncivil behavior. Thereafter, Manju had returned to her father's house without raising any objections. Narendra's father-in-law was a goods clerk in the Nayanpur goods yard. It was from Nayanpur some months later that Narendra had got news of his daughter's birth. But these weaknesses never found a place in his life. He had forgotten Manju long ago. But on some days, he couldn't help but remember her gentle, kind nature, and her willingness to serve. His mind would grow unnaturally soft. He wished he could be relieved of this bondage and get lost in some unknown corner of this vast earth. He had made several attempts to get over his past barbarity and written several letters, feeling repentant for all the mishaps he had been responsible for, and to return to Manju. But this had come as an insult to his manhood and self-respect.

Shymal got up abruptly. He asked the silent Narendra, 'When did you get back?'

Narendra replied in a calm voice, 'I removed six fish plates from Milepost no. 472 of the Megha bridge and threw them into the river. The five-down Masudgarh Express is supposed to arrive at Masudgarh at 2.57 a.m.'

Making a jubilant sound, Shymal shouted, 'The neta is supposed to arrive by that train today. He will address a meeting of labourers tomorrow. The neta will be able to understand now how terrible the punishment for conspiring against the revolution is. Do you know, Narendra, how much blood and sweat I have poured into the moulding of this workers' union? But the agents of the mill-owners and capitalists were determined to sabotage our revolution. They were trying to set up a parallel organization here. Well done, Narendra! Bravo!

Tired, Narendra lay helplessly on the canvas bed in his wet clothes. The timepiece on the shelf overhead sounded its alarm: 2.30 a.m.

Another twenty-seven minutes to go.

There was no light in Bindia's hut. Kamala's mother might have returned.

Narendra re-entered the 'cell'.

2.45. Another twelve minutes to go.

Shymal said, 'Narendra, we'll have to organize a meeting of workers on a large scale tomorrow. What do you say?'

2.47. Ten minutes more.

Narendra collapsed on to the canvas bed, with his face down. The Nayanpur Express was rushing through his head at 80 miles an hour. Heartless, ruthless and cruel.

* * *

Akhil Mohan Patnaik (1927–87)

'Flowers of Ficus'

(Translated 'Dimiri Phula' from the Odia by Bikram K. Das)

The woman was convinced that I was Sanjay and nothing I said could make her change her mind.

But let me tell you the story from the beginning.

I was a post-graduate student at Allahabad University, visiting Gauhati on a holiday during the Puja vacation. I found myself in what appeared to be one of the posher localities in the city. What supported this conclusion was the fact that all the newly built houses, standing in neat rows on both sides of the street, looked equally impressive. They seemed to have stepped out of a catalogue of modern architectural design and taken up positions along both sides of the street. They provided evidence of expensive and modern tastes, but the unvarying uniformity of their design was quite fatiguing. The sense of liberation which the word 'home' should provide was missing. I could never have felt relaxed if I had to live in such a grand neighbourhood!

But this story is not about houses. Let me return to the main theme.

I had found a room in a hotel in that locality and was about to return to my room. It was almost evening and I walked with measured steps.

Suddenly, a mass of black clouds appeared in a corner of the sky to the north and almost simultaneously, a strong wind began to blow. Huge drops of rain came down, making me feel that it would be difficult for me to reach my room.

I decided to make a dash for the nearest house on my side of the street. Normally, I would have hesitated to try to enter an unknown house, out of fear of the armed guards or fierce Alsatian dogs protecting the property, but that fear was forgotten now. I pushed the gates open and ran up the steps to the front verandah in order to avoid getting soaked in the rain, feeling a sense of relief.

The verandah had been decorated in an attractive manner. The wide mosaic corridors, thickly carpeted, were furnished with luxurious chairs of woven cane. On the wall, just beneath the nameplate of polished teak, hung a letterbox. Across the screen of wire netting, some flowering creepers of radha-tamal hung down into the verandah. Rare varieties of cacti had been planted in vases made of expensive porcelain. Outside the house, the dance of the raindrops continued uninterrupted. Occasionally, there was a momentary flash of lightning which split the sky wide open. To my surpise, the large house seemed to be completely unoccupied. One might have expected to hear the sound of a radio being played or at least the tinkling of glass vessels being shaken by the wind. Someone inside the house should have shown some alacrity and closed the doors and windows to shut out the wind and rain, but there were no sounds or movements at all. The gossamer-thin curtains hanging over the doors fluttered in the wind, as though in joy. Through the doors, one could see the pages of illustrated magazines and newspapers fluttering wildly about the room, carried aloft by the wind. Anyone listening to the sounds would think there were large flocks of pigeons flying about the room, trying in vain to escape through the windows.

The rain continued to splash and dance, producing a medley of sounds. They reminded me of one of the melodies that could be heard from a dance hall during a performance of rock-and-roll music. In the distance, one could see strings of raindrops trickling down to join the swiftly flowing stream that was gushing down the street. From time-to-time droplets of rain stood out against the flashes of lightning, only to shiver into powdery fragments the next moment.

After a few minutes, a large old limousine entered through the open gates and came to a halt inside the portico. The car's bright headlamps continued to glow even after the engine had been switched off. The light, reflected against my body, seemed to pierce every atom of my being. I felt like the son of the *katual*[liii] in the stories which I had heard as a child, who had lost his way in the jungle and while looking for a place where he could find safety, had wandered into the demon's den.

The car's headlamps were extinguished and as the darkness grew around me, I tried to gather up into the recesses of my consciousness the confused picture that was beginning to form itself in that brief medley of light and darkness.

From inside the car came the excited sound of a woman's voice: 'Arre, Sanjay, is that you?' She alighted from the car and as she led me into the soft light outside the house, I saw her for the first time.

She seemed to be in her forties—though she had spared no effort to preserve her looks, there could be no disguising the effects of time. We looked at each other in the dim light but made no attempt to say anything. But how could I tell her, in just the opening moments of our meeting, that she had erred in calling me 'Sanjay'? The thought continued to agitate my mind, however. Just then, without giving me time to collect my wits, she began: 'You haven't changed a bit, Sanjay—you look exactly as you did earlier!' Then, calling out to her cook or valet, she ordered coffee to be brought. 'You see, Sanjay, I remember well that you don't drink tea! Parents remember

[liii] Kotwal/policeman.

every detail of their children's likes and dislikes. But let us see whether you still remember how many spoonfuls of sugar I like in my tea?'

I preferred not to reply rather than come up with a wrong answer. Within the few intervening moments, the lady's eyes had taken on a distant and wistful look of sadness. Leaning back slightly against the back of her couch she said, 'Sanjay, I know very well that, at your age, it is not natural for people to try to keep the memories of ancient people like us alive. But, can anyone defend what Manju is doing? After all, what earth-shaking research could she be carrying out? Couldn't she have found the time even once in these last four or five years to come and visit us? *You've* managed to come, haven't you? Her father told me he had sent the plane tickets to her so she could come early. The vacation is about to end, but there is no sign of her yet!

I was listening to her mutely. The puzzle was becoming more and more complex. I found myself trapped. There could be no escape for me unless the rain stopped.

The lady continued her story. 'Manju knows perfectly well that she is scheduled to leave for England this December. Her father has made all the arrangements. Could anyone tell me when we would be meeting next? How pleasant your childhood days were, when both you and Manju were here together in this house! Is it right to let such distance develop between your parents and you just because you are being educated somewhere far away?'

The lady's tone of voice as well as the expression in her eyes hardened as she said, 'Sanju, I could have stopped her allowances and compelled her to return at any moment I chose, but you can't do something like that when you are a mother, can you?'

The rain had receded slightly. One could hear the sound of the large drops of water clinging to the edges of the cornice falling into the garden below. I was announcing my intention of leaving by looking at my watch repeatedly and told her that it was necessary for me to go as I had an appointment with a friend. When the lady asked me for my address, I told her that I was staying in Room No. 14 in the Tea View Hotel just round the corner. She was probably going to say something more but by then, I had already reached the bottom of the steps.

She made another attempt to stop me. 'No, Sanjay,' she said, 'you can't possibly walk home through this heavy rain! Get into the car. My chauffeur will drop you at the hotel. That will also give him a chance to see where you are staying!'

I had no option but to sit in the car. While I was sitting there, I found it to be a real struggle to contain my curiosity about the lady and her family.

The next morning, the waiter in the hotel had barely come and placed the tray containing my cup of tea on the table next to the bed when I heard a knock on my door. I heard a man's voice ask, 'May I come in?' I hurriedly straightened my bed-clothes. 'Please come in,' I said.

An elderly gentleman walked into the room. One look at him was enough to tell me that his age had been advanced prematurely by several years from the impact of some great sorrow. His dhoti, panjabi and the glistening walking stick in his hand gave clear indication of a long tradition of refinement. The gentleman removed the spectacles he was wearing, wiped the lenses clean with his handkerchief, and made his walking stick lean against the chair before he had another look at me—a long one.

I gestured to him to be seated.

While sitting down, he said, 'I felt quite sure my wife was making a huge mistake—yes, the house where you took shelter from the rain last night is my house and the lady you met is my wife. She practically compelled me to come here this morning. She is quite positive that you are Sanjay.'

I said in an apologetic tone, 'Sir, my name is Ashok. I am truly embarrassed about what happened last evening. But I found so much affection in your wife's behaviour that I found it quite impossible for me to admit that I wasn't Sanjay.'

The gentleman said, 'Yes, I admit there are surprising resemblances between you and Sanjay. A close look at you might reveal that. But that's no reason for you to apologize or to feel embarrassed. Ashok, this is a cruel joke being played on my wife and me by destiny. The marriage of my daughter Manjushree had almost been finalized with Sanjay, but for some reason, it could not happen.'

His voice trembled and he seemed to be staring fixedly at some point in the distance.

I prepared a cup of tea and offered it to the gentleman. Absent-mindedly, he took the cup of tea close to his lips, and said, 'There is no point in my telling you all this! But it was after a very long time that I found my wife in a truly happy frame of mind yesterday. When she looked at you yesterday, she felt quite certain that her only dream was about to come true. I did not want to shatter that dream. If she can spend the rest of her life happily, thanks to an innocent error that she might have made, what could be better?'

The gentleman was quiet again. He seemed to be speaking inaudibly to himself. While cleaning the lenses of his spectacles again, he said, 'You are like my son in many ways, and I shall call you Ashok—no, I have made a mistake—Sanjay! The last thing I want is to make some reckless error that would result in my wife's happy illusion being broken!'

'Sanjay, please listen to me. From this day on, your only introduction, as far as this family is concerned, will be that of Sanjay. And I will have to beg you to grant me something. From time to time, you will *have* to pay us a visit here. I have never been in any financial difficulties, and there are none now. But any difficulties that might arise will have to be tackled by you. Only you could do it.'

The pathos in his voice was indescribable.

'Give me a promise, Sanjay. Promise me that whatever difficulties you might have to face, you will come here from time to time and play Sanjay's role.'

'I give you my promise. You can rest assured.'

An enormous weight seemed to have been lifted off the gentleman's chest.

'Sanjay, there is something else. I hear you are going to Delhi by this evening's flight. My wife wishes to send a package for Manju. She and I will meet you at the airport this evening. Well, I'll waste no more of your time. Let me be off!'

I escorted him to his car and returned to my room in the hotel.

* * *

At the airport lounge that evening, I was looking around and trying to spot the mysterious couple. Suddenly, I heard someone say, 'Hello, Sanjay!' Startled, I turned around. A light hand was resting on my shoulder. The lady I had met the night before was standing by his side. She seemed the very image of feminine affection and tenderness.

She put an elegantly packed package into my hands and said, 'This is for Manju, Sanjay. Hope you don't mind the trouble I am giving you!' Only two large letters, in Bengali script, had been inscribed on the package: Man-ju.

There was an announcement then, asking the passengers to board the flight.

I hurriedly called the elderly gentleman aside and whispered softly: 'Pardon me, sir, but there is no address written on the package. I don't know her address. It would help if you could give me her address.'

I have never seen human eyes looking so inert and lifeless—like eyes made of glass. The next moment, there was a loud burst of laughter from him. He brought his head closer to my ears and whispered, 'I don't know Manju's address either. No one does. One year ago, my wife suffered a stroke and lost her powers of reasoning completely, Manju was killed in a train accident. My wife has never been told of it. Manju was a student of third-year science then. Three years have passed since she began her research—today is when she was supposed to submit her report. Then she was supposed to go to England for another project—a more advanced one.

Another boarding call was given. The passengers were running up the aisle. My name was called out. I was last on the list. I climbed the last three steps with one big leap.

There was barely enough time for a last look at the line of those who had come to see us off. Someone was waving her hand. I turned around and entered the plane.

* * *

Santanu Kumar Acharya (b. 1933)

'Snake-Mobile'

(Translated 'Sarpa-Yaan' from the Odia by Bikarm K. Das)

On the same evening on which Commander Rakesh Sharma, India's first cosmonaut, completed the first leg of his voyage through space in the Soviet spaceship, Soyuz 11, Sadhu Mahanta, an inhabitant of Rasam Tola village in the subdivision of Karanjia, in Mayurbhanj District, Odisha, was headed towards the dense jungle, mounted on the back of a gigantic serpent.

After that first circuit of the earth, Commander Sharma went on an extended cosmic tour around the universe and each time his craft passed over the Indian subcontinent he sang out, in a voice quivering with patriotic pride, the anthem: '*saarey jahan se achcha, Hindustan hamara . . .*' Sadly, we have no record of where Sadhu Mahanta went, what he saw, which patriotic song inspired him, etc. However, when questioned about Sadhu's disappearance, his wife and several of her female relatives went round the village, shedding copious tears telling the villagers, 'The serpent came and went straight through the house. Mahanta got out his bed and seated himself on the serpent's back, like a man riding a horse, neither smiling nor weeping, and as we watched, the snake slithered away with Mahanta on his back, the same way he had come!'

Seven days passed.

Rakesh Sharma returned to earth. While his landing on earth was being flashed on the news, someone came to the village in Karanjia and reported: 'Sadhu Mahanta has been found lying unconscious outside the Shiva temple, otherwise known as the Sri Rasikeswar temple, at the far end of the village.' Everyone in the village, as well as in neighbouring villages, walked out of their homes to confirm if the report was correct. They saw Sadhu Mahanta lying on the ground in deep slumber in front of the temple. His breathing was normal and there was not a scratch on his body. Surprised beyond belief, the people looked around in wonder. Sadhu Mahanta had left the village on a serpent's back, but how had he returned? While trying to solve this puzzle, their eyes travelled beyond the temple walls. Clear traces were visible of someone having been dragged along the ground. Some stray shrubs and bushes had been crushed flat, as though under a heavy weight. Could there be a doubt in anyone's mind after this? The same serpent that had carried Mahanta away must have brought him back and deposited him in front of the temple.

For several weeks after this incident, the entire world was busy celebrating Rakesh Sharma's journey through space. He was the recipient of numerous titles, medals and prizes, and praised in glowing terms by India's president and prime minister. There were no such celebrations in Rasam Tola village after Sadhu Mahanta regained consciousness. No one thought it necessary—so much so, that reports of the incident did not reach even the subdivisional headquarters of Karanjia town, only 3 miles away from the village. In other words, the official circles took no notice of the incident at all. Even if the reports reached some people, they lacked the courage to give them prominence. This was because many such incidents, important as well as trivial, took place from time to time in this part of the world and were never heard of. If the outside world came to know of them, they would dismiss the reports as 'inspired by *handia*'[liv]. So, the higher officials, mindful of

[liv] Home-brewed liquor.

their prestige, preferred to remain uninvolved and the news of Sadhu Mahanta's serpent-ride remained unknown.

After Rakesh Sharma returned from his voyage around the cosmos, he never received a second chance for such a voyage.

But elsewhere, a most surprising thing happened—the serpent that had carried off Sadhu Mahanta was back! He made his appearance unexpectedly one day in Sadhu Mahanta's bedroom. Several hours before the serpent's return, Sadhu Mahanta had called his wife to his side and said 'I have a strange feeling inside. The same feeling I had on the day the serpent visited us for the first time. I think he is about to return!' When she heard this, Sadhu's wife got up and hurriedly bolted all the doors and windows. Panting frantically, she said to her husband, 'If that wretched snake comes back today, he will have to carry both of us on his back! I am not going to let him take one of us alone!'

Sadhu Mahanta felt reassured when he saw his wife in this aggressive mood. There were reasons for him to feel reassured. Ever since his first adventure with the snake, the people of his village, including his children and his parents-in-law, had developed a new respect for him. Their attitude towards him was one of fear and reverence, mixed with scepticism and envy. That is how ordinary people regard *babajis*[lv] who have extraordinary powers.

Sadhu Mahanta had been transformed into a sannyasi without anyone's knowledge. And he was no ordinary sannyasi either—the gods were sending him personal invitations through snake messengers! This was enough reason for fear, and envy. And for scepticism too. People were telling each other, 'Strange things are happening! Sadhu Mahanta is not known to be a holy man with extraordinary powers. He's just an ordinary man, like any of us. He eats, drinks, sleeps,

[lv] Holy men.

laughs, loses his temper, tills his land, is greedy for money like the rest of us, and doesn't mind cheating people, given the opportunity. Which stupid god is sending snake messengers to fetch him?' Sadhu Mahanta heard the gossip but didn't feel disturbed at all. However, he did say to himself: 'These stupid people understand nothing! The gods who send snake messengers to earth—are they like the ministers of today that they should send motor-cars or horse carriages to fetch their touts and agents from the earth below? The world that I was taken to is unique—the only one of its kind! I didn't see any gods seated on thrones, and those snakes were unusual too! Did they ever give us a hint—where they were from, who had sent them, where did they take us, etc.?'

Nevertheless, Sadhu Mahanta was in a thoughtful mood for some days. What if the snake did not return? What would the villagers think? They might dismiss the whole thing as a dream. Dreams are meant to be dreamt by people but this dream was different—it had been seen by a lot of people at the same time. Does that make a difference? Don't such things happen every day? Imagine, everyone in the house is asleep and dreaming. And something unusual happens just at this time! What if everyone were to see the same dream instead of their private dream? When the sleepers got up in the morning and narrated their dreams to each other, they would all turn out to be the same! This might seem to be a wonder, but only for a limited time. Then they would all get used to such unusual happenings! If someone made an attempt to remind others of the uncommon events that had taken place, the others would say, 'What's so special about that?' If things are to be regarded as uncommon, they must happen again and again and again.

For these reasons, Sadhu Mahanta had been apprehensive that the unusual experience might not be repeated. But if the snake had appeared twice, without due reason, why couldn't it appear again?

Just then, Sadhu Mahanta heard a scraping sound, like something crawling or creeping. He jumped up, startled. His wife was clinging to him in a tight embrace. He whispered in her ear 'Is he back? It seems he called out to us but we couldn't hear! He says he'll break the door down if we don't open it. Let go of me! Open the doors and windows! Let me go!'

Which wife would have released her husband from her grip after hearing such dreadful things? Sadhu Mahanta's wife gripped her husband with double the strength. One must not forget that she was the daughter of Mahanta parents as well as the wife of a mahanta husband. It is said that all mahantas are well-versed in tantra—the cult of secret rituals that may have originated with the forest tribes of central India. In addition, mahantas have mastered the unseen world that can be conjured up through chants and are extremely hard-working. It is said that 'If you throw a piece of rock at a mahanta, the barren rock will come back to you as a piece of fertile earth.' Mahantas are the earthworms of the earth. The inside of the earth is seething with activity where there are mahantas in abundance. For this reason, they are known as 'krumi-kshatriyas'—members of the Kshatriya tribe who perform the role of earthworms. Their language is known as 'kuru-mali'. Kuru-mali women are known to be as tough and fearless as they are soft and sweet-tempered. It was no surprise at all that Sadhu Mahanta's wife had been able to cast a spell over him that made him powerless to move. She warned him, 'If the snake is able to make its way into this house even with the doors bolted, then that would show that this is no snake but a ghost. Let me see which ghost can carry you away while I am here to guard you.'

Sadhu Mahanta was trapped in doubt. Suddenly, his wife's reasoning seemed incontrovertible to him. He said to himself, 'What she says is true! If it was a mere snake, could it have entered this house? And it is not a snake of small size either—not a petty cobra or *tampa* [viper]. This snake is the grand-daddy of the world's biggest python! How could such a snake gain entry into this house in the first place, with the doors and windows closed? No, this is no snake! It could be a god, a ghost or some other such supernatural creature. Gods and ghosts are regular visitors in this part of the jungle. Each house in this village is haunted by a ghost. As for the gods, they come down to chat with the people every other day. If this snake turns out to be just another ordinary god or ghost, there will be absolutely no benefit in our trying to cultivate a friendship with him.'

While Sadhu Mahanta was still debating the best course of action, the door flew open with a loud clang. Or was it ripped off its hinges—who knows? Both husband and wife saw that the door-frame had collapsed, and like an ocean tide sweeping all barriers aside, through the open door, entered an enormous snake! Which human being could have retained his senses and kept his eyes open after seeing such a scene? But the mahantas are no cowards. They have been fighting battles since the beginning of time, which has ensured their survival as true Kshatriyas. You will find a mahanta in the distant tea gardens of Assam, the plantations of the north-east or in the trackless jungles of Bihar, chanting their timeless ballads. You need more than strong arms to combat the unknown dangers of the forest—you need great strength of mind, of which there is no dearth in any mahanta man, woman or child.

Sadhu Mahanta's wife had been able to, thus far, keep her husband tightly bound in her arms and prevent him from going out to face the serpent waiting outside their door. But suddenly, she released him and leapt from the bed on to the floor. A large part of the gigantic serpent's body was already inside the room and her agile leap placed her directly on the serpent's back. A few days earlier, she had seen her husband leap from the bed on to the serpent's back—he had parted his two legs like an athlete and gripped the serpent's back between his legs. She had remembered the manoeuvre and was able to imitate it perfectly. And immediately, the serpent twisted his body around in a 180-degree loop. What was surprising was that this time, he had not come for Sadhu Mahanta but for his wife. As soon as she was seated on his back, the serpent crept out through the open door into the courtyard and from there, into the jungle. Sadhu Mahanta sat on the bed, staring ahead.

The next morning, Sadhu Mahanta made his appearance at the village square. People listened to his story patiently, but no one was in a hurry to believe what he told them. The older villagers said, 'We can tell you what it is that you have seen—ghosts playing games to amuse themselves! Some ghosts can disguise themselves as snakes; what's surprising about that? There are ghosts who will steal a man away from his home while he is sleeping! There was a *bagalia*[lvi] in the village—the ghosts stole him from the jungle as he slept and kept him prisoner for fourteen days. People searched for him everywhere, even on the banks of the village pond, but couldn't find him. Finally, the lad appeared on his own one afternoon. When asked by the people, "Where were you?", the bagalia narrated a long story of how the ghosts had kidnapped him and carried him away, and how they had made him invisible so that he could be sitting next to you, seeing you clearly and able to hear every word you said, but you wouldn't be able to see him or hear him! All these are wonders which ghosts can perform. Sadhu, it was this kind of ghost that carried you away as well as your wife. There's no snake, Sadhu—it's all done by ghosts!'

Sadhu could not believe everything that the people of the tribe told him about ghosts but neither could he dismiss everything. As a child, he had heard stories in his tribe of the

---

[lvi] Cowherd.

magical deeds which ghosts could perform. With the recent experiences he had gone through, he was convinced that ghosts were responsible for his wife's disappearance as well. Of all these experiences, however, one stood out prominently. As soon as Sadhu had taken his seat on the serpent's back, his entire weight seemed to disappear and he felt as if he was floating in space. And after he had experienced this loss of weight, he had another strange sensation—he could *see* a new world which had been invisible to him before. This invisible world contained everything that you could find in the *visible* world (trees, rivers, animals and birds), but only one thing seemed to be missing—human beings! Sadhu had forgotten that he was human himself! But his experience ended as abruptly as it had begun—he found himself lying in front of the Sri Rasikeswar temple. It was then that he remembered who he was.

These varied experiences of Sadhu slowly made him feel convinced that somewhere in the cosmos, there must be a place or a country (call it what you like) where an entire creation had already been brought into existence, but human beings had not been created yet. The creator had thought of a plan to save himself some unnecessary labour. Instead of creating a totally new species of human beings to match the new patterns of creation which He had already brought into existence, He had hit upon the idea of 'importing' some existing specimens out of the species which He had already completed. These would be the 'seeds' that He would spread and propagate across the new universe that He was engaged in creating. And in that list of 'seed human beings', two names which had been included, we know not how, were those of Sadhu Mahanta and his wife, both of Rasam Tola, Karanjia.

A new universe, new creation, new earth—call it what you will; where one seemed to be invited to become the first inhabitants—the first pair of human beings from the Mahanta species, Sadhu and his wife, who had been found fully fit to discharge that responsibility. Maybe it was to spread this piece of information that the serpent had dropped Sadhu's wife at the old 'landing ground', the Sri Rasikeswar temple outside the village. When they heard the news, the inhabitants of the village dashed to the temple. By this time, Sadhu's wife was in such a deep sleep that she seemed to be unconscious. Sadhu pushed his way through the thick crowd and reached his wife's side. He sat down on the ground, lifted his wife's head and placed it on his lap. Then he said, 'This time he has gone back. But the next time we'll go out together.'

It took Sadhu's wife some time to return to consciousness. But when she finally did come back to her senses, they were convinced she was someone else entirely; a stranger that the serpent had brought back. When she called out Sadhu's name while unconscious, the alarmed women of Rasam Tola shouted that a ghost had entered the body of Jui.

It was obvious that the criticism of Sadhu Mahanta's wife would continue among the women for quite some time. Jui Mahanta had always called her husband by name and often exhibited traits of masculine behaviour, which the men in the village found shocking.

Meanwhile, Jui had caused another serious worry for her husband. After her experience in riding serpents, her behaviour towards her husband was no longer the same. She had not only started to treat herself as his equal, the kind of behaviour she had begun to manifest towards him could be labeled dominating. 'My place is far above yours; it is only out of kindness that I am holding your hand.'

Sadhu's masculine pride had been gravely injured, but he was not an arrogant man and did not feel resentful of the change in his wife's behaviour. He also made no accusations. Sadhu's problem was that the serpent had not reappeared for a long time. As a result, he was not able to return as soon as he would like with his wife to the new planet or satellite that had been specially created for them. On the other hand, Jui had been creating problems for him too. He had attempted repeatedly to discuss the problem with her, but each attempt had been futile.

'No, brother,' she told him. 'You and I no longer share the relationship we had. You go your way and I'll go mine.'

'Who will look after you if you go alone?' he would ask her. 'Won't you feel afraid?' When Sadhu made any attempt to reassert his proprietorship, the reply came: 'Fear? What fear? You saw with your own eyes, didn't you? I travelled on the snake's back to the same place where you had been? Did you see any signs of fear there? Did you and I know there was such a place in the universe?'

'Look, all that is the generosity of the Sarparaj—the Snake King!' he said. Sadhu's eyes went into a dreamlike state as memories of the snake kingdom returned. But if they did return there, Jui would no longer live with him as his wife—as of old. He said to her, 'Very well, I'll have to look for a new wife in case you don't wish to come with me. I have no intention of living alone.'

This statement did not have the desired effect on Jui. She told him, 'You can take another woman, but I shall not go looking for another man. Do you know what it is that I require?' She had been groping for the right word, but it had eluded her. Her struggles to find the word gave the clue to Sadhu. So it was he that supplied the word on her behalf: 'What is it that you want? Is it freedom?'

With a sweet smile she said, 'I envy you, Sadhu! How are you able to know exactly what's in my mind? How I would love to gain freedom!'

An angry Sadhu raised his voice, 'Oh, I see—you want freedom! That means, you wish to turn into a *dahani*[lvii] now! You've reached the right age to become a dahani!'

[lvii] A witch.

Jui burst into a laugh. Since she knew that Sadhu had acquired the ability to read her mind clearly and supply the right word when she needed it, her behavior grew mellow. In a sweet voice, she said, 'So far, we have had no dahanis in our village, Sadhu. I shall be the first! Do you know who the dahanis in this village are? What causes a woman to turn into a dahani?'

'The desire to feed on excreta!' Sadhu roared out.

'What's that you said?' Jui Mahanta produced a strange sound, which was neither a laugh nor a sob. And with that sound, an unknown power seemed to enter her body.

It was already midnight. In the summer moonlight, Jui leapt off the bed on which she had been lying, threw open the doors and disappeared outside.

At first, Sadhu was alarmed. Then he stepped out of the house through the open doors. Searching for Jui, he turned in the direction of the forest. He had gone only a little way when he saw a pack of wild bears digging up the earth around the roots of a mahua tree. Surprisingly, Jui had walked straight through the pack towards the forest, with no signs of fear. Earlier, she used to be afraid of the dark. Where had her new courage come from? Sadhu Mahanta went closer to the pack of bears only to realize they were a group of naked women, all of them with their heads bowed low towards the ground. Their long hair had come loose and was dragging along the ground. They were crawling on their knees, creeping . . . Some were walking on their hands, with their legs pointing at the sky. Exactly as dahanis are supposed to do in stories!

Sadhu Mahanta returned home without a sound. Lying on his bed, he waited for the morning and his wife to return.

Dawn came. The cuckoo's cry again. The doors, which had been closed lightly, opened. Sadhu Mahanta jumped back on to the bed. In his hand was an enormous stick.

'Well, Jui, you are back? Had your fill of excrement?'

'Be careful!' she said. 'Look straight ahead or you'll be burnt to ashes! I haven't gotten off the serpent's back yet!'

Jui removed the bunch of clothing that she had tucked beneath her armpit and put it down on the floor. She was looking for the woven border of her sari.

'Don't tell me lies,' Sadhu said. 'The serpent never came here! I know where you have been! Who were the bunch of women with you? There are no dahanis in our village—you are the first!'

'They are all from our village,' she said. 'You didn't know about it and neither did I. The snake has been going from door to door and taking women to that unknown kingdom.'

'Don't talk rubbish!' he said. 'I did not see a single person in that unknown kingdom. That snake was only testing whether any of us deserved to live there. He found me first, then you. We were dropped off at the temple. No one else has been seen.'

'We are not discussing who was dropped off at the temple and who was left at home. This is a question of, what is that word that you had used?'

She had wrapped her sari around her waist and the other end was hanging from her shoulder. Gripping it between her teeth, Jui Mahanta was putting on her blouse when Sadu Mahanta said, 'Freedom? You seem to have become very conscious of your freedom suddenly, Jui!' 'Why shouldn't I be?' she said. Her smile was like the dawn. Some unknown power seemed to have dropped off her person, leaving her brighter yet softer.

'You men have been free since your birth while a woman's freedom begins at forty. You show surprise when a dark corner of the house reflects the light of freedom after forty years. Why should the cuckoo sing in the middle of the night? But the dark night will return. I shall go out again.'

'Then you are not coming with me to that new world? A new creation awaits us there—the house is ready, waiting. Only inhabitants are needed. I had thought that you and I . . .'

'You can occupy that new creation!' Jui had the lilting laugh of a young girl. She said, 'People only visit that world; they cannot live there, you idiot! They must return! A new life begins after they have returned. My new life has already begun. I shall roam at will in the moonlight, in the dark phase of the moon, with the rain and thunder overhead. When I was a child, I heard the cuckoo call, I heard the *dahuka*[lviii] call and I wondered where they were. Could I join them? But I felt afraid then. I have no fear now. Praise be to that serpent which rid me of my fear! Very well, go to bed now. I'll prepare a pitha for your breakfast.

* * *

[lviii] Greater coucal.

Manoj Das (1934–2021)

'The bridge in the Moonlit Night'

(Translated 'Janha Ratira Setu' from the Odia by the author)

At times, the moon appeared so big and so close to Ashok's balcony that he thought he could say hello to it, and even reach it in a few bounds and shake hands with it. Since it evidently had no hands, he wondered if it would do to plant a kiss on it.

Relaxing in his easy chair Ashok loved to chitchat with the moon, particularly when it shone appreciably bright. He had just told it, 'I crossed eighty some years ago. What about you?'

There were moments in such moonlit nights when he could see young fairies of both sexes—he was surprised that they never aged—playing hide-and-seek amidst the milk-white clouds and atop the star-lit trees on the dusky horizon. He enjoyed their frolic to his heart's fill. He would doze off sometimes, but, intriguingly enough, wouldn't cease to see them. His only problem was that he could not say how much of those games he saw while awake and how much in sleep.

He was aware of the fact that this queer brand of forgetfulness had slowly begun to affect his other activities—even those purely physical in nature. For instance, that evening he had been delighted at the alluring colour of his cup of tea reflecting the sunset sky. He had had a warm sniff of its steam. But his happiness had driven him into one sudden snooze and he found himself sipping the tea in a dream. A little later, upon being reminded that his tea was going cold, he felt amazed to find that his satisfaction at having drunk the tea in a dream was not a whit less than the satisfaction he derived from actually drinking it.

But whatever the condition of his memory, he was proud of the fact that age had not dimmed his vision to any considerable extent. He attributed this to his feeding at his mother's breast till the age of five as he was her last child.

He had, however, suddenly developed doubts about his vision. The bridge on the small river two furlongs away was no longer visible to him. Every time he woke up, he rubbed his bleary eyes and tried to locate the old familiar bridge but failed. Was the moon playing a trick with him and withholding its beams? He glared at the moon. He then looked at the clump of bushy trees on the horizon where he was accustomed to seeing the silhouette of the Taj. He could see that all right. This was an annoying problem. He solved it by quickly dozing off.

The footfalls dragging up the stairs were enough to rouse him. They were Sudhir's—as familiar to him as the thwacks of his walking stick. Although younger than him by a decade, Sudhir gasped for breath while climbing up. But to Ashok, the ascent was hardly different from that of normal walking. What is more, he had lately begun to have the most unusual experiences while climbing the steps. For example, on the last occasion, he had fallen asleep midway up the stairs, although for no more than a minute. But that had been sufficient for his mind to lose track of events. He had just returned from a delightful drive in his son's car. But on reaching the balcony he had concluded that he had just got down to the portico. He had looked for the car and had succeeded in rapidly recovering the sense of perspective, and complimented himself on that score. To mistake ascent for descent and vice versa was no hallucination of any alarming proportion, he assured himself.

'Come on, Sudhir, shouldn't we go out for a stroll?' Ashok extended his hands for Sudhir to help him stand up.

'Where on earth to go? The bridge was the only place.' Sudhir lamented looking in the accustomed direction.

'Yes, yes, the bridge. Let us go there.'

'Look here, Ashok bhai, you must fight off this forgetfulness of yours—what they call amnesia. Where is the blessed bridge? Why do you think we haven't gone out for a stroll for a whole month? They have pulled down each brick of the dear old bridge. They plan to build a new one—a stylish one with a number of jetties on both sides for the taxpayers to enjoy their evenings around crotons and bougainvillaea, cracking nuts and sucking at ice-cream sticks. In no time, it will turn into a fish market, I'll bet.' Sudhir spoke with some anguish.

'Say that! The bridge is just not there! That explains why I cannot see it. No doubt my memory is fooling me. Your case is different. You are young!' commented Ashok.

'Not as young as you think. Ashok bhai, I will be eighty in a year or two.'

'Well, at your age I could . . .' Ashok's muttering grew feebler and he fell into his snooze halfway through his observation.

'You are under an exaggerated impression about your age, Ashok bhai. It is so common to read about centurions nowadays! What are you before them, a mere octogenarian? Ashok Bhai, are you falling asleep?'

'Oh no, Sudhir, I must confess though that I doze off from time to time. But that keeps me fresh. Should we make a move—towards the bridge?'

'Ashok Bhai, did I not tell you for the umpteenth time that the bridge has disappeared? How fast you forget!' Sudhir sounded disappointed.

From the restless doddering of his limbs, it was obvious that Ashok felt embarrassed. But soon he regained his composure. 'You are right, Sudhir,' he said, 'I keep forgetting much of what people tell me. There was a time when it was necessary to forget a fat lot of things. But then the mind proved too diligent to let a single item slip from its possession. And now when it is imperative for you to remember at least a few things—who else would care to remember for you when you are old and out of tune with the rest—the mind betrays you.'

'But you lack no care, Ashok bhai. Hasn't providence placed you amidst a host of kind souls who would remember for you all you need?

'A host of kind but colourful souls. Despite all their goodwill for you, they must dab your affairs with their tint and tone, so much so that you will fail to recognize what was yours. No, Sudhir, others cannot remember for you, just as others cannot forget for you!'

'Ashok bhai, after a long time you are sparkling as before, much like your university days. How dramatic you were!'

'Dramatic, was it? I don't remember. And look here. Sudhir, on second thought, there is so much peace in forgetting things! I am in peace, believe me, with my what do you call—amnesia. My instant snoozes of which you complain are nothing but a sign of my peace. Would death prove gracious enough to close in on me while I was in one of those snoozes?'

Sudhir understood from the volume of Ashok's voice that he would not feel sleepy for some time to come. He dragged his chair closer to him and, after a little hemming, said, 'Ashok bhai, for over a long time, I've been trying to make a confession to you. No longer can I keep the anguish bottled up in my heart. Will you kindly bear with my babbling for a few minutes?'

'Go on, Sudhir.'

Sudhir hemmed again, rolled up his sleeves and readjusted his position. He passed a few more seconds ensuring that there was nobody in the vicinity to overhear him except for a cat on the sofa. He waggled his stick at it and it walked away more in disgust than in fear.

'Ashok bhai, you remember Meena, don't you?' There was no response from the listener.

'You remember her, don't you? Meena, my distant cousin, two or three years older than I, the beautiful Meena! Wasn't she a student when you were the star of our college—a young lecturer? Who could have outshone you in gait and glamour, in that spick and span look you carried about yourself! But let me go back to Meena. We had put her up in our house. To cut the story short, I mean the very Meena you were in love with. Ashok bhai, you have not fallen sleep I hope!'

'How can I, Sudhir? Go on.'

'But will you first tell me whether you remember Meena or not?'

'What a silly question! Did you not say that I was in love with her?'

'Thank God. Yes, Ashok bhai, you loved her and you grew thin yearning for her.'

'And I never grew fat again!'

'But you fattened me—and I have remained fat all my life. Feeding me like a pig because you used me as the courier of your love letters to her—and how wonderful those letters were! I have rarely met with such galvanizing sentiments in either fiction or poetry!'

'Sudhir, don't you tell me that you were unkind enough to read my private letters to Meena!'

'Pardon this sinner, Ashok bhai, I did read them. I read not only your letters but also the one—the solitary one—she had written to you in reply. Of course, that was how I learned that she too had come to set her heart upon you.'

'No, Sudhir, she had not. And she did not ever write to me.'

'She did, Ashok bhai!'

Ashok sat silent without taking his eyes off the moon, which had grown brighter emerging from a fragile scrap of cloud. The lone eucalyptus that stood touching the balcony persisted in its monologue in the steady breeze. The grandfather clock rang out a resonant half-past seven.

Ashok suddenly spoke out in a vibrant tone, 'I am lucky. I don't care to call for any proof of the veracity of your statement, Sudhir. But I wish you had told me of her love earlier. I could have considered myself lucky over a longer period, that is.'

'There lies the knot, Ashok bhai! What do you think I am feeling so awfully guilty about? You certainly remember how shy Meena was. But she had at last yielded to your entreaties. She had written a small but sweet reply to your epic love letters. In fact, she had agreed to meet you at the bridge.'

Sudhir paused for a moment and then continued, 'And she had come, but had to go back feeling humiliated, for you did not turn up.'

'How do you say so? Sudhir, I never received any letter from her!' Ashok asserted in a trembling voice.

'How could you have received the letter, Ashok bhai?' Sudhir faltered and tried to clear his choking throat. 'Did it not fly away, while I was crossing the bridge, in a sudden gust of wind?'

'Fly away? Let us go and look for it!' Ashok made an effort to get up.

'After sixty years?' Sudhir laughed nervously. Ashok fell back into his chair.

'Ashok bhai, I must confess that the letter flew away only after I had read it and torn it to shreds. In fact, I let the shreds fly into the rolling flood of the monsoon. I can still see them flying away like butterflies and disappearing under the bridge.'

Ashok kept quiet.

Sudhir hung his head and muttered, 'I do not know why I did such a thing. You will certainly agree that I was not mischievous. No doubt, I had a deep attachment to Meena. I could not have wished for anything but her welfare. My affection for you was no less, but that was tinged with a fear.

I was perhaps afraid that should Meena marry you, she would be lost to me entirely. It was sheer stupidity, of course . . . In any case, I was to lose all contact with her the moment she left our house—which she did before long—on the receipt of a message about her father's fatal illness.'

Sudhir fidgeted with his stick before resuming, 'Ashok bhai, all this hardly mattered to me as long as I was engrossed in my vocation. But since retirement, whenever I have visited the bridge, the memory of my treachery has assumed a terrible dark form and haunted me like a ghost. For ten long years have I been plagued by it. I still feel puzzled if I try to hit upon some convincing explanation of my conduct that evening sixty years ago. Ashok bhai, will you pardon me? I wonder. But believe me, if I was a rascal, over the past years, by pretending to be good, I have become good.'

Sudhir stopped. Someone was climbing the steps. It was Mahindra, tired but excited.

'Ashok babu, if I am still capable of walking quite fast and even climbing, it is entirely due to the inspiration I draw from your example. Now, tell me, Ashok babu, how on earth could you reach home so soon? I saw you from the other side of the dismantled bridge and called out to you. It appeared you were too engrossed in looking for something on the dry of the river to respond to my call. I just took a turn to avoid trudging. You were gone. You will overtake a hurricane, Ashok babu. Who will believe that you are older than I?' Mahindra observed, still panting.

'But Ashok bhai hasn't been out at all this evening! You must have seen someone else,' said Sudhir.

'Ha! Can I ever mistake someone else for Ashok babu? And in this bright moonlight? Well, Ashok babu, you couldn't but have reached here only seconds before me! Isn't that so?'

Mahindra waited for a minute for Ashok to reply and then observed, 'Surely, he has fallen asleep!'

'But he never sleeps so deep at this hour! Ashok bhai, do you hear?' Sudhir called.

'Ashok babu!' Mahindra joined in.

'Ashok bhai!' Sudhir called louder and gave a shake to his old professor and friend. The next moment, he screamed out, 'Who is there? Phone the doctor, quick! Where is the switch for the light, Mahindra? O God, I forget everything!'

* * *

Rabi Patnaik (1935–91)

'Barren Gandhari'

(Translated 'Bandhya Gandhari' from the Odia by Aditya Nayak)

I am talking about something that happened five years ago.

It was around 11 in the morning, Bina Panda dragged Kuna Sahu out from his shop in the market and stabbed him. Kuna Sahu had screamed, 'He is murdering me! Someone please help!', as his entrails spilled out on the unpaved red path. He kept saying, 'I am dying, someone please give me some water.' Then his voice grew feebler and feebler.

The place was crowded but it became eerily deserted very soon.

The sound of a single voice whining had swollen into a loud chorus. Kuna's father and a few relatives bound his wounds with a towel, put him on a string cot and carried him to the government hospital, which lay a couple of furlongs away.

A few women from the neighbourhood came out, held Kuna's mother in their arms, comforted her and led her back to her house. Soon, everything in the marketplace went back to normal. Once more, things were bought and sold, and it seemed as if nothing unusual had happened. Subdued fear had gripped everyone. Nobody talked about the incident. No one answered questions put to them by curious strangers. Some would say, 'I was not here when this happened. I came just now.' Others put on masks of stony silence and completely ignore the questions. Why should anyone risk one's life and limb? Who would like to be hassled by the police? Also, if Bina Panda comes to know of this, you get your shop looted in a day. We should care only about our own business and never poke our nose into matters that do not concern us. Who knows, maybe Bina's henchmen might have secretly warned everyone around. Word about this has somehow spread through muffled whispers. Bina had issued a threat—he would cut off the tongue of whoever testified against him and he would also do to their family what he had done to Kuna.

Two hours later, a police party comprising an inspector, his subordinate and four constables arrived at the bazaar. At the sight of the police, shops at the scene of the crime closed their shutters. The inspector settled on an empty bench lying in front of Madan Sahu's closed shop and instructed his subordinate to inspect the crime scene. Surrounded by four constables, the assistant sub-inspector of police looked around the place and took some notes. By this time, Kuna's fresh red blood had become indistinguishable from the loose red gravel of the street. However, in one spot, a little blood had congealed and a dark red film had spread over it.

At first, nobody dared appear before the policeman. But gradually, one after another they stepped out on to their balconies. A small crowd gathered around the inspector in a short time. The inspector started his investigation. 'Who murdered the victim? Has anyone seen the person who committed the murder? At what time did the crime take place?'

But the only answer to his questions was, 'No sir, we haven't seen anything and we don't know anything!' Someone said, 'Sir, I came just now when I saw you.' Another joined him, saying, 'Sir, I was busy doing things in my shop. Again, how could I see what happened here from such a distance?'

No one had seen a thing.

A subdued murmur filled the air. A swirling crowd of people busy talking to each other. People whispered, 'The police should investigate and find the murderer. We do not understand why they are asking us questions. They are paid salaries by the government. So, it is their job to nab the culprit!'

The inspector asked again, gravely, 'Someone killed a person in broad daylight and you are telling me that none of you have seen who has done the crime! Do not be scared, we are here to protect you. Give me his name, I will arrest that scoundrel and lock him away in jail.'

Someone in the crowd remarked in a low voice, 'Bullshit! Don't we know what you do? We know you will pocket 5000 or 10,000 rupees and let him off the hook, and then our life would be hell.'

The inspector repeated the question, 'Do you really mean to say that none of you have seen who committed the murder?'

A girl, about eleven years old, who stood near a pillar of Madan's Sahu's shop, screamed out loud, 'Sir! Sir! I have seen who did it! It was Bina Panda who stabbed Kuna Sahu.'

Suddenly, a deafening silence descended on the crowd. All eyes turned to the corner from which the voice had emerged.

A thin, fair-skinned girl, having witnessed the murder of a human being for the first time in her life, stood trembling in fear and apprehension. Her face had turned red, her eyes were dilated, her nostrils flared and her lips quivered. She stared unblinkingly into the distance. It seemed as if after having uttered those two or three words, she had turned into stone.

After a few minutes of silence, someone from the crowd shouted, 'Hey you, Bharati, what are you doing here and why haven't you gone to school?' Saying so, the middle-aged man walked up to the girl and gave her a stinging slap. It was as if this slap broke something within the girl. She dropped her bag and clasped that man screaming 'Father,' and burst out crying inconsolably. That man, who was shivering with rage, calmed down in no time, lifted his daughter and started to comfort her by saying, 'My dear one, please stop crying, big girls do not cry.'

The crowd silently kept watching until the father and daughter left the scene.

After a while, the inspector and his party went back to the police station. The crowd dispersed.

Gangadhar babu had been sitting on the verandah of the inspector's residence for over two hours. The inspector had not returned home yet. It would not matter how long he took to come home, but the matter must be sorted out today.

The inspector's quarters lay 200 metres away from the police station. The inspector returned to his residence at 8 p.m. As soon as he stepped on the verandah, Gangadhar threw himself at his feet.

'Respected sir, the child is utterly ignorant and knows nothing about the world. Please do not involve her in this case. She is a girl, after all. Her life will be ruined if she loses her reputation and my family will be disgraced forever. Think of your children and save her. You will not be here to protect us forever. One day, you will get transferred. After that, Bina Panda will destroy me and my family. I am not going to leave this place until you give me your word of honour that you will spare us.'

The inspector listened to him silently for a while, shook his leg free and walked into the house. But the undeterred Gangadhar kept sitting on the verandah.

When the inspector stepped back into the verandah after changing his clothes and having a cup of tea, he found Gangadhar still sitting there. The inspector said, 'This cannot be done. This is no case of theft or burglary. This is a murder case! She took Bina Panda's name in the presence of hundreds of people and she is the sole witness to the case. I may lose my job if I oblige you.' At last, he took the few pieces of paper Gangadhar placed in his hands and assured him that his daughter Bharati's name would not be mentioned anywhere in the case records. Gangadhar returned home around 11 p.m.

The same evening, a group of Bina Panda's henchmen were sitting in someone else's house. When they were opening the last bottle of liquor, Chintu Mohanty said, 'Brother, if you give me the green signal, I will make sure that the body of this wicked girl hangs from the branch of a mango tree growing near her house.' Bina Panda downed a glass of liquor at one go and said, 'Shut up you idiot! I will make that truth-telling bitch my wife. Go and tell this to her father tomorrow. If he marries his daughter to someone else or sends her away, I will kill his other children.'

Since that day, Bharati stopped going to school. Her father, Gangadhar Mishra, who was the headmaster of the primary school, had to keep her confined in his house and give up his dream of his daughter becoming a doctor. A lively, garrulous girl like Bharati now suddenly grew unnaturally quiet. She too did not want to step out of the house. If she had to marry a murderer in order to protect her family, she had no option but to do so.

Who knows what will happen in the future? Bina Panda might die an untimely death. He might end up being sentenced to life imprisonment. She was desperately praying to God that something terrible should happen to him.

But nothing happened to Bina Panda. Due to lack of evidence, he was acquitted by the court and continued to throw his weight about in the village. Every month, shopkeepers would go to his house and pay him his extortion money in gifts and cash.

As luck would have it, panchayat elections came to be held a year after his acquittal. Members of various political parties flocked to his house. 'Bina babu, nothing can be done without your support!' Bina Panda took money from all the parties, but after accepting a huge sum from the ruling party, he helped it win the election. He was informed that the Bauris and Muslims were planning not to vote for the ruling party, so, on the eve of the election day, he arranged to set fire to their colonies. That year, the ruling party won by an absolute majority in the election.

After this, Bina Panda's clout and influence grew rapidly. He visited Bhubaneswar frequently, met ministers and even the chief minister with ease.

Soon, he gave up wearing jeans and nylon shirts, and took to putting on white kurtas and pyjamas. He now began managing transfers of government servants—from BDOs and doctors to *gram sevaks*[lix] and primary school teachers.

Those days, Bina Panda spent a lot of time with government officials and often dined with them. In the course of time, his manners and deportment underwent a visible change and soon he emerged as an unchallenged political leader of the area. Although people whispered about his indirect involvement in several rape and murder cases, everyone continued to support him out of fear. Through Bina Panda's exertions, the primary school, which Gangadhar babu was serving, got upgraded to an English-medium middle school. A private high school for girls was also opened in the premises of the same school. Bina Panda was elected unopposed as the secretary of the managing committee of the school. People slyly hinted that the lady teachers at the school were warming Bina Panda's bed at night.

Bina Panda won the election to the legislative assembly with a handsome majority. One month after the election, he sent word to Gangadhar babu to begin preparations for the wedding. Over the last five years, Gangadhar babu's resistance to the idea of having Bina Panda as a son-in-law had weakened somewhat, especially after he was promoted to the post of headmaster of the middle school. Moreover, Bina Panda was no longer seen as a murderer. Rich and powerful, he had now become a responsible leader and lawmaker, and was a respected figure of society. He was a man after all. One

[lix] A man employed to advise and assist villagers in matters of community welfare and development

should not hold against him something he had once done in a fit of blind rage. He was now a reformed person. Apart from that, to be known as Bina Panda's father-in-law would earn Gangadhar babu a lot of prestige!

Now, Gangadhar babu, with a clean conscience, set about making arrangements for the wedding. Chintu Mohanty, the trusted henchman of Bina Panda, came and assured him that he and his friends would come and make all preparations for the wedding. Then he asked him to ensure that the bridegroom's party would receive proper hospitality. The party would include five ministers and twelve MLAs, who would come all the way from Bhubaneswar. 'Here, take these 5000 rupees. Feel free to ask for more money if you need it. Bina Panda does not care how much money is spent—his prestige should never be tarnished,' Chintu added.

Word spreads that Bina Panda was a man of his word. See, he had vowed he would marry Bharati five years ago and he kept his promise. When he grew rich and powerful, many affluent families wanted their daughters to marry him, but he turned down all these proposals.

Preparations for the wedding were in full swing at the same time as Bina Panda's charitable work. With only a month left to the wedding, Bina Panda organized a family-planning programme, which was inaugurated by the deputy health minister. Panda himself delivered a speech on the benefits of family planning. It was the first time that such an interesting event had taken place in the area and everyone, especially village women, talked excitedly about it. The air was thick with apprehensions and fears, which were expressed through anxious whispers. Some said, 'All will be rendered impotent. If this happens, women will run out of control and go berserk.'

'After all, children are gifts from God. If we prevent people from having them, there will be no one left on earth and mankind will perish.'

For a couple of days after the meeting, a few men and women from Bauri *sahi*[lx] were forced by the goons of Bina Panda to come to the hospital and undergo surgical procedures in keeping with the family planning schemes. But no one came on the third day. Not even one person from Karana, Brahmin and Khandayat sahis could be persuaded to come to the hospital. Bina Panda, for his part, soon lost interest in the programme. As far as he was concerned, the minister inaugurating the program was all that really mattered. A list of 400 names was prepared in consultation with the doctor. It hardly mattered if some names in it were fake. In any case, the money was to be divided equally between him and the doctor.

It was around 9.30 a.m. The premises of the hospital were completely deserted. The nurse, compounder and dresser were busy gossiping in a room inside the hospital. Seated on a chair, his legs resting on the desk, the doctor was absorbed in reading a film magazine. Around this time, a girl whose face was covered fully with the end border of her sari, entered the doctor's chamber.

Laying down the magazine on the table, the doctor asked her, annoyed, 'What do you want?'

The young lady replied in a low voice, 'I want to get sterilized.'

The doctor sat up. Pulling the half-opened register, he asked, 'Your name?'

The girl: 'Bharati Mishra.'

Doctor: 'Age?'

The girl: 'Nineteen.'

Doctor: 'What! Only nineteen?'

As it is, people in villages did not record their age correctly. Even a forty-year-old woman may say that she is fifty-two or twenty-two. So, the doctor wrote twenty-nine in the column

[lx] A colony in town.

meant for recording age. He could not see the girl's face properly and her body was draped in a coarse cotton sari.

Doctor: 'How many children do you have?'

The girl: 'I have no children!'

Doctor: 'What, you are unmarried?'

The girl: 'No, I'm going to get married.'

Doctor: 'Are you joking with me? Should I ask the sweeper to throw you out?'

The doctor was angry this time.

Bharati now uncovered her face and leaning on the table, gave him a fixed stare. Seeing such a breathtakingly beautiful woman, the doctor was struck speechless. He simply kept gaping at her.

'Doctor sahib! I am not a mad woman nor am I a woman of loose character. I come from a respectable family. My marriage is fixed with a murderer and the marriage will take place after a month. To save my family from being ruined, I agreed to marry this murderer. I do not mind being the wife of a murderer, but I can never bring myself to become the mother of killers and criminals, nor can I give birth to sons who are cowardly and impotent. The world is peopled by timid, spineless persons like you and murderous criminals like my would-be husband. Doctor sahib, please save me from such a terrible fate by sterilizing me. I want to remain a barren woman for the rest of my life.'

* * *

Binapani Mohanty (1936–2022)

'Patadei'

(Translated from the Odia by Urmishree Bedamatta)

No one knew where Patadei was—it was as if she had evaporated into the ether. It was the evening of Dola Punei[lxi] and the moon cast an ethereal glow upon the village hamlet, which basked in a mesmerizing radiance. The deities, having indulged in their share of hospitality within the dwellings of the villagers, convened in the *melana*[lxii] ground, resonating with the pulsating rhythm of drums and *jhanja*.[lxiii]

There were bustling crowds all around—the children, their tiny bodies weary, would momentarily rest on the ground only to rise again, compelled to venture out and discover what was happening. Each person carried a handful of *abira*,[lxiv] clandestinely smearing it on the faces of unsuspecting passersby. Yet, the mirth and jubilation of the Holi festivities seemed somehow greater than those of the days preceding Holi. This cherished occasion arrived just once a year, an elusive treasure that slipped through one's fingers all too swiftly. Even if one wished to partake in its enchantment endlessly, it was a privilege denied. The festival, like a fleeting breeze, dissipated in no time. Reluctantly, one could not escape its presence—it seemed to engulf even those

[lxi] Odia version of Dola Purnima; a swing festival celebrated during Holi that is dedicated to the divine couple of Radha and Krishna.

[lxii] A place of confluence of village deities.

[lxiii] Cymbal.

[lxiv] Coloured powder.

who sought to evade its grasp. Throughout the year, the weight of life's burdens and impurities accumulated within one's body and soul, unseen and unnoticed by all. And so, Patadei, much like a spectre looming over countless years, concealed her sorrows and worries beneath a painted smile.

Under the radiance of a moonlit night, so luminous it rivaled the sun, Patadei ventured forth. Amidst the thronging chaos, she sought solace in making offerings to the deities and partaking in the festivities at the melana ground. Earlier in the evening, she had consumed a bowl of water rice accompanied by fried greens. Claiming an ailing stomach, she squirmed on the mat spread across the verandah, just outside the kitchen. Her father, carrying the deities upon his shoulders, had been absent since morning. Within the confines of her desolate home, there was no one to share her burdens with. Her sister-in-law, Mani bhauja, had come to extend an invitation for a game of cards, but Patadei, feigning illness, declined. As Mani bhauja and the others departed, one of them chuckled and remarked, 'Ah, she's just pretending . . . If not for her charades . . .' Their laughter resonated, carried away by the boisterous wind. However, Patadei continued to lie there, her gaze fixed upon the moon, her mouth agape. It appeared as though the revelry and merriment in the streets held no sway over her. She inhabited a world of her own, wherein her sole concern was herself, detached from the cares of this realm.

The village resounded with the sound of drums and jhanja being played during the *kirtana*.[lxv] Men with abira-smeared faces were present everywhere. In such a moment, without any concern for foxes, dogs, spirits and sorcerers, Patadei securely closed her house and departed to witness the jatra. Throughout the night, no one had entered the house

[lxv] Devotional chanting using a medley of musical instruments.

nor had anyone taken the trouble to inquire about Patadei's whereabouts.

The fair continued throughout the night. In the early morning, once the Holi celebrations had concluded, everyone returned to their homes to rest. That night, there was to be a *pala*[lxvi] competition between two villages, leaving no one any time or opportunity to check on Patadei's whereabouts.

After spending the entire night outside, Jagu Behera leisurely made his way back home around noon. His anger flared when he discovered the house was locked. He bellowed for Patadei at the top of his lungs, but his voice echoed back, unanswered. He proceeded to visit each person's house in search of Patadei.

What other option did he have but to shout? He had sold off a fifth of his land to arrange her marriage. The groom appeared princely, owning over two acres of land, and they possessed a considerable amount of pawned gold. However, Patadei didn't even spend two months at her in-laws. No one knew what issues she faced there. Within a month of her marriage, she grew pale. When asked, she would remain silent and stare blankly, as if she knew no one and had encountered a human for the first time. Jagu believed that since he had raised her with great love and affection, she couldn't handle the challenges of married life. Without a mother or brother to confide in, as a father, Jagu felt helpless. Furthermore, he wasn't a king or landowner to confront Patadei's in-laws. Amidst everything he did, Jagu was constantly anxious about her.

Jagu remembered the scene very well. There had been absolutely no news of Patadei. In the middle of the night, a persistent knocking on the door had startled Jagu. It was drizzling, with a dark sky overshadowed by clouds, and the

---

[lxvi] A folk form of theatrical commentary on mythological or current events.

bullfrogs bellowing near the ponds. The weather was damp, and Jagu was sleeping, fully covered from head to toe. Upon hearing the knock, he woke up and inquired about the identity of the visitor. No response came. Jagu suspected it might be a ghost and settled back to sleep. After a while, the knocking resumed. He grew annoyed. This time, holding the garland blessed by the Lord in his hand, he cautiously opened the door. What he witnessed in the darkness left him astonished. It was indeed his own daughter returning to him. Recognizing her instantly was no challenge. Overwhelmed with shock and wonder, he whispered, 'Pata! Pata, it's you . . .'

Without uttering a word, Pata walked past her father and locked the door from the inside. A concerned Jagu inquired, 'Dear daughter! Why have you come in the middle of the night? Did you sneak out after having a fight with your husband?'

Pata, her face turned down, leaned against the wall. Her features were not clearly visible to Jagu, who sat down, exhausted. As Pata began to enter the house, Jagu softly asked, 'Dear Pata! Why won't you say anything? Did the elderly couple mistreat you? Are you well?'

Pata departed without responding. Jagu sensed that something was amiss. She would speak when she was ready. Perhaps she hadn't eaten anything. She had always been stubborn. Unable to restrain himself, Jagu rose to ask his daughter, who sat on the floor near the kitchen, 'Dear! Won't you have something to eat? There may be some cooked rice in the pot . . .' Pata buried her face between her legs and burst into tears. She had never cried so much, not even when she left her father's house on her wedding day. Jagu wiped away her tears with his gamuchha and remained silent. All he grasped was that his daughter was hurt and had left home as a result. He needed to be patient for the truth to unfold. She was still young, unaware of how to manage a household, Jagu thought. Surely, the groom or his father would come looking for her in the morning. Jagu imagined giving them a piece of his mind.

But a year elapsed since Patadei left home, and no one came inquiring about her. Jagu tried his best but failed to discover why Pata had left in the middle of the night. When asked, Pata wore a blank expression on her face. Her eyes welled up with tears, her lips trembled, but she refused to utter a word. Whenever the villagers questioned him, Jagu remained silent. When the inquiries became too much, he would respond that the groom had gone to Madras and would return to fetch Pata once he found employment there. However, not even a letter arrived from Pata's husband or in-laws, and no one was sent to check on her. For some unknown reason, Jagu himself never ventured to Pata's marital home to investigate the cause of her predicament. The elderly Jagu worked as a daily wage labourer and often went hungry to provide for both. Pata never seemed to care about the troubles she caused him, but Jagu couldn't be angry. Despite his grief, he didn't want to add to his daughter's burdens. What if she committed suicide or ran away? Jagu had no one else to call his own. However difficult or stubborn she may be, Jagu had to care for her and bear the blame on her behalf. Consequently, the once talkative Jagu gradually fell silent. Upon Pata's return, the villagers cast accusations at her. Some claimed she was expelled from the house due to misbehaviour, others said she disobeyed her husband and was thus abandoned, while some alleged she had affairs with men in the village and was subsequently evicted. Jagu would glance at Pata, contemplating whether any of it was true. He considered berating her, or dragging her back to her marital home, but refrained from doing anything when he saw the sorrow on her face. Every day, with the cawing of crows at sunrise, Jagu would rise, go to work and return in the evening with a prayer in his heart that all would be well. After all, he wouldn't be present forever to care for his daughter.

Now, after two exhausting days of work, and without any food, Jagu felt utterly drained. His daughter should have been waiting by the door, holding a pot of rice for her father, but she was nowhere in sight. Jagu grew furious at the notion that she might have run off with someone or be playing frivolous card games. Would he have to continue to toil until his lifeless body was carried to the graveyard? Would there be no one to look after him?

Jagu Behera cried out, 'Pata! Oh, dear Pata! Where are you? Please come back soon . . . Pata, my dear Pata!' There was no response at all. After searching through every home in the village, Jagu returned home in the evening and surveyed his surroundings. The house remained locked, just as before. It appeared as if the doors were contorting their edges, gnawing into each other, determined to stay shut. The sun descended and darkness extended its embrace over the entire house.

Jagu Behera remained seated on the verandah until he eventually dozed off, leaning against the wall. As dawn broke and the birds began their melodious calls, he woke up to find the door still locked, just as it had been before.

According to the villagers and onlookers, Jagu remained seated, leaning against the wall and became unresponsive. When the village elders attempted to engage him in conversation, he would simply stare at them. When the village girls and women arrived with rice to feed him, his lips quivered, tears welled up in his eyes, but he remained silent. Rumours spread that Jagu had become deaf and mute due to his daughter's alleged adultery. Tragically, after enduring ten days without food or water, Jagu collapsed and fell into an eternal silence. His gaze remained fixed on the locked doors while flies buzzed persistently around his face.

Three years have elapsed since Patadei departed from home, and Jagu Behera departed from this earthly realm. Since that fateful day, three melana festivals have been celebrated on the melana ground, mango trees have borne fruit and shed their ripe offerings, and the river waves have crashed upon the banks before flowing into the vast sea. Mani bhauja has now become a mother to a young boy but has also become a widow, and friendships have been forged and lost in the course of marriages. However, no one has witnessed Patadei's return, and no one has taken the time to ponder why she left home or if she found new matrimony.

Hence, the sun has risen, and the seasons have passed in their usual rhythm. Patadei remains an enigma in the minds of all. Neither does she possess the answers herself, nor does anyone in this world hold the key to unveil her secrets.

Jagu Behera's house has remained locked since the day of his demise. It was a humble abode comprising a room and a half. Inside, one could find a tattered shawl, a few bamboo mats and an open tin suitcase. The entire village had witnessed this sight, yet no one had the desire to claim these accursed belongings. After all, everyone feared the spirits that were believed to roam the village outskirts at night, and Jagu Behera's house happened to be situated at the far end. There used to be a flowering tree near the entrance of his house, but even its blossoms had ceased to grace the surroundings. Otherwise, perhaps someone would have been enticed by the blossoms and ventured inside to investigate if there were any remnants belonging to Patadei.

Standing isolated, the house emanates an eerie presence. Travellers, both men and women, begin to catch glimpses of Patadei's ghost in the darkness, sometimes even hearing Jagu Behera's mournful cries.

Suddenly, on one fateful day, a buzz of excitement filled the air. Three years had passed like three distinct epochs, and people had almost forgotten the events of the past. Those lacking in knowledge added embellishments to the tale, while the wise chose to distance themselves from such gossip. It was reported that Patadei had been spotted mopping the verandah of her house. Accompanying her was a two-year-old boy, his fingers habitually finding solace in his mouth. Patadei's figure had gained some weight, with her face and abdomen exhibiting signs of rejuvenation. However, her eyes still held tears and a weariness burdened her, as if carrying the weight of her sorrows. News rapidly spread. Jagu Behera's daughter, Patadei, had returned from the realm of the departed, and she had brought a child with her. It must be her own, for what other reason would she have brought the child along? In the dead of night, she had abandoned her handsome husband, without cause. Unable to find solace in her father's home either, she had struck a deal with someone and left. It was difficult for anyone to provide for her sustenance throughout her life. Patadei was growing older, lacking the strength to use her body for earning a living. Thus, with the hope of finding a safe haven, she had returned to her father's home.

Patadei has undergone a profound transformation. There exists an undeniable contrast between the Patadei of the past and the Patadei of the present. She no longer concerns herself with the opinions of others. When the village elders approach her with questions, she covers her head with her sari and positions herself at a distance. When the women from the community come to visit her, she lays out a mat for them to sit on, all the while gazing off into the distance. In the midst of idle chatter, she remains silent. Occasionally, a faint smile graces her face, while at other times, she becomes distant and engrossed in drawing something on the floor.

Everyone claims she is a woman of ill repute. Since her separation from her husband, no one knows who the father of her child is. What purpose do her vanity and pride serve? Ram! Ram! She is cursed! She is no divine deity who can transform all evil into good. She cares for nothing and yet dares to dream of a contented existence . . . Ha! It's utterly disgraceful! Couldn't she find a trace of poison to consume . . . If she remains silent about everything, how long will she continue to live?

Since Patadei's education only extended to the third grade, it does not prove advantageous for her. Additionally, she lacks the support of a protective family. Eventually, the villagers reach a decision one day that she must depart from the village in order to continue living. If she chooses to stay, they threaten to set fire to Jagu Behera's house. They are determined not to let the women of the village bear the consequences of Patadei's wrongdoings.

On that fateful evening, as dusk descends and the villagers congregate at her doorstep, flinging accusations her way, Patadei scowls while gripping the tattered end of her sari between her teeth. 'Yes, I have given birth to this boy,' she declares defiantly. 'When my husband departed for Calcutta the day after our wedding, my in-laws locked me away in a room for fifteen days, depriving me of food and water. That is why I escaped from their clutches in the dead of night and sought refuge in my father's house. My father was filled with dread and had to endure your unkind words as long as I remained under his roof. To support me, he toiled tirelessly until his bones ached, yet he could never satisfy his hunger or live with dignity.'

Patadei swallows a lump in her throat, lowers her veil and continues speaking. 'I had no words, no course of action. I couldn't end my life to spare my father from his toils . . . and this merciless world has sent me back with a baby in my embrace.' An elderly man, adjusting his gamuchha firmly around his waist, emerges from the crowd. Placing his hands on his hips, he exclaims with a sharp voice, 'How dare you utter such words? Did you say that the earth bestowed upon you a child in your arms? Was there no other place for the child to go? Why did it have to come here? I can perceive you are a shameless individual. Tell us, whose child is this?'

She pulls her veil even further down, her hands trembling, and sinks down to a seated position. The baby in her arms chokes on his tears, his cheeks stained as the stream flows, yet his cries go unheard by anyone.

Suddenly, with great force, Pata's waist is kicked by none other than Mani bhauja's mother-in-law who is also Pata's *khudi*.[lxvii] As Pata gets up, tears streaming down her face, the elderly woman bellows, 'Hey you! Why don't you speak? The timid young girl that you once were, you couldn't bear to live with your in-laws for even a month, which led to your father's demise. And now you have the audacity to claim that this child is yours, bestowed upon you by mother earth! Shameless creature! Speak the truth and reveal the identity of the child's father. Otherwise, I will slice you to pieces with a kitchen blade. Keep this in mind, for your own sake.'

The elderly woman continues to scream relentlessly, her leg exerting pressure on Pata's neck. They are encircled by men and women from all sides, their gaze fixated on the scene as if watching a macabre spectacle.

Pata's neck is being forcefully pushed down, almost as if it were to be buried beneath the ground. Her breath grows shallow, and her vision starts to fade. But within herself, she musters the determination and declares, 'No, I will not endure this any longer . . . I refuse.' She knows that the earth won't tear itself open to offer her sanctuary, nor will Hara and Parvati come rushing to her aid.

Something inside Pata is ignited, prompting her to forcefully push away the old woman's leg and rise to her feet. In an instant, the petite woman of 5 feet stands tall, her face flushed with a mix of courage and indignation. She fixes her gaze firmly on the villagers, takes the crying child, cradles him against her waist and proclaims, 'Do you all wish to know who the child's father is? All of these men standing here are the child's fathers—Ramu, Bira, Gopi, Maguni, Naria, and all those standing behind them. How can I single out one father? On the night of the punei festival, while the

---

[lxvii] Aunt.

pala fight was underway on the melana ground, it was Ramu who forcefully gagged me with a gamuchha and abducted me without any reason. In the bushes near the graveyard, all of these men surrounded me, tearing away at my flesh, consuming me greedily. My voice was silenced, but before I lost consciousness, I recognized each one of them . . . So, who then is the father of the child? What am I supposed to say? Why don't you ask Haria or Bauri, khudi? Put your hand on your heart and let someone step forward and claim to be the father.'

When the gravity of the situation sinks in, the elderly and middle-aged men exchange uneasy glances with each other, while the young boys feel embarrassment. No one has the words or the courage to speak up or pose any questions. Khudi, wearied by it all, slowly lowers herself onto the verandah, exhaustion evident on her face. Ramu, Bira, Gopi, Maguni and the others hang their heads in shame, unable to meet anyone's gaze.

Wiping away her tears, Pata resumes mopping the verandah, even as her baby continues to cry. Setting aside the broom, she gently wipes her baby's nose with the tips of her fingers and showers him with affection. 'Why do you cry, my dear? Are you afraid of these men?' she whispers. 'Don't be afraid, for I am here. None of these men possess the strength or character to call themselves your father. Don't cry, my dear, for you have your mother by your side.'

It remains unclear what the baby comprehends, but he ceases crying instantly. Raising his tiny hand towards the moon, he emits a burst of joyous laughter. The spectators are taken aback by the baby's laughter, causing them to turn around and depart in astonishment.

Just two days prior, the tarata tree has burst into bloom, with a handful of flowers blushing delicately in the gentle breeze. Mani Bhauja's mother-in-law, stooped with age, releases a faint sound with her walking stick as she silently walks away.

Patadei glances around and spits a mouthful onto her baby's chest to ward off the evil eye. 'Oh, my little prince has grown pale under the intense scrutiny,' she thinks. 'No one will come to our aid anyway. I am the mistress of my father's house, and my baby is my prince,' Patadei whispers to herself, finding solace in her own determination.

On that day, time seems to freeze in its tracks. Patadei gazes upwards to the heavens and downwards to the earth, her emotions in a tumultuous whirlwind. She finds herself caught between tears and laughter, alternating between sorrow and joy in a blend of emotions.

* * *

Bijay Prasad Mahapatra (1938–2013)

'A Game of Dice'

(Translated 'Pashakhela' from the Odia by Aditya Nayak)

Hari Gumasta's pukka house stood next to Mata nani's *mutt*,[lxviii] which had two wings. The mutt had an earthen verandah and a huge courtyard, and its backyard was overgrown with gangasiuli and durlava plants. Red roses bloomed in abundance in the courtyard, at the centre of which stood a tulsi platform. In the past, this belonged to Jhanjapita mutt, and legend has it that Bhakta Charan Das, an ascetic, had composed the famous poem 'Mathuramangal' here. When Mata nani came to our sahi as a daughter-in-law, a *mahant*[lxix] named Purushottam babaji lived in this mutt. The mutt owned vast landed properties in Kesakara and Bankura. Lots of men and women from neighbouring villages came carrying rattan baskets on their heads, on the day of *Akshaya Tritiya*[lxx]. They spent a day or two on the verandah of the mutt. There, they would cook rice and dalma,[lxxi] and wait for the mahant to whisper mantras into their ears. Once the rite of initiation was over, they would put on necklaces of wooden beads and leave for their villages.

One day, Mata nani's young husband suddenly died. He had a hearty meal and had gone to bed the previous day. When dawn broke, he was dead and gone. Some said that he

[lxviii] Monastery.

[lxix] Abbot or head of the monastery.

[lxx] An annual Spring festival in Hinduism.

[lxxi] Lentils cooked with vegetables.

had gone to the temple of Baliharchandi and on his way back, had encountered a deadly ghost. Others said that he had bhang laced with lethal poison and a few others claimed that his wife had mixed his rice with a paste made of poisonous kaniar seeds. Mata nani did not wail in grief, nor did she withdraw into a dark corner of the house. She was a very young woman at that time, bursting with youth—tall, fair-complexioned and with striking features. Her thick shiny hair fell on her back and was tied into a knot. She was neither unlettered nor feckless. She lost none of her strength of character even after becoming a widow. Three or four months after her husband's death, she decided not to stay confined to her house and stepped into the world outside. Every day, she would take a bath in the morning, put on a coarse cotton sari, lock the front door of her house and go out. She would return home in the evening. No one knew where she went, with whom she associated herself and how she spent her day. Whenever Kartik Mahatmya or the Bhagavad was recited at the mutt, she would sit with a few other women on the verandah and listen reverentially to the recitation. When the recitation would come to an end, she would leave after spending a long time offering up prayers to the lord. No one saw Mata nani face hardships, she never got into a quarrel with anyone or suffered from any ailments. Before the rains came, she got the roof of her house thatched with new straw and gave her walls a fresh coat of paint. Nobody ever dared to point a finger at her. Whenever someone in want of a little money approached her or the boys of the sahi asked for a donation on the occasion of a festival, she would never disappoint them. It is not that people didn't gossip behind her back, but they didn't have the guts to say anything to her face. Three years passed in this manner.

The condition of the mutt was going from bad to worse. Purushottam Babaji took ill frequently. His hands and legs had become thin like reeds and his belly had bloated. He also started to look deathly pale. His disciples, who lived in villages nearby, came to see him and sometimes spent two three days at the mutt. Doctors had asked babaji to abstain from taking salt, oil, chilli and spices; he survived on a little rice and a few boiled slices of papaya. Ever since the caretaker of the mutt stole the gold crown of the deity, Dolagovind, and ran away, even such a frugal meal couldn't be cooked for the mahant on some days. Vaidyas and *Kavirajs*[lxxii] said that the mahant's belly was filled with fluid and that he was suffering from dropsy.

Grass had grown on the verandah of the mutt, and holes had appeared on the thatch where monkeys had pulled out the straw. The rose bushes and the tulsi plants had gone to seed. The mahant said, 'The mutt won't be able to celebrate the jhulan festival this year.' Nobody bothered to organize the festival. The residents of the sahi were more interested in the treasure that they thought lay buried under the mahant's seat. They believed that the treasure comprised two brass pots filled with silver coins stamped with the face of Queen Victoria. They didn't rule out the possibility of finding gold bricks or nuggets. They told each other, 'This is such an old mutt! So many mahants have headed it—who knows what one would find under its floor?' Some expressed the opinion that neither gold nor diamonds lay buried there. If one would dig the floor, one would find a bunch of palm leaves, which Bhakta Charan Das wrote his famous poems on.

One day, the sahi witnessed a lot of hustle and bustle. People learnt that, like every year, this year too, the jhulan festival would be celebrated at the Jhanjapita mutt. Like every year, Balila the house painter, arrived at the mutt carrying earthen pots containing coconut shells full of paint and glue made from tamarind seeds. Loka Mohanty and his nephew

---

[lxxii] Traditional medicine men.

had brought two loads of pith, white like the wings of storks, which lay drying in the sun. They sat in the mutt making a *jambura*[lxxiii] from yellow and red sheets of paper, which lay spread before them on the floor. These sheets glittered in the bright sunlight of the rainy season. Kadamb and champak flowers were crafted for the jhulan festival.

The gossips now fell silent. What Balunki, the *moharir*[lxxiv] said silenced everyone around. Mata nani, they were told, had undergone a rite of initiation on the twelfth day of the month. She had shaven her head, started wearing the loincloth and putting tilak on her forehead. She also now wore a necklace made of holy tulsi twigs. The mahant handed her two keys and told her, 'O handmaiden of the lord Dolagovind, He draws you towards Him. I can hear the call of Lord Brajabihari, who wants me to join Him.' On the first night of the jhulan festival, boy-dancers began dancing as Lord Dolagovind was placed on the swing pulled by the devotees. Mahant maharaj was summoned by Lord Krishna to heaven. *Sankirtan*[lxxv] parties arrived, red powder was scattered and earthen ghee lamps were lit. Babaji Purushottam Das's soul soared into the heaven in the midst of ululation and devotees shouting 'Hari bol'. Since that day, Jhanjapita mutt came to be known as Mata mutt.

We children used to play in the open and loved to run beside the long verandah of the Mata mutt. There were other reasons why it was our favourite place. Sometimes, Mata nani would appear on the verandah carrying a basket full of offerings made to Lord Dolagovind. She would call out, 'Come to me my dear little Gopals!' and we would go running to her. She would give us handfuls of the offerings, which

[lxxiii] Pattern.

[lxxiv] Deed-writer working in law courts.

[lxxv] A form of song or chanting that praises god.

would contain sweetened roasted rice, slices of bananas and cucumbers, a few sugar crystals, and other sweets. We would play and run eating the offerings. She would say, 'Run carefully, my dear ones or you will have a fall.' However, she would never allow us to enter the mutt. In the recess of a wall of the verandah, she would keep garlands for the deity to prevent us from touching and defiling them. She was scared that we might break branches of the tree growing in the middle of the courtyard, make noise that would wake up the lord from his midday nap, tread upon rice drying in the courtyard to be pounded, or scatter with our feet the powder of five colours placed in the sun. Only those whom Mata nani herself called into the mutt could step inside.

One day, Mata nani whispered to me, 'Come inside, Kalia.' There was a naughty look in her eyes and it seemed as if she had slyly taken me away from my friends. It was as if a yellow pennant cluttered the crown of her chariot and like *Akrura*,[lxxvi] she was trying to spirit me away. I would run into the mutt, Mata nani following me and carrying a few sweets or nuts in her hands, but I would rush out the moment she would hand me these. Mata nani would shout, 'Kalia, you little thief, I will punish you tomorrow. You will be taught a lesson.'

When the month of Kartik would arrive, we would sit below the verandah of the mutt and Mata nani would distribute offerings made to the lord to us. She would make pictures of parrots, bhadabhadalia birds, and the images of Jagannath, Balabhadra and Subhadra using five kinds of coloured powder around the tulsi platform. She would place offerings on a leaf and sitting on the verandah, a pandit would read aloud the Kartik purana. A lamp would be raised to the top of a tall bamboo with the help of a rope. The light of the

---

[lxxvi] Uncle of Lord Krishna

lamp enabled human beings to glimpse the dark immensity of the universe. It was to remind them that they had been living on borrowed time and that God had descended on earth to make them render proper accounts. Mata nani, who would be fasting during this month, would serve us offerings. She would tell us, 'Eat, children. If you take even a grain of rice, I will feel as if I have eaten my fill.' On festive days, Mata nani would deck me up. She would take off my shorts, make me put on yellow silk clothes and use a length of diaphanous fabric as a waistband. She would decorate my arms and wrists with bracelets made of glass beads. She would sit me on her lap and lovingly hold my chin, painting holy marks on my cheeks and forehead. Between my eyebrows, she would draw a black line and adorn my neck with a medal. Tucking a flute into my waistband and a peacock feather on my head, she would ask me, 'O Kalia, did you spend time with *Brundabati*[lxxvii] in her bower yesterday?' Tears would streak her cheeks as she said this. Uttering, 'O Krishna! O Krishna!' she would clasp me to her bosom. Then she would take off the clothes she had made me put on and looking away, she would say, 'Go away.'

For over three days now, the mutt had gone very quiet and it seemed as if nothing happened there. Mata nani had gone to her village, the village where she was born. It lay 6–7 miles from Sakhigopal. We were told that her parents were alive, and she also had brothers, sisters and their children living there. Five days later, Mata nani returned to the mutt late at night. She was accompanied by her young niece. Although this girl came from a village, she appeared quite confident. She was the daughter of Mata nani's elder sister and resembled her aunt. Her name was Ujjwala. A grown-up girl, she never stirred out of the mutt.

[lxxvii] One of the gopis.

The mutt became active once more—offerings were made to the deity, cymbals were played in the morning and evening, and the dried-up tulsi plants came into new leaves. Now and then, Mata nani would step out of the mutt and come back carrying a few things. If someone asked her what she held in her hands, she would say, 'I went out to buy a dress for the girl, then I thought I should buy her a couple of bangles too. One finds few fancy things in a mofussil village like mine. That's why my niece looks so plain. Her parents didn't even give her an extra dress when she came with me. They must have thought I own a bazaar here. A beautiful girl like her doesn't even have a few bangles to adorn her wrists.'

It was midday. Mata nani tiptoed out of the mutt and blinking at me, said, 'Kalia, come to the mutt today. You will see what I have kept for you.'

I went in and saw Mata nani in the sanctum holding many things in her hands. She said, 'Come in, you will see how I will deck you up.' I said, feeling hesitant, 'No, your niece is here, I will feel awkward in her presence.' Mata nani couldn't hold her laughter and said, 'How strange, my naughty little Krishna is feeling shy!' Taking me by hand, Mata nani tied around my waist a length of embroidered cloth. I asked, 'Tell me what you have kept for me today?' Mata nani smiled and replied, 'Have patience my little Kanha, I have kept these things only for you.'

After she dressed me up, she led me through the courtyard to a room in the corner of the mutt. The anklets I wore kept tinkling. I was wearing a garland of wild flowers on my neck. She pushed me into the room and shut the door from outside. I kept staring, feeling dazed. I thought that I would break down and weep. I found Ujjwala, a paper crown adorning her head, standing in front of me. Her bosom was covered with pearl necklaces, and bangles adorned her arms and wrists. Four decorative laces were tied around her waist. Her lips and her cheeks were painted with lac dye. She looked every inch like a nautch girl.[lxxviii] At her feet on the floor, lay spread out a dice board, on which were arranged, the dice and cubes. We looked at each other and a smile lit up Ujjwala's face. She said, 'You really look like a boy dancer.'

'Shut up!' I told her.

Her face broke into a smile again and taking my hands into hers, she said, 'Come, let's play a game of dice.'

I shook off her hands and told her, 'I don't know how to play this game.'

'Neither do I,' said she, trying to make me feel confident.

She added, 'You will roll the dice. I will count the numbers and then you will move the cubes.'

I agreed to do as she said and told her, 'First take out my necklaces. I find them prickly.'

She replied, 'I can't do that. My aunt will scold me if I do so. In any case, I too am wearing necklaces and they don't prick me.'

We sat down facing each other on either side of the board and got immersed in playing the game. We were utterly unaware of how much time had passed, as if absorbed in a performance of a play featuring Krishna and Radha.

Mata nani opened the door a crack and peeped into the room. She told Ujjwala, in a voice full of mock anger, 'You adulteress! So you have stolen my darling Kalia from me!'

* * *

[lxxviii] A dancing girl.

Pratibha Ray (b. 1944)

'The Ring'

(Translated 'Mudi' from the Odia by Bikram K. Das)

He lay flat on the hospital floor, undisturbed by the hum of visitors, the traffic of nurses and attendants, the stench of disinfectant, and even the buzzing of the flies that swarmed around his face. The other inmates of the ward, denied sleep by their assorted pains, aches and other complaints, looked at him enviously as he slumbered blissfully through the afternoon.

Overcrowding everywhere, from maternity ward to mortuary. So what if he had been denied a bed and dumped on the floor? Was it such a calamity? Even that seemed a luxury to the old woman. When she had set off with her young son in the back of the old truck for the great hospital in Cuttack, everyone in the village turned out to offer instructions. She wouldn't be able to get a bed for her son, she was warned, unless she knew some doctor in the hospital. She ignored them and rode off after she had pawned her few bronze utensils. Although they didn't get a bed, they did manage a place on the floor, enough for him to lie in. And that without a single acquaintance! She felt as though she had successfully crossed the ocean in a frail dinghy without an oar. Did her son need a bed anyway? Had he slept in one at home? Wasn't the smooth concrete of the hospital infinitely cleaner than the soggy mud floor of her hut? They had given him a plump cotton mattress to sleep on, instead of his filthy cotton quilt. At home, the sun and the moon peeped through the thatch, but here he had a solid roof overhead. Wasn't that enough? Why covet a bed in the temporary home that the hospital was? Greed led to sin and sin to death.

As soon as the word entered her mind, her heart began a furious drumming against her ribs. What an inauspicious thought! She cursed herself. May she be consumed in the flames of her own foul mind! What evil there lay in a woman's tongue!

To drive the thought away, she turned to look at the people around her in the ward. The sick and the maimed everywhere. Some with bandaged heads, others with layer upon layer of dressing encrusting arms, legs, backs, bellies . . . peeling away, like insects moulting. Hollow eyes peeped from scarecrow faces encased in bandages. How frightening! As if they were masquerading as ghosts to scare you. But no, this was no masquerade—the wounds beneath the bandages were real. By comparison, her son was unscarred. Not a scratch on him, not one scrap of bandage. Bare he had been, except for a loincloth, when he clambered up the babu's roof in the village to mend his thatch in return for a day's wages, and slipped and fell into the stone-paved courtyard. And bare he lay now on the hospital floor. By the grace of the goddess Jagulei, not even his skin had been broken by the fall. He had merely fainted from fright. The village kaviraj had tried in vain to bring him back to his senses, but his charms and spells had been equally ineffective. The lad had always been restless and fidgety, even as a child. And who could blame him—hadn't he lost an older as well as a younger brother? He must have been scared out of his wits, the rascal. Well, he would soon be up once he got over the fright. The babu's daughter, who went to school in Cuttack, had made a black-tongued remark—after a fall like that, she said, people often remained unconscious for months; they could even be paralysed! It was she who suggested they go to the hospital in Cuttack, where he would be cured. The old woman was furious at first. Who had ever heard of a man remaining unconscious for months? Was he a human being or the demon Kumbhakarna? But who can retort to the powerful? Besides, once the remark, however silly, reached the woman's ears, she simply *had* to take her son to the hospital. She had a mother's heart after all, even though she knew quite well it couldn't be anything serious. If he had bled or broken some bones, she might have been worried. She had seen people being knocked unconscious from a blow on the head—not just seen but suffered it as well. Her own husband.

The family home was being partitioned and a fence would be erected across the courtyard. The brothers were disputing a patch of the courtyard no wider than a hand-span. Words led to blows and lathis were raised. She jumped in to intervene. 'Stop!' she shouted to her husband. 'Your elder brother has already claimed the lion's share in everything else. Does it matter if he gets an extra hand-span of the courtyard? Is it worth fighting over?'

The courtyard was crowded with menfolk and her husband couldn't afford to be seen listening to the counsel of a mere female! 'Go away, woman!' he roared, giving her a shove, making sure it was observed by everyone. 'Who asked you to mediate in the affairs of men? Don't forget your place!' And turning to his brother, he said 'The fence will be raised where I draw the line, or else . . .'

The words were scarcely spoken when his brother's lathi had descended on his skull. Like water from an overturned pot, the blood streamed, bathing him from head to foot. He fell like an axed tree and never regained consciousness. The corpse was carried out through the door and the fence rose where he had drawn the line in his blood. She remained, reluctantly, to bring up her fatherless boy. Not knowing why or for whom she had survived, she grew into a ripe old age, never once allowing herself to think of death but hoarding her happiness like a miser through all her sorrows, until she saw the face of a grandson. Well, that's life—if one were to abandon it for the sake of another, would the world continue? The Almighty's *maya*[lxxix] be praised!

Since her son hadn't even bled, how could life ebb away as he lay unconscious? She bit her tongue again. How could she have such black thoughts when her son was sleeping beside her?

Her gaze turned from the bandaged patients in the ward to her son. How meek, how gentle he looked in his sleep! Not that he was any different awake. She stroked and caressed him from head to foot. His face looked exactly as it had in his childhood. Was it because they had shaved off his hair? It had been shorn once before, when he was seven, when his father had died. His tears had been more for his flowing locks than for his father. She had made a vow to offer his hair at the goddess' shrine when she could afford the ceremony. So, for seven years, no blade touched his head and he romped free like the infant Krishna, dangling his shoulder-length curls decorated with crow and pigeon feathers. Holding to his lips the short whip which his father used to drive the bullocks as if it was the infant God's flute, the boy stood with one leg crossed across the other, torso, hips and knees triple-bent in the *tribhangi* posture[lxxx] he had seen in the village jatra. 'Look!' he lisped, 'I am Ma Yashoda's darling son!' The proud parents laughed at the child's theatrics. How charming those thick hanging curls looked against his chubby face! And how he had treasured them! Poverty allowed him no other indulgence so he pampered himself through his hair. He had not even a rag to cover his back, but he would comb and preen his hair

---

[lxxix] Illusion.

[lxxx] A much sought-after pose in Odissi dance showing the three-way split of the body of the dancer

with infinite care before he set out to work. Passersby stopped to admire his crowning glory. Starvation robbed him of flesh and blood, dimmed the glow on his face but not a hair of his head could it touch. And then the doctors in the hospital had to shave it off! Why on earth? They had insisted it was necessary as they would have to take a picture of his head to find out if there was any injury inside. How odd! How could there be an injury inside the head when there was not even a scratch on the outside? God alone knows what the doctors found in the picture, but all they did afterwards was to lay him down flat on the floor. Not one drop of medicine did they give him, nor a drop of milk. No attempt to bring him back to consciousness. Doctors and nurses trooped past him to attend to the other patients, giving them medicines, injections, milk, fruit and biscuits, but no one so much as looked at him. As if there was nothing the matter with him, as if he was lying there for the fun of it or as if he would get up and walk away when his sleep was over. Well, God grant that it be so! But how could he leave in his present state?

She pestered the doctors and nurses with her questions but the reply she received was: 'We have to wait, Aunt, until his consciousness returns. Trust us, we will give him all the care he needs. But at the right time.'

'I know,' the old woman said, 'but if he were to get some medicine or some milk, perhaps it would make him stronger so that he could regain consciousness sooner.'

'Be patient, Aunt,' they replied. 'Can a man swallow anything when he is unconscious? Wouldn't it stick in his throat?'

She prayed to her gods as she continued to stroke him. 'Please, god, make him conscious now so he can have something to eat. He must be starved!' All he had had since morning, when he went out to mend the babu's thatch, was some water in which they had soaked rice overnight. The rice itself was gone—her two grandchildren woke up before the first crow cawed to gobble it all up. The gluttons! Her poor son had nothing. But why blame the children? That was the fate of the poor. Their pots were always empty but never their bellies. Hunger filled them up! How strange God's ways were!

The stroking and caressing continued. Suddenly, she felt his fingers tightening, as though he was trying to clench his fist. Was his consciousness returning? She massaged his palm and fingers, trying to straighten them out, to pass on the warmth of her own body into that cold hand. Her fingers came to rest on the middle finger of his left hand. For ages now, the old silver ring had gripped his finger tightly, as steadfast as an old friend that had sworn undying loyalty. Their hopes of getting a gold ring for his dowry were foredoomed, for providence had already chosen a poor widow's daughter to share his handful of rice. Where was her mother going to find a gold ring? The boy's mother understood her plight. Since she was happy with the daughter-in-law, she chose not to make a fuss over the ring. Before the wedding, she had her old pair of silver toe-rings melted down into a solid ring for her son, which he accepted without a murmur. Thus are the golden dreams of the poor turned into silver or brass, or even mud and gravel. Compromises have to be made or life would be impossible.

The flat ring of beaten silver burned on his dark skin like a ruby. No ring of gold could have shone as brightly on his grimy, sweaty, knotted finger as the silver; at best it would have looked pale, like brass, or like a faded gourd flower.

When he cleansed his teeth each morning with ashes from the earth, he scrubbed and polished the ring as well, but gently, lest the metal should wear off. But no amount of care could avert the inevitable—hard work was scraping the flesh off his bones and along with it, the silver from the ring on his working finger. It was wearing thin. When it was new, one could see some fine engraving on it but not anymore. The upper surface had been scrubbed as flat and shiny as a tamarind seed. Being pure silver, it was naturally soft, like her son. What a misfit he was in the present age! Other labourers might shirk but he would do the work of five. The more hard-working one was, the sooner one was worn out—aged before one's time. Why did he have to climb onto the babu's roof? Couldn't he have remained on the ground and flung the bales of straw onto the thatch? There were other labourers working too; surely one of them could have mended the thatch. But bow your neck once and the whole world will rush to strike you down! Someone as meek as her son was bound to attract trouble.

She went on caressing his face, his hands, fingers and the ring. The visitors were beginning to leave; it was already evening and it wouldn't be easy to find a bus back to the village. Kala Miyan, the truck driver who lived in her village, was leaving for Bargarh with cargo when the mishap occurred and it was in his truck that she and her son had travelled to Cuttack. He had left them in the hospital and driven away, telling her not to worry as he would inform a few of their fellow villagers who were now working in Cuttack and would come to the hospital to look after them. Medicine and food for patients were provided for free at the hospital. The old woman would have no need for money other than the bus fare back to the village for her son and herself.

She would have liked to buy a few of the sweets wrapped in shiny paper for the grandchildren as well as a whistle for her grandson, but where was the money? She had a two-rupee note folded and tied up in a knot in the tail end of her sari, but that was all. The children would sulk if she took nothing for them. They had insisted on accompanying her to Cuttack—they even ran for a distance behind the truck shouting 'We want a ride!' Her nine-year-old grandson was a regular imp, while the granddaughter, two years younger, was as quiet as a lamb. Her brother had outran her as they ran behind the truck, and as she tried to catch up, she tripped and fell on her face. The blood streamed from her split lip and the scream of pain was so long-drawn, the old woman thought the child wouldn't breathe again. And that stupid daughter-in-law of hers had stood there like a log, looking at the departing truck with wide eyes instead of picking up the child and soothing her. 'I'll get some sweets and toys for you,' the old woman shouted as the truck went round a bend in the road. She couldn't see their faces any more. Poor dears! How would they manage without her? There wasn't a grain of rice in the house. How long could she beg and borrow? They would be waiting anxiously for her to return.

Her own stomach was churning with hunger. A few lumps were all she ate normally but since the night before, it had been a complete fast. Her son would have bought some rice for them with the wages he would be paid when . . . Well, that was all over now.

The hospital provided meals for patients but not for the relatives or friends who tended to them. As for her son, he was sleeping so soundly, there wasn't even a rustle. That afternoon they had served rice, dal and curry to the patients. The hospital had skilled cooks—though she hadn't tasted the food, she could tell from the aroma. She had tried to shake him awake; if he had been fed she could have had something to eat as well. She wanted to tell the attendants: 'Is he going to lose his share just because he is asleep? If *he* can't eat now, there's always his mother!' But she was too shy to ask. What if they refused? She had never begged, even during the worst times. Would she bring disgrace upon herself now that she had come to the city? Everyone in her village would come to know.

But where *were* the people from her village that Kalu Miyan was supposed to have informed? He had been in such a hurry to leave! How would she manage without help?

She felt a slight tremor in his hand. The breathing quickened. Was his consciousness returning?

The nurse doing her rounds stopped to look. She quickly ran to fetch a syringe and gave him an injection. Two men in white aprons rushed to his side and pressed down heavily on his ribs. Good god! Even a healthy person would collapse under such rough handling! Was this how they treated patients at the hospital? And was it for this she had brought him here?

'Babus, you'll smash his ribs!' she shouted angrily. 'Do you want to cripple him? Who'll look after his family? Can't you be more gentle?'

They left him and walked away. Had she annoyed them? But how could she remain quiet after what they had done to her son?

He wasn't stirring now. The nurse covered him from head to toe with a clean white sheet. The patients in adjoining beds craned their necks and peeped curiously like tortoises. All eyes were on that white sheet. But why? Couldn't he have even a clean sheet because he was poor? It was the government that provided it, not them; why should they whisper and mutter? Her son wasn't going to walk away with that sheet—he would surely return it when he left. He wasn't the sort who took what didn't belong to him.

That nurse seemed always to be in a great hurry, rushing madly around the ward. In her haste, she had even covered up the boy's face with the sheet. Wouldn't he suffocate? Even in the coldest winter, he liked to sleep with his face uncovered. 'I'll choke to death in *my* sleep *if my* face is covered,' he would say. 'When I depart, it'll be in broad daylight, and not like a thief in the night,' he had always joked. As *if* it was a joking matter! She quickly uncovered his face, folding the sheet back. He felt cold to her touch. The fever must be coming down. Thank God!

The nurse came back looking anxious, as though a debtor was about to run away with her money. 'Aunt,' she said to the old woman, 'do you have any relatives in town? Send word to them.'

'I have no one here,' the old woman replied, not comprehending. 'All strangers. What do you want me to tell them?'

'You have no relatives in Cuttack then?' the nurse repeated. 'And in the village?'

'No one who can help,' the old woman said. 'The daughter-in-law is a simpleton; her children are babies. This son is the only support I have.' She stroked him fondly. Poor lad! she thought, has he had one decent meal since his father died, or a day's rest? Carrying the entire family burden on his shoulders.

'Do you have any money?' the nurse asked again.

'Of course!' the old woman replied. 'Could I have come to Cuttack empty-handed?

There, that's a two-rupee note. You can have it if you need some money; the medicine and food are *free* here.'

'No, no, you keep it!' the nurse said hurriedly. 'I don't need it. It's you I was thinking of.'

'Me?'

'Yes. There's no point in taking him back to the village now.' She saw the confusion on the old woman's face, hesitated and went on firmly, 'If you have neither money nor help, how will you manage here?'

'Well, if I could bring my son to Cuttack without help, I should have no trouble taking him back!' the old woman said emphatically. 'Once he's awake, we'll go back. What do I need relatives for? Has anyone ever come to help?'

'Your son is no more, Aunt!' the nurse said in a strong voice. 'There's no use taking him back! You have no money. The funeral can be done here; the hospital staff will remove the body.'

She couldn't understand at first and only stared. Then the great rasping sobs came. She lay down flat, covering up his body with hers. Pulling the sheet away, she caressed the still, unconscious body with both hands from head to foot, foot to head. She covered the pale face with her kisses until they glowed red with blood. Pressing her face down on his, beating her forehead against his shaven skull, she howled out a lifetime of grief, reliving the past, flooding him with tears and memories of the games he had played in the dust as a child, the games that a cruel divinity had played on him, of laughter, tears and hunger. Her fingers tore at the earth, ripped it apart. Then she beat the earth with her head. Scooping up a handful of dust, she smeared it on her son's face and body, howling madly, complaining, 'Listen, you 300 million gods, wherever you may be . . . Bring my son back to life! I don't ask for wealth, for palaces to live in. Only for a little air. Let him breathe again!'

Her grief touched everyone in the ward. Eyes grew moist as they looked at her.

Her sobs subsided as she became exhausted. The sound of her sobbing changed. Grief turned to anger—she cursed her treacherous husband, the murdering brother-in-law . . . her son, whose treachery was greater even than his father's. She cursed the cruel gods who held in their hands the keys to life and death, the people of her village, the other labourers who had been repairing the babu's thatch, the babu himself, Kala Miyan the truck driver, the doctors and nurses, the hospital attendants, and even those wretched patients in the ward who were witnesses to her grief. Pain wrenched her ribs, her bowels, her flesh and skin, and milked her entire being dry.

The curses flowed in broken strings:

'May you find no peace in the three worlds, O father of my wilful son! If you *had* to abandon me in my youth, why did you come in procession to my door with music and lights? Who asked you to parade your manhood, you eater of my happiness? Wasn't it enough that you stripped the bangles from my wrists? Didn't that satisfy you? You had to leave your seed in my womb, you cheat! And that son of yours, fourteen times worse than the father! What did you gain from cutting my throat, you rascal? Was it for this day I nurtured you in my womb? And what did you profit from devouring my son, daughter-in-law, you wretched widow's offspring? Is your thirst quenched now, husband-eater? And that demon, my husband's elder brother: are you happy now? May the gods strike you with their thunderbolt . . .'

The sounds and language of her grief changed constantly, tender at one moment, harsh or obscene at the next. The onlookers watched in silence. Did grief have so many faces?

Anger turned into a mother's tenderness, tenderness into hurt pride: 'Go! Go where you please, wherever you can find happiness!' she said indignantly to her son. 'Let your mother suffer! Let her face the world alone! How does her plight affect you? Can't you see for yourself how strong she is? How did your conscience allow you to abandon her, with the burden of three helpless souls on her shoulders? What tricksters you proved to be, father and son! Shirkers both! You were too cowardly to face the world so you left a feeble woman to carry your burden! Why did you build a nest? Well, go, go! If you had no time to think of me why should I be bothered with you? Does one have any claim on another in this world? It's all deceit, all maya! Nothing but lies!'

She consoled herself into silence. Turning away from her son, she fixed her vacant gaze on the darkness outside, as though she had not a care in the world, or was too exhausted to care. Thus she sat for hours, immersed in her own thoughts. When she seemed to have recovered her composure a little, a nurse and two attendants approached her. 'Aunt,' the nurse said, 'We will have to carry the dead body away. The doctors won't allow a dead body to lie here all night among the living patients. Your son's funeral rites will be performed well, Aunt. Don't be worried!'

She looked up, startled. In a pitiful voice she said, 'All I have is this two-rupee note. Will it be enough?' She burst into tears.

'There's no need for money, Aunt,' the nurse said. 'It'll all be free.'

'Don't delay now!' the nurse said to the attendants, 'Arrange to remove the dead body.' She left.

The two attendants bent low to whisper to her, 'How can it be entirely free, Aunt? Give us whatever money you have.'

Eagerly, she untied the knot in her sari and gave them the two-rupee note. There was not a trace of miserliness in her. He had never been anyone's debtor while he lived; would she allow him to be a debtor in death? Why should strangers remove his body free of charge?

She caressed him one last time, pouring every drop of love into that last kiss. 'Go, my son,' she said, bidding him farewell, 'You never knew what happiness is. Perhaps you'll have some happiness now.'

The attendants reached out to lift the corpse. Bending, they said, 'Aunt, let him go now!

It's getting late. Why such fondness for a mere lump of clay?'

Slowly, gently, she brushed her hand across his face and body, gripping his rigid, half clenched fist in her quivering fingers, allowing the last tender drops of love to drain away. Then she got up and shook herself free.

The attendants lifted him off the ground; one gripped his arms, the other his feet. The old woman's fingers were still interlaced with his, as though locked into them. She could feel the ring, so dear to her son. Suddenly, as though she had abruptly come to her senses, she clutched the ring and tugged at it with all her strength. The attendants had been eyeing the ring hungrily. 'How greedy you are, old hag!' they said. 'Robbing your dead son!' But she ignored them. Finally, the ring came free.

The onlookers, who had been numbed by her grief, were shocked. Sympathy turned into loathing. 'How mean!' they said. 'Is she a mother or a block of stone?'

The attendants carried the corpse away.

'Where are you taking my darling son away, you wretches?' she howled as she followed the attendants through the door, out into the street, for a short distance. 'May Death take you!' The mother's grief stunned sky and earth, tree and leaf, into silence. The darkness swallowed up her son. Only the ring glistened in her fingers.

With infinite care, she concealed the ring within seven folds of her sari's tail end and tied it up in a knot, her eyes focused on the path along which they had taken her son away.

How dark it was!

* * *

Kanheilal Das (1947–75)

'Dhrutarashtra's Eye'

(Translated 'Dhrutarastrara Akhi' from the Odia by Manu Dash)

Those who dwelled by the riverbank awoke one fine morning from their beds to find that the colour of the water had changed. It had turned the colour of *catechu*[lxxxi] and there were clouds of foam floating around everywhere.

Everyone—tonsured pundits, public servants, politicians and litterateurs—came together at the riverbank and began investigating.

They arrived at the conclusion that there must have been a dead body whose blood had mingled with the river water and turned it that shade of dark red, the colour of catechu.

However, it remained to be ascertained where the dead body was.

A selection process was duly carried out in a democratic manner to assign this responsibility to a suitable person.

Unanimously, they selected a writer to discharge this duty. The reason behind selecting a writer was that writers did not act as the middlemen of any political party. Besides, a writer also possessed a powerful vision that saw through everything. He could visualize the past, present and future at one go, and see each scene, incident and character unerringly.

Therefore, the people chose him.

Finally, the author set out on his journey carrying a backpack packed with rations and instruments to write. His objective was to trace the source of the body fluid.

[lxxxi] Cachou.

He set out from the riverbank and proceeded across the knolls and forests toward the direction of its source.

Days passed and the author persisted in his relentless journey.

* * *

Dhutura is strutting ahead and is accompanied by Chutia. Every morning, they move like this—Dhutura with his arm on Chutia's shoulder. Dhutura's bona fide name is Dhrutarashtra, given to him by his parents because he was born blind. No one knows who his parents are, where they reside or what his origins are.

Everyone sees Dhrutarashtra leaving for town in the morning hours and returning at night—for Dhrutarashtra is a beggar.

Over the years, the name Dhrutarastra had shortened itself to Dhutura as it cascaded down from tongue to tongue.

Dhutura has no remorse for being born blind. He knows that human beings with eyes are the real blind ones—the government is blind, the ruler is blind and blind is our culture.

He realizes every bit of it. Both his sightless eyes sparkle when he is happy and his eyelids quiver when he is sad.

Dhutura is marching towards the capital. He has a salt-and-pepper beard and coarse, straight hair. Chutia puts on a tattered shirt with a picture of a leopard on it. Some kind-hearted soul must have donated it.

Chutia seems very cunning. His eyes keep blinking every now and then, always awaiting an opportune chance. His hair droops over his eyes. On the crown of his head, a lock of hair hangs straight like straw. Dhutura walks ahead with his hands on Chutia's shoulder. There is a mended bowl in Chutia's hand, into which the liberal donations of some generous people will fall.

Along the rear of the main road, buses and vehicles packed with passengers and trucks are moving in the opposite direction. Pounding along, Dhutura moves ahead. How far would the assembly house be now?

Dhutura pauses under the banyan tree in front of the assembly house. Patting him on his back, sometimes, the leaders passing him ask about his wellbeing.

Dhutura knows everything. Poor people come to their leaders from faraway villages to vent their sufferings. They speak about relief arrangements, problems in the schools, release of library grants, and at other times, seek aid after drought or floods.

While the people are following the leaders and narrating their woes, at that precise moment, Dhutura's hand reaches forward to ask for alms.

The leaders drop a 25- or 50-paisa coin into his bowl to show how benevolent and generous they are. Dhutura can make out what coins are being tossed into his bowl from the clink itself.

Chutia is a bit more cunning than him. He stretches out his begging hand for the coin whenever he gets the chance, without allowing the coin to hit the bowl.

This ultimately becomes the extra income that slips into his pockets without Dhutura's knowledge. Afterwards, Chutia buys ice cream for himself with the money.

Dhutura realizes everything, but fails to catch him in the act.

Like every other day, Dhutura and Chutia stand today in front of the assembly house. The assembly session will begin soon. A minister is hurrying past the gate when Chutia's long hand with the repaired bowl reaches out to him. The minister looks at him in irritation and stops for a moment. He mumbles, 'Whatever help you may extend, it seems impossible to eradicate beggars from this country.'

Saying so, he calls out to a policeman and gives some instructions. The policeman comes and ask Chutia to leave the place soon!

Dhutura knows well that the police's harshness won't be for long.

He stares at the direction where he imagined the minister is standing and says loudly, 'Sir, give some alms to this poor, blind beggar!'

The minister doesn't mind giving him alms, but begging in front of the assembly hall must be stopped. What would the chief minister think if he were to see?

The minister looks back. A huge crowd of people are following him.

He gropes in his pocket and gets a 50-paisa coin. Pushing it aside, he gropes further but there finds no other coin.

Wearing a broad smile, he drops the coin into his bowl and moves ahead.

The several feet of sycophants follow him. Following the minister, these people drop the coins into his bowl as well—10 paisa, 5 paisa, 3 paisa, 2 paisa and so on.

Looking at Dhutura, Chutia rebukes those who dropped 2- and 3-paisa coins in the bowl. 'Are you so penniless? Why don't you come with a begging bowl and stand beside us? And toil yourself under the sun and rain with us?'

Chutia sees Dhutura's eyes whirling inside their sockets. A soiled leper is passing by their side. Chutia gestures with his finger to come nearer to him. Looking at Dhutura's eyes, he silently takes a 5-paisa coin from the bowl and throws it at the leper.

Picking up the coin, the leper smiles at him. Chutia feels as if he has become the chief minister. What a sheer joy to donate the money collected through beggary!

Suddenly, a commotion is heard. Dhutura leans his head in that direction and asks Chutia, 'What's this noise all about?'

Chutia steps up to the base of the nearby banyan tree and looks in the direction of the commotion.

He announces that people carrying red flags are approaching the assembly.

Dhutura puts all the money into a knot in his gamuchha and fastens it around his waist. He tells Chutia, 'Let us disperse, they are marching towards here.'

Hundreds of hungry people are marching towards the assembly, carrying posters and placards in their hands.

The man leading the procession is the rebel numero uno, hovering his heavy hand in the air and then bringing it down like lightning.

All indications of breaking the laws, rules and regulations of the administration are evident in his body language. Behind two or three persons, a young man, of the age when smart, young persons crave to be leaders, is accompanying the procession. His face is red and he is exhaling hot air as a police van moves past.

The faces of all those in the procession have turned red in the sun, Similar people are found in all such processions. Maybe they have no other business. Marching in a procession is their sole profession.

They wear rubber shoes and carry haversacks on their shoulders, in which they keep a gamuchha, beaten or puffed rice and *gudakhu*, a toothpaste made of dried tobacco leaves mixed with jaggery.

As the revolt happens, unfurled flags dance above the torrents of the huge crowd.

Some people in the procession are walking worry-free, watching the people, offices, shops and the bazaar nearby. That's the way the revolution goes on.

Gradually, the procession stops in front of the prohibited hall of the house, which is cordoned off by the police force.

The police stops the procession by demarcating a line while the slogans suddenly increase.

It is as if all the bogies of a train stand still after a sudden brake.

The leader at the front of the procession tries to move forward but the police pushes him back with the tip of a staff pointed at his abdomen.

Two or three persons behind the leader are also pushed back. Suddenly, the previously mentioned smart, young man breaks away from the line and runs swiftly like a cow twitching its tail.

Suddenly, panic breaks through the procession. A few of the provoked people break away from the line. They collect stones and boulders from the roadside and hurl the stones at the police, shouting slogans like, 'Stop police atrocity' and 'Won't tolerate police excesses'.

Dhutura and Chutia had decided to run away from the spot, but Chutia informs him that the police forces have already cordoned off the spot and that there is no escape route.

He whispers, 'You better be here, let me find the way to leave the place.'

So Dhutura waits for Chutia and stays there surrounded by the police forces. Dhutura can make out, through his ears, that the commotion is increasing gradually.

He can hear the creak of heavy boots moving rapidly.

A policeman, perhaps, bumps against his body, and he somehow manages to stop himself from falling.

He now understands that he is surrounded and trapped in an altercation between the police and the protestors.

Suddenly, he feels his head being smashed and something dribble out.

He touches his head and knows that the blood is oozing out as a pelted stone has hit him.

He starts tottering and groping the air blindly. He feels his head swirling.

While falling, he senses someone charging at his back with a staff. He falls and quivers with pain as one or two men walk over him.

Before he loses his senses, he can hear the exchange of gunshots in the distance and the smell of the smouldering; he feels the waves of the ocean passing over and the sky surrounding him like a mosquito net.

Waves after waves pass over him like white noise and lastly, a giant wave jumps over him but its crest does not collapse. It remains at a standstill.

Gradually, everything becomes calm and quiet when the big drops of rain descend from the sky. The rebels fall apart and leave. A few dead bodies and some wounded rebels are carried into the police van.

Only the dead body of Dhrutarashtra, Dhutura, is left flat on his face there. The blood oozing out of Dhrutarashtra's head flows down the roadside gutter.

Gradually, the drain-water passes through all the alleys of the town and mingles with the small river at the outskirts of the city. Finally, it joins with the big river and turns the water red.

The author from the riverbank, who walked in the opposite direction, finds the origin of the blood in front of the assembly. He scribbles the details in his notebook. The dead body of Dhrutarashtra is lying there, a stream of blood oozing out of his head and spreading all over the country.

The author notes everything that he witnessed, gathers all the stories, and marches ahead to reveal this news to the people of the country.

* * *

Tarun Kanti Mishra (b. 1950)

'Lyrical Ballad'

(Translated 'Lalita Akshyan' from the Odia by Sunanda Mishra)

Evening had fallen as the droplets of frozen rain made their way down to the earth.

It was around 5 p.m. The icy blast from the north chilled us to the marrow. Standing tall and dignified, the maple and cedar trees lining the road faced the north wind and snowy rain stoically.

We had travelled 100 miles from Lake Champlain. Our destination, the city of Albany, lay about 40 miles ahead.

It had been a bright autumn day, cool yet sunny. The majestic mountains covered with green foliage and patches of nameless yet lovely, blooming flowers enraptured us.

Switching lanes on the wide highway, Chinmoy asked if I could recollect a poem, 'The Road Viewed from Inside the Car' by Ramakant Rath. He went on to recite a few lines:

Our car races fifty miles an hour,
Anointing the road with a layer of light,
Like butter shining on bread
Fifty miles an hour along the road
Towards an empty wilderness.

I stared at him, surprised. A professor of physics at a New York university, Chinmoy could recall Ramakant Rath on the road meandering through the mountains from Montreal to New York!

'I have travelled this road at least twenty times,' he said, 'yet it feels refreshingly different each time—each journey reveals something extraordinary. Look at the hillock to your left—doesn't it resemble a playful penguin with its wings outstretched?

As we were driving and chatting, we noticed an unexpected change in our surroundings. The sun took cover behind thick gathering clouds, a biting cold wind started blowing, and soon, heavy rain and snow followed.

I had come to New York to attend a petrochemical seminar. My wanderlust had led me to explore all the interesting destinations in this fabulous city. Chinmoy suggested a trip to the Great Lakes in upstate New York.

I had no idea that upstate New York is dotted with thousands of lakes, big and small. It was late September. The trees had donned autumnal hues, slowly transmuting into a riot of colours—the famous Fall colours of upstate New York.

We had planned to spend the night in the city of Albany and drive down to New York City in the morning. I was heading to India the next day.

Our car suddenly screeched to a halt, hitting a road divider. The storm had escalated into a blizzard, reducing visibility. We were stranded on a desolate road, enveloped by the darkness and falling snow. Our luxurious car did not sustain any damage, but it was clear it would not be safe for us to go further. The GPS monitor showed that Albany was 28 miles from here. The nearest human habitation was Saratoga Springs, about 3 miles away. Pulling the car back onto the road, Chinmoy said, 'We can't go far in this weather. Do you want to see Saratoga Springs?'

I had read about Saratoga Springs. It hosts some famous springs, rich in rare minerals. It is also famous for its casinos, race courses and nightclubs.

We had no option. We needed shelter till the snowstorm passed. The satellite radio predicted that it would blow over in a couple of hours.

Chinmoy exited the highway and stopped the car in front of a building. The place was neither a bar nor a casino or a restaurant. In a narrow, dimly-lit lane off Fila Street, was a bookshop that was rather empty.

'I want to show you this amazing place', said Chinmoy, as he unbuckled his seat belt and turned the parking lights on. '*Lyrical Ballads*. Remember the book by William Wordsworth?'

Honestly, literature does not interest me very much. All I could recollect about Wordsworth was the poem 'Lucy Gray', which was given in college. My professor had been frustrated at my failure to respond warmly to Wordsworth's views on 'spontaneous overflow of powerful feelings'.

The chilling wind assailed me as I stepped out of the car, but Chinmoy was unfazed. He was standing on the sidewalk, beckoning me to the bookshop.

'It's cosy and warm inside. Hop out!' Chinmoy urged me. 'We will have a nice hot cup of coffee at the Starbucks cafeteria in the bookshop.'

I moved on, zipping my overcoat.

The entrance to the bookshop was narrow, like the back door of an old bank building. Engraved on the glass front door was the name, 'Lyrical Ballad'.

It was indeed warm and cosy inside. Not many customers were to be seen. In this weather, one would prefer to settle down comfortably in a casino or a restaurant.

The place did not look exactly like a bookshop. It resembled a rather quaint, disorganized library. Heaps of books lay scattered all over the place, most of them old.

'This bookshop is very old. Some of the books here were first published 100 years ago.' Chinmoy spoke in a low voice as he led me towards a tunnel-like passage.

I was intrigued that this part of the bookshop bore an uncanny resemblance to a tunnel. One narrow and long room led to another, each having different dimensions. It was like a maze of rooms lined with books of every possible kind.

'This used to be a bank a long time ago where the rooms were stacked with currency notes inside heavy vaults. This place has metamorphosed into this amazing bookshop that is noted for its rare collection. The name "Lyrical Ballad" adds to it a fascinating charm. "Lyrical Ballads" embodies the collaborative effort of Coleridge and Wordsworth. Written 200 years ago, the book celebrates the feelings and idioms of common people, ordinary men and women. It envisioned a new age in the world of poetry and poetic imagination. And the poets were right. Truly, a new era was born.'

Chinmoy continued, 'I am sure you have not forgotten our impressive language teacher who talked about spontaneous overflow of powerful feelings, while discussing Wordsworth's "Daffodils" and "The Solitary Reaper"!' In the preface to "Lyrical Ballads", Wordsworth wrote that spontaneous overflow of powerful feelings is the mainstay of all creative pursuits.'

The crammed bookshop seemed to be overflowing with books. Books littered the floor, were piled on tables and spilled over from the shelves. A few customers were scanning the books, flipping them over carefully.

'How many books do you think they have in this library, I mean, in the bookshop?'

'Nobody knows, not even the owner.'

I was surprised to see books costing as little as a dollar a piece and some as much as $750.

'The joy of visiting this shop lies in searching and unexpectedly finding a book you would love to read. Sometimes, you would find a rare gem of a book hidden in the piles of old, almost disintegrating volumes. You may suddenly chance upon a piece you have been looking for years in an unlikely place. Stephen Hawking's *A Brief History of Time* would be concealing itself in the stack of history books and Aristophanes' play *The Birds* could lie hidden in the Zoology section.'

'I would love to have a cup of coffee,' I said.

'Oh yes, I forgot about coffee.'

Chinmoy replaced the book on the shelf and looked at me. 'Let's go to the other section of the store'.

The narrow corridor led to the interior of the store, books crowding all over.

Someone brushed too close to me as I was navigating the congested passage. The gentleman appeared completely lost. I turned back to look at him as he was rummaging in a big wooden chest that was crammed with old books.

He looked up at me, a pair of pensive eyes. He seemed to be utterly unaware of his surroundings, even his own existence. A faded denim jacket covered his lean frame. His watery eyes seemed full of dejection, almost despair. His wrinkled brow was crowned with snowy white hair. He could be anywhere between sixty and seventy.

'We are sorry, it was our fault.' Chinmoy apologized.

The man said nothing. His misty eyes were vacant.

Standing at the coffee counter, Chinmoy mentioned that the man's name was Kevin. Kevin Parker Anderson.

'Do you know him?'

'Most people here do.'

The inside of the bookshop was fairly visible from the coffee counter. I could see Kevin. His slight body was moving like a pale shadow.

'He is a regular here. He visits this shop at least once a week. Has been doing so for the last forty years.'

'I presume he is a professor and a book lover, like you.'

'No, he is a college dropout.'

'What kind of books does he pick up from here?'

'He comes here searching for a single book, a certain book of poems.'

Chinmoy looked out of the glass window. The storm had blown over, leaving behind a calm, tender night.

'We should leave before another spell of rain.'

Chinmoy picked up three books for a paltry $7. We walked back to the car.

The road to Albany stretched out in front of us, glistening in the headlights of our car.

'Did you say Kevin is searching for a poetry book in the store for the past forty years?'

'Exactly.' Chinmoy replied briefly.

'I should think he is really passionate about poetry!'

'Alas, that is not so. Kevin does not intend to read the book. He wants to destroy it.'

'That sounds strange!'

'That's why he searches for it desperately. If he ever finds the book, he will tear it into a thousand shreds and throw them into the Hudson river.'

After a brief silence, I asked, 'What does he do for a living?'

'He is an undertaker . . . you know the guys who take charge of funerals.'

Our car raced ahead on the empty highway—the darkness intermittently lit up by moving beams from the headlights of cars. Chimnoy was humming a tune that could be Elton John. Returning to Ramakant Rath, he recited:

Fifty miles an hour in space desolate
We travel,
Soulless spirits surround.

An SUV overtook us on the wrong lane, gradually vanishing from our view.

'I think this guy is back from a gambling den. His pockets are probably empty, but his belly is full of cheap alcohol. Let us pray he does not bump off someone.'

'Why does the man wish to destroy that book of poems?'

'Which man? Oh, you mean Kevin Parker Anderson!'

Chinmoy fell silent for a minute. He checked out the GPS to ascertain the exact location of our car.

'It is hard to believe he was passionate about poetry once upon a time. And fairly good at it, too. He was a student at the City College then, and in love with a girl two years his junior. Elena was one of the most attractive girls in town and came from a prosperous family as well.'

The automated traffic signal ahead forced us to stop despite the deserted road. The dark, eerie silence was broken only by the sound of the freezing rain outside. An ethereal presence seemed to be knocking at the door, pleading for access.

The traffic light turned green. Our car surged forward.

Inside the car, the darkness seemed to weigh us down. Chinmoy broke the silence by recounting to me the story of Kevin Parker Anderson.

A quiet, shy boy, Kevin was doing reasonably well in college. His true passion, however, was poetry. He started writing poems at an early age. His first poem was published in Saratoga Times when he was seventeen. One day, an unknown girl, Elena, spoke to him at the college's coffee house. 'I read your poem, "Epitaph". It's lovely. Just a small mistake, chrysanthemums do not bloom in December, at least not in our city.'

Kevin was surprised. He looked at the bright, beautiful eyes of the girl, and asked in a low voice, 'Did you like my poem?'

'I loved it!'

Kevin was quiet for a moment and then said, 'I know chrysanthemums do not blossom in December. But would it not be just wonderful if they did?'

Elena stared at Kevin.

Kevin was not a prolific writer. He wrote sparingly. Every time he published a poem in the local magazine, he would wait impatiently to hear a few words from Elena. He found in her a sensibility and charm that were alien to him.

Such was his enchantment with Elena, he realized that, without her, his poetry had no meaning, no purpose. Elena was his creative self, his muse.

On his twenty-first birthday, Kevin put together twenty-one of his best poems and brought out a slim volume by a local publisher. A wave of pure joy rose in his young, tender heart when he received the first copy of his book. He took out his pen and carefully wrote out the words 'To Elena' on the first page. The precious gift in hand, he hurried to meet her.

Delighted, Elena thanked him lavishly. She also gave him the good news. She was getting married the coming Sunday at St Patrick's. Kevin was cordially invited to the ceremony.

That Sunday night, a devastating fire broke out in the storehouse of the local press. Flames engulfed the stocks of books. A heap of ashes was all that remained of the books, including 999 copies of Kevin's book of poems. Only one copy of the collection escaped the wrath of the ravaging fire. The one with the words 'To Elena' written on its first page.

Not a single line of poetry did Kevin write after that night. After some time, he dropped out of college and followed his father's footsteps to become an undertaker. He established himself as the most reliable and professional undertaker in the town. Kevin could engrave beautiful epitaphs on headstones and offer coffins at the most reasonable rates.

The twinkling lights of Albany appeared on the faraway horizon. Then came the lights atop the hillocks, lights floating on the shimmering surface of the Hudson.

The rain and snow had stopped their incessant assault on our car. The night was silent. The restless spirit seeking shelter seemed to have slowly melted into the darkness.

'Did Kevin ever meet Elena afterwards?' I asked Chinmoy.

'No, and it is improbable that they would ever meet again. Elena left for Australia with her husband a few days after the wedding.'

'And that poetry book . . .'

'Well, people here donate, or cheaply sell away used books or the books they'd never read. Books arrive in bunches at this used bookstore, swallowing every nook and corner. Over time, they are picked up by interested customers. Some are never sold, gathering dust in some unnoticed niche. Elena must have done the same before leaving for Australia. She must have left all her books here.'

Chinmoy remained silent for some time. The only sound one could hear was that of the crunching of soft snow under the car's wheels.

It had been an eventful day. My tired eyes were heavy. I don't know when I began to doze off. An elderly man slowly emerged in my dreams. He was searching for a book amidst stacks that looked like mountains—an old, discoloured book of thirty pages.

As he was delving into the piles, he grew frail and wizened. The pages of the books crumbled and fell apart as the long nails of his unkempt hands tried to turn the pages. The covers fell out and the letters cascaded down onto the dusty old carpet.

Suddenly, a look of relief lit up his misty eyes as he picked up a book—the one he had been searching desperately all these years. Ardent desire made his eyes glow as he opened it, ever so gently. He was amazed to see that the print on the pages was completely obliterated, every alphabet from each page had faded away, lost forever. It was a blank diary of thirty pages.

Dismay and sorrow would not overpower Kevin Parker Anderson. He knelt down on the floor. Pulling out a feather-tipped pen from his pocket, he began writing on the pages. He seemed to write with such passion, as if he had had lived this long only to write on the blank pages of this book.

I woke up. In my mind's eye, I pictured Kevin with his precious book in his withered, sensitive hands. Could he really tear and burn the book before casting the handful of ashes into the waters of the Hudson? Or would he simply hold the book close to his heart, the broken remnant of a priceless treasure lost and found after a long quest?

I did not ask Chinmoy.

I did not want to burden him with a question that none could answer.

* * *

Jagadish Mohanty (1951–2013)

'The Hero in Meltdown'

(Translated 'Stabdha Maharathi' from the Odia by Himansu S. Mohapatra)

Handing over his own goods to others
Lord Shiva went away naked.
(Folk saying of Odisha)

Sivananda's book and Dibyendu made their entry into Arunav's house together.

The book *Practical Lessons in Yoga*, a paperback edition in crown size, propped up on its inside page by an English bio of Sivananda, carries an account of philosophy, yoga, penance, trance and the pathway to the realization of God. And Dibyendu! Well, he is 5 feet and 4 inches tall, stocky and dark, with high-powered glasses; busy preparing for his examination in costing and accountancy as a non-collegiate candidate; cooks his own meals in his Icmic pressure cooker; a self-pitying type, and rather ordinary—so ordinary as to be unmindful of the current trend and close-crop his hair, smear it thickly with oil and wear drain-pipe trousers with a 14-inch bottom. Not surprisingly, he is a clerk in the accounts department.

Arunav cannot be compared with either of the two entrants into his house. To start with, he is a technical adviser. He keeps his hair long, wears bell-bottoms and is something of a bohemian. He is prone to bumming around, without caring to look for a job here and there, and is certainly not bothered about his future. He never allows himself to get drawn into a debate on the existence of God. The most remarkable thing about him is that there is absolutely no order in his life, and he writes stories and poems. Arunav thinks that people do not understand him. He wonders if there is something about him that at first pulls people towards him like a magnet, only to scare them away when they come close enough—the way it is with static electricity. In fact, they retreat in such a manner and so fast as to not only put themselves at the furthest remove from him but often to turn into his enemies. So Arunav prefers to stay alone, although it can be said that aloneness is a part of his bloodstream and bone marrow. He wonders if he can live easily without solitude for a companion. Tossed in the waters of his thought, he fails either to plumb the depth or reach the shore.

It is to such an Arunav that Sivananda and Dibyendu happened in unison.

At first, Arunav was in some dilemma—what will he do with these two who didn't fit into the tenor of his life? He had no taste for yogic penance before. But after hearing a two-hour lecture on yoga recently, he was influenced, and thought that if not God, at least a super consciousness existed and could be felt. The very day that he had this changed perception, Dibyendu came to him with his plea—he was preparing to sit for his costing examination and was not able to find a fit house to rent. He had not been allotted a quarter by the company, and wanted to know if he could share Arunav's quarter for a few days. Arunav was no doubt weary about the prospect of adjusting with somebody but couldn't say 'No' to Dibyendu on his face. The next day, Arunav picked up Sivananda's book at the market. Dibyendu too arrived at his house the same day, bringing with him his table, bed, bedsheets, bedding, cookware, books, notebooks, paper, pen, etc. It thus came about that Sivananda's book occupied Arunav's mind while Dibyendu took possession of his entire dwelling.

Arunav's quarter is located in the upper portion of a flat-type building. It was the type of living unit that was seductive for the middle-class residents of a town like Rourkela. The unit had one bedroom and one other room that could be called a drawing room, with a space alongside the rooms that was slightly larger than a passage and can surely accommodate a dining table. A kitchen and a bath-cum-latrine were thrown in for good measure. There is a ceiling fan in the bedroom. The unit was called a 1-BR-quarter in the local lingo.

Dibyendu's first job after moving in was to drag Arunav's bed from the bedroom to the drawing room and to put his own bed in its place. There was no space left in the room for Arunav's bed after he installed in it a table, measuring 3.5 x 2.5 feet, and two chairs. So he said to Arunav in a sort of commanding tone of voice that he hoped that Arunav would not face much difficulty in the drawing room. Arunav felt hurt, but he was someone who couldn't utter a word of protest or dissent to someone's face. So he couldn't say anything to Dibyendu. The next thing Dibyendu did was to push Arunav's books, manuscripts of his writings and magazines to one corner of the book rack, and arrange his books on costing in the cleared space in a neat row. He also removed Arunav's clothes from the pegs on the wall from which they were suspended and hung them from the nails on the drawing room wall. Arunav kept quiet, but he knew that the time had now begun for him to live the life of a refugee in his house.

Arunav faced his first major test on the very first night of their shared existence on account of mosquito bites and terrible heat. There was no fan in the drawing room, and he found himself faced with the stinging bite of mosquitoes without the net and unbearable heat with it. Dibyendu did, of course, ask Arunav to sleep in the bedroom and even went to the extent of clearing a space on the floor by gathering his table and chairs into a pile in one corner of the room. He spread a *sataranji*—a coloured, striped carpet made of coarse cotton—on the floor. But Arunav couldn't bring himself to accept the offer. He couldn't stomach the idea of him sleeping on the floor of his own house while the guest occupied the bed—especially with the slippers of the guest on the floor next to the sataranji, staring him in the face. It was like being treated like a servant in his own house. But then how nonchalantly Dibyendu went on about it—as if there was no reason for Arunav to take umbrage at such an arrangement!

Out of anger, hurt and a sense of injured pride, Arunav carried his cot, mattress, sheets, mosquito net and the book by Sivananda on to the rooftop and made his bed there. To read a few pages before going to sleep was a longstanding habit of his, so if he didn't read, he couldn't fall asleep. But there being no light on the rooftop, he tried to sleep by closing his eyes forcefully. Failing in that, he went down to his house and returned with a candlestick. He lit the candlestick and placing it on one side of the cot, got into the net carefully to guard against a fire hazard. While reading Sivananda's book, he was also feeling morose thinking about Dibyendu's behaviour. At this point, his eyes fell on a poem, the first stanza of which ran like this—

> Adapt, adjust, accommodate,
> Bear insult, bear injury, this is the highest *sadhana*.

The lines made such a deep impression on his mind that he not only recited it repeatedly but also started to prepare himself for *sadhana*[lxxxii] mentally.

Whatever else they may not accomplish, the changed circumstances brought at least two tangible benefits. One, Sivananda's book brought order to Arunav's life, and two, Dibyendu brought cleanliness to Arunav's home. Arunav had always tended to give orderliness a short shrift. There was neither order in his bathing, nor in eating or even in writing

lxxxii Penance, religious training or discipline.

stories. He didn't even tidy up his own bed and clean-forgot the daily duty of sweeping and dusting the floors of his house. It may be that the tedium of the daily routine made him recoil from these mundane chores.

Now, the same Arunav got up at 4 a.m., and as described in Sivananda's book, washed his face and sat down to concentrate his mind without either brushing his teeth or taking bath. But his mind started to race every which way like a disobedient school student after the final bell. So Arunav consoled his mind with the thought that he would develop a concentration with continuous practice and that he should not give up on it.

The house came alive with Dibyendu's touch and looked squeaky clean. The books didn't get strewn about all through the quarter like before; the floor was rid of cigarette ashes and stubs; the corners of the ceilings were brushed free of soot and even the ceiling fan looked shiny after being dusted off twice during the day. But after all this also, Arunav felt that something was broken somewhere in such a manner that the house remained no longer his, that he had become a shelter-seeker in his own house. This sent him headlong to those lines of verse from Sivananda for the sake of solace.

Arunav started to adjust and didn't even utter a word of protest against Dibyendu's selfish actions. Sometimes, he slept at night on the rooftop and sometimes, he slept in the drawing room, braving the heat. And Dibyendu acted aloof to all this as if these discomforts were not too much to bear for Arunav.

Arunav used to sit at Dibyendu's study table to do his reading and writing. He sat at one end while Dibyendu took the other end. Dibyendu was, however, a stickler for his own rules. Exactly at 11 p.m., he would switch off the light as he couldn't sleep with the light on. Arunav had no such fixed rule. There were days when he would fall fast asleep at 8 p.m. and days when he would remain awake all night to write his stories.

A day's incident: It was 11 p.m. Arunav, sitting at one end of the table, was in the throes of writing his story. Dibyendu, at the other end, was yawning. Dibyendu hemmed and hawed for some time before he got up, got to the light switch and flicked it off. While getting inside the mosquito net, he said, 'Arunav, go to the other room and work. I'm sleepy.'

His words, issued out of the womb of darkness, seemed to indicate he was afraid to look Arunav in the eye. Arunav found himself powerless to turn on the light in defiance of Dibyendu's wish and to say to him, 'Dibyendu, this is my house. Everything here will run according to my sweet will. I will read or write for as long as I want. I will sit wherever it pleases me to.'

But he couldn't say anything, although, hurt and humiliated, he seethed inside in terrible rage. Instead, he left the room like an accused, carrying his papers and pen, and tried to resume his writing while sitting on the bed. But by then, the muse had deserted him. He went on to the rooftop and started to pace to and fro there. While he declared war against Dibyendu, looking up at the sky and uttering his war cry up on the roof, Dibyendu slumbered inside.

Arunav's practice of yoga sadhana didn't escape Dibyendu's notice. When Arunav sat in the drawing room, seeking to concentrate his mind, Dibyendu would cross right in front of him, making him extremely jittery, as if the yoga he was doing was some kind of sin or childish prank. Although Dibyendu's presence gave his mind a series of jolts, he couldn't openly tell Dibyendu not to disturb him. Sivananda's book, in fact, said that yoga sadhana was best conducted in a separate room, a room meant for the sole use of the *sadhak*—the practitioner, with its door and windows shut. It would be good for the room to have a picture or image of God,

Jesus, the cross, Mother Mary or a mosque. A blanket, meant for sitting on while doing yoga, may be kept in the room. Incense stick should regularly be lit in the room. Care should be taken to keep the room free of clutter. The idea was that when you enter the room, you can feel the fragrance of purity pervading inside. The book also said that in the absence of a separate room, a small enclosure in the room could be created by wrapping a portion of the room with black cloth.

Instructions such as these filled Arunav with remorse. If Dibyendu were not staying in his house, then it would surely be possible for him to mark out a separate room for his yoga. But under the circumstances, getting an independent room was out of the question. When he thought of this, the old feeling that Dibyendu existed as a dead weight on him, and that he had handed him the key to his likes and dislikes, was intensified.

The matter didn't simply end there. One day, Dibyendu spoke tauntingly about Arunav's yogic exercise. Even after an agitated Arunav explained everything about yoga, starting from *pranayama* to *samadhi*,[lxxxiii] Dibyendu started to ridicule him by calling him Mr Sivananda.

The next morning, when Arunav sat in *padmasan*—lotus—pose, got both of his eyes to fixate on the spot in the centre of his brow and began to meditate on the formless image of Lord Jagannath for unifying his focus, his mind, dressed in the robes of Dibyendu's taunt, started to wander away, and he thought he heard somebody shouting into his ears, 'Mr Sivananda, Mr Sivananda'. The echo came back to bump against his head and seep into his consciousness.

Arunav was bound to suspend his meditation and get up in the face of Sivananda's book telling him: 'He has hurt only

---

[lxxxiii] A fusion of mind and matter in yogic mediation, and the practice of breath regulation in yoga.

your body, mind and petty ego. You're not limited to these. He has not hurt your real being. Because he too is contained in that pure being. Rather by hurting your petty ego, he has helped you to differentiate yourself from it.'

So, after consulting Sivananda's book and thinking deeply about the matter, he decided that he would try to remain silent and keep conversation with Dibyendu to a minimum.

Sivananda's book had this to say: 'By denying the material reality of the world, man can expand his consciousness. Hunger and thirst solicit your mind. So exert control over your desire, instinct and feelings, and you will see that there has been an unprecedented increase in your mental power. It is this mental power you need for your sadhana.'

So the day Arunav, following Sivananda's book, removed every item in his bedding except the sataranji, put them in the bed-holder and shoved it under the cot, the same day Dibyendu hauled home a thick and foamy mattress for himself, not forgetting to sing its praise for half an hour. Not only that—while cleaning the house, he picked up Arunav's bed-holder and dumped it on the rack near the ventilator.

This ill treatment of the bed-holder may have been a small matter. To Arunav, however, it looked as if Dibyendu had hurled a huge boulder at his chest out of utter hatred and disregard. Sleeping on the sataranji, he thought about whether or not he should get cross with Dibyendu's action. Yes, why not? Of course, he must. Dibyendu's action did really call for anger. Or maybe it should not, if it was inner calm that he was trying to achieve through yoga.

Seesawing thus between the yes and no of conflict and dilemma, Arunav picked up Sivananda's book and recited: Adopt, adjust, accommodate, bear insult, bear injury, this is the highest form of sadhana.

However, many little things like the dumping of the bed-holder did agitate Arunav. Like, for instance, Dibyendu's habit of reading aloud—although it was true that Arunav could have a radio playing while writing stories and had penned many good stories while listening to Hindi film songs coming out at full blast from the radio. Another thing: Dibyendu had deprived him of the hangers he used for keeping his clothes, leaving him no other choice but to hang his shirts and trousers from a rope strung between walls or from nails driven into them. Yet another thing: Dibyendu had slipped his own soap into Arunav's soap case, thus compelling him to keep his own wet soap in the paper wrapper as a way of keeping it apart. Finally, a bleary-eyed Dibyendu's uncharitable and resentful words and gesture while opening the door every time Arunav returned from his *adda*[lxxxiv] late at night tended to hurt him deeply, making him reach for the advice of Sivananda to be egoless, unselfish, and rise above worldly weal and woe to the level of a *sthitapragyan*.[lxxxv]

That day, of course, things were carried to an extreme, with Sivananda's book cutting no ice at all. Arunav returned home at 11 p.m. to see his house secured with a different lock on the door. Dibyendu was out.

Arunav had given a spare key to Dibyendu. Yet, at this midnight hour, Dibyendu had put another lock on the door and gone out. Arunav climbed down the staircase, carefully counting the steps in the dark, and started to loiter on the road while waiting. After a while, he returned to find the house under lock and key still. While moving up and down like this, Arunav felt pissed off, mentally showered the choicest expletives on Dibyendu, and decided that when he saw Dibyendu next, he would tell him to clear out of his quarter right away. Finally, after being tired of waiting, he knocked on his next-door neighbour Nayar babu's door and

lxxxiv A hangout place.

lxxxv An unruffled person of steady wisdom.

woke him in the dead of the night. Briefing Mr Nayar on his plight, Arunav requested him to let him find his way to the rooftop through his house, as the roof shared by them could be accessed through both their houses.

Thanks to Mr Nayar's kindness, Arunav gained access to the rooftop that night. For how much longer could he wait? He took off his shirt and lay down on the bare floor and drifted off to sleep amid mosquitos, stargazing and myriad thoughts that included wishing death on Dibyendu.

The next morning, he confronted Dibyendu in extreme rage and asked him the reason for his going out like this and putting another lock. Dibyendu, however, disarmed him by telling him nonchalantly that he had to go to the station for some urgent work, and being quite in a hurry and not finding the right key, had put his own lock on the door.

What did Arunav do? Well, he could not give Dibyendu a dressing down, ask him to vacate his quarter or throw out Dibyendu's personal effects, even though he stood face to face with Dibyendu. He didn't say a word; couldn't say it. He went back to the book and spoke aloud the familiar lines.

Then there was this other day. Arunav returned habitually at 11 p.m. and knocked on the door. After quite a delay, Dibyendu opened the door. The moment Arunav entered the house, Dibyendu moved close to him and spoke confidentially and sotto voce: 'Arunav, a girlfriend of mine has come. She will stay here tonight. Make adjustment on the rooftop tonight. Please.'

Girlfriend? Or call girl? What kind of girlfriend could there be in this town who would want to spend a night with a man? The door of Dibyendu's room was ajar. It was dark inside. The sound of the moving fan could be heard. Arunav couldn't figure out what he would do in this situation. He took off his shirt and trousers, and slipped into his habitual informal wear, a lungi, while Dibyendu remained standing there. Having washed and towelled himself, he picked up his cot, mosquito net, sataranji and pillow, and left for the rooftop without speaking a word to Dibyendu. He could hear the door to the rooftop slam shut, bolted and latched from inside.

Suddenly, a wave of anger surged through his body at the sound of the door being closed with a thud. What would he do now? Could he call all the residents of the block and tell them that Dibyendu had brought a cheap woman into his house?

While he wanted to do that at first, he later curbed that desire. As he slept on the sataranji spread over the cot and inside the net, he suddenly felt helpless. Reducing him to a refugee in his own quarter, Dibyendu slept happily with a woman of loose character in his own bedroom. For how long would he carry the dust of humiliation and apathy in every atom of his being? For how many more days? No, he would have to speak up. He was not such a coward that he would tolerate the indignities that Dibyendu heaped upon him. He too was a human being and did have a few things entirely personal—why would he forfeit his claim on these?

No, it was time for action now and he would bang on the door of Dibyendu's room and, the moment he opened the door, he would drive him out of his own house along with his things and that loose woman, accompanying the action with these words: 'I'm the master of this house, do you understand? I let you stay in this house rent-free out of sheer pity. You should have at least realized that.'

Arunav stood up, shaking in anger. He moved towards the door. He was about to bang on the door when he had this strange and surreal feeling—his feet were starting to turn into jelly; he was having a meltdown, as if he didn't have the power to even raise his hand to rap at the door; the soles of his feet were melting, turning into water and flowing away; a chill was cascading downward towards his knees. Sivananda's book was not with him at the moment or else he would have reached for it for solace and advice. With great difficulty he tried to cry out: 'Sivananda, what will I do, Sivananda?'

But the cry remained stuck in his throat. He remained immobilized in that painful pose. His feet were dissolving like ice thawing out.

* * *

Satya Misra (b. 1952)

'The Cross'

(Translated 'Jisukhrista' from the Odia by the author)

They break into houses and steal. Their method is simple. They employ a bit of stealth but not much by way of skill or finesse. Their targets are middle-class households, pre-identified in daylight. They approach their target in the darkness of night and glance furtively around to ensure that the coast is clear. Rocky enters first, through an open skylight or window, which too would have been located during their reconnaissance. Peter follows when Rocky signals. Scaria waits outside, her alert eyes searching furtively for any passerby who may disrupt the operation. Her sensitive ears sometimes detect muffled sounds. This scares her but she keeps staring into the darkness with hesitant anticipation.

She imagines fearful sights and sounds. An ominous bat noisily fluttering its wings just below the pointed gable of the town church! Or an angry dog howling into the dark midnight. Or perhaps it is a jackal, not a dog, with its primal growl, somewhere in a jungle. Even a vampire bat may suddenly fly out of the dark cavity now invaded by Rocky and Peter.

There is no reason why such a thing should happen. But happen it will.

But nothing happens. After some tense moments, her hallucinations fade away as two shapes emerge from darkness. Like a painful delivery after a lengthy labour, Peter and his pet monkey Rocky come out from the unholy womb of darkness with their modest loot.

They don't face any problem. Peter has trained Rocky well. Once inside, Rocky peers into the darkness searching for anything worth stealing. Peter has taught him to identify things that can be burgled and that should not be touched. They aren't greedy, so they remain satisfied with just one or two valuables which can be exchanged somewhere for cash.

They have never been caught. The police constable on the night beat gets no chance even to suspect. Rocky takes hold of stolen goods and hides in some dark alley before the constable can know of his existence. Peter and Scaria keep walking with practised nonchalance.

Not to take any chances, the constable flashes a torchlight, stamps the ground with his heavy boot and shouts, 'Who's there?'

Peter replies, 'Returning home from our village, Master. Search us if you want.' Beams of light scurry back into the round glass of the constable's torch and the darkness speaks, 'Okay, Go ahead.'

Rocky joins them silently after a few yards.

Both Peter and Scaria know that with Rocky in their gang, their nocturnal vocation will continue smoothly. Peter strongly believes that Rocky has a great future in the enterprise of burglary, and will certainly grow into a cunning and competent thief.

'My Rocky, my mate,' he proclaims.

Scaria analyses the relationship and agrees, 'Monkey, the mate of man.'

Peter adds, 'Monkey, the ancestor of man.'

'But the Bible doesn't say that', protests Scaria.

'Who cares what the Bible says?'

'I do. It is our holy book. Tells us about Jesus Christ.'

'Jesus Christ? Who cares?'

'Don't say that. You are not even going to the church.' Scaria's voice now has a tinge of anger.

'Church? I shall go there only if there is something to steal. With Rocky, of course.'

'Oh My God! Jesus! What sacrilege.' Scaria prays, fear writ large in her large round eyes.

'God? Eh? Jesus! Haha!' Peter utters the words like spitting out a tasteless, unchewable lump.

But Scaria will have none of it. She picks up that invisible lump and swallows it up in one eager gulp. 'You don't mean that. It is pure blasphemy. Jesus had given his life for us.'

'Rocky is giving his life for us.'

Finally, they enter into unwritten agreement and drop the topic.

But the situation takes a different turn one night.

Peter, the slinking, low-lying thief that he was, lived mostly by hiding and escaping. But in their tiny bedroom, his nightly transformation into a hyper male was routine. Scaria relished his earthy vigour and machismo. That night, when Peter's wild ecstasy was rushing madly for a violent release, Scaria felt her body melting into a putty under his hard embrace. Man's first sin. Bible says so. But her bliss was rudely interrupted as she cried abruptly, 'Hey, look.'

Pushing Peter's excited body to one side, Scaria stared at the wall as though she was seeing a living ghost there.

'What's the matter?' asked Peter, losing his body tension.

'My God! How did he come here?'

Peter turned his eyes to the spot Scaria was staring at. From a dimly lit corner of their dingy bedroom, two eyes, burning like embers, were looking at their lovemaking.

Rocky!

'How did he come inside? He sleeps outside.'

Peter didn't have an answer to his own question. The sudden discovery of this unwanted intruder in their deeply private space had jolted him. Almost simultaneously, both looked at each other. The mutual realization of their nakedness was abrupt and deeply disturbing. They felt like Adam and Eve, who had eaten the forbidden fruit, committed the primal sin and got caught in the act.

They dressed fast. Rocky looked at them accusingly, like God seeking an explanation from the sinners.

Peter kicked Rocky out and bolted the door from inside.

'Oh God, Oh God', Scaria muttered to herself and wandered aimlessly inside the tiny room. Then she pulled out an old, torn Bible from somewhere and leafed through its crumpled pages seriously.

Peter stared at her in astonishment. Scaria had kept a copy of the Bible hidden somewhere! It was good that this secret got exposed today. Peter was offended by this unexpected discovery. He was not the type to tolerate a girl who worried herself with such trash as God and Jesus.

He rolled on the bed and called her, 'Scaria!'

'No Peter. No more.'

Peter didn't understand.

'We haven't married, Peter.'

'So what?'

'This is sin.'

'Sin?' Peter expelled the word from his mouth like spittle. 'Sin? Sin?'

He was angry but didn't know who the subject of his anger was. The offending word escaped from his mouth again and again like fireballs coming out of a dragon's mouth.

By then, Scaria had started reading aloud from the pages of the Bible.

Peter didn't bother her anymore. He was amused to find that he could utter the word 'sin' in so many different ways, bringing several meanings into his articulation. It is a sin to sleep with a woman whom you haven't married. It is sin to steal things. It is sin to cheat the constable on duty. There are sins of many flavours. His life could be a menu of sins.

Peter was lying listlessly on the bed while Scaria was squatting on the floor with the Bible in her hands. Without any interest or curiosity, he started listening to what she was reading.

And when they come to the place which is called Cavalry, they crucified him there; and the robbers, one on the right hand and the
other on the left.

Peter didn't follow much of it but thought it unfair that the robbers were crucified—one on the right hand and the other on the left. He watched Scaria's moving lips as she went on reading.

And the people stood beholding, and the rulers with them derided them, saying: He saved others; let him save himself, if he be Christ, the elect of God.
And the soldiers also mocked him, coming to him and offering him vinegar,
And saying: If thou be the king of the Jews, save thyself.

'That's that, then,' Peter thought. He was losing the thread, but listened on.

. . . blasphemed him, saying: If thou be Christ, save thyself and us.

Peter felt suffocated. Abruptly getting up from the bed, he set out on a pensive stroll along the silent streets. With no specific destination, he just wandered off counting the lamp posts that were glowing weakly through the night. Every lamp post looked like a cross. He was angry with himself and decided not to surrender his night to the invisible forces that were torturing him. Sheer anguish propelled his weary steps to the prostitutes' colony that was still open for business. What difference did it make? After all, he had not married even Scaria, his live-in mate and partner in crime. Was it only marriage which entitled a man and a woman to copulate?

He didn't need much time or effort to reignite his aggression and masculinity.

Holding the woman in a tight embrace, Peter asked, 'Honey, do you know about Jesus?' But his lip-biting kiss didn't allow her to reply. Not that she wanted to. Peter kept mumbling. 'Scaria keeps a Bible hidden from me. But you are so gracious, darling! I hope you haven't hidden a Bible somewhere. Do you know that Jesus saves the sinners? I wish Rocky were here. Rocky is my pet monkey. You should see him sometime, darling. Monkeys, if you don't know, are our ancestors.'

It was past midnight when he returned to the forlorn streets.

While trudging back, his brain felt like a trash can with assorted thoughts about sin, Jesus, Scaria and the Holy Bible dumped inside. He could not help blaming Scaria, who seemed to consider Peter as the sole beneficiary of all her sins. This attitude implied nothing but her alliance with Jesus. It was clear that the allies viewed Peter as an adversary. Why else did Scaria have to pull out a Bible and read aloud at midnight?

But soon, Peter found a dependable stakeholder for all his sins.

Rocky.

Rocky helped them in burglary. Rocky in fact was the real burglar. He also cheated the constable on the road by hiding their booty. That was sin. And then, though slightly less sinful, in the entire universe of the living, Rocky was the only eyewitness of their fornication.

Rocky is sin incarnate. The thought gave him some comfort.

But what happened the very next day changed all that.

Possibly, Rocky didn't consider himself in any way different from Peter, nor did he hesitate to demonstrate this unique feeling of oneness with his master. Peter was sitting outside, staring at the tall steeples of the church which made him depressed. In a proud posturing quite unbecoming of them, the spires had penetrated deep into the bluish evening sky.

His reverie was shattered by a sharp cry of terror from inside his home. It was mixed with an inexplicably rough guttural sound which appeared to be that of Rocky.

Peter rushed inside. Rocky was trying to disrobe Scaria with his claws. Scaria was struggling to ward him off and protect her modesty while crying helplessly. The sharp nails of the animal had scratched her body at places, some of which were bleeding.

Peter pulled Rocky away from Scaria and threw him roughly on the floor. With a sharp cry of agony, the primate scampered away to his resting place.

The animal could not be tolerated any further, friend or whatever. Peter was mad with fury. Sensing that his fury might get diluted by an affection that he had nurtured for Rocky all along, he resolved not to be overpowered by any such weakness. Rocky was the ultimate sinner.

Peter knew sin was neither evil nor offensive. It could be sweet and rewarding as well. He would even worship sin as a deity if it appeared before him with a visible shape. Some sinners were clearly more sinful than others.

The next day, around noon, Peter summoned Scaria, 'Come Scaria, look at Jesus on the cross.' His voice was loud but unsteady.

Scaria was not available to respond, but when she came after sometime, a macabre scene awaited her. She could actually see the crucifixion.

A wooden cross was perched against the wall of the outer room. Rocky was crucified, his limbs grotesquely nailed at appropriate spots on the cross. Like Jesus. Blood was still dripping from the body, forming a puddle on the floor. Rocky was gasping in a desperate attempt to cling to whatever was left of his life. His mouth was wide open, with its grotesque smile of death, exposing two rows of teeth mocking his human partners. Scaria could hear the soft ominous splashes of blood dripping on the crimson puddle. Peter stood like a sorcerer, glowing with animal blood splashed all over him.

Peter took his own face close to the monkey's and spit hard on the dying creature's face. He started mocking him in a hoarse voice that didn't sound like his own. 'You have saved others. Now save yourself if you can.'

Pulling out half a bottle of cheap rum from the shelf, he poured it in a tumbler. He held the tumbler close to the monkey's mouth and repeated, 'If you are the saviour, then save yourself.'

Scaria ran away in horror before Rocky's body became still. Peter kneeled before the cross and prayed, 'Hallowed be thy name, thy kingdom come'.

Scaria had no doubt that Peter had lost his mind. He would do something more ominous if she didn't tend him back to his normal self.

As the night deepened, she bolted the door from inside and checked herself before a mirror in the dim glow of a bed lamp. She climbed on the bed and hooked a leg seductively around Peter while undressing.

Peter pushed her with a savage kick and shouted, 'Wretched whore! You want to crucify me, don't you? But you can't make a Jesus of me.'

* * *

Dash Benhur (b. 1953)

'The Crow'

(Translated 'Kau' from the Odia by Jatindra K. Nayak)

Udia would wake up with a start even in the middle of the night. It seemed to him as if a crow had flown in from somewhere and cawed near him. Its loud cawing brought the whole place down. But when Udia would get up and prick his ears, he would hear nothing at all. Everything would seem eerily quiet. Phagu Nana would lie like a log on a bench over there, absolutely still. A stray dog would bark intermittently somewhere. A leaking tap in the hotel kitchen kept dripping on the dishes in the sink.

Udia would remind himself that he must get up early, and do the dishes and the cooking pots. Or else his employer would hurl the choicest abuses at him.

He would try to close his eyes and go back to sleep. But sleep would elude him. In the thinning darkness, he would sometimes see the smooth round eyes of a crow; at some other time, he would see a lone crow flying off into the distance.

The sky would be covered with dark clouds. A roof of clouds shut out the light of the sun. A single crow winged its way through the thin darkness. It flew endlessly towards some strange far-off land. It spread its wings as if it was getting ready for a bout of wrestling. At times, it suddenly came face to face with Udia and stared at him out of its deep black round eyes, tossing its head from side to side. It talked, opening its beak. Then it flew off, flapping its wings.

This happened a number of times. But every time the crow would fly off, Udia's heart would pound. He would feel as if he suddenly crashed down from a great height.

It was five years since Udia came to work in Adarsh Hotel in Cuttack. He had started by cleaning the tables. Later, he graduated to doing the dishes. He was twelve when he had first come here. He was dark-complexioned, had spindly legs and was narrow-chested. He also had big, bulging, staring eyes.

Madan Rout, who belonged to a village near Udia's and worked as a peon in Cuttack, had found the latter this job. Madan had brought Udia to Cuttack with the promise that he would find him a good job. The owner of Adarsh Hotel was known to Madan and he gave Udia work.

Udia recalled the hard words the hotel owner had said to him when he first set his eyes on him. 'What work would this crow-footed boy do? He looks famine-stricken. His hands and legs are stick-like, but see what a large belly he has. The rascal would devour everything. Well, let him work. We will see about his wages later.'

That very day, Udia was given the job of mopping the tables. In the beginning, he was not at all good at this kind of work. While cleaning tables, he would often rub left-over food on them. When this happened, the owner and sometimes even the customers, would charge at him, shouting. Whenever he slowed down, the hotel owner would scream, 'You stupid useless fellow.'

One day, while putting the dishes on the table into a bucket, Udia dropped them all. A few customers made a racket. The owner boxed his ears and gave him such a stinging slap that everything for him became a blank and he nearly fainted.

The hotel had five or six employees. Phagu nana was the cook. Dhumal cut vegetables, ground spices, and brought provisions from the shop. Linga served the customers. Natha doubled as a waiter and a water-carrier. A boy called Loka worked for a daily wage. Except on holidays, he cleared the tables and wiped them clean.

Of them all, only Phagu nana was fond of Udia and looked after him. The day Udia received a slap, Phagu nana rushed in and led him away from the owner. Not that others ill-treated Udia, but none of them looked upon him with affection as Phagu nana did.

Udia got his ears boxed if he made even the slightest mistake. On occasions, he received a slap or a kick. After wiping tables for a year, he was given the job of washing utensils in the backyard. After doing this for six months, he received a monthly wage of 20 rupees. Ghana Lenka, the hotel owner said, 'You get trained during the first six months. You don't get paid for this period.' Udia said nothing. He only stared at his employer, who shouted, 'Why do you gape at me like that? Bastard, you are staring at me like a crow.'

Every month, Udia sent his wages to his father through Madan Rout.

Flocks of crows gathered around Udia whenever he washed the dishes sitting by the drain in the backyard. He threw bones, leftover rice and fish bones at them. The crows gratefully accepted the gifts. They came down whenever they felt like, ate whatever they found and flew wherever it suited them. He said 'hush' and they flew off. Why should they linger in a place where they were not wanted?

Earlier, the crows would not dare approach him. But these days, they came, stood close to him and circled over his head. Udia had never seen crows from such close quarters. After he left his village, he had lived like a prisoner. Now, the crows made him feel as if he had found a lot of friends. Udia worked in the backyard all day long and played with the crows, watched them, admired their tough beaks, looked at their black eyes, which resembled glass beads.

He noticed that all crows were not alike. There were some among them who were clever. When he threw bones at them, he saw that a particular crow caught them in the air before they fell on the ground. The others would not have a chance. One of the crows had lost a leg, but it got the better of other able-bodied crows when it came to pouncing on a delicacy.

Ever since he was given the chore of cleaning pots and plates in the backyard, Udia's life seemed to change for the better. He had grown to like the crows. It no longer hurt when his boss called him a crow. Rather, the birds appeared in his dreams as intimate friends. On some days, he saw red, blue, violet, yellow and green crows in his dreams. At times, the sound of a crow cawing suddenly roused his from sleep.

There were many like Udia who worked for a living in Cuttack. In some places worked boys even younger than him. On his days off, when he wandered about in the streets, he often came across some of them. His thoughts turned to his own lot. He would comfort himself somehow.

Udia's body had undergone many changes in the course of the last five years. His chest had grown broader and he had grown taller. He had now the beginnings of a moustache under his nose. His calf muscles had become stronger. His workload in the hotel had also grown heavier. But his wages had not kept pace with these changes. His nails had worn away and the gaps between his toes were inflamed due to always being exposed to water. Whenever he fell ill, he would curl up like a python and endure the pain until it went away on its own. Once or twice, Phagu nana brought him medicine from a homeopath's shop close by. During the last five years, he had visited his village only twice. The condition of his family had not improved. His father said, 'Why don't you ask your employer to raise your wages? You have worked for so long. How can one make do with only 40 rupees?'

Once, after coming back from his village, Udia felt bold and said to his boss. 'Sir, my father wants you to give me a little more. We can't manage with what I get.' Ghana Lenka lunged at him, saying, 'Get lost, you bastard. If one has enough stale rice in his pot, there won't be dearth of crows flying in. How dare you talk about increasing your wages? What work are you doing here, anyway? Get out. There is no shortage of hands these days. So you can't scare me.'

Udia did not utter a word. He went into the backyard and started doing the dishes. He threw leftover rice to the crows. For some strange reason, the crows looked pitiable today. Ah, poor creatures! The other birds moved from place to place, toiling hard to gather food. But these crows waited for crumbs to be flung at them. True, there will always be crows around if you have enough rice in a pot.

As Udia grew older, many thoughts crowded into his mind. His thoughts often turned to the crows. When the day dawned, he went and sat among them till evening fell. Now and then, he went inside to collect pots and plates, and after washing them, took them back in. Crows came and went, but Udia worked away, sitting by the drain.

Worries oppressed Udia when he thought about his own situation. Back home, there were his parents and two sisters. His sisters had reached marriageable age, and his father was keen to marry them off. But where was the money? Udia was convinced he should get at least 100 rupees per month. Young men like him were paid 150 rupees, even 200 rupees. But Ghana Lenka would not listen to his request for a raise. Who else could he approach? Maybe he should go back to his village. Even if no one hired him there, he could try to do something on his own.

Phagu nana had told him the other day, 'Who bothers about us? If only all of us who work in this hotel get together and say, "This is the wage we are entitled to. Pay us a fair wage, or else we won't work for you." But that is not going to happen. Whoever opens his mouth will be kicked out and a replacement will be quickly found.' Udia had heard what Phagu nana said, but he kept quiet as if he understood nothing. He thought to himself, 'How did it matter if poor wretches like us get united or not? The bosses will never care to listen to us. Again, who knows who works where, and how could anyone bring them together? The boss was right after all. We are no better than crows. We will live on leftover food and flock around leftover rice. And we would scatter scared the moment someone so much as hissed at us.'

Udia seemed preoccupied these days. Sometimes, he wondered if there was any point in worrying at all.

One day, he decided that, come what may, he would ask his boss to give him a raise, and that he would say it firmly. If his boss said no, he would go to his village and never set foot in Cuttack.

One day, Ghana Lenka was smoking a bidi, sitting by the cash box after taking his midday meal. Udia approached him, saying, 'I get very low wages. People working in other hotels here get 100 rupees, even 150. Please pay me at least 75.'

Ghana Lenka exploded and rushed at him, screaming, 'What did you say, you bastard? You want 75 rupees a month? Has your father ever received 75 rupees? How dare you? Get lost.'

Udia repeated what he had said earlier. 'No. Give me 75 rupees. Other hotel owners pay their employees this much. Why would you not do so?'

This was the limit. Ghana Lenka lunged at Udia and dealt him two resounding slaps. He shouted, 'Take your wages. You want more? Do you?' He rushed at Udia again, but Phagu nana and Linga pulled him away, or else Udia would have received a few more blows.

Udia sobbed uncontrollably. Ghana's five fingers had left red welts across his cheek. Phagu nana tried hard to make him see reason, but something had snapped inside Udia. He decided he would leave the hotel before dawn the next day.

Udia went to the backyard without saying so much as a word and busied himself with washing plates. Tears streaked his cheeks. He considered his hands and legs. He was now seventeen years old—a fully-grown man. But his boss had thrashed him as if he was a mere child. The shame of it withered Udia.

He went on doing the dishes. He threw leftover rice at the crows who had gathered about him. Suddenly, he saw that all the crows flew off and settled on the road. In no time, thousands upon thousands of crows assembled there. Udia ran to the road to find out what had happened. But there were so many crows around that it was difficult to see what was going on. Someone said to him, 'A crow flew into a telephone wire and broke its wings. So the crows have now encircled him.'

The racket made by the crows went on till evening. When night fell, they dispersed. The crow with the broken wings also disappeared.

All afternoon, Udia did his allotted chores. He did not say a word to anyone. There was no need, for he was to leave the next morning.

At night, in a dream, he saw that thousands of crows had surrounded him. He was lying wounded. The crows were trying to raise him using their beaks, which slowly turned into hands. The crows themselves slowly got transformed into human beings. They all looked like Udia, tall and dressed in shorts. Their nails had rusted away. The gaps between their toes were covered with sores. They all cawed and said, 'Get up. Rise to your feet. We are all by your side. We will come running to you if you call us.' Caw. Caw. Caw. Caw. Hundreds of crows cawed.

Udia woke up. The darkness was thinning out. The eastern sky in front of the house was slowly becoming light. In that weak light, Udia looked at himself, felt his body with his hands and said to himself, 'Wait for me, Ghana Lenka, you bastard. I'll show you what a crow like me can do.'

* * *

Sahadev Sahoo (b. 1959)

'The Amrit Mahotshova in the Tehsil Office' (Translated 'Tehsil Officere Amrit Mahotshova' from the Odia by Snehaprava Das)

The Independence Day fell on a Monday.

Since it followed the Sunday and a second Saturday, it meant that there were three consecutive holidays for the office workers. Pramila, Sudhir's wife, had made the plan to visit her parental home in those three days much in advance. Her sister, who had settled in USA, would also come to India at that time. They would enjoy a good time together. She had also planned for a sightseeing tour through Puri and Konark. Sudhir had been transferred to Purangarh as the *tehsildar*.[lxxxvi] He was now the office head. It had not been mandatory for him to attend the Independence Day meeting when he was posted at the old headquarters. Nobody questioned him. It was the duty of the head of the office to hoist the flag and address the gathering. If the head of the office remained absent for some reason, some other employee did the job on his behalf. He himself had hoisted the flag once when the office head could not make it.

But here, he was the head of the office. He had to hoist the flag and take care of the other formalities. This year, the nation was celebrating the seventy-fifth anniversary of its independence. The office staff were more excited about obtaining a day's leave than being inspired about celebrating

[lxxxvi] A revenue official.

the occasion. But the government had, at least, taken all steps to inspire a feeling of jubilation in them. The stringent rules about tricolour hoisting were slackened. The tricolour would not have to be taken down in the night as was the practice. People could keep the tricolour fluttering in their terraces and premises for three days. Replicas of the tricolour were being sold at the post office and there was a long queue before the counter for the national flag.

Since he was the head of the office, Sudhir had to be present at his workplace and hoist the flag. There would be serious consequences if the programme was cancelled. Anyone with a mobile was a news reporter these days. Such news travelled in social media with the speed of lightning. Anyone could click a picture or interview the employees at the office and post the item on Facebook, Instagram, Twitter or WhatsApp. It would reach the masses in an instant and hurt their patriotic sentiment. The action would be denounced with vehemence as anti-national, and he himself would be trolled mercilessly on the social media sites. The news would reach the higher authorities of the department in no time, and they would take disciplinary action against him. He recollected a recent episode of a school mistress getting suspended for dozing off in the class room. Someone had captured her snoozing in a video recording and the government authorities had suspended her from service. Sudhir did not want to suffer similar consequences.

'The country celebrates the Amrit Mahotsav on the occasion of the seventy-fifth anniversary of Independence on 15 August. I shall have to remain present in the office to hoist the flag. My absence here on that day may be regarded as negligence of duty by the authorities. I think I will stay back. You take our daughter along with you,' Sudhir said to Pramila.

Pramila glared at him for a long moment. The look in her eyes was eloquent enough. 'You speak as if you are the only one who does a government job. What is the meaning of earning money if you cannot fulfil such small wishes of your family?' Sudhir interpreted the glare in his wife's eyes.

He tried to explain it to Pramila before she could voice her displeasure, 'There is no other officer here who could be entrusted with that duty. It would have been easier for me, had there been an additional tehsildar here. I know how you must be feeling, but it is truly difficult for me to find a substitute who would hoist the flag.'

'Which tehsildar would be staying in this godforsaken place on holidays?' Pramila said glumly. 'They must be making some alternative arrangement when the tehsildar remains on leave. My sister and brother-in-law are coming to India after three years. God knows when they will come again. They will feel very bad if I do not come to meet them.'

The look in Pramila's eyes was a blend of request and resentment.

'You are right. Let me see what could be done,' Sudhir said without much confidence.

Reaching the office on Friday morning, the first thing Sudhir did was to call the head clerk to his office. 'It will not be possible for me to be present here on 15 August. I will go to my parents-in-laws' house with family. You will have to hoist the flag on my behalf.'

'I cannot afford to stay back, sir. I am very busy. My father is to undergo a surgery on that day in a nursing home at Cuttack. The date had been fixed much before.'

The refusal was polite, but firm.

Sudhir could not compel the head clerk. He had decided to get the date for his father's surgery fixed during that period because he would be getting three consecutive holidays. The next option was the revenue inspector. Sudhir made a phone call to him and repeated his suggestion.

'I have submitted my leave application in the office, sir,' the R.I. returned, 'I am going for a *darshan*[lxxxvii] of Goddess

lxxxvii To have a glimpse of a deity in a temple.

Vaishno Devi. I will join back on the eighteenth. I am already on my way.'

Sudhir looked questioningly at the head clerk. 'Yes, sir, he had submitted his application for leave last evening. You had left the office by that time. I will put it up in the file and send it to you for your approval in a while,' the head clerk said.

Sudhir asked the junior clerk if he could perform the duty of flag hoisting.

'My mother is not well, sir. I will go to my village with family during these three-day holidays. We hardly get three consecutive holidays in our job.' The junior clerk smiled sheepishly.

Who would hoist the flag? Sudhir was worried and displeased. His subordinates had made plans to use the three days' holiday to take care of their personal engagements. What irritated him most was that they had not cared to ask for the consent of their superior officer, the office head. They had taken things for granted. Sudhir was not rigid about his staff leaving the headquarters on Sundays and other public holidays without prior permission. But the Republic Day and the Independence Day were not ordinary holidays. The office staff had to remain present in the office for the flag-hoisting ceremony. It would create a furore if the flag hoisting in the office was cancelled. Notorious people like unemployed young men, petty political leaders and small-time news reporters, who love to turn unimportant issues sensational, might make a video recording of it, and post it on social media sites. The office head would be put under the gallows for sheer negligence of government duty, as if to celebrate the occasion was the sole responsibility of the head of the office! Sudhir thought sourly.

'Subala can do it, sir,' the head clerk suggested.

'Subala? The office peon?' Sudhir asked.

'Yes, sir.'

Sudhir thought about it. Subala worked as a peon in the office. He was a glib talker. On the day Sudhir had joined duty, Subala had narrated a proud panegyric about his warrior ancestors who were *paiks*, the peasant militias of the Gajapati rulers of Odisha. He told of how his forefathers had rendered military services to Buxi Jagabandhu during the paika rebellion of 1817. The British government crushed the rebellion and got the chieftains hanged and their property confiscated. 'The old Banyan tree where they were hung to death still stands at the end of the village as a testament of their undaunted spirit,' he said. Time has cast a patina over the past glory and forced him, their descendant to take up the job of a peon in the Tehsil office, but people still regard his lineage in respect.

'But he is a peon. Won't people disapprove of it if he hoists the national flag?' Sudhir asked warily.

'Why should they, sir? He too is a citizen of the country. Besides, it is not his first time. He has done it more than once. He hoists the flag when the tehsildar and the office staff remain absent on such occasions,' the head clerk assured Sudhir.

Sudhir was in two minds. He had a fear of social media. 'These days social media has become very active. If someone finds something untoward, he may capture a picture of it in a mobile camera and post it on different social media sites. The news will spread around like wildfire. A disciplinary proceeding might be initiated against us by the department if it catches the notice of the authorities,' he said.

After a long deliberation, he called Subala to his office room.

Subala entered the room and wished him politely.

'None of us will remain present in the office on 15 August for the flag hoisting ceremony. Could you hoist the flag on behalf of the office?' Sudhir asked looking at him.

'I will do it, sir,' Subala agreed readily. There was no reluctance in his voice—he sounded happy.

'You must be very careful. There should not be any slip. You know how active the social media is these days. There is a news reporter in every house. It will be immediately made public if anything goes wrong,' Sudhir cautioned him.

'Don't you worry, sir. Everything will be perfect. I will see to it that no one raises a finger at us. Why should anyone find fault in it, sir? Which family in this region other than ours has a significant role in India's freedom movement? Our ancestors have shed their blood for the freedom of this country. We are the descendants of the famous paik chieftains. Circumstances have compelled me to work as a peon here, but the blood that flows in my veins is that of the paikas. Those who move about flaunting a mobile phone, and brag about the rights and wrongs are mere nobodies. They depend on the charity of the government to survive. They live in houses acquired free of cost through the Indira Abasa Scheme and use a toilet through the Swachha Bharat Mission. They live on the one-rupee-per-kilogram-rice, and the allowances the government gives out to the old and the decrepit. I may be a peon, but no one in this area has the pluck to utter a word against me.'

'Well, then,' Sudhir said resignedly, 'I trust you. Manage the situation somehow.'

'You rest assured, sir. Nothing will go wrong. You will see when you get back.' Subala sounded convincing.

They had all left the headquarters on Friday night entrusting Subala with the responsibility.

Sudhir spent a happy time with Pramila's sister and brother-in-law. They had gone to Puri on 14 August and spent the night there. After a darshan of the Lord Jagannath the following morning, they went to the sea beach. Subala had posted the pictures of the flag hoisting ceremony on WhatsApp. There were pictures of schoolchildren and other people standing in front of the flagpole, and pictures of Subala hoisting the flag. There were photos of snack packets being distributed amongst them too. Sudhir felt relaxed. Subala had organized the function flawlessly.

He joined back the office on 16 August. There were two neatly folded newspapers on his table. One of them was a local daily where the news of the flag hoisting ceremony at the tehsil office of Purunagarh was published. The other newspaper which had a wide circulation across the state had given good coverage to the event. On its regional page, there were several pictures of the flag hoisting event, followed by the news in detail. Sudhir was pleased with Subala. He might be a peon, a glib talker, but he had done a good job.

Sometime after, Subala submitted an account of the expenditure incurred.

14,500 rupees! It gave Sudhir a jolt.

He knew there was only 200 rupees in the office contingency fund for such functions. Since it was too paltry a sum, the head of the office and the other staff members who had some secondary income besides their regular salary, would contribute from their pockets to meet the extra expenses. But the amount had never been this big.

He called for Subala.

'What is this? Why has such a big amount been spent just for a flag hoisting ceremony?'

'Sir, you know that the Amrit Mahotsav was celebrated this year on the occasion of the Independence Day. The function had to be something grand. You have seen how the newspapers have given it a wide coverage. All students from the schools in the neighbourhood had attended the function. 400 snack packets had been ordered. Then there were the journalists and news reporters. They needed special treatment. 12,000 rupees had been spent only for the refreshment. You know how expensive it is!' Subala smiled sheepishly.

'Okay,' Sudhir said dismissively. Subala left.

Sudhir waited for a while and then called for the head clerk.

'Have you seen this bill?' he asked when the head clerk came.

'Yes, sir. The total expenses would not have exceeded 3000 or 4000. He says that he has spent 12,000 rupees for refreshments. Who can verify that? Who knows how many packets or, if at all, he had ordered the snack packets? A few days back, he was asking me for a loan of 10,000 rupees for his father's treatment. I refused him since my own father had to undergo a surgery and I needed the money for the medical expenses. It was a golden opportunity for him when he was asked to take the responsibility of the celebration of Independence Day in the office. He made the best use of it.'

Without making a remark, Sudhir took out 2000 rupees from his wallet and handed it to the head clerk. 'Ask others to contribute their share and give 14,500 rupees,' he said.

* * *

Paresh Kumar Patnaik (b. 1960)

'Sermon'

(Translated 'Prabachana' from the Odia by Snehaprava Das)

There was still some time left for the recital of Ramacharitmanas to begin.

The stage was ready. Pasted against the backdrop was a large banner that displayed the glowing images of Lord Ramachandra, Goddess Sita, Lakshman and Hanuman. The stage was extensively decorated with flowers and streamers. The seat that was placed in the middle of the stage looked like an ornate throne, from where the famous preacher Ramabhakta Das would deliver the holy sermon.

Elaborate arrangements were made in front of the stage for the devotees, a good number of which had arrived at the venue. All eyes were immersed on the stage. The devotees were eagerly waiting for the holy recital to begin—some enthusiastic devotees were shouting Jai Shri Ram intermittently. The women devotees were ululating every now and then. The environment had turned spiritual. The devotees were getting impatient. 'Why are the organizers delaying? Let the programme begin. Let the miserable souls stuck in ignorance and the falsehood of the illusive world get redeemed with the enlightening preaching. Let the sublime words wash away the sins.'

Suddenly, there was a commotion in one corner behind the stage. The sound of loud hailing and sloganeering was heard amidst the beating of gongs and ringing bells. The man of wisdom, the great preacher Pundit Ramabhakta Das, followed by his entourage, ambled on to the stage in a royal grandeur from that corner. He was dressed in an expensive and shiny ochre-coloured robe. Raising both his hands up in a posture of blessing the audience, he advanced towards the throne in the middle of the stage. The audience, now spiritually stirred, cried out the name of Lord Rama and hailed the preacher. His face lit up with a beatific smile, Pundit Ramabhakta Das settled on the throne. The sound of the gongs and bells had subsided. An important figure of the village and the president of the Rama Charita Manas committee, Shyamaghana Das climbed on to the stage now to deliver the inaugural speech. In his address, he spoke extensively about Lord Ramachandra, his devotion to his father and his commitment to fulfil his father's wish. He tried to prove that despite his rural background, he had enough knowledge of the Ramayana and had read all the seven volumes. 'The character of Ramachandra presents an illustrious example of obedience of a son to his father,' he said. He explained that one's parents are the most important people in one's lives. One who does not love and obey his parents is doomed to suffer in hell. Our devotion for the Lord is of no value unless we follow his ideals and practice his principles in our own life. Parents are living gods. Worshipping them should be the motto of our life.

A ruckus amidst the audience interrupted Shyamaghana Das's speech. Someone flung a few unsavoury comments at him. Shyamaghana babu paused and pricked his ears to listen.

It was not easy to get a clear view of the people there from the stage. The stage was brilliantly lit, but the audience arena was in semi darkness. It was also heavily crowded with devotees. Some were standing in the back and would not sit down and remain quiet despite several requests from the volunteers. 'The comments must have been made by someone from that section,' Shyamaghana guessed. He threw an open challenge and demanded with aggression:

'Who is the one that commented? What did you say exactly? Could you repeat it?'

'It was me, sir!,' a voice sounded from the dimly lit space at the back of the audience arena. 'I have said it.'

Shyamaghana stretched his gaze to trace the source of the sound, but it was not easy to make it out.

'Would you say it again?' he flicked the question at an indistinct figure who he guessed to be the one that had commented.

'Sir, weren't you advising a little while before to respect and obey one's father like Lord Ramachandra did?'

'Yes, I did,' Shyamaghana said. 'Did I say something wrong?' His voice was sardonic.

'No, sir. There was nothing wrong with that. It seems you have learnt the Ramayana by heart.' The spectator's voice was no less sarcastic. 'You should have just made a small correction in that. You should have said, "Everyone except me must follow the ideal of Lord Ramachandra and revere his parents."'

Shyamaghana was surprised at the frank accusation made by an unknown person, but he was not ready to reveal his embarrassment. He curled his lips in a derisive smile and asked, 'What do you mean by that?'

'I mean to say that what you say amounts to hypocrisy. Last night, you beat your father and the neighbours saw it. You have thrown him out of the house. No one knows if you have given the old man something to eat or not. Most of the time, the loud noise of fights and arguments is heard from your house. People have also heard your old father crying pitiably. What an irony it is that today, you are delivering a sermon from this platform to this large gathering to worship parents,' the mischievous man retorted.

Shyamaghana was a bit nonplussed. He peered at the crowd of faces rendered unrecognizable in the thin darkness. Who could have been bold enough to offend him in this manner in public? He was both disgruntled and curious. The man who questioned him was hidden in the darkness and Shyamaghana could not detect him. But he was not a character to admit defeat so easily. He enjoyed the repute of a respectable and philanthropic figure of the village. He also donated large amounts to the cultural and spiritual institutions of the village. He was offered a seat in the front in the functions organized by these institutions. He, like the zamindars of older times, owned a huge, landed property. He could deliver enlightening discourses in meetings. He had connections with political organizations too.

The unexpectedness of the incident and the insulting accusation of the young man shocked him, but he did not look defeated. The expression on his face was one of arrogance and stubbornness.

'How dare you insult me in this manner? This is *my* native place, my homeland. Don't you forget that,' he shot back at the invisible offender.

The man who challenged Shyamaghana was still hidden in the darkness. Some of the other spectators, who vouched their loyalty to Shyamaghana, got up from their seats and began looking for the man amongst the crowd, even though Shyamaghana had not asked them to do that.

'Why shouldn't I sir? Did I say something wrong?' The man asked from the darkness.

Shyamaghana's lips twisted in a mocking smile.

'But why do you bring in the private issues of my family here in this public gathering?'

'Shouldn't I?' the man from the darkness demanded. 'Then why do you speak glib lies in this public gathering? Why don't you admit that you have beaten your father?'

Shyamaghana admitted his mistake but not without making an argument to justify his act.

'Yes, I hit my father. I was compelled to. I do not think it is a heinous crime. If all sons were to be as revering as Ramachandra, then their fathers too should have to be as noble as King Dasaratha. Do all sons obey their father? Did

Prahallada obey his father's command? We worship Prahallad because he defied his father. You do not know my father. He is a demon within a *Hiranyakashyap*.'[lxxxviii]

'In that case, you should first advise the son to examine if his father is a King Dasaratha or a Hiranyakashyap and treat him accordingly,' the man said obstinately and laughed out loud.

Shyamaghana was unfazed despite these sarcastic assaults.

The hubbub in the venue had given way to a strange silence. Only a few random murmurs infiltrated it. 'Who is this man? Where from he has come and why is he asking such intriguing questions?' Some were doubtful if at all the programme of Sri Ramacharita Manasa would be conducted. Beads of perspiration had formed on the face of preacher Ramabhakta Das. Visibly disturbed, he mopped his face with his expensive mantle, taking care not to spoil the makeup.

'Am I the only sinner in this entire earth?' Shymaghana demanded, throwing away his ostentatious calm. 'Am I the only hypocrite? You say that I speak only lies, that I am a fraud. Are all those present here epitomes of divinity? Are they holy sages without a speck of blemish on their character? What about this preacher here? Is he a saint? A noble character like Lord Ramachandra? You brand me a sinner because you have seen me beating my father. Has anyone seen what this man has done?'

Pundit Ramabhakta Das, who was preparing to recite and explain the holy Ramayan looked embarrassed and insulted. He reacted to the remarks of Shyamaghana with unconcealed hostility.

'You have invited me here as a guest. But now you are offending me with your unkind words. Does it suit you?'

[lxxxviii] Hiranyakashyap was a demon king and a staunch hater of Vishnu. Vishnu slayed him in the incarnation of Narsimha or lion-man.

'Guest, my foot!' Shyamaghana sniggered, a bitter smile on his face. 'You have not obliged us by coming here. You have been paid for that. You had bargained about the payment. Hadn't you?'

'Who would come to deliver a religious speech in such programmes without being paid?' Pundit Ramabhakta Das scoffed. 'No one becomes a guest in these programmes for free. Only a few desperate ones might be doing that. I have always been regarded with respect wherever I have gone. This is the only place where I am treated so disgracefully.'

'Could you claim that you are an illumined soul?' Shyamaghana retorted.

'I am a spiritual speaker. A preacher of divine commandments. Why should I claim to be an illumined soul?'

'Preacher indeed!' Shyamaghana sneered. 'Didn't you ask me last night for a couple of bottles of foreign liquor? You have also asked to get you 2 kilograms of dry fish to take to your home. Not only that, but you have also smoked weed this evening before coming here. No one is a saint here!'

'Shame! Shame! It is a sacrilege!' voices were heard from the audience. People were getting impatient. The gentle murmur in the audience had now grown to a loud buzzing.

'An untoward situation has defiled the aura of spiritualism even before the programme has begun. It would have been such a satisfying experience to hear the recital of the Ramayana. But one wicked man has spoiled it, making a mention of irrelevant topics. Why don't the organizers catch hold of the man and drive him out of the place? What should have been a spiritual discourse is now reduced to an exchange of bitter altercations on his account.'

The voice that was flinging challenges to the stage from the darkness seemed to have gathered strength. It was now distinct and solemn. Another slashing comment was shot at Pundit Ramabhakta Das from that area of invisibility.

'Revered Pundit! Now it is your turn to say something.'

'What should I say?' Pundit Ramabhakta Das looked flustered.

'Do you practice your holy preaching in your personal life? You preach the glory of Lord Ramachandra and advise people to follow his ideal. Do you follow the noble ideology of the Lord in your life? Do you really regard your parents with reverence?

Pundit Ramabhakta Das took a thoughtful pause. He braced himself to confront the truth:

> My dear man, I do not know who you are. But I thank you for the courage you have shown to ask me the questions. You too should thank me for braving the adverse consequences of my candid confession. I am not at all a saint. But I can enact the role of one with expertise. You are moved by the tattered garb of a beggar, and your heart melts with pity. In the same way, I too garb myself in the robe of a holy man, a saint, and the spectators are spiritually motivated. They become eager to listen to the holy words I spill out. The beggar changes his garb in the evening and goes out to watch a movie in a modern outfit. You cannot recognize him. Would you listen to me or pay me any respect if I come here in a pair of jeans and a T-shirt to recite the divine texts?

Yes, it is true that I had drunk alcohol last night. But there is a reason behind it. Drinking alcohol gives me the boost to preach with conviction. I smoked weed some time ago for the same reason, to sound convincing to you and to make my words impressive enough to awaken a feeling of spiritualism in you. Your favourite movie actors are taking banned drugs to bring perfection to their acting and impress the viewers. Do you reject them or the movies? They act better because of that.

You have questioned me if I regard my parents with respect or not. I had once been an obedient and dutiful son. But everything turned topsy-turvy after my marriage. My wife could not adjust well with my parents. There were constant fights over small issues. Despite all efforts, I could not find out a solution to the conflict. I tried to change my wife's mind by reading to her episodes from holy texts but failed pathetically. The same thing happened with my mother. I was compelled to live in a separate house, away from my parents.

> And now about the dry fish. I am not a seer or a divine figure. I am an ordinary human being. I have not relinquished the material world, even though I am regarded as a *brahmachari*[lxxxix] in places like this. Devotees will not be motivated to attend these events if the sermonizer is not a brahmachari. The marital status of the preacher must have to be kept a secret. My wife is fond of dry fish. 'What have you brought for me?' she would inquire when I reached home. I have to please her with the gift of dry fish in order to avoid squabbles at home. The status of a preacher does not help a husband to escape the tantrums of his wife.

'Why don't you preach your gospels to your wife?' the impish questioner would not give up.

Pundit Ramabhakta Das heaved out a sigh. 'I do not have the nerve to do that. It is she who preaches gospels to me. For husbands like me, the words of the wives are the holy command.'

The sound of raucous laughter rose from audience arena.

'Judged by strict ethical parameters, I may be branded as a sinner, a phoney,' Pundit Ramabhakta Das resumed. 'But I wear the persona of a man of virtues. I can deliver moving

---

[lxxxix] The one who abstains from carnal pleasures, a celibate.

sermons. I can elaborate and interpret the sacred texts with expertise. I can recite poems. I can sing, too. I can hold the audience overwhelmed by my talents. All the while, I wear a mask of falsehood. Unfortunately that mask has dropped today. It now depends solely on your wish whether this programme will be conducted or not.' Ramabhakta Das stopped and waited for a response from the audience.

There was a mixed reaction amongst the people. 'Shame! Shame! A group condemned the so-called godmen. 'All of them are frauds,' some others snorted. 'All sinners have gathered here today at this marketplace of Kandarpur.'

Shyamaghana took the cordless microphone once again and spoke into it.

'Everything has come out to the open now. Nothing remains hidden. You have no misconception now about the true nature of the men present here. Now the question is whether the programme will continue or not.'

Piercing the commotion in the audience, voices rose demanding the continuation of the programme.

'Yes. The programme must continue. We are waiting here since evening to listen to the holy recital of Ramacharitmanas, and prayers and kirtans. The event must not be cancelled under any circumstances.'

The cordless microphone exchanged hands. Now it was in the hands of Pundit Ramabhakta Das.

'My dear devotees! You are interested to listen to the words of a sinner like me. That shows how liberal, how God-loving you all are. It proves that you are true devotees of Lord Ramachandra. I must make a small request before I begin. The truly virtuous ones must leave the place. This is not a fit place for them to be in.'

There was a furore amongst the audience. But no one left the place.

'It was decided prior that on the day of this spiritual programme everyone in the village should follow the path of honesty. They should eat vegetarian food, not sin, show respect to their parents and elders, and not hurt them with unkind words. They should conduct themselves nobly like Lord Ramachandra. They should not be moved by hatred, resort to any form of violence, or be engaged in fights. I request the people who have followed these instructions to leave here,' Pundit Ramabhakta Das said.

Once again, there was a commotion amongst the audience but nobody left the place.

'Those who are inclined to listen to my holy words and adopt those principles in their lives must not stay back,' the Pundit advised.

'Only those who would applaud me and sound slogans hailing me should be present here. Only the ones who would be inspired to forget themselves and dance like crazy but would let my preaching move past without entering their ears, should remain here. The rest must leave.'

A loud cry of joy and excitement erupted from the audience. The devotees clapped. The women ululated. The place throbbed with slogans of Jai Shri Ram. Some devotees, overwhelmed with reverence, began to dance raising their hands. But nobody left the place.

'Quiet! Quiet!' Pundit Ramabhakta Das requested in a solemn voice.

'My dear devotees! We have now acquired a pretence-free status. We have dropped our masks of falsehood. It is a unique and rare experience. It happens once in a long time. In my case, it has happened here, in this village. I make this announcement here that tomorrow's preaching will be even more unpretentious, more genuine. I will take this camouflage off my personality. Tomorrow I will deliver the sermon in a pair of jeans and a T-shirt. I will even smoke weed on this platform. I will be more candid and true to my own false self.'

'Well said!! Well said!!' the audience chorused.

The recital of Sri Ramacharita Manasa was carried on as per the programme after that. The bells and gongs were sounded. Devotional songs were sung. The women ululated and the devotees got drunk with the potion of the holy words of the Ramayana. Pundit Ramabhakta Das preached divine messages. There was a shower of sermons. The audience was charmed. All agreed that there was not another preacher and devotee of Lord Ramachandra to match Pundit Ramabhakta Das. No one had such expertise in elaborating and explaining the passages from the sacred scriptures. No one had interpreted the sacred texts in this way.

As scheduled, the programme came to an end after two hours and the devotees, as if blessed with a new life, returned home in a state of spiritual intoxication. 'Listening to the spiritual tales and to be in the company of holy personalities are experiences of absolute joy, and to surrender oneself at the feet of God is the ultimate goal of life,' they discussed as they walked back from the venue.

The next evening, when the programme began, Pundit Ramabhakta Das took his place on the stage in a pair of jeans and a T-shirt instead of the shiny saffron robe, as promised. He wore a leather belt around his waist and a pair of leather shoes. The mark of sandalwood paste he wore last evening on his forehead had vanished, as had the flower garlands that adorned his neck. The graffiti on his T-shirt said, 'Kill and Kiss'. There was a picture of a knife and a bottle of wine with its lid open under the graffiti. A hookah was kept by his side. Songs from Hindi movies, instead of devotional ones were played in the background.

But the audience space was empty. There was not a single person there. Even the convenor of the Ramacharita Manasa programme, Shyamaghana Das was absent from the scene.

Pundit Ramabhakta Das waited for a while and then stepped down from the stage. The few volunteers present there turned off the lights.

* * *

Gourahari Das (b. 1960)

'Merchant of Lies'

(Translated 'Bepar' from the Odia by Snehaprava Das)

It had happened about a year before.

Narendra Prasad sat on a cement bench on the railway platform of Bhubaneswar, waiting for the train. He bought a newspaper and was about to open it when the man made his unexpected appearance before him. The face of the man was a mask of abject misery. Tears of distress trickled down his cheeks. 'I am in deep trouble sir,' the man said, his voice suffused with sorrow. 'Please, help me, sir. My only son is critically ill. He will not survive unless he gets immediate medical attention.'

Narendra Prasad was moved by the pathetic appeal of the man. 'Do not cry,' he said consolingly.

'Tell me what I can do for you.'

'I am a very poor man, sir. I can at least get my son to a hospital if you give me 100 rupees. Rest is in the hands of God. Be kind to me sir. Divine blessings will be showered on you. I will remain grateful to you forever.'

Narendra Prasad took out a 100-rupee note from his wallet and gave it to the man. The man was overwhelmed with gratitude as he took the note from Narendra Prasad. He wiped the tears with the back of his hand and poured words of gratitude on Narendra Prasad.

'Please get his son cured, God!' Narendra Prasad prayed silently.

He was, in those days, doing a business in children's garments. He used to come from Nayagarh to Bhubaneswar by a taxi. After attending to some sundry works at Bhubaneswar, he travelled to Kolkata by a night train. He bought the garments from the wholesale shops there and returned to Nayagarh. He had set up a sophisticated kids' wear shop at Nayagarh that did good business.

An incident of a similar nature occurred a month after this.

Narendra Prasad came across another unfortunate man on the railway platform of Bhubaneswar. The man implored him to extend some help for the treatment of his ailing mother. Narendra Prasad noticed that the man looked a bit older in age than the man he had met a month before. His face was covered with a frizzy, messy beard, and he wore a pair of heavily creased trousers and a grubby half shirt, and was begging help from people to meet the expenses of the treatment of his sick mother.

That day too, the train was late, and Narendra Prasad stood at the book stall to buy a magazine.

'Kindly help me, sir. My mother is very ill. She is not able to breathe. She will surely die if she does not get early medical treatment. I will be orphaned unless you extend some help, sir,' the man whined pathetically.

Like last time, Narendra Prasad was overwhelmed by the man's sorrow. He handed him a 100-rupee note and left the place hoping for the early recovery of his old mother.

The next month, he met another such distressed fellow on the same railway platform. He wore a shabby shirt and a pair of shabbier trousers, and had wound a cloth-towel around his head. A sling bag hung from his shoulder and there was a mark of vermilion on his forehead.

As usual, Narendra Prasad stood on the railway platform waiting for the train. The man approached him, and without any preamble, started to tell his tale of woe.

'I live in village Baghamari of district Khurda,' he began. 'My mother died. I do not have a penny with me to perform her funeral rites. The priests say that she has died in an inauspicious hour. They advise that some special rituals are to be performed to counterbalance its negative impact, and for the salvation of her soul. Where shall I get the money to spend on these special rituals? Have mercy on me, sir. It will be a great help if you could spare only 300 rupees. The good deed will fetch you good fortune.'

Narendra Prasad felt sad for the man. Poor fellow! He had become motherless. He remembered the pain and the sense of loss which he had experienced after his father's death. The priests and brahmins had advised performing a special ritual since his father too had died at an inauspicious time. A sacred fire was lighted with the ghee made from buffalo milk, while the brahmins and priests chanted slokas from holy scriptures.

'What was the problem with your mother?' Narendra Prasad asked consolingly.

'She succumbed to cancer. It was detected very late. How could I help even if it had been detected early? I had no resources to draw upon. I begged everyone I knew. It is a selfish world, sir. No one came forward to support me.' The man broke into tears. The arrival of the train was getting announced. Narendra Prasad gave 200 rupees to the man and hurried away from the place.

'Have trust in the goodness of man. All are not selfish in this world.'

The next month was the month of Dussehra. The air was festive. There was a large crowd on the platform. The train was an hour and a half late. It was announced that the train would reach Bhubaneswar around midnight. Narendra Prasad waited on the platform, feeling desperate and vexed.

A man approached him. He wore a lungi, and his hair was oiled and combed neatly. 'Sir, I am in a terrible situation.

I am plunged in an ocean of sorrow. My world is going to crash . . .' he spoke in a south-Odisha accent. Narendra Prasad looked closely at the man. He noticed the big black mole below his neck. It looked familiar.

Narendra Prasad stopped him before he could stretch his whining further.

'What happened? Why do you say that your world is going to crash?' he asked.

What Narendra Prasad could gather from his indistinct whimpers was that the fellow was a native of Chhatrapur in south Odisha. He had come to Bhubaneswar with his wife. A speeding autorickshaw hit them as they were crossing the road after disembarking from the train. His wife was lying in the hospital with a broken leg.

All the while the man was narrating his sad story, Narendra Prasad's gaze was fixed on the mole under his neck. The mole looked distinct and bold. Narendra Prasad tried to recollect. The face of the man bore a semblance to the face of the fellow whom he had met earlier on the same platform who was grieving his mother's death. Could it be so that one man is duping him impersonating different characters? But he was not much aggrieved. He must have been cheated, he thought, like this quite a number of times by some other people. It was no big deal if the fellow had swindled a few hundred rupees from him. The tale of his wife being hit by an autorickshaw and breaking her leg might be true. In that case, the money he gave the fellow would be of some use. He pushed the episode out of his mind and directed his thoughts to his business. 'The customers these days are bargaining a lot. The price tags attached to the articles from now on should have to quote a 30 per cent increase in the margin rate,' he decided.

The man, despite his carefully worn disguise, was finally caught in the month of December. The big black mole below his neck betrayed him.

He came to the spot where Narendra Prasad stood waiting for the train and began to narrate the sad tale of his mother's sickness.

'Didn't you tell me about your mother's death about a month ago?' Narendra Prasad cut in.

'You have already spun stories about your mother, wife and son. Try something new or leave this place.'

Any other fellow at his place would have felt ashamed and embarrassed. But to Narendra Prasad's astonishment, the man retorted unabashedly.

'You are a strange person,' he said accusingly.

'Why do you say so?' Narendra Prasad asked.

'Why did you pretend to believe in my stories if you had already recognized me? Why haven't you pointed this out before?'

Narendra Prasad felt a mild prick in his heart. He knew he had a credulous nature—he easily believed what people told him. He did not, however, admit it before the fellow.

'To trust someone is a satisfying experience. I believed your false tales in the beginning and let myself be robbed by you. Later, it became a pleasant engagement that reduced the boredom of waiting for the train. People these days are spending thousands in restaurants, theatres and other such places to enjoy a good time. I enjoyed the tales you told me, and they cost me only a few hundred. What is so odd about it? What is the harm? You are caught red-handed this time because of your carelessness. You should have taken care not to narrate the same episode before the same listener more than once.'

The fellow was busily trying to find an excuse to get away from the place. But Narendra Prasad was not finished with his admonitions.

'You may get arrested by the police if you continue to cheat people in this manner. You seem to be healthy and capable. Why don't you find out some other means to earn a living? You could start with a small business.' Narendra Prasad's tone was conciliatory.

The man burst into tears and slumped on the floor of the platform. 'I am an ill-fated fellow,' he stammered through his sobs. 'I was orphaned when I was a child. I did not have a home or a patch of farmland of my own. I did the job of washing plates in a hotel. I got married too. Soon after my marriage, I suffered from various ailments that made me physically weak. I was not able to do hard work. My wife ran away with the cook. I searched several possible places but failed to find her. I was filled with an acute bitterness. I am living here on this railway platform for the last four years. This has become my home. I try to impress people with the sad tales about my wife, mother and son, and draw their sympathy. What business can I do? I neither have the capital for starting a business nor have the recognition to earn the trust of people.'

Narendra Prasad was not sure if what the man was saying about himself was true or he was concocting another story to impress him. It appeared he was telling the truth.

'Don't worry,' he consoled the fellow. 'For a person with intelligence and an acumen for doing business, capital is not a very big issue. You can start a business even with scraps. But resorting to falsehood in this manner will land you in big trouble one day or other.'

The fellow, like an obedient pupil, stretched out both his hands towards him. 'I will follow your advice. You are my mentor. Give me something as a token and I will start my business using it as my capital.'

'What is your name?'

'Sanatan.'

'But that day you said your name was Narottam,' Narendra Prasad said.

'Narottam too will do sir. You can call me by any name.'

'That is weird. You must have a specific name.'

'I used to have one, sir. But I have impersonated so many characters with different names in the last few years, that I myself am confused what my real name is.' The fellow took a pause.

'My original name is Santosh, sir. Santosh Majhi,' he said, as if remembering something long-forgotten.

'Okay. I believe you, Santosh. Here, take this umbrella.' Narendra Prasad held out an old umbrella. 'It has lost its utility for me. You can start your business with this if you are serious about it.'

Santosh, alias Sanatan, alias Narottam, took the umbrella from Narendra Prasad, his face lighting up with a new-found enthusiasm.

Narendra Prasad walked away from the place. He turned abruptly. 'Santosh!,' he called out.

'Yes, sir,' the man responded. 'Tell me please.'

'Nothing. I just wanted to know if Santosh was your real name.' Santosh went away carrying the umbrella.

This had happened about eight months ago.

Narendra Prasad got down from the train at Bhubaneswar. He had gone to Kolkata on the thirteenth and had returned after a couple of days. It was 15 August, the Independence Day.

Narendra Prasad had not travelled to Kolkata for the last eight months. The business manager at the wholesale garment shop at Kolkata was getting the stuff delivered at his garment shop in Nayagarh from time to time.

Narendra Prasad's searching gaze travelled around the platform, hoping to see Santosh Majhi. He had developed a kind of interest in the fellow in the past few months. He wondered how a man could change his guise with such expertise, narrate tales with a brilliant oratorial skill, and to top all that, invent ingenuous stories to impress people.

Santosh Majhi was not there on the railway platform.

Narendra Prasad came out and hired a taxi. He would travel to Nayagarh by taxi as he often did.

Bhubaneswar was celebrating Independence Day with pomp and splendour. The road from Master Canteen Square to Mahatma Gandhi Marg was decorated with festoons and flowers, and was lined with the tricolour on both sides. The political leaders would deliver speeches there after a while. Some major roads were barricaded and the police were directing the vehicles to take different routes. A policeman stopped Narendra Prasad's taxi and advised him to take a diversion through the Raj Mahal Square. Narendra Prasad looked out of the window of the taxi as it rolled on.

A makeshift shed close to the old office of the block development authority caught his eyes. It was made with white sheets. A man wearing a Gandhi cap[xc] was announcing something in a loud voice. Narendra Prasad could hear him as the taxi crawled closer to the shed.

'Come and buy the mementos of the freedom movement of India. Keep them with you and cherish the valuable experience for a lifetime.'

Narendra Prasad was mildly surprised. There are quite a number of national museums across the country that preserve such mementos. What was so special and unique about the collections the man displayed in his makeshift shop and lured people to buy? Driven by curiosity, he asked the taxi driver to stop by the shop. The driver grumbled but Narendra Prasad assured him of an extra payment and got out of the taxi.

He looked at the items displayed in the shop.

There were a couple of sling bags, a walking stick with a curved handle and two wrist watches on a table. Just in the middle of those objects, there was an old umbrella.

[xc] A Gandhi cap is a white cap pointed in back and front and having a wide band.

Narendra Prasad recognized the umbrella instantly. It was the same one which he had given away to Santosh Majhi eight months ago.

'Hello, there,' Narendra Prasad said. 'Can I have a word with you?'

The man turned to look at him. Despite the Gandhi cap, Narendra Prasad recognized him. It was Santosh Majhi alright. Santosh Majhi was stepping out after giving instruction to the young man in the shop. A customer approached him at that moment. 'What is so special about that umbrella?' he asked Santosh Majhi.

'Mahatma Gandhi came to Odisha in 1943. There was a light drizzle when he arrived at the railway station of Cuttack. Gandhiji carried an umbrella with him. Acharya Harihara received Gandhiji and had held the umbrella over his head as they walked from the station to Bidyadhar Pur. When the rain stopped, Gandhiji gave this umbrella to Acharya Harihara. 'Keep this umbrella with you, Harihara,' he said. It was in the custody of Acharya Harihara since that day. We have collected it with much difficulty after the sad demise of the Acharya. It is a holy relic. A precious memento of the father of the nation. The price is only 3000 rupees.'

Santosh Majhi rambled on without the slightest hesitation.

Narendra Prasad could not believe his ears.

'Santosh,' he called out a bit loudly.

'Please take a look at these. I will just have a word with sir,' he said to the customer and hurried out of the shop.

'What is all this you are doing, Santosh?' Narendra Prasad asked without a prelude.

'Please do not blame me, sir,' Santosh Majhi said trying to explain. 'I wandered through this capital town trying hard to earn my living by honest means. But I did not succeed. I discovered that people here need stories, interesting and enjoyable. My old business of duping people at the railway platform with false stories was doing well just because of that. Do you know why people who were reluctant to spare a rupee or two were ready to give away hundreds to me when I told them the sad stories of my life? It was the art of narrating a false story with honesty that fetched me hundreds of rupees.'

There were both amazement and wonder in the eyes of Narendra Prasad.

'Why was it so?'

'Everyone wants to believe that they are having a better life than others. It gives them tremendous satisfaction. And they believe it only when another person tells them his own sorrowful tale. The belief is born out of comparing their own condition with that of the man that bemoans his troubles.'

Santosh Majhi paused briefly here.

'"How are you?" they ask others and secretly expect to listen to a negative reply. They derive a sort of happiness out of the suffering of others. That is the reason I made my tales as pathetic as possible and won their trust,' he added.

'Is this man a psychologist? A mind reader?' Narendra Prasad wondered.

'It may be so,' he said, hiding his thoughts. 'But you must not link an ordinary, old umbrella to Mahatma Gandhi. That is cheating.'

'There is no such object on earth which is useless or a waste. Things which fools believe to be of little value could be transformed to priceless objects when presented cleverly. It depends on how wittily a story could be concocted to describe its worth. Didn't you say the other day, that to trust someone is a satisfying experience? One must know the art to awaken that trust in a person. When handled with cleverness, that trust can turn an ordinary thing to extraordinary.'

'What you are doing is fraud. You may get arrested for it one day.'

'It seems you can never come out of that fear. Hundreds of political leaders are exploiting our trust and ruling this country for the last seventy years. They are trying to convince us of the worth of their worthless promises. No one arrests them. Why should I be arrested then? Let someone come forward with a challenge that Gandhiji had not used this umbrella.'

The sound of drums and music came floating in the air. The jubilation of the Independence Day celebration blurred the words of Santosh Majhi.

Narendra Prasad understood that arguing with Santosh Majhi was of no use. He was no longer interested in countering his absurd claims.

'I have realized that the art of telling a lie with conviction is my strength. I need people to believe the lies I tell them. That is the capital I do my business with. It is another thing that you do not approve of it. But the world is a vast place,' Santosh Majhi said.

Narendra Prasad walked back to the taxi without saying anything.

* * *

Dipti Ranjan Pattanaik (b. 1961)

'Magic Slippers'

(Translated 'Kuhuka Chati' from the Odia by the author)

My eyes were still bleary when the doorbell rang. It was not as raucous as I thought, but the journey was rough. The movie on the TV of the bus had been playing very loudly, and I could not steal a wink of sleep throughout the night. I thought of catching some sleep in the morning after I reached Jadu's place. But now, there was this doorbell. The whole world had conspired to murder my sleep, I thought. I was beginning to curse the visitor. Then I saw her. Jadu had answered the door and let in a bewitching form of feminine perfection into the ramshackle apartment that had been his dwelling place for the last two years. I had read about breathtaking beauties in popular romances. Now, it was my turn to lose a heartbeat or two on seeing the beautiful woman who had just come in. So, the bastard has been entertaining such beautiful friends so far away from home. That is why he has been turning down offers of marriage for such a long time! I was growing jealous. I winked at him. Jadu winked back. My suspicion grew thicker. I silently complimented him on his choice of a girlfriend.

When the girl entered the kitchen and started making tea, I caught hold of his neck and tried to smother him.

'So, you've been hiding her for such a long time. You think I will steal her away or what?'

'Hey, don't have ideas,' Jadu could barely manage to blurt out between bouts of coughing. 'She is the domestic help.'

'The domestic help?' I was appalled. I thought only Bollywood could imagine such beautiful domestic help.

'Yes, she works in the mornings for some extra income. She really doesn't have to. But we have kind of started liking each other. She thinks I'm her elder brother or something.'

'Don't bloody feed me that postmaster, Tagore crap. Will you tell me how far you have gone? Or I'm gonna kill you and run away with her.'

'Honest. I swear.' Jadu was trying to be earnest. He didn't need to. In college, all the beautiful girls were dying for him and he had succeeded in securing *raakhis*[xci] from everyone. I didn't have much reason to imagine Jadu had changed.

The girl came in with the morning tea. I really did not need the tea to drive fatigue away—her presence itself had ensured that. I was just lapping up her beauty with my mouth gaping in awe. The fact that she was a maidservant made her look more exotic, and yes, more desirable.

Jadu started introducing me as the friend he had earlier talked of—a big businessman who plans to set up a chain of beauty and massage parlours. He also informed her that I was looking for a suitable manager to assist me in the business. Apparently, the crook had been feeding her a lot of crap; had boasted of rich friends keen to enter this business of beauty parlours. And this girl was training to become a beautician. Now that I had arrived, I had to step in as one of those imaginary businessmen.

Jadu has always been like that. He had been selling dreams to people right from his childhood. In fact, when in college, he had claimed the best palace in our native town as his grandfather's. It took me years to find out that he had lied. This time around, he did not even allow me to make whatever little attempt I could make to establish my true identity.

[xci] An ornamental wrist band tied by a woman to her brother.

There was no problem being a rich businessman when Jadu was around, for he did all the talking for me. But once Jadu left for his office and the girl was left alone with me in the house, it was unbearable. Her beauty was already a source of trouble, but her attempts to strike a conversation with me between her chores made it troublesome. My imagination had to work overtime to create huge palatial bungalows, foreign cars and beauty parlours for myself. I chose to feign a headache and went to bed. There was no respite even after that. The girl fished out some balm and started applying it on my forehead. Apparently, she was quite used to this chore with Jadu. I don't know what effect it might have had on Jadu, the saint, the yogi, but it was really shattering me. I had not come in such close contact with females other than my mother. She had just touched my forehead, but I discovered my legs melting, and then the body turning into jelly, only the hard skull remained. The stuff within the skull, however, had turned to molten lava. I was sinking into a labyrinth of oblivion, an opulent bliss, but did not have any sense to map out or enjoy that bliss. I fought desperately to retain my sense of me. My fight led me first to her hands, her breasts, her entire body. The next moment, I was holding her face and planting a kiss on her half-opened mouth. Then it was her turn to melt. Her lips were the only part of her body that had any semblance of solidity about them. The rest of her body started flowing beside me like the small village stream of my childhood.

At this point, I became conscious that our lives had started resembling Samuel Richardson's novel, *Clarissa*. I could see through the game of power which had sealed our lips. The only difference was that the source of Richardson's protagonist's power was real. The source of my power was imaginary. I was not as wealthy or vile as Clarissa's rapist. Moreover, my Clarissa was less resistant to my advances than

Richardson's. So I concluded that my confession should be more in the mould of a fairy-tale than a realistic narrative.

I disengaged myself from Nirmala. Incidentally, that was her name. I went down on my knees and said, 'Nirmala, I'm the prince charming. I don't promise you a crown or a fabled kingdom of happiness. In my kingdom, hunger still strives for food, sex still closely searches for the other in the deeper recesses of the soul, the big fish eat the small, but I promise you a pair of slippers which sometimes takes wings and could take you wherever you want to go. What of Tata, Birla or Ford, you can dance with *apsaras*[xcii] if you like in those moments. Will you marry me?'

Before Nirmala could respond in any manner, all my fairy-tale moments were exhausted. When I came to myself, I realized I was holding a broken tape that was tied to my slipper with a safety-pin. Since the last two days, I had been thinking of attaching a new tape to my slipper, at least before my trip to Dibrugarh to meet Jadu. I must change the tape today on my way to the Blue Hill transport service counter to reserve a bus ticket. I suspect I have also developed this habit of gossiping and spending time slothfully, like Jadu. Let me stop this cock and bull story. I have to get ready for the journey to Dibrugarh. Oh, how tiresome, these night journeys by bus!

But first of all, I have to get up from bed. It is already too late in the morning. I have to get rid of my sloth, which is the mother of all such day-dreaming.

* * *

xcii Heavenly nymphs.

Paramita Satpathy (b. 1965)

'The Testimony'

(Translated 'Sweekarokti' from the Odia by Ganeswar Mishra)

Was it a train or a bus? It was a running vehicle. You were sitting inside, your face dark and pale—strangely pale. Your eyes were clouded with a tinge of yellow; the pupils seemed to have vanished. You looked ghastly. You got up from your seat, paced up and down, and sat down again. I woke up with a start. I was trembling all over. I felt sick and had a splitting headache. I did not try to sleep again. I was scared at the thought of dreaming of you again. I felt restless throughout the day. Why did I have such a dream? What could this portend? Did some harm come your way? All evil possibilities flashed through my mind. Something might have happened to you on the road. You never carried your helmet. I would be reminded of this every time I heard of a road accident. I could only pray that everything was all right with you.

The next day was a Tuesday. We used to meet every Tuesday and I assumed you would be home in the evening. The road was being repaired near the bridge about a kilometre from your house. So I had to leave the rickshaw there and walk down to your house. It was late evening when I reached your place. It had started drizzling. Your lane was pitch dark—not a single street light was on. *I should have carried a torch with me*, I thought, and cursed myself for being so unmindful. I reached the gate of your house and was startled to see the house was totally dark. When I came on Tuesdays, Sharat would ask me to sit down even if you were not there. Today, the door was locked from outside. *Both of you must have gone somewhere*, I thought. I was thoroughly disappointed, for it had never occurred to me that both of you could be away. I felt depressed at the thought of walking back to where the road was dug up and then having to wait there for a rickshaw. It was still drizzling—who knew when it would begin to pour! I decided to ask your neighbour about you. I knocked on their gate and a girl—you had mentioned her to me—opened the door.

'Where have they gone? The gate is locked,' I asked.

'They left some seven or eight days back.'

I remembered the smell of fresh paint on your verandah. I have not met you these last two weeks. But how could you shift house without informing me?!

'Do you know where they moved?' I asked.

'He has been transferred,' she said and smiled as if she had known she would have to pass this information to me. 'I do not know exactly where they have gone. But I think he has been transferred to some place outside Odisha.'

It made no sense to me. Your face flashed in my mind's eye that instant.

'I came all the way thinking they would be home.' My voice must have sounded miserable.

'I am alone,' she said with sympathy, 'my younger brother has gone for his tuition, or else I could have walked you home.'

I remembered you telling me about another newly-married friend of yours living nearby. I now asked the girl to show me his house.

I knocked on the door; your friend's wife came out but she did not appear too friendly. 'My husband is not at home and our servant is not here either,' she said brusquely. I did not feel like asking her anything.

The girl offered to give me company part of the way, but I politely declined. 'Thanks, but do not take the trouble. I think I can find my way.' I started walking back.

The road was never-ending. I felt as if I was climbing a mountain and would reach my place only if I could cross it. I was trying my best not to think of you. Just beyond the point where the road was dug, a group of people were huddled on the road. A petromax[xciii] light burnt at a distance. At the centre, a middle-aged woman, her hair flying loose and her blouse conspicuous by its absence, was waving her hand and shouting in a high-pitched voice. 'Wait, wait,' she screamed as I passed by. She held my hand tight.

'What is it?' I asked with annoyance.

'Sit down here,' she said and made me sit down. The men and women sitting around now focused their attention on me.

'Come on, hold this,' the woman handed me a small looking glass without a frame and a hibiscus flower. 'Sniff the flower once and look into the mirror,' she commanded.

'What nonsense is this? Leave me out of it.' I tried to get up.

'Just look into it once and then you will know.'

I had no option but to sniff the hibiscus flower and then look into the mirror. The glass seemed to expand. In it, I could clearly see myself reaching your house and everything that had followed. A cold shiver ran down my spine. 'Who are you?' I asked, amazed. She looked at me as if she had won a battle. 'Come on, have another look,' she ordered me.

Once again, I sniffed the flower and looked into the mirror. I found myself standing in front of the locked door of a dark house. It was not like your house. Neither the road nor the trees nearby looked familiar. I could also feel that the reflection in the mirror was not exactly mine.

[xciii] Petromax is a brand name for a type of pressurised paraffin lamp that uses a mantle.

'I had told you this earlier, too,' said the woman in a knowing voice. 'It is no use being born again and again; you will have to return from a locked door not once or twice, but again and again—as many times as you take birth. But you did not pay any heed. You thought things would happen the way you wished them to? You thought the door would open for you this time, didn't you?' The scorn in her voice was unmistakable.

I was burning with shame and indignation. I could not say anything; I tried to get up.

'Wait, wait—where are you going? Take another look,' she screamed.

I covered my face with my hands and started sobbing.

'Leave me alone; please leave me alone. Why are you talking to me like this? What have I done to you?' I was crying now.

'Look! Look at the silly woman! She is asking me if she has done me any wrong.' She laughed. 'What wrong do you think you can do to me, eh?'

I knew I had to move now. I experienced a sudden, powerful desire to go back home. Pushing away the crowd, I started running blindly. I missed the road to my house. I started to run along the detour you and I used to take when we had a little more time on our hands. The road now appeared endless. I was thoroughly exhausted. I looked this way and that for a patch of grass or a concrete culvert so that I could sit down for a while. But I did not dare do so. I felt as if that sibyl of a woman was chasing me at the speed of wind.

* * *

4
Essays

Gourishankar Roy (1838–1917)

'Obstacles Towards the Promotion of Utkal Language'

(Translated 'Utkal Bhasar Unnati Prati Byaghat' from the Odia by Manu Dash)

There is no limit to the degree to which the local people and the government are taking care to promote the literature of Utkal. The way schools are being established and the books printed, all have a strong belief that there shall be progress in the Utkal language very soon. I feel that the real means are yet to be followed and there remains a serious obstacle in the progress of the language.

Before giving an example of this obstacle, we deem it proper to rectify the misinterpretation of a few people. The readers would have remembered how Rajendralal Mitra of Calcutta visited our province last December and addressed the Cuttack debating club. We had appreciated his ability to deliver lectures in the English language, but we had not given any opinion about his address at that time. We came to know a few days back that many people are following his address and considering it as an intellectual discourse. That's why we thought it necessary to point out the flaws in his address. Babu Rajendralal Mitra said, during his address in the meeting, that real well-wishers of Utkal would do great service to the state if they promoted Bangla literature, ignoring the literature of Utkal. In his opinion, there shall be no development of the state if the standard of the Utkal language has not reached a particular level, and there shall be no possibility of progress in the country.

Justifying his opinion, he said that according to the census of the drought commissioner, the population of Utkal is 20 lakh. If the women and children are taken away from this lot, there will be ten to twelve lakh of people who are potential readers. Can such an insignificant number of people actually protect any language? It is impossible for any author to be successful in the profession of writing because of this number. Bengal, on the other hand, is a vast province with significant progress in its language. If Bangla is implemented here, then the good books in Bangla will be abundantly available for the people living here. He mentioned that 300 books have been published in Bangla in the last three months whereas in Utkal, no more than three or four books were published. It is a glaring example that the Utkal language can never make any headway in such circumstances.

We had thought that after coming on a visit to Utkal, Rajendra babu would be aware of many things, but we were surprised to hear the above information. It is now very difficult to make out whether he expressed his intimate feelings or tried to thrust his personal opinion upon us by citing false examples, carried away as he was, by the love for his province. Was he not aware while talking about the population, which was confined to the Mogulbandi area, that the Utkal language is spread out up to Medinipur on the north border, Ganjam on the south border and Bengal to Sambalpur on the east-west border? If he was not aware of the fact, why did he damage his reputation by sharing his ignorance with people? A person should not speak about any subject in which he is not well conversant. In fact, it is observed that the area of Utkal-speaking people is no less than the area of Bengal province.

So, there is every possibility of the development of the Utkal language. Whatever he said about the publishing of books is nothing but misinterpretation. We have said time and again that for long, the Government has had a soft corner for Bengal and the Utkal language lags because of it. Rajendra babu's version would have been appreciated had there been the same appreciation for both languages. Could this be expected to be achieved without taking the time and situation into consideration? After the famine, the state government extended its help for development. Had these endeavours been initiated ten years ago, Rajendra babu would have found it difficult to find the reason to bring his arguments home. What we want to say is that his opinion is wrong and those who are following this opinion are swimming through the fog, causing unnecessary difficulties for themselves.

But what's the obstacle in the promotion of the Utkal language? We believe the Utkal language has been three-pronged. It is not getting its due for no reason. Three separate governments have become its saviour. This language is not read with evenness as one segment comes under the ambit of the Bengal Government, another under the rule of the Madhya Pradesh Government and the third under the rule of the Madras Government. Each area has its own rules and regulations, and different books are read in different regions.

Apprehending this proposal is getting a little too lengthy, we are constrained to proceed no further. We will publish next week whatever proposal we have in mind.

* * *

Utkal Dipika, 1869

Fakir Mohan Senapati (1843–1918)

'Vulgar Idols Inside the Temples'

(Translated 'Mandira Manankare Kutshita Murti' from the Odia by Manu Dash)

Nowadays, the way the revolution goes on in the system of idol worship in the Hindu religion, there is no doubt that at one point in time, this religion will be there for namesake only. Among the main destroyers of the Hindu religion is the *panda*, or the servitors who perform the rites at the temple. We have not imagined this but in fact, witnessed it in the course of our journey to various ancient shrines in India. Whatever it may be, we shall speak about the stigma linked with the Hindu religion. Vulgar idols are usually kept when a temple is constructed. Had it been done in cases of common insignificant temples, we would not have taken the pain of describing it here. But these are the temples decorated with vulgar idols, where people from all parts of India come to visit. To keep such unsightly idols inside the temple is neither sanctioned by any religious scripture nor validated by any rational thought. We are unable to know the reason for which these rituals continue to be there.

We can only guess that the concept of idol worshipping might have been introduced to inspire a sense of devotion to the formless Almighty, and these rituals were started first for the lecherous with a view to creating in them love and devotion for God. This implies that vulgar idols are kept within temples to attract those who would otherwise have no inclination to go there.

This sort of imagination, however, is erroneous. Because our senses have such an intimate relationship with our instincts, specific natural reactions are caused by certain sights. A sense of hatred is caused in us when we see excrement and a sense of fear seizes us when we view the dreadful. There is no doubt whatsoever that it does much damage to the public instead of doing any good when the temples are full of vulgar idols. People generally enter the temple along with their family members for a *darshan*[i] and one can well imagine the shame and embarrassment it could cause when one goes there with one's sons and daughters when seeing these idols all by oneself causes such a sense of utter shame. This tradition is the main reason behind the destruction of the Hindu religion, and it is a matter of endless disgrace for the Hindus.

* * *

[i] To pay a visit.

Radhanath Ray (1848–1908)

'The Conscientious'

(Translated the condensed form of 'Bibeki' from the Odia by Asima Ranjan Parhi)

Who can assess the trial, trouble and tribulations of humankind in its entirety? Who would fathom the extent to which it is bowed down by adversity?

We anticipate finding hope in essays and narratives that help us during such hardships. On days when a particularly violent rainstorm lashes on our wall, it seems like a perfect day to write an essay. In a home that is content within itself, a heavy lashing barely comes off as trouble; it rather seems pleasurable. The human soul bears with the adverse. Such a shocking phenomenon is not exclusive to this objective world alone. The spiritual world too is quite familiar with adversities and traumatic situations that continue to affect it.

In times like these, *pothis*[ii] pose as great companions. They stand by us during our material and spiritual trauma. When we are confined by the rain, they delight us. If we are sad, they heal us. Dear readers! Would you like to be a part of the pleasure I get? My joy will increase if you find reading pleasurable. When we see the pothis, we visualize the great men and women they describe. They are resourceful and permanent company to humans. When you read them, you might feel they are exhaustive. While much of the rich

[ii] Pothi refers to a written work, typically in the form of a manuscript or a book, containing literary or religious material.

content of the pothis remains unexplored, the human mind to its boundless extent too remains unquenched in its quest for knowledge.

There are people who think they won't be shaken by thousands of troubles and can handle everything with patience. Many think they would not get tempted by external pulls of any kind. Such overconfidence is not good before it is tested. What is the basis of such self-confidence? Would everyone assume that I am not smart enough? If I act rationally, I shall succeed. My work shall be ethical and I won't bother about criticism from 'others'. But after a few days, new thoughts visit us. Initially, one hopes to prove one's worth by acting prudently. Seeing eminent people trapped in their wrong habits, the inexperienced ones pity them and behave with a child's confidence, as if they would not err ever in such circumstances.

The novice innocently assumes that they would be capable enough to accomplish the task. The new entrant always acts with a childlike dream, fails frequently only to realize that looking after the matters of the world is way easier than taming one's own mind.

With age, human beings learn how to be mindful of one's health. So, there is a saying in Odia, 'At forty, some attain the skill to be a saviour of lives like the doctor, while at forty, some are cursed to let go of life itself. The same rules apply to both body and mind. The mind realizes its role and potential, its strength, and rules through new experiences, modes and habits. This is the conscience. It teaches that 'I cannot find any remedy to this harmful thing. Better to forget it. When left alone, the same questions will captivate me. I will engage myself in the anticipation of a possible pleasure that is beyond the material. It may look faithful from a distance but not so actually. I am experiencing the same pleasure that I was not able to find before. And that which i found pleasant by not being trapped by mere attention then, still seems pleasing, though a greater, enticing energy of joy is lacking in such an experience.' All such ideas and thoughts ensnare the mind. It creates multiple perspectives and then only people find it easy to control the mind.

If we are aware of the exact nature and measure of our distractions, we can control them. In this case, we do not find this material pain mixed with wonder. Many avid readers of fiction remain unaware of the greater pains of life. They fail to fathom that the world of fiction is vastly different from nature itself. But nature is always unmoved. The morals we learn from the world of fiction are different from those we receive from nature. Some say calamities don't linger and loiter, they come and they go. But those with a deeper view of the world would differ. Some calamities stay forever and cause pain for a long time. One does not fall from the hill straight without stumbling. Slowly, he falls, tries to hold on to anything and everything he comes across, a stone, a tree, a herb or a branch, and thinks he will not fall again. Gradually, he learns that he has fallen to the feet of the hill. This analogy is crude but still fits the context.

Only a handful can ever attain true happiness. The rest are fated to experience trauma along the way. Some get pain due to failure despite their sincere efforts. Some are bankrupt due to court cases. Wayward children and their nuisance create constant anguish for their parents. Some are unable to get over the shameful acts they got involved in the past. Many go on cursing their birth due to the failure and lapses experienced in their life.

The lawyer and a minister might have to put in an equal amount of hard work. While the lawyer's concerns or duties rise and set along with the sun, the minister's concerns transcend beyond the sun as he has to plan policy measures for the state in an apt manner, lest everything should crumble. And a mistake in the process results in its failure. The pain of it is always immense. The intelligent and conscientious always gain from a failure and accept it as learning. Napoleon Bonaparte suffered this pain. We need to remember how our loss gives us enough insight and hope for the future. The darkness that follows the sunset also enables us to see other precious objects. One that is self-illumined cannot be blank or dark.

Dear reader, I may fall short in my search for a suitable simile and rhetoric to put this forward but it will all lead to one meaning, that our adversities are our true teachers. It teaches us knowledge. It is our only unpretentious benefactor.

The knowledgeable are always polite. True knowledge remains in remembering our lapses and lackings. Only the competent commander knows how to steer safe and achieve the highest pedestal. Just the knowledge of it isn't enough; it's just as important to put things into action.

There may come a day or two in everyone's life when they come and say something to cross a few hurdles. The weak may feel broken inside but it's also important to remember that in times like these, they have to bring themselves up and realize that society as a whole is evolving every day. People who are close to you won't change their minds about you as easily. It isn't easy to wait for the day when society changes, but if the person is right; sooner or later society will realize the truth.

It is important to note that jealous rage doesn't originate from where we think it does. It is in fact wrong of us to assume that people are always plotting against us. There seem to be three reasons that give rise to an angry mind, namely ignorance, narrow-mindedness and near-sightedness. Therefore, instead of thinking of it as injustice, one should rather brush it off as simple bad luck.

Anybody who has to take up a lot of responsibilities would face reproach from others. To hope to live a life without any hurdles is wrong. Among all the people we come across in our lives, there are a lot of people who are ignorant or jealous, who might fan the fire of hostility, but that doesn't originate from hatred towards you. It is, in fact, a sadistic pleasure they derive out of the miseries of other people. Since we live in a society with people of all kinds, we must accept that not always are things going to be simple for us. You might fail even when you are right. In times like these, you might have to invoke the same conscience that picked you up during a calamity. Time is the greatest healer, and when the time is right, things will fall right back into place. Patience is the key.

* * *

Biswanath Kar (1864–1934)

'Literature and Criticism'

(Translated 'Sahitya O Samalochana' from the Odia by Sanskruti Pujari)

Criticism is biased. We criticize whatever we see or hear. A child with his little knowledge and wisdom voices her opinion, notwithstanding the fact that the other person is doing his best to control his laughter, still, she is not afraid to present her thoughts with utter seriousness. A woman confined to the inner quarters remains within that limiting border of this world. But even then, she indulges in criticism—a dissection of character—because why wouldn't she? We have barred them from positions of high authority, nevertheless, they have been born with the same human characteristics offered by God. That is, in her own limited space, she engages herself in exercising these natural characteristics—for the right or for the wrong. There are certain characteristics of humans that make them different from animals; criticism is one among them. The more humans evolve from their animal origins, the more this characteristic will be ingrained in their bones. To see this flourish in the minds of civilized people would only make someone awestruck.

As society develops, people avoid engaging in the criticism of the trivial, and instead engage in the criticism of a higher faculty. They understand the importance of life and do not indulge in things that have nothing to do with life. Earlier, the things that had an undebatable hold upon them, are now charged with a question—tell me what profit would I get from you occupying such important parts of my invaluable life? They do not accept or reject anything without giving it a thought. This, in turn, leads to the rise of many revolutions in society.

A person without knowledge would feel satisfied even if he has dirt and pebbles in his mouth—they cannot differentiate right from wrong. If anybody tries to remove the dirt and pebbles from their mouth, they become impatient with anger and agony. Even if they are offered a beautiful, sweet thing instead, their mind is not contented. Even if you try to give them a lengthy speech on the ills of eating dirt and pebbles, it would not reach their ears. The sound of their crying would send the sky quaking. It is the business of what's real and what's visible in the case of an unknowing child that applies to the unknowing society. Now, we will put everything aside and focus on the discussion of certain aspects of literary criticism.

It is seen in civilized countries that their renowned journals are filled with criticism of contemporary literature. It is not necessary that any thought would exist undebated in society. The one who has survived the blow of the weapon of criticism alone can garner respect at the highest position in society. The minds of many great learned men have been eternally engaged in this important task. Several meaningless books exist in civilized countries but their reception is limited only to the lower ranks. Only a few volumes of ancient books have been written about criticism. Nevertheless, it is endless. In essence, literary criticism is one of the prime and most vital parts of civilization. The growth of civilization leads to the development of literature, which, in turn, leads to the growth of criticism.

The best of writers wish that their works be criticized in the most impartial manner. A great female novelist in England used a pseudonym because she didn't want people to criticize her works based on her gender. Those who think like this can alone understand the true value of literature. Criticism bodes well, both for writers and readers. Whether a work of literature deserves a place in this society or not is defined by how it is criticized.

Writers have the freedom to propagate their opinions. But just because they have written something, it does not mandate the reader to blindly accept what is written. The reader, too, has the freedom to reveal his opinion on it. The aim is not to belittle, but it is in fact, a mark of respect to the author, to be discussed. Criticism reflects the varied tastes and interests of the readers. But if one wants to be a good critic, one must not shy away from making an enemy or two.

In our language, we do not have a culture of critical discussion. With the little literature that is being produced, people are not interested in their criticism. Those who love to read and write read works in either English or Bangla. They believe that there is nothing realistic or acceptable in the words written by Odia writers. That is, it is unreadable, and hence there is no question of criticism there. There is another category of people who do not analyse what is good and what is bad; they read whatever they find—in it, whatever essence they find or don't, whether it matches with their perspective or not—they never give it much thought. In whatever way we see it, the dreary state of Odia literature and the disrespect it receives from the part of its readers makes it clear.

The main purpose of criticism is to bring out responsible writing in a writer's works. Those who fear or shy away from criticism are not fit to be called good writers. Presently, it is the dawn of Odia literature; but to think that whatever one writes is correct and to say a word in its criticism is a sin, is nothing but an unbearable revolution. Those who think like this, we should request to read Rabindranath Tagore's *Europe Pravasir Patra*. If the criticism is groundless, then the writer has every right to speak against it. There is no reason to shy away from a debate. A healthy debate does more benefit than harm. Those who consider Odia literature to be too raw for criticism, we might not agree with. But those who misuse their freedom of speech in the name of criticism are even more disgraceful. For those who are inclined towards Odia literature, it is extremely necessary to agree to these two things—to impartially criticize whatever they see and if someone criticizes them, then to patiently analyse it. Otherwise, the pace at which contemporary Odia literature is heading, in a short while, it will become a rare appearance.

* * *

Chandramohan Maharana (1870–1929)

'Qualities of Literature'[iii]

(Translated 'Sahityara Guna' from the Odia by Tyagraj Thakur)

The complete history of the Utkala Sahitya series has not been published yet. But those who are engaged in the pursuit of this literature know what lies in the literature of our mother tongue and what deficiencies it has. There is no iota of doubt that there is an acute deficiency. Most of the educated people in this country today have gained moderate competence in the English language. Many educated Odias keep speaking and discussing while speaking in Bengali. Since certain educated people are fans of the Sanskrit language, they are engaged in the discussion of poetic figures of speech, philosophy and scriptures written in that language. From the discussion of these languages, the educated Odias must be able to effortlessly experience the deficiency in their mother tongue. It is our duty to fulfil this deficiency. The signs of some people making this fulfilment of the deficiency a mission of their life are already visible. Some are biased towards the old, and among them, some are blindly biased. In this context of bias, some look at the old with the eyes of disobedience while considering it to be inferior and are solely biased towards the new. The wise people follow an appropriate middle path with a calm mind while quitting both the above categories. The thoughtless

[iii] Lecture delivered at Utkala Sahitya Samaj, 1926.

ones are biased towards the old saying, 'What didn't we have?' In their opinion, we do not have any deficiency. But Odisha seems to have overcome the times of blind bias as educated Odias have recognized deficiencies in the mother tongue. The mother tongue has already been invoked to fulfil the deficiency by entering the work field with cooperative perseverance. The ornamentalists[iv] of the Sanskrit language have mentioned poetry as the one to offer the fruits of the four objectives of life—*Dharma, Arth, Kaam, and Moksha*, which mean righteousness, wealth, desires and liberation. There is no need to think about the justification of this proclamation now. However, it has at least this much truth in it that the ones with expertise in the composition of true poetry, fill the human heart with pure bliss as well as ensure spiritual upliftment of the individual, by interweaving invaluable pieces of advice in appropriate places with their skill in their poetry. If this yardstick of poetry is applied, then many poems of the English language and some of the Bengali language will be discarded. The Vedas and the Upanishads had been written first in the Sanskrit language and the pundits were spending time discussing and studying those. The pioneer of the era and revolutionary, Valmiki, knowing the Vedas and the Upanishads to be extremely incomprehensible to the common people, took the mission of composing the oldest epic, the Ramayana. To date in Odisha, nothing has lasted in its richness as well as its poetry. Of course, it cannot be claimed that any poetry has gained the same status as the Valmiki Ramayana. This is because all the ancient writers of Odia poetry, or most of them, discussed in the Sanskrit language first, and then they picked up the pen/stylus to write in Odia. Thus, whoever had whichever ideology for them in the Sanskrit language, keeping

---

[iv] The ones who prefer or advocate using ornamental language.

that in front of their inner eyes, wrote their own poetry. I am, of course, not saying that it does not have a special method.

Bhanjakabi (Upendra Bhanja) was a great disciple of epic poets; there is a shadow of epic poetry on 'Baidhehishabilasa'. But that does not mean that Bhanja was incapable of composing phrases in a lucid style. If the lucid style in some places of his creations like 'Koti Brahmanda Sundari' etc. is perused, the readers will have the illusion of reading a modern text. In the poetry of Baishnaba/Vaishnav Kabi, the creator of 'Bidhagdha Chintamani', there falls a shadow of Baishnaba/Vaishnav religious scriptures or Baishnaba/Vaishnav philosophy. Later, his phrases became easily comprehensible because Dinakrushna was not biased towards such ideology. Jagannath Das is a writer with a special independent class. He himself is a Baishnaba/Vaishnav and has scripted the Odia poetic rendition of the Bhagabata, originally written in Sanskrit by Vyadadev/Vedvyas. The spirit of the Bhagabata in Sanskrit is there in Jagannath Das's Bhagabata.[v] However, the bone, marrow, etc. are different. In the opinion of many, this Bhagabata of Odia language has taken the place of the standard Bible of the English language. The write-ups of writers before Bhanja, Dinakrushna, Sarala Dasa, Jagannath Das and Samanta Sinhara have not been printed or published till today. If these are published one day, commentaries or translations will be needed along with that.

Literature is like a mirror to society, drawing its subjects from it. It is the key to the composition of a language's history, grammar and vocabulary. The important political, material, psychological, spiritual, and many such institutions and timeless reforms or changes in society are reflected more or less in literature. The national literature is a great warehouse;

[v] Bhagabata, written by Jagannath Das in Odia, is a sacred text of the Hindus that records the narrative of Krishna and the mythology of the Dwapara age.

many precious gems and pictures/images are preserved in it, such as The Mahabharata by Vyas. We come to know about the conditions, politics, artillery skills, expertise in scriptures, spiritual discussions, human hobbies and interests etc. of the then society from this epic. Taking palmfuls of water from this ocean, many writers have received the title of a great poet. The body is perishable, but the embodied soul is unperishable. The physical body decays and perishes, but the soul cannot be annihilated. This is the opinion of the philosopher pundits as well as the common people. Those who are weak, are in subordination to the strong just like a family, where the head supports the other members. One has to serve the king in a kingdom, and the many members of society must serve its leaders. Wherever there is the custom of receiving initiation, the disciples have to come under the subordination of the guru offering the initiation. The influence and deeds of each and everyone are reflected in an individual's life, in the community, race or society. In human life, the influence of religious preachers is the highest among all and distinctly clear. Below the religious preachers, there is a seat for the poets and the doyens of literature. However, the influence of poets and doyens of literature is not as obvious as that of religious preachers. Eloquent speakers and poets are people of almost the same class; the difference is that the impact of eloquent speakers runs at lightning speed in the arteries of the audience, but that is momentary and transitory; however, the impact of good poets is everlasting for ages. When the discourse of any speaker gets a place in national literature, it becomes national property and stays forever. There is probably no difference of opinion in the fact that the influence of poets and great poets is permanent. That influence does not exist in their perishable body—it exists in their immortal soul, in their poetry, and in the books of literature created by them. Their souls get reflected and dictated in their writings. They remain immortal in those write-ups, poetry and literature. Valmiki, Vyas, Bharavi, Kalidas, Upendra, Dinakrushna, Sarala Dasa, Homer, Virgil, Shakespeare, Milton, Socrates, Kabi Surya, etc. have remained alive with the body of their fame and glory. The crematorium has devoured their perishable physical structures only. Whichever races they were born in, as long as the literatures of these races prevail on earth, they will remain immortal till then.

* * *

Gopalchandra Praharaj (1872–1945)

'First April'

(Translated 'April Pahila' from the Odia by Manu Dash)

1 April 1936 is an auspicious day for the Odia people. I remember those hardworking dedicated leaders like Madhusudan Das, Biswanath Kar, Raja Hahihar Pardare, Narasingha Das, Gadadhar Bidyabhusan, Fakirmohan Senapati, Maharaja Ramachandra, Shyamasundar Rajaguru, Parala Second Prince Chandra Maharaja, Sribatsa Panda, Gourishankar, Ramakinkar, Ramachandra Das—all now dead—had apprised the government thirty-four years ago of the agony of the people, and their strong desire to bring all the Odia speaking people under one government and make a politically separate state on a linguistic basis on 1 April 1936.

About thirty-four years ago, the Odias were under the Bengal Presidency, while those of Singhbhum were under Chotnagapur. The Odias of Sambalpur, Ganjam and Visakhapatnam were under the Madhya Pradesh and Madras rule respectively. This group gradually expanded to include the kings of Manjusa, Dharakot, Surangi, Chikiti and Vizag, and their presence was conspicuous. The Utkal Sammilani, the congregation of Odias, passed the resolution of bringing all Odia-speaking areas into one fold and accordingly sent the proposal to the then government. Sambalpur merged with Odisha after a prolonged political movement. By virtue of the investigation and report of the Language Commission, led by Philip, the British, the ray of hope dawned about the

Odia region of Ganjam to merge with Odisha.[vi] The ray of hope became clearer after the Montagu–Chelmsford and Morley-Minto reforms. Finally, this awakening among the Odia-speaking people of all concerned regions propelled Philip during the visit of Lord Simon to India (in 1928). It was so destined that the Congress organization, which had been formed for the development of the whole of India, turned hostile against the fate of Odias. Congress, which was espousing the formation of provinces based on the languages, did not look upon it favourably and finally engaged in bulldozing the hope of Odia-speaking people's demand for a separate state.

The rules that were considered legal for other Indian regions were dismissed as illegal for Odias. After many arguments, sloganeering, conferences, commissions and reports, the British parliament announced the formation of a separate province comprising all Odia-speaking regions. Had the brothers of other regions not stood against this movement, all Odia-speaking regions would have merged with Odisha. But the Odias luckily broke themselves free from those who were taking undue advantage of their name. Who would have been the hewers of wood and drawers of water for them? Nevertheless, they exhibited their protest and celebrated for the regions that did not merge with Odisha. As a result, the Odia-speaking regions of Singhbhum, Midnapur, Madhya Pradesh, Ganjam and Vishakhapatnam remained outside the ambit of Odisha rule. Our woes did not end there. The brethren and cousins of our Gajapati, and rulers of princely states also severed themselves from Odisha.

[vi] C.L. Philip, a political agent of the British Government along with A.C. Duff, collector, were the members of the Philip–Duff Committee which gave a favourable report in 1924 for the merger of Ganjam district (then part of Madras Presidency) with the Odisha province.

This matter was pending (*huliyat*) before the government for the last thirty-four years, and it was not easily believed that we would ever get what we have achieved today. One thing became clear to us—that by creating a province exclusively based on the language, the British government, British parliament, the emperor of Bharat and the government of India accepted unequivocally the importance of Odia language, civilization and culture.

Based on this general statement, regions like Cuttack, Puri, Balasore, Sambalpur, Angul, Jeypore, Ganjam, Parala and Khariar came under one province. Based on the same general statement, the Odisha province will come under one flag in the future. There is no iota of doubt in it. The day when Odias staying outside Odisha province would hoist the flag of federal India in unison and prove their distinct Odianess, they will certainly come under one fold.

The rich resonant voice of ancient Utkal, Koshal and Udra would return if the Odias living inside and outside of Odisha worked in tandem, keeping this ray of hope alive. We are bound by duty to express gratitude and *rajabhakti*, devotion to the state, to the government of India, the British people and their parliament and emperor of Bharat. Today's day shall be remembered forever in the history of the Odia community. 150 million children of Odisha will pay obeisance before the creator of the universe as the foundation stone of the development of Odisha is laid down today.

* * *

Mohini Mohan Senapati (1881–1945)

'Odia Folk Tales'

(Translated 'Odia Kahani' from the Odia by Mousumi Patra)

Folk tales appear out of place in the present age in view of the inconsistent and absurd ideas found in them. But this is a total misconception. If not for anything else, folk stories are necessary for the amusement and entertainment of children. We have to understand the wisdom and imaginative mindset of the ancient people to trace the evolution of the human psyche and its tendencies. Folk tales truly reflect the thoughts, emotions, customs, morals, manners and codes of conduct of our ancestors. They are therefore essential tools with which to understand human psychology and this is where their relevance lies.

We discern several similarities in the folk tales of different countries. Some themes common to folk stories of most of the countries may be listed here. The youngest of the sons in the family is ill-treated, but he comes out triumphant at the end and inherits his share of ancestral property. Brides are interchanged by using the identity of one bride for another in marriages. A daring young man kidnaps a maiden whose demonic father chases them simply to be outwitted by the young man. A celestial husband or wife has to depart from their earthly spouse due to some mysterious reasons. Some forbidden doors have been unlocked leading the intruders to face unanticipated danger. People have descended to some murky subterranean realms and suffered immensely after consuming some magical food there. A couple has been prohibited from meeting or uttering each other's names. The souls of dead people have transmigrated into the bodies of animals. One living creature has metamorphosed into another. Human beings and animals have tied the nuptial knot. Women have given birth to animals and animals have given birth to human beings. Non-living objects have accomplished the impossible after coming under the spell of some incantations and are able to communicate just the way human beings do.

What can be the reason behind such close resemblances? Some people are of the view that the aboriginal Aryans composed ancient tales during their stay in Asia. When they migrated to the different regions of the world, these primordial tales travelled to other territories with them and assumed diverse forms in due course of time. There is another view that suggests that adventurous merchants used to travel from one country to another peddling their goods, which often included men and women who then played a vital role in carrying tales from one country to another. Some scholars attribute the similarities of such themes in the stories to other factors. They point out that the human imagination (just like inanimate objects) is governed by the laws of nature. If two people are endowed with the same level of mental faculty and face similar external circumstances, they will imagine alike, and the outcome of their imagination will be identical. If a Greek poet and an Indian poet are kept in the same environment of a civilized society, they are bound to think and imagine in the same manner, and their creative output will be almost indistinguishable. Those who are amazed at the similarities between Homer's Illiad and Valmiki's Ramayana should take the aforementioned reasons into account. We are not biased in support of any reason. All the reasons mentioned above have played a role in shaping the history of the world and giving rise to the resultant affinities across religions, imaginations and literature of different nations.

According to some people, all these stories of Odisha have been composed within the state of Odisha. Odisha is a region of great natural beauty abounding in hills, rivers and lakes. We find the depiction of various aquatic creatures living in these rivers and lakes, as well as wild animals like the tigers and bears from the forests of Odisha. The sea and the coastline also play an important role in these stories with the depiction of the 'deserted island', the mythic bird 'Gandabhairava' and many other sea-related episodes. But the rivers, the sea, the lakes, the forests, etc. are not the exclusive properties of Odisha but the whole of India. That is why we do not subscribe to the view regarding the exclusive natural resources of Odisha. Some of the Odia tales may have originated in Odisha but many others may have been imported from other countries. It is not possible now to ascertain the place of origin of most of the stories i.e. whether they are indigenous or alien.

The central characters in such tales are the king, the minister, the *katuala*_and the *sadhaba*.[vii] Between the prince and the son of the minister, the prince is more generous whereas the minister's son is clever and acts as an adviser to the prince. There is usually a profound friendship between the two young men. As the central protagonist, the prince is capable and brave; he finds his way out of forests and out of difficulties, and wins the throne and the princess. Women have a characteristic flaw in their nature and that is, once they get inquisitive about something, they cannot rest unless the mystery is unveiled. It is said that Lord Jagannath became deformed only because of this feminine flaw. The queen could not rein in her curiosity to have a glimpse of the idol before

---

[vii] Sadhaba means trader/merchant and katuala is the police superintendent or the head of the royal force.

it was completed. This resulted in the disfigurement of Lord Jagannath.[viii]

Shiva and Parvati are portrayed as the supreme deities among all gods. They come down from heaven to take a tour of the earth in the silence of the night. They help anybody in any plight. But demons are regarded as the eternal enemies of human beings. They are omnivorous, cannibalistic and have a fear of weapons.

Elephants are the best among all animals. When a kingdom has no heir to the throne, it is customary to place a pitcher of holy water on the head of the royal elephant. The lucky man on whose head the elephant pours the pitcher's water becomes the next ruler of the kingdom. A suitable groom for the princess is also selected with the help of the elephant. The fortunate young man on whose head the elephant pours the sacred water is selected as the groom and gets to marry the princess. The elephant was always associated with good luck. It is not certain if there really existed such an implausible system or if it is merely a figment of poetic imagination.

In those tales, even inanimate objects used to play active roles like living beings. A gem, by the order of a merchant's son, could amazingly construct a palatial mansion overnight. The same gem could ruin the merchant's son when it came under the control of another man. The stories enlighten us about the past. People were not so materialistic in those days. Their universe was divided into four spheres—at the top was the Devlok, which is the abode of the gods. Below it was the Pitrulok, which was inhabited by the souls of the forefathers. They are considered to be the first creators of human beings.

[viii] This story refers to the mythic narrative concerning the establishment of the Jagannath Temple at Puri. While the images of the three deities—Balabhadra, Subhadra, Jagannath—were being carved by the celestial sculptor Vishwakarma, Gundicha Devi, the queen of King Indradyumna, tried to see the sculptor at work, which was forbidden.

They have created the human race with the help of their extraordinary mental power. Hindus pay homage to their ancestors by performing the *pitru tarpan*[ix] during the dark fortnight in the month of Ashwina.[x] Of course, modern science has a different theory about the origin of man. The Naralok or the earth is located just below the Pitrulok, where human beings have their habitation. The Nagalok or the abode of serpents is found below the Naralok. The serpents who live there speak and behave like human beings, practising the same kind of rituals, customs, systems and manners. The ancient man used to conceive of the universe in his own image. It is called anthropomorphism and is used to ascribe human attributes to everything. In the opinion of many people, God has been created in the image of man. Science has dispelled this misconception of the primitive man.

These folk tales make repeated mention of temples but never refer to mosques. Were Muslims not part of Odisha in the ancient times of folk tales?

We hear about the maritime trade of the sadhabas of Odisha in the stories. Merchants from Odisha used to travel across the seas for the purpose of trade and commerce in distant lands in past times when these stories were composed. On the full moon day of *Kartika*[xi], the people of Odisha set afloat miniature boats made of sponge wood and banana stems in the rivers and ponds to celebrate the maritime glory of Odisha. A princess has been portrayed to have travelled to foreign countries by riding a horse. There is no mention of the purdah in the tales. There are innumerable folk tales of Bihar

---

[ix] Offering libations of water and til (gingely) to the *pitrus* (deceased parents and ancestors) to satisfy and elevate them to higher spiritual planes.

[x] September to October.

[xi] Months of October–November.

in which robbers and dacoits have been frequently mentioned, but there are no accounts of fights or such encounters with dangerous people.

Although it is quite impossible to trace the origins of Odia folktales, their importance to literature can be judged from the following lines in a poem written by the eminent Odia poet Nandakishore Bal:

'Telling each other tales, the simple little girls
Played and brought joy to all around them!
Their days of merriment are now over,
Who knows whither, they are all gone.'

* * *

Girija Sankar Ray (1886–1967)

'The Language of Literature'

(Translated 'Sahityara Bhasa' from the Odia by Animesh Mohapatra)

Writers express their thoughts and feelings through language. However, authors adopt different writing styles in order to communicate diverse shades of feeling and ways of thought. The writing style of some is marked by lucidity and lyrical grace while pungent acerbity characterizes the style of others. Some are fond of using the simple idiom of the countryside and others are partial to the use of a heavily archaic diction to lend an old-fashioned flavour to their works. Even when two writers appear to be using the same kind of diction, one's sentences could be interminably long and the other's, crisp and rhythmic. Some authors prefer elevated thoughts and sonorous diction, which remind one of the majesties of the sea, whereas, in the writings of others, one hears the sweet sounds of a river gently flowing by. One comes across several theories which prescribe certain styles and diction, and some that prescribe others. In reality, great writers display command over different kinds of literary styles and types of diction and know how to present their works to readers in an aesthetically pleasing manner. The extraordinary versatility exhibited by celebrated writers expressing themselves in various languages convinces us that all languages are perfectly capable of affording aesthetic delight to readers.

Some general principles regarding the language of literature are worth reflecting on. It is of two types—some texts are more realistic and therefore, the language of such texts has to be natural and unadorned; the language of some other texts could be more sentimental, idealistic and lofty. Generally, one finds the employment of language used in day-to-day life in novels, stories and plays. In poems and essays, on the other hand, sentimental expressions are preferred. Moreover, since authors follow certain rhythmic and metrical patterns while composing poems, their focus rests more on the elegance of form than on the richness of content. Although some writers may possess the ability to communicate their thoughts with lucidity and grace in other forms of literary expression, poetry cannot be created without divine blessings or inspiration. The language of poetry and that of prose and plays differ from each other in significant ways. In literature written in prose and drama, writers enjoy the privilege of expressing themselves competently. However, since writing poetry requires conforming to specific rhythmic and metrical patterns, poets deviate from the prevailing rules of syntax and language, and the poems in their hands behave in unusual ways and acquire an aura of strangeness and novelty. Adopting different mechanisms, poets try to maintain symmetry in their works and afford aesthetic delight to readers. Therefore, even when the readers know poetic language to be artificial, they overlook its unnaturalness as a result of the abundance of pleasure they derive from reading poetry. Aesthetic rapture enables readers to ignore the complex and unusual use of language one finds in poems.

Two questions concerning the language of literature spontaneously arise in one's mind: (a) In what ways is the language of literature different from ordinary spoken idioms, and (b) Can dialects be legitimately employed as the language of literature? The answer to the second question is quite easy. Through their extraordinary talent, many great writers have proven beyond doubt that local variations of a language can be used effectively in literary texts. Even the Nobel Prize-winning author Gabriela Mistral (1889–1957) has used such language to wonderful effect. Every language cherishes a model or a standard which most authors adhere to. Though several regional variations of English can be identified within England both in terms of usage and accent, the English spoken in London is considered the standard version. Similarly, Odia is used in different ways in different places; the language spoken in Puri varies significantly from that in Sambalpur. One finds certain expressions used in Puri, that one would not come across elsewhere in Odisha. The same is true of other places as well. Thus, the spoken idioms of Puri, Cuttack, Ganjam and Sambalpur vary from one another. However, the way Odia is spoken in Cuttack has become the standard version of the language used in literature. If a powerful writer starts using the idiom of Puri in an aesthetically compelling manner in a literary work, the language of Puri may soon be recognized as a language perfectly suitable for literary purposes. The fortunes of a dialect depend on the virtuosity of an author who uses it in a literary text. Although it is convenient to use the 'standard' version of a language, several authors have achieved fame using regional variations in their works. Such writers transform a language through the power of their imagination lending it new dimension and depth.

It is not easy to find a solution to the conflict between formal and colloquial modes of linguistic expression. The language which is used by educated people, is replete with Sanskrit words and is strikingly different from the simple idiom used by country folk. While this can be termed formal, the speech which is used in our day-to-day conversations may be described as colloquial. Writers should choose an idiom in which they are able to express themselves adequately and with ease. Moreover, authors should use words in such a way that readers are deeply moved, and a sympathetic response is aroused in their hearts. For this precise reason, some writers consider the prevailing colloquial idiom more suitable for literary use. They think general readers would not face any difficulty in following texts written in everyday speech. However, many a time, the profundity of thoughts and feelings cannot be conveyed through colloquial idiom and the writer fails to leave the intended impact on readers. Moreover, colloquial idiom often proves inadequate to express new concepts or thoughts, for which an equivalent cannot be found in the existing vocabulary. Rustic speech is simple and unadorned, and it is not easy to coin new words for users of this kind of language. Therefore, colloquial idioms are not always suitable for use in literature. Again, the occurrence of a highly refined expression in text written predominantly in everyday speech or vice versa immediately strikes a discordant note and such incongruity is generally frowned upon. For these reasons, most authors prefer to employ formal or literary language in their texts. In fact, there is no real distinction between formal and colloquial uses of a language, but one can discern some difference between its spoken and refined versions. Though in literature, the use of formal language is prevalent, these days, many writers are trying to employ colloquial idiom and the language of peasants in literary texts. In the process, the language of the countryside also gets enriched and reaches a higher level of excellence. Some authors also blend formal language with colloquial idioms in their writings, but the success of such texts depends on the quality of their artistry. Truly powerful writers can deftly use rustic idioms as the medium of creative expression and render it mellifluous, but lesser writers follow the well-trodden path and resort to using conventional literary language in their works. A comparison of the writings of Madhusudan Rao (1853–1912),[xii] who is famous for his devotional lyrics, and

[xii] Madhusudan Rao is an eminent Odia poet who wrote 'Re Atman, Nidra Parihari' (Thought of Life).

those of Gopalchandra Praharaj (1874–1945), who compiled the multi-volume *Purnachandra Odia Bhashakosha*, would adequately illustrate this point. However, both writers are equally popular in Odisha and their works occupy an elevated place in the Odia literary canon. Therefore, it can be safely claimed that any mode of linguistic expression can serve as a medium for literary art. The success of a literary text depends on the ingenuity of its author.

Literary language possesses certain distinctive characteristics. An author always writes with the aim of providing pleasure to readers and therefore adopts a language and style that would be agreeable to them. Affording delight being one of their primary aims in literary texts, authors, thus, tend to avoid using language that would appear vitriolic, coarse or infused with extreme sadness. In addition, they eschew difficult and opaque expressions and try to make language refined and delicate. In order to make their texts more appealing, authors use various evocative figures of speech to establish parallels between the realm of their imagination and the world of external nature. In consonance with the aesthetic sentiments they are embodying, authors adorn their narratives and discourses with various rhetorical devices and other compositional techniques, to make their works more euphonious and alluring. Embellishments distinguish literary language from ordinary language and render a piece of writing engrossing. Some authors make excessive use of literary embellishments while others use it only sparsely. Some believe that language turns unpleasantly opaque through the immoderate use of alliteration and assonance and fails to convey emotions effectively. Just as excessive use of jewellery obscures the loveliness of a beautiful woman, overindulgent employment of literary embellishments contributes to impeding full appreciation of the depth of feelings. Some writers, though, do not consider the use of literary embellishments a shortcoming. In pre-colonial times in Odisha, poets made their works so felicitous and mellifluous through the liberal use of figures of speech and other compositional techniques that one cannot help being enchanted by the use of literary adornments. Though one finds a preponderance of literary embellishments in pre-modern texts, in modern literature, they are used in a more restrained manner. Modern authors set a high value on the propriety of expressions and profundity of feelings. Therefore, modern texts affect the intellect more deeply. For general readers, it proves exceedingly challenging to appreciate a text encumbered by a profusion of literary embellishments and grasp its essence. Such texts may bear evidence of the author's virtuosity and exceptional command of language, but these fail to elicit a favourable response from readers. In fact, excessive use of literary embellishments may indicate a dearth of feelings and emotions. Since modern literature sets out to address social issues, there is not much room in it for the employment of ornamental language.

Intimate inwardness and rich imagination are vital components of a literary language. Without sincerity and inwardness, a writer's linguistic virtuosity may beguile readers for a brief while, but it would fail to leave an enduring impression on them. A literary text can never become a source of true delight unless it is transformed by the powers of imagination. Exploiting various figures of speech and other compositional strategies, an author attempts to render language more harmonious and lyrical. This is what sets literary language apart from everyday speech and renders the task of writing a literary text of the highest quality so complex and challenging.

* * *

Bepin Vehari Roy (1887–1975)

'Beauty'

(Translated 'Soundarjya' from the Odia by Asima Ranjan Parhi)

It is difficult to know the origin and time of humanity's search for beauty and gratification. The history of all civilizations reveals the extent to which music, poetry and objects of beauty occupied them, even though it is hard to get any information about the eternal practice of art education anywhere. Many times, art as a skill gets affected when a nation is caught struggling in the throes of a nationalist movement. Art is for a time of peace; a time when a country and community get settled, and safe from external forces. The taste of beauty is an ability human beings acquire from birth. Its mode of presentation, representation or underrepresentation varies from place to place. An Egyptian sculpture is different from that of India. But the *rasa*[xiii] evoked out of beauty is inherent both in the civilized and uncivilized. Civilization, in itself, is not a cause of the art, for it is found in the uncivilized too. But civilization helps in the growth and spread of its taste and practice. The inherent nature of appreciating beauty is seen in the way a child acts. The perception of the child and primitive human beings match quite well. They are delighted by the dazzle, the colourful and the ornamental.

[xiii] Rasa is the aesthetic realization of a feeling. Taken from the famous Indian aesthetician Bharata's Natyashastra, rasa theory examines all kinds of human emotion and feeling with equivalent emotion aroused in a character's dramatization.

An object in itself is not beautiful. Beauty cannot exist in exclusion. It emerges from the comparison between objects. Beauty does not exist independently of its environment. It owes its symmetry to its background, and the objects that do not have symmetry with their surroundings generally repel onlookers. A star is beautiful when we see it against the vast sky, and the sky is beautiful when it is seen in comparison with the thousand stars that dot it. Beauty lies in each element complementing the other. A lot of variation and repulsion among objects make them look stale. An integration and order among objects magnify beauty. A kind of unity in diversity, an assimilating force rather than discordant digressions makes the artistic object beautiful. In an educational institution, if you see the chalk, pen, book, newspaper, table, almirah, chair, and inkpot kept here and there, it would appear to be in a mess. They also have a suitable place for themselves. Various disparate objects, when arranged in a harmonious setting, can unexpectedly yield beauty. In Odia, there is a proverb, *Gotie chaula re gadha*[xiv]. This is the quality of accommodating and assimilating everything in the external as well as imaginative world. This quality makes one beautiful and this innocent balance is the basis of beauty. Thought and imagination can materialize this integration of objects. The proportionate assimilation happens in the fertile imaginative skill of the man. The artist in this case seems to have prepared a formula, a model that foregrounds the objects as part of one beautiful entity. Beauty belies a workmanship of thought and imagination on the part of the artist, which creates an interface of both in his mind and gets reflected in the artwork. The temples of Konarka in Bhubaneswar are the outcome of such a skill. The man who is more equipped with this skill is the greater artist. Man's exceptional skill of

[xiv] Made up of one grain of rice, pointing at the seamless nature of the grain and its speciality.

converting objects of the world to beauty is nothing but a transition and integration of objects and laws. The perception of such beauty is also exclusive to man and is available neither to the inanimate world nor the animal species.

There lies an inherent link between the external world and beauty. The lifeless worldly objects too evoke a sense of beauty by the mere touch or smell of them. Only the people with a special sense to recognize it gratify the world of beauty.

Both the skill of the *purusha*, which is the characteristic of any artist irrespective of gender and its assimilation with *prakruti,* create an embedded state of consciousness in us to appreciate beauty.[xv] The following lines from the 'Thought of Life' will explain this:

> Oh! *Brahman*,[xvi] our soul
> shed your illusive sleep
> remove your worries
> and see deep.

The poet creates a sense of nature, i.e. a kind of feeling in his thought to produce the rasa by the use of words like 'reflect' (*lochana*) and 'enquire deep' (*nirikhyana*). In a similar vein, the lines below are from 'Chilika', an outstanding poem by Radhanath Ray, a nineteenth-century Odia poet.

> At your hint,
> the ocean runs to you with a fleet of waves
> both complement each other
> by their beauty
> as the pride of the east
> to the proud people of the east

[xv] Purusha means manly, energetic and charismatic. Prakruti is womanly, nature and earth. Both complement each other.

[xvi] Brahman means supreme soul of divine origin with ultimate knowledge.

Where the words 'hint', 'pride' and 'run' are the traits of purush that get embedded with prakruti.

A poet confined in the physical, practical world cannot create beauty. The worldly and the ideal get churned and mixed, and both purush and prakruti come in tandem to produce great art that speaks of both the present and future.

This is how the imagination makes real art. True beauty is in the domain of the ideal. A painting's worth lies in its implicit essence, not in the nature of colour or lines drawn over it.

Hence, the essence of beauty is an organic thing. It has a deep structure of its own. Mere ornamentation cannot turn the ugly into the beautiful. Beauty is neither hidden nor obvious. Poetry or other arts unveil ingrained qualities and produce beauty. This play of the visible and invisible, and the thought behind its surface is the aim of the artist.

The artist and the sculptor realize this relationship and make it visible. There are two kinds of beauty: One comes out of our senses and the other from imagination. The former happens because of the physical response of our body to the objects. The other comes out of our mental, thoughtful, imaginative connection with them. In our childhood, we are influenced by the external elements and react to them, but as we grow older, we realize the significance of both the external objects and the evocation of our four extraordinary feelings towards them. We also come to find out how sometimes the external object is a kind of deception when its worth is tested.

This worth of bodily beauty is a matter of personal gratification. It is also changeable. But beauty born out of pure values and quality is universal and eternal. It lasts for a very long time.

Idol worship may be attractive to many, but the quality of worship remains a talent forever. The place, Bhagabata

Tungi,[xvii] may not be in use but the essence of Bhagabata is not a matter of extinction. Gold-enamelled objects are more beautiful than brass ones because they are made of a superior material. But the beauty of a world-class architectural marvel like Konarka or a temple in Bhubaneswar is because of the use of its material by the skilful artist and his artistry. It is an equal combination and mixture of object and art.

Imagination can be yet another essence of beauty. This has nothing to do with the beauty of the body, face, structure or features. A lover finds his beloved beautiful even if she may not look so to others or appears ugly. This featureless beauty is born out of our imagination. It cannot be described though sensitive minds try to describe it. It is a personal taste and a matter of self-realization. A lover finds his partner beautiful because of the association of the person with many other objects, places, contexts, memorable past and future prospects.

We cannot say that beauty comes out of only sense perception. We ordinarily perceive certain objects to be more beautiful than others. There is an intrinsic relationship between colour, shape and the object itself. To say that a particular measure of the shape has made it beautiful is ignorance. The beauty of a flower doesn't lie in its petals only. It is there in its 'flowerness'; in other words, a quality that even the actual flower as an object does not exemplify. Once it creates a feeling of delight and contentment in our hearts, it then illuminates the world by its inherent quality which we recognize to be beautiful. It cannot be an outcome of our mechanical and intellectual faculty.

[xvii] Bhagabata Tungi is the place in every Odia village where the scripture Bhagabata is placed, worshipped and chanted, whether there is an audience or not, as part of an everyday routine.

Literature is a site of imaginative beauty. The use of language and rhetoric may attract us and place such writing as beautiful but a literature that creates a novel feeling, a text that evokes an ideal state of thought and converts the old to a new model, transforms the matter-of-fact properties to an ideal vision is superior. Valmiki's epic, Ramayana, is based on the ideals of a noble state, filial gratitude, truthfulness and victory of good over evil, which is why this kind of literature has remained beautiful and will continue to be beautiful for all times to come. Even if human beings differ in their sense perception, there would still be unity in their imaginative state of being. A kind of music that is based only on its auditory quality may or may not be liked by all or gratify everyone, but music that presents a special imaginative splendour would certainly entice all. That which captivates all is an eternal creation.

Beauty is a matter of universal appreciation and realization. Parts of an object do not create beauty. Rather by breaking it into parts, we spoil its essence. A beautiful idol or a sweet flower loses its sweetness if perceived as a mere head, waist, hand and feet or root, stem and petal. An analysis of these is the nature and duty of the scientist. It is required for an explanation of the object. That is why such an analytic process results in removing the object's beauty. Physicists are usually deprived of the evocation of beauty because they seek truth. To reach the truth about the object is the task and purpose of knowledge creation but the realization of rasa is the precursor to beauty. Knowledge depends on the brain. Beauty depends on imagination. Science discovers. Art creates knowledge.

Still, that which is true is beautiful and the best. The true, the beautiful and the best serve humanity. Truth is not an asset of the individual but of the whole of mankind. Beauty is not the monopoly of one but attracts the entire humankind.

The best is capable of the well-being of humanity. In the ideal world, they are united. Like beauty, knowledge too is inspired by an ideal significance, and engaged in the creation of an ideal state. The visible world is always imperfect. So, these faculties are involved in bringing an ideal fulfilment to complete the incomplete. At a moment when the ideal gets nearer, we get an assimilation of the worth of the object, of what its beauty and superiority accomplished. This is proved as we can say God is simultaneously true, beautiful and the best.

Suniti Kumar Chatterji (1890–1977)

'The Oriya Character'

(An excerpt taken from 'The People, Language and Culture of Orissa', Artavallabha Mahanti Memorial Lectures, given originally in English)[1]

The great qualities of Orissa's people are no less manifested in peace than in war. The Oriya character is essentially that of industrious and peace-loving people. Their spirit is of innate gentleness and patience. Their attitude of acceptance on the spiritual level of all approaches to the unseen forms is fundamental in Hindu culture. This has been a great elevating and civilizing force in the formation of the 'national personality' of the Oriya people as much as in other parts of *Hindudom*.[xviii] This has enabled the Orissans to be firm without blatant aggressiveness, and gentle and kind and well disposed towards all. It certainly is a great virtue in the world of man. There are some other fine traits of the Oriya character, which would at once strike an outside observer-simplicity with inventiveness, adaptability and accommodation, and a general friendliness for all. In a word, the mental atmosphere and outward behaviour are that of the Vaishnava faith at its best.

[xviii] The realm or sphere of Hindus.

Orissa in the Pan-Indian Set-Up

The all-round contribution of the Oriya people to the development of India, both in culture and in economy, has been quite considerable. In ancient times, the maritime enterprise of the people of Orissa, along with that of the people of Bengal and of Andhra, took some of the most characteristic things of Indian civilization and culture to Indo–China (Burma, Cambodia and Siam), and also to distant Indonesia. This connection was established through Orissan merchants and sailors, as also through the merchants and sailors, from Bengal and from Andhra. In both Bengal and Orissa, they had the same word to mean a sea-going ship, *buhita* or *bohita*, which is from the Sanskrit *vahitra*. Buhitas from eastern India were sea-going crafts without riggers such as we find depicted in that well-known frieze from Boro-Budur in Java.[xix] The stream of the Oriya settlement in the lands of Indo–China appears to have been stopped after the advent of the Turks, who had the same effect on the people of Orissa as they did on other people of India. But Orissa maintained, during the rule of the Karas (8–10 CE), connections with China, and we have the account of a Buddhist scholar from Orissa who went to China in the year 900 CE. In the Konarka sculptures, we have a figure of a giraffe, which was evidently brought in as a great curiosity to India and offered to the King of Orissa by Arab merchants, particularly from South Arabia who had business connections from times before the Prophet Muhammad, with South India and Eastern India. Chittagong, as an important port in Eastern India, had Arab merchants as a settled community. It is exceedingly likely that Orissa shared in these international connections, which were faintly

[xix] Borobudur, also transcribed Barabudur, is a ninth-century Mahayana Buddhist temple in Magelang Regency, near the city of Magelang and the town of Muntilan, in Central Java, Indonesia.

maintained even after the loss of freedom by Hindu India. After the establishment of a Pax Britannica[xx] in Burma and other countries of South-eastern Asia, along with the Telugus and Tamilians and people from North India–Bihar, UP and Punjab, Oriya people of humbler ranks went to Burma and Malaya as agricultural labourers, and many of them made these places their homes. But after the recent Burmese policy of driving out all Indians, all these ancient contacts have become disorganized. Within India, the Oriya people, in their attempt to spread out for economic reasons, established themselves over the greater part of Bengal and even in Assam, and a good number found their way into other parts of India including Maharashtra—although the Oriya settlement there has grown in driblets. Oriya labour had a great contribution to the development of a great town like Calcutta as well.

But all this was due to the economic pressure of the modern times on the Oriya people. Their great qualities, which have been dormant for the last few centuries, are once again manifesting themselves. At one time, the Oriyas had built up a great empire which spread from the lower reaches of the Bhagirathi river right down to the frontiers of the Tamil country in South India, and in Central India, it extended over considerable parts of what is now Madhya Pradesh. But what is still more important and valuable for India, was that, like the Vijayanagara empire founded jointly by the Telugus and the Kannadigas in 1336 CE, the Ganga empire and its subsequent developments in Orissa, gave stubborn and effective resistance for some centuries to the spread of Islamic power by the Turks and North Indian Muslims towards Orissa and South India. The Hindu Ahom state in Assam and

[xx] Pax Britannica was the period of relative peace between the great powers. During this time, the British Empire became the global hegemonic power, developed an additional informal empire, and adopted the role of a 'global policeman'.

North Bengal, and the Koch and Tipra states of Hindu Bodo tribes in both North Bengal and East Bengal, checked Turks and Bengal Muslims as well as the Mogul aggression and extension of Muslim power in North-Eastern India.

The powerful military organization of the Orissa people, based in economic solidarity and its innate spirit of nationalism was, for some centuries, a thorn in the side of the Moslem state in Bengal. For years, the Orissa kings repeated the feat performed by Kharavela as a sort of Asvamedha for Indian rulers of the Kali age. They used to bring their armies and march to the beat of drums into the enemy's country (as the Rajputs boasted in the fourteenth century when they entered Delhi in force—*Dholla maria Dhilli-maha caliyo Bira Hammira*, which translated to 'The hero Hamir marched into Delhi beating his drums') and would make their war elephants drink from the waters of the Gangas at Triveni near Hooghly (*Magadhanam ca vipulam bhayam jane(n)to hathisu Gangaya payayati* [engendering a terrible fear among the Magadhan people, he made his elephants drink from the Ganges], as Kharavela's inscription says in the 2nd century BCE). It was from the internal disorders in Orissa, and through the instinct of self-preservation from the expanding Mogul empire under Akbar, that the Pathan rulers of Bengal made (traditionally, under their general, the renegade brahman, Kala Pahar, who had developed a violent antipathy towards his own people) a final attack against the weakened Orissa, and conquered the territory in 1565. Around the said time, the Battle of Talikota, was a watershed fight between the Vijayanagara Empire and an alliance of the five Deccan sultanates. Despite the Vijayanagara army being larger, they were comprehensively defeated. Later on, Sivaji and the Peshwas revived the Hindu state. It was just three years before the overthrow of Orissa by the forces of the Pathan Sultan of Bengal in 1569.

The Orissa empire in its great days, vis-a-vis the Muslim states of Bengal, Bihar and Jaunpur, was a haven of refuge for the Hindu people of Bengal. It was also (Like Mithila, which somehow retained its internal control right down to the Mogul period) a centre of Sanskrit learning and Hindu culture. During this time, Puri became completely integrated with Bengali Hindu culture and religious life, as much as Varanasi was. As said before, Chaitanya virtually found an asylum in Puri under King Prataparudra, so that he might carry on his work as a devotee and religious teacher in peace. Orissa on the one hand, and far away in the North East Assam on the other, became the repositories of Hindu culture and religion, with much greater conservation of the ancient Hindu world in Orissa, which was strengthened by its association or contact with the Telugu states in the south.

This empire, of course, does not exist anymore, but the Orissa country is now awake in seeking to bring about an industrial revolution, signs of which are apparent everywhere. The peace and harmony with which the present state of Orissa is carrying on its affairs, without any problems with her neighbours in Madhya Pradesh, Andhra, Bengal and Bihar, is a sufficient testimony of the working of the principle of peaceful co-existence, which forms one of the great messages of India in world politics. With all her high traditions of civilization and culture, her pre-eminence in the arts and crafts, and in the art of peaceful living, Orissa, as a state, possesses the fundamentals of civilized and cultured life and fully upholds the great traditions of India.

* * *

Gobinda Tripathy (1899–1962)

'Lies'

(Translated 'Michha Katha' from the Odia by Sanskruti Pujari)

Many wise men have proclaimed that honesty is the best policy. One is bound to abide by the wise men and their wise words, but you cannot force a threshing horse down somebody's throat and expect them to swallow it. Nevertheless, if someone claims in fear or in a manner of bragging that they can swallow a threshing horse, they surely are some fire-swallowing liars. It becomes impossible to get by in this world without lies. Lies are sweet, but the truth—the absolute truth—is like the scorching desert sun, dry and depressing. A lie or two feels like a drop of water in that desert. This broken dilapidated world once arose from a bottomless depth of water. From that day onwards, lies have held onto an unshakable throne of their own.

According to the written word of our truthful great saints in ancient times, the world was filled with water; *Mahaprabhu*, our Lord, used to float over this world perched on a gigantic leaf. One day, the Lord decided to play. In his play, he miraculously created this world. We are the educated mass, and hence we understand that all of these are nothing but lies. It is the same in the Bible. At first, there was only water and darkness all around. God was seated within that darkness. Maybe all that idle sitting made him restless and he made up his mind to do something. Then *ti' bing faat*![xxi] God said, 'Let there be light' and there was

---

[xxi] An onomatopoeia used for magical revelation. An English equivalent would be *tada* or *bibidi-bobidi-boo*.

light. Let the winds blow, and the wind blew. All the science that we have read has made us capable of knowing that these are all lies. We know that religion is a lie that floats on the cloud of falsehood. People say that in the *Satyayug,* not a soul would utter a lie. That lies are the treasured property of the *Kalyug.*[xxii] Even this is a lie. To say that Rama was a righteous, truthful man. That he could figure out if Sita was pure just through a fire ordeal. But when they came back to their kingdom, when a random person uttered a few words against her, he left Sita in the forest believing that she was not pure. Does this fall under the banner of truth? To say that Krishna is the Mahaprabhu himself. In the great war of the Mahabharata, it was he who fibbed that the very much alive Ashwathama was dead. How much more should I write? The entire humankind is alike, who has the time to count every single hair?

In sooth, it is in a lie that a person's courage shines. 'I went, I came back, I just said what I saw'—that's what they'll all say. What did you achieve by feeding your educated brain with all the bookish knowledge that you could acquire? Your education is put to the test when you lie. Twisting and turning the lie to make it appear as the truth is the mark of real wisdom. The greatest liars of our land of wisdom, *Bharatvarsha*, are the enlightened sages. Following them closely are the epic poets. Kalidas, Bhababhruti, Bharabi, Shriharsha—they have all been frantically running on the same lines. To say despite being such great sages and poets, what is all this huff and puff about lying? The thing is the brighter knowledge burns in the mind of a person, the better dances their restless imagination. All that is beautiful and sweet in human life is rooted in imagination.

[xxii] According to Hindu Cosmology, *Satya Juga* or 'the age of truth' is believed to represent the pinnacle of human civilization, where people lived in accordance with dharma (righteousness), and were free from greed, deceit and other negative traits. *Kali Juga*, on the other hand, is a period of darkness and degradation, where virtues are diminished, and vices prevail.

Real happiness doesn't reside in earning money for a living. The very act of imagining what all one can do when that money is earned, and eventually fulfilling those desires, is what makes one content and where happiness resides. Kissing your lover's lips isn't half as pleasurable as staying away from your lover and imagining that you are kissing her lips. To say my thoughts aloud, to attain fruits after doing some labour doesn't make one happy. Real happiness is in the imagination that goes behind the task, much before the labour yields some fruit. It means that we attain the fruits of our labour even before we actually do the task. When a farmer takes his plough to his farm, his imagination for the outcome knows no bounds, right? What kind of paddy his fields will have, at what rate he would sell his yield, what all he could do after he gets that money, and in this imagination, he overcomes all the kicks and blows, and all the petty shaming of this world. He takes a handful of grain back home. That's when all the tribulations settle on his head like a mountain. With this handful of yield, how will I repay the landlord, how much revenue will I pay, how will I repay my petty loans, and what will I eat? His happiness is not in his harvest. Whatever happiness he had was before he procured his harvest, but that happiness is a lie. That's like going down the dark rabbit hole of imagination. But this lie, this game of imagination is the only hope in his life. Deal with this lie, tell him the truth, say, '*Bapa*! Dust thou art, to dust thou returnest' will be your fate all year. Whatever you earn will fill the pockets of others. The wet cloth you have tied on your stomach today will stay put to that day and beyond. This is the unbending truth. If you utter this unbending truth, the farmer will crumble into a corner of his hut with his palm on his forehead. He'll say, '*Jaa, ho*![xxiii] If all the roads lead to my misery, then why work?'

[xxiii] *Jaa Ho* is an Odia exclamatory phrase used to convey discontentment, renouncement, anger and even dismissal, depending on the tone. In the context of this essay, it denotes renouncement.

As we understand, this imagination or this lie of life doesn't just make one happy, but it also provides the strength to keep striving. It is an encouragement that serves as a whip that gets one going. To understand this, one does not need those saints with dry lives. One needs romantic poets and litterateurs. There is no one as treacherous as these saints and sages. They spend their lives with tigers and bears chasing after the imagination of a power called God. They believe that if they perform this penance, they will go to heaven. They will witness the Mahaprabhu indulging in an eternal nap floating on an ocean of milk. No one has seen that before. If anyone has ever felt the presence of God, they have done so in their imagination. We have heard that Ramakrishna Paramhansa had made Vivekananda experience the existence of God.[2] The reason is that Vivekananda had a great power of imagination. If he had not been swayed by the river of religion, he would have become a highly regarded poet or novelist. It is said that when Galileo went around telling people that the earth goes round the sun and not the other way around, the learned men of that time accused him of sacrilege and imprisoned him. A wise man visited him in prison. Galileo told him, 'See, I can feel that the earth is moving.' That experience of his was simply his imagination. A certain learned man from our country once said, 'I can hear the flapping sound of the wings of birds.' Even that is imagination. Imagination is often a lie. But these learned men cling to lies and proclaim, '*Satyam Shivam Sundaram*' (truth alone triumphs). That is why I had called these saints and sages treacherous. They will feed their stomachs with lies but will sing the merry song of truth. Of course, if they agree that truth can only be achieved through imagination, and that truth is God, I am ready to lick their feet, because it is only at the end of this tunnel of imaginary lies that one can find the truth. You'll say, in life what is the difference between imagined truth and the absolute truth? The difference that exists between the human body and the soul, moonlight and the moon, the smell of a flower and the flower itself—that is the difference. That is the difference between truth, that is, what appears to be the truth and the absolute truth—the truth that is palpable. I am lying dead, Ram came, he saw me and went away. He went and told Shyam, 'I went to see Gobinda.' He is speaking the truth. But what he has really said is a lie because does Gobinda even exist?

Now, there are three things—the truth, the untruth and the lie or imagination. A lie is not the opposite of the truth. Instead, if a lie is the body to which life is given by the truth, it is by tackling or using this lie that one can achieve the truth. Untruth, on the other hand, is the opposite of truth. Only a litterateur can understand this. This is because the actual purpose of literature is to assign the truth, the untruth, and the lie to their proper places. The writer of the Christian Bible; the creator of Gita, the poet Vyas; the writer of Ramayana, the poet Valmiki, are all worshippers of the God of lies.

You might want to chase me down with a stick after this. The creator of Gita and the writer of the Bible have not said this just once or twice but a thousand times: 'Say the truth, say the truth, don't you ever lie! That's your fault.' They have said to not say what is untrue. If you have not understood this and you believe that what is untrue is a lie, then it is the fault of your brain. The ancient saints and poets used to behave like a bull that has seen red when they came across untruth. But for the real poets, lies are as beautiful as untruth is grotesque. That is because what is true is not beautiful, and what is ugly is unlovable.

We say, *satya bruyat priyam bruyat, ma bruyat satyam apriyam* (utter the truth, utter what is lovely, never utter a truth that is not lovely). If you have to say the truth, saying what is pleasant to the ears and mind alike should be uttered. If one is to always say the absolute truth, then one would have to forcefully shut one's mouth, because there is no reward for absolute truth in this world. And the only prize of uttering mind-pleasing untruths is getting beaten with shoes. This is why I have said that untruth is grotesque.

We are all poets. The reason is that we all wish to acquire things that are beautiful. I will have a beautiful bride, beautiful children, a beautiful house, and in that house, a beautiful bed and on that bed, a beautiful soft mattress. My beautiful lover would be seated on it adorned in beautiful attire, a beautiful moonlight falling on it all, etc.

* * *

Krushna Chandra Panigrahi (1909–87)

'Literature of Odisha'

(Translated 'Odishara Sahitya' from the Odia by Manu Dash)[xxiv]

While making a close study of the ancient literature, history and archaeology of Odisha ever since my childhood days, I have learnt one thing: they are dovetailed in together. If we don't understand one subject out of those properly, we cannot follow the other subjects as well. History gives ample proof that literature is the mirror of society. Whenever any historic movement has caused the new renaissance, impacting national life, it has created brilliant literature in the said society. The great poet Kalidas was born in the kingdom that dazzled with the light of knowledge in the Gupta Age. *Mahakavi*[xxv] Sarala Dasa had scripted his magnum opus the Mahabharata only during the period of King Kapilendra Deba, whose kingdom extended from Ganga to Kaveri. The genius of Shakespeare came to light during the golden period of Queen Elizabeth's rule in England. The great saint poet Tulasidas had written his classic epic, Ramacharitmanas, in the kingdom of Akbar. When the renaissance of knowledge made an appearance in India, great poets like Michael Madhusudan Dutta and

---

[xxiv] A lecture given on the occasion of the Gopabandhu Das centenary in 1976–77.

[xxv] The great poet.

Rabindranath Tagore were born in Bengal, which received all the privileges of this cultural era.

While making a critical analysis of ancient Odia literature and history, the same inter-relationships are easily revealed. Odisha's literature, much like Odisha's history, has travelled all along an uneven road i.e. the genesis of the history of Odia literature is not easily traceable.

Taking a few short, scattered writings and examples, some literary pundits have made exaggerated statements that these writings belong to a pre-Sarala period, but their existence is very negligible. These writings could neither be treated as sacrosanct sources nor evolved into a sacrosanct stream in Odia literature. From the gigantic/ majestic source of Sarala literature, the stream of sacred Odia literature started flowing. In the aftermath, this ever-growing stream has been continuing to expand and swell. At times, its stream has been narrowed down after facing the unprecedented and the great *Nanka* famine.[xxvi] But it has never stopped flowing.

From its beginning, Odia literature has moved in three major eras of history. The first phase is from 1435 CE, the initial period of Gajapati Kapilendra Deba's reign till 1568 CE, the last phase of Odisha's independence; the second phase is from 1568–1947 CE, the dark period of Odisha under Muslim, Maratha and English rule; and the third phase is post-Independence India. While Odia literature has carried the definite marks of these three historic eras, often, we do not make proper interpretations of these certain marks, being carried away by mere emotion. Painting the past as excellent is not only a misrepresentation of the truth, but it is also a sign of an inferiority complex. Without critical analysis,

---

[xxvi] 'Na-Anka' Durbhikhya (The Great Famine of 1866) of Odisha, which took place during the ninth year of the rule of Gajapati of Puri, Dibyasingha Deba, killed over a million people in eastern India.

eulogizing the whole of ancient literature is like making a travesty of truth.

The great stream of Odia literature has been formed over the years and we are part of this flow. In the olden days, scholars believed that history does not repeat itself. The style and the content adopted by the great ancient poets cannot be replicated. But their sacrifice, labour, effort, sincerity and talent will be always respected. The creators of ancient literature that dates back to 1568 CE were talents of great eminence. They addressed themselves as Das, or slaves of the people, such as Batsha Das, Markand Das, Sarala Dasa, Jagannath Das, Balaram Das, Jasobant Das, Ananta Das and Achyutananda Das. Humility was a common enough trait shared by them; they referred to themselves as ignorant or even illiterate and never made attempts at donning honorifics like Mahakavi or Kabisamrat.

In the later years, this ideology underwent a sea change. The poets of the *riti*[xxvii] era had clearly written that their literary works were not meant for the illiterate and fools, but for the wise, the knowledgeable, scholars and discerning people only. Their work was more layered, and more complicated. Literature was now of *utkat rasatmaka*.[xxviii] Though camouflaging Sita–Ram and Radha–Krishna with religious fervour as hero and heroine in this literature, we also envisage all the dirty games played in the bedrooms of the then kings of Odisha.

In the last phase of the British rule, knowledge and science found their way to Odisha. In the backdrop of its light around India, it made the poor plight of Odisha crystal clear and perturbed the hearts of the poets. A stream of melancholy flowed in Odia literature, particularly in the writing of

---

[xxvii] 'Riti' is known as the age of style in medieval Odia literature. Dinakrushna Dasa and Upendra Bhanja are among the greatest poets of this era.

[xxviii] Grotesque feelings.

Radhanath, Fakir Mohan, Chintamani, Gangadhar and Gopabandhu.

Modern Odia literature today has thus been enriched by a history of poetry, short stories, novels, drama, essays, historical criticism, folklore and children's literature. Only I fail to understand the development of modern poetry. It might be because of my ignorance. Lagging far behind the advanced path of a new endeavour of leading youth, I have perhaps no energy to understand it. Ancient poets of Odisha have written poems for the welfare of all people, animals and the world. I would like to congratulate the Odia poets if they are writing having been inspired by this motto.

* * *

Prabhat Mukherjee (1914–84)

'Chaitanya in Oriya Literature'

(An excerpt taken from the *History of Chaitanya Faith in Orissa* originally written in English)[1]

The Oriya literature sources supplement our knowledge of the Chaitanya period in Odisha. We learn from these sources that Chaitanya had a large number of followers headed by Jagannath Dasa, Balaram, Achyutananda, Yasovanta and Ananta, who were called *Pancha Sakha* (five comrades), that Chaitanya passed away before the image of Jagannatha, and that Chaitanya was also considered to be Buddha–Jagannath.

(1) Sunya Samhita by Achyutananda

Achyutananda incidentally refers to Chaitanya in his *Sunya Samhita*, which is a masterpiece of esoteric Vaishnava literature. In the *Sunya Samhita,* Achyutananda attempted to synthesize the concept of Buddha Jagannatha with that of Chaitanya. Sunya Samhita was probably written during the reign of King Mukundadeva (1560–68), whose son-in-law was Achyutananda's patron.

Achyutananda was an eyewitness of the passing away of Chaitanya. The master has been defined in the *Sunya Sunitha* by Achyutananda, who writes that Chaitanya the master is the Lord himself. He has appeared to redeem the sinners.

Achyutananda rights that he participated in the *kirtana* processions of Gauranga Chandra along with his comrades Ananta, Yasovanta, Balaram and Jagannath. According to his narration, he was one of the first to receive the grace of Chaitanya. The Ananta, Yasovanta, Balarama, and Srivatsa aka Jagannath Dasa also participated. Thus, all the five comrades were present and by the order of Chaitanya, the chanting of the name of Hari from every house sounded in the air. The *Sunya Samhita* makes no reference to the prominent followers of Chaitanya such as Nityananda, Ramananda and Svarup Damodar.

(2) Mahabhava Prakasa by Kanhei (Kanai) Khuntia

Kanhei Khuntia was a servitor of the Jagannath temple. The last part of his work, the *Mahabhava Prakasa* is lost. Only the first two cantos and a portion of the third have been published. The work deals with the idea (*tattva*) of Radha, which the writer had heard from Chaitanya himself. The master explains to Kanhei Khuntia that Radha is the embodiment of *Mahabhava* or supreme bliss.

The work refers to Kesava Bharati and Madhavendra Puri, who are called devout Vaishavas. It corroborates the statement in the *Chaitanya Charitamrita* that Ray Ramananda was devoted to Krishna and could not properly manage the affairs of the province of Rajamahendri (canto 2). Kanhei vividly describes the *bhavavesa* (emotional ecstasy) of Chaitanya at the sight of Jagannath. He at once noticed that the effulgence from the eyes of Jagannath fell upon the face of Chaitanya! He refers to Svarup Damodar and to Govinda. He praises the king of Orissa for his devotion to the Master. Kanhei writes that Chaitanya, after taking *sannyasa*,[xxix] reached Puri in

[xxix] A life of renunciation.

the year 918 (*Naasa athara sale prabesa hoila*). The Umlee (Islamic) year 918 has been obviously interpolated after the Muslim conquest of Orissa. Kanhei is silent about Kasi Misra, Tulasi Parichha and other attendants of the Jagannath temple. Historically, the importance of the work lies in the description of the Muslim invasion of Orissa in 1511 CE.

(3) Chaitanya Vilas by Madhava Dasa

B.B. Majumdar first traced a copy of this manuscript. He attributes the authorship to Madhava Patnaik, who has been mentioned in the Vaishnava Vandana and works as a pious Vaishnava. In his opinion, Lochan Das has followed Madhava while narrating the sannyasa of Chaitanya. There is not sufficient evidence to justify such an inference. To justify this, it has to be established that this Oriya manuscript reached Lochan Das before 1566 and he considered it important for narrating the incidents which took place in Bengal. No contemporary writer, Oriya or Bengali, refers to the *Chaitanya Vilasa*. On the contrary, Madhava himself admits that he had translated into Oriya language what Thakur had said. It appears that a portion of the *Chaitanya Vilasa* is based on the *Chaitanya Mangal* by Lochan Das, who respectfully addresses his preceptor Narahari Sarkar as Thakur (spiritual guide).

(4) Mayura Chandrika by Sri Hari Dasa

The writer probably flourished towards the end of the sixteenth century. He calls Ray Ramananda his teacher and refers to Ramananda's religious discourse with Chaitanya, whom he invokes as Krishna Chaitanya (canto 6). The poet writes that Chaitanya has manifested himself as Nadia, concealing his (dark) complexion (canto 14). He refers to

Gauranga's contemplation of Radha and Krishna with tearful eyes (canto 1). Sri Hari Dasa makes obeisance to Advaita and Nityananda at the beginning of the poem. He writes that Radha and Krishna are manifestations of Jagannath (canto 12).

(5) Chaitanya Bhagavata by Isvara Dasa

The *Chaitanya Bhagavata* was probably written in the second half of the seventeenth century.[xxx] The author writes that, at the time of the completion of the work, Chaitanya's passing away was still talked about. When he showed his manuscript in the *Mukti Mandapa*[xxxi] of the Jagannath temple, Vasudeva Tirtha, a *sannyasi*,[xxxii] expressed his doubt about Chaitanya's merger into Jagannath. Isvara Dasa, like Achyutananda, describes Chaitanya as the embodiment of Buddha–Jagannath.

The poet's source of the book has mainly been stories and names collected from traditional hearsay. The book is more a devotional account than real history. Chaitanya perhaps became a legend when the poet came to the field. Isvara Dasa's account suffers from extreme credulity for all miraculous legends relating to Chaitanya. The work, being a Bhagavata, is written in the form of a dialogue between the sage Agastya and an unnamed king of Sampurna Nagara. The writer borrows the character, stage Agastya, from Sarala Dasa's Mahabharata, where he is the story-teller to

---

[xxx] The Chaitanya Bhagavata refers to Virabhadra, son of Nityananda (canto 64). In Isvara Dasa's time, the conception of Buddha–Jagannath had not lost popularity.

[xxxi] There are many mandapas or pillared halls on raised platforms within the Jagannath Temple complex that are meant for religious congregations. The most prominent is the Mukti Mandapa, the congregation hall of the holy seat of selected learned brahmansm, who would help and advise the king in in different fields of life at the time of requirement in state administration.

[xxxii] A hermit who has accepted the life of renunciation.

Vaivasvata Manu. By the time the work was written, the deification of Chaitanya was firmly established in Orissa. In the Dvapara Yuga, Devaki bore Krishna in her womb, but could not bring him up. Sachi, the mother of Chaitanya, dreamt that Jagannath came into her womb in the form of Krishna (canto 1).

Isvara Dasa's *Chaitanya Bhagavata* has a distinct value. Behind a mass of facts, loosely arranged and at times incredible, we glean valuable information regarding the history of Vaishnavism and allied sects in Orissa. Isvara introduced a large number of persons in his work without caring for historical sequence. Nanak, Kabir, Buddhist Virasimha, Virabhadra, Jangali, Nandini, Jagai, and Madhai are all introduced indiscriminately.

Isvara Dasa's *Chaitanya Bhagavata* is an important contribution to Oriya Vaishanava literature for the following reasons. Firstly, Isvara writes that Chaitanya is the embodiment of Jagannath. The Puri deity has been identified with the ninth incarnation of the Lord (Bhagavan), who says that in that incarnation, He will embody compassion and talk of enlightenment. He will also be known as Bodhavatara. Secondly, Isvara gives a detailed description of Chaitanya's association with five comrades (Pancha Sakha). Thirdly, Isvara is the only writer who rises above sectarian feelings. In his *Chaitanya Bhagavata*, the Gaudiya Vaishnavas and five comrades mix freely and participate in the kirtana processions led by the master.[xxxiii] To this extent, Isvara Dasa alone states historical fact. Lastly, by the time the *Chaitanya Bhagavata* was written, Nityananda had been identified with Balarama. In Canto 2, Vishnu (Ksirthna) says to Narada that he would

[xxxiii] One kirtana party was attended by Uddata (Uddharana Dutta), Aditya (Advaita), Vakresvar, Gauridas, Sundarananda and the five comrades. In another kirtana party, shortly before Chaitanya's passing away, Srivas, Sarvabhauma, Gauridas, Gadadhar and the five comrades were present.

be born at Nadia for the salvation of mankind. Balabhadra would be born as Nityananda. In Canto 47, it is again stated that Nityananda is the embodiment of Sankarshana.

In Canto 46, Rama Ray meets Chaitanya at Navadvipa and has a religious discussion with him. Because he gave *amanda* (joy) to Chaitanya, the master named him Ramananda. In the same canto, Isvara Dasa describes Chaitanya's journey in Orissa. After bathing in the Vaitarani River, Chaitanya visited the temple of Adivaraha. After spending a night on the outskirts of Cuttack, he continued his journey. He bathed in the river Kusabhadra, which is stated to be as sacred as the Ganga. Therefore, he proceeded to Bhubaneswar and visited the Siva temple. From Bhubaneswar, he proceeded to Konarka. On his way, he worshipped twelve Siva lingas near the mouth of the river Parchi.

In canto 47, Isvara Dasa describes Chaitanya's first visit to the Jagannath temple, accompanied by Advaita, Vasudeva, Sarvabhauma and Ramananda.

In canto 49, King Pratapa Rudra came with a large retinue to Puri. He visited the Jagannath temple. He heard an oracle 'Listen, O king. Fall at the feet of Chaitanya and take the great mantra from him. The king accordingly met the Master. Chaitanya, the Lord Himself, *(Chaitanaya ape Bhagavana)* embraced the king and imparted the mantra. But suddenly, an elephant started to run amuck. Balarama Dasa chanted the names of Hari into the ears of the mad elephant. It became pacified and bowed at the feet of Chaitanya, who addressed Balarama as Matta Balarama. The king presented the elephant to Chaitanya, who was at first unwilling to take the elephant as he was an ascetic.

(6) Jagannatha Charitamrit by Divakara Dasa

Divakara wrote the biography of Jagannatha Dasa—one of the five comrades. It is the first biographical work in Oriya literature. He belonged to the 'Ati Badi' sect founded by

Jagannath Dasa and was the fifth in preceptorial descent from him. It is generally held that he lived in the middle of the seventeenth century.

Divakara writes that Jagannatha Dasa first met the Master at the age of eighteen. He was, at that time, reciting from the Bhagavata under the banyan tree within the Jagannath temple premises. Chaitanya used to come to the temple for the sight of Jagannath every day. He listened to the exposition of the (Bhagavata) Purana and stayed there with overflowing love. For eight years, Jagannatha constantly served Chaitanya.

The first seven cantos of the Jagannatha Charitamrita refer to Chaitanya's life in Orissa. He asks Balaram Dasa to initiate Jagannatha Dasa (canto 2). Accompanied by Jagannath Dasa, Chaitanya goes to the house of Sarvabhauma and learns from him the principles (tattva) of Jagannath worship (canto 4). Chaitanya explains the implications of the Hare Rama Krishna mantra to Nityananda in the presence of Jagannath Dasa and other Vaishnavas. He explains *Prema Panchatmaka* (five modes of love) to the Vaishnavas (canto 6). Pratapa Rudra pays homage to Chaitanya and arranges his accommodation in the Vakula Math (canto 7). Chaitanya's disappearance is also described in this canto.

Like the Chaitanya Charitamrita of Krishnadas Kaviraj, the Jagannatha Charitamrita was written for the glorification of a sect. While Krishnadas utilized the source materials of Chaitanya's life, Divakara's references to Chaitanaya are based on stories, legends and his own imagination.[xxxiv] Divakara knew Sanskrit well and quoted a large number of shlokas in the work. However, he did not consult the Sanskrit

---

[xxxiv] Chaitanya's grandfather Vishnu Panda named him Chaitanya after his birth. Divakara describes Jiba Gosvami as one of the followers of Chaitanya. It is stated that after taking sannyasa, Chaitanya visited many places, including Vrindavana, but found *prema bhakti* (devotion based on love) nowhere. So, he came to Purushottama Kshetra and settled there (canto 2).

biographies of Chaitanya written by Murari Gupta and Kavikaranapura.

Divakara writes that one day, Chaitanya asked Jagannath about his past birth. With humility, Jagannatha replied: 'Suffer me to recount the facts, O Master, which are known to you. Once, while I was meditating on Radha and Krishna, I realized that Radha and Krishna were gazing coyly at each other's faces. From the laugh of Krishna, you were born. Radha smiled prettily and from that laugh, I was born. You have appeared in the Kaliyuga for the salvation of the sinners. Chaitanya exclaimed. You are then a partial manifestation of Sri Radha—the supreme object of Krishna's love! Only the adepts are able to comprehend the mellowness of Radha's love. In sooth, you are a great person. Then taking off his red-ochred wrapper, he tied it round the head of Jagannatha and said, 'You have spoken great words. So you shall be known as very great (*ati badi*).'

The matter did not end there. Divakara writes that the Gaudiya Vaishnavas became jealous of Chaitanya's intimacy with Jagannatha Dasa. They told Chaitanya, 'Master, let us not stay only in one kingdom. We should visit other holy places such as Gaya and bathe in the mouth of the Ganga. But Chaitanya turned down their suggestion and refused to leave Jagannath Kshetra. At this flat refusal, the Gaudiya Vauishnavas decided to abandon Master. They blamed Chaitanya for his close contact with the Oriya Vaishnavas. Out the spite, they decided to go away to Vrindavana. On their way, they halted at Jaipur. Chaitanya sent a messenger to persuade them to come back to Puri. But they refused and made their way to Vrindavana. They used to come to Puri during the chariot festivals. But the Master's partiality for Jagannatha Dasa made them hasten their departure.

Divakara Dasa's statement is highly embellished, motivated by sectarian differences. Divakara did not cite the source on which he based his accusation against the Gaudiya Vaishnavas. There is no doubt that Chaitanya honoured the translator of the Bhagavata with the title of *Ati Bada* for his erudition and it appears that some Gaudiya Vaishnavas became jealous. However reliable evidence is necessary to corroborate the fact that the Gaudiya Vaishnavas left Puri for Vrindavana and defied the request of Chaitanya to come back to Puri. Few Gaudiya Vaishnavas had settled at Vrindavana during the lifetime of Chaitanya. It is curious that the Jagannatha Charitamrita shows the influence of the Chaitanya faith, which it tries to discredit.[xxxv]

Divakara Dasa refers to a table of preceptorial descent in canto 7 of his work. Chaitanya is stated to be the teacher of Gauridus Pandit, who was believed to be an embodiment of Chaitanya–Nityananda. Haridayananda was the disciple of Gauridas[xxxvi] and the spiritual guide of Balarama Dasa.

[xxxv] Divakara Dasa describes Jagannatha Dasa as an embodiment of Radha. It is stated that Jagannatha used to put on female dresses to imitate the feeling of Radha. But Jagannatha does not refer to Radha in his translation of the *Bhagavata*. According to the Chaitanya faith, Gadadhar Pandit is the embodiment of Radha who used to dress as Radha. This fact has been stated by Isvara Dasa in his *Chaitanya Bhagavata*, canto 62. Gadadhar spent his last year at Puri.
Divakara writes that Jagannatha once physically became a woman by his occult power. There is a similar story about Nandini and Jangali (male disciples of Sita, the wife of Advaita). They dressed and lived like women to imbue the feeling of the gopis. Isvara Dasa refers to them in his Chaitanya Bhagavata, canto 64. Nandi settled at Puri to worship Gopinath and died there.

[xxxvi] The table of preceptorial descent is also mentioned in the *Nityaguptamani* (Canto 19), a Sanskrit work which is ascribed to Divakara Dasa. Hridayananda was a nephew of Gadadhar Pandit. He lived for some time at Puri. Then he went to Kalna near Santipur in Bengal and became the pupil of Gauridas Pandit. Hridayananda was also the preceptor of Syamananda.

Though a non-Brahman, Balaram was made the preceptor of Jagannath Dasa, one of the greatest Brahmans of Orissa.

(7) Yasovanta Dasanka Chaurasi Ajna[xxxvii] by Sudarsana Dasa

This unpublished manuscript was probably written towards the end of the seventeenth century. There is a reference to Salabeg, who became a disciple of Yasovanta. Salabeg, a Muslim Vaishnava poet, lived in the middle of the seventeenth century in Puri. Thus, Yasovanta of the sixteenth century cannot be this preceptor. *The Chaurasi Ajna* contains a number of miracles to show the occult power of Yasovanta. It also refers to Chaitanya's association with Yasovanta and four other comrades.

(8) Eighteenth-Century Works

Towards the end of the eighteenth century, Sadananda Kavisnrya Brahma delineated the Chaitanya faith in his writings. In the Prema Tarangim, he describes the glory of the Gaura–Avatara. He writes that Krishna incarnated himself to be Radha and Krishna in one body.

In the Nistha Nilamani (canto 3), he makes it clear that devotion to Gauranga is fruitless without the grace of Gadadhar Pandit, from whom he traces his preceptorial descent. In the Visvambhara Vihara, the early life of Chaitanya has been described.

[xxxvii] Eighty-four is a conventional number. At Balarama Dasa's command, an idiot expounded eighty-four mantras ('Vedanta Sara', *Gupta Gita I*).

In the eighteenth century, Raju Govinda Bhanja of Keonjhar composed the *Charans Sudhania*. He reveres Chaitanya as an incarnation of Krishna.

Bhagavan Dasa wrote the Gauranga Bhagavata describing the last years of Chaitanya's life when he was lovesick. It is a free translation of the *Chaitanya Charitamrita*. The author is likely to be Bhagavana Dasa, who lived at Puri in the middle of the eighteenth century and became the Mahanta of Gangamata Math. He used the obsolete word Chadeiagiri instead of Chatak hill. His Guru was Govindadeva, the author of *the Gaura–Krishnodaya Kavya* in Sanskrit, which was written in 1680 Saka (1758 CE). This Kavya is based on the Chaitanya Charitamrita. Furthermore, B.B. Majumdar refers to *Sri Chaitanya–Sarvabhauma Samvada* and places it in the eighteenth century. The writer tries to make a synthesis between the principle of void and the Chaitanya faith. Chaitanya explains Sunya Brahma to Sarvabhauma.

(9) Nineteenth Century Works

In the nineteenth century, the following manuscripts were written by devotees. Historically, these works are not important.

1. Sri Chaitanya Gita: Bhramaravara Das
2. Chaitanyavali: Govinda Bhatta
3. Manasiksha: Bhakta Charan Das
4. Chaitanya Panchaka: Bisvanath Deo, Raja of Athgarh

* * *

Natabar Samantaray (1918–2000)

'Modern Odia Literature'

(Translated 'Adhunika Odia Sahitya' from the Odia by Sandeep Sahu)

Modern Odia literature did not emerge upon the literary scene suddenly. One can assess the distinction between ancient and modern Odia literature on the basis of the uniqueness of expression, tools of depiction and, in short, terms of form and soul.

The origins of the two were entirely different. Furthermore, medieval and ancient Odia literature was merely a provincial version of its rich Sanskrit predecessor. Its movement, its distinguishing features and its life-flow were sustained by the aesthetics of Sanskrit literature. But modern Odia literature was beholden to Western literature and both in form and essence, was heavily influenced by its notions. The spread of Western education and literature in this country brought about unprecedented changes in the thinking and perception of its people. Wedded to this new thinking, the educated middle class was able to produce a new kind of literature by following the ideals of Western literature. This was what was called modern Indian literature. Modern Odia literature was a regional variant of this new-age literature. When one analyses the evolutionary history of this new brand of literature, a new life history spread over many years is clearly discernible. The evolution of this new literature is built on the foundations of this life history. It is hard to believe that the evolution of this literature would have been possible without this history.

Therefore, the birth of modern literature was not a sudden occurrence. Remnants of the history were visible in both the withering away of the old lifestyle and the emergence of a new life flow. The foundations of that history were visible in the spread of modern education, the publication of modern textbooks in tune with such education and the emergence of an educated middle class. This new lifestyle did not get an opportunity to grow organically in Odisha till 1870 due to the political subservience of the state, its misfortune of being clubbed with Bengal, and above all, the illiberal attitude of the Bengal government towards Odisha. There was a change in the generic apathy of the Bengal government only during the movement against the effort to kill the Odia language. The recognition given to the Odia language was the clearest possible indication of it. The flow of life, which had been reduced to a small stream for nearly half a century between 1822–72, assumed the dimensions of a wide, free-flowing river after this governmental recognition. The *Utkala Darpana* monthly magazine launched in 1873 was merely an artistic expression of this flow of life. Hence, the emergence of this new genre of literature was neither accidental nor surprising.

What we call modern literature today is nothing but a happy culmination of the clash between the educational and cultural systems of the East and the West. This literature is an artistic expression of the harmony achieved between Eastern and Western thinking. A new and unique thinking permeated multiple facets of life through the new education system of the nineteenth century. Over time, harmony between the twin strands of thinking manifested itself in a new brand of literature and lent it a new look.

But for nearly forty years (1822–60), modern education did not receive popular support in Odisha. Efforts by the government too were only notional during this period. After 1861, people were attracted to this new system of education and modern Odia literature was born with the publication of *Utkala Darpana* in 1873. The history of half a century (1822–72) is essentially the history of the first phase of the harmonization of thinking. Modern Odia literature had its origins in the favourable atmosphere that this harmonization of thinking created through textbooks. The period from 1871–95 may be called the second phase of the synchronization of thinking or the first phase in the evolution of modern literature.

The world view, the creative ideas and the aesthetics of medieval Odia verse literature were influenced by Sanskrit. But the spread of modern education, which followed with the advent of British rule in the country, created in the public mind a craving for new life philosophy and a thirst for new aesthetics. Though the people continued to enjoy the aesthetics of the old literature, they did not follow the norms of that literature while creating new literature. Modern Bengali literature influenced by the notions of Western literature was the first and main source of inspiration for modern Odia writers. The literature produced by the modern Odia writers—wedded to a new taste, illuminated with the light of modern education and steeped in the new industrial culture—following in the footsteps of modern Western and Western-influenced Bengali literature, was completely different from medieval Odia literature in both its form and its soul. The period from 1871 to 1895 marked the first phase in the evolution of this new-age literature. Since *Kabibara*[xxxviii], Radhanath Ray was the pre-eminent poet during this period, new-age Odia literature has been named after him. There are two clear strands visible in the literature written during this period; one was creative and the other critical. The poetry, plays and novels written by Radhanath, Madhusudan, Ramshankar and Umesh Chandra Sarkar et al. belong to the first category.

[xxxviii] A title conferred on an eminent person that means 'poet of poets'.

The new creation was inevitably accompanied by two different reactions moving in two different directions. While creating new literature, there was a strong reaction against the old literature in the mind of the creator. Therefore, the new-age writer built his/her creative edifice on the foundations of a critique of old literature. The ruthless criticism of medieval literature in general and the writings of Upendra Bhanja, in particular, was nothing but a reflection of this reaction in the minds of the educated middle class with its modern tastes and sensibilities. On the other hand, the public, with its old tastes and fondness for old-school literature, was unable to accept and appreciate the form and novelty of new literature. A strong reaction against new age literature was an inevitable consequence and the criticism of the 'Radhanath' literature was just an expression of this reaction. The two contrasting reactions that began against the literature of Upendra in 1871 and against that of Radhanath in 1880 acquired greater vehemence after the publication of *Utkala Prava* in April 1891. The publication of two magazines, *Indradhanu* and *Bijuli* (1893–94), was a rather ugly outcome of this reactionary fire. The fight between *Indradhanu* and *Bijuli* was not merely a matter involving two magazines, but an indicator of the clash between modern and ancient sensibilities. There were three undesirable and unavoidable consequences of this fight:

1. The modern age was the only age of literary growth; going back to the old times while being sustained by the elements of this age—the water, the air, the breathing—was nothing but an act of monumental foolishness. Because the new age was not conducive to the resurrection of the old age, the literature produced by those who sang paeans to Upendra Bhanja bore no relation to old literature in terms of its craft and creative impulses.

2. Radhanath was the foremost architect of modern literature and his literature was the true harbinger of modern literature. The first phase of modern literature stretching from 1871 to 1895 was acknowledged by all sides as a separate genre of literature only during this controversy. This literary acknowledgement placed all modern literature, including Radhanath literature, on a sound foundation and welcomed a new literary trend.
3. Notwithstanding the richness of Radhanath literature, the love of the alien, the incomplete characterization of men and women and above all, the anti-nationalist trait in it led to a fierce reaction among critics of that period. They started assessing his literature not in terms of its literary and creative merit, but on the yardstick of nationalism. This strong criticism built against this genre of literature paved the way for Odia literature to move on to an altogether different track. The writings of Fakir Mohan, Nandakishore, Gangadhar, Gopal Ballav et al. were not just examples of a new literary trend but were also a silent protest against the literature of Radhanath. From here began the third phase in the assimilation of thoughts and the second phase of modern Odia literature. Unless we acknowledge the three major consequences of the *Indradhanu–Bijuli* tug of war—the desirability of a new form of literature in the modern age; the recognition of modern literature, including the literature of Radhanath, as a new genre of literature; and, last but not the least, the advent of a new current of literature—we cannot really appreciate modern Odia literature in its entirety.

* * *

Golok Behari Dhall (1921–74)

'Odisha, Odia Language and Language Movement'

(Translated 'Odisha, Odia Bhasa O Bhasa Andolan' from the Odia by Manu Dash)

Very few people thought Gandhiji would succeed when he started his agitation against the emperor of British dominion. When man fights for his very birthright, none can deprive him of that—with this faith and conviction, Gandhiji fought and won.

Freedom is the birthright of a man, and so also is his language. The way the non-cooperation movement continued till independence was achieved, the fight for freedom of one's language will be continued until it is achieved.

Until people are given the right to communicate in their own language, a movement will persist. Those who have knowledge of the history of freedom movements would agree that the movement was not smooth sailing all through. Sometimes, it was passing through like a whirlwind and at other times, it was sluggish. There were times when revolutionaries found themselves in low spirits while those opposing it rejoiced. Today, too, there is a storm that is moving forward from the Hindi-speaking hinterland of Delhi, where the consciousness of sleepy people like us is also awakening. We go into deep slumber again when there is a lull in those areas, and we keep rising as and when the occasion arises.

The interesting fact is that the amount of energy the progressive states spend to uphold those different measures to sustain their languages is equalled by our state, albeit for the contrary purpose of checkmating opposing views on language. Some people emphatically say that they would unseat the Odia language as long as they are alive, and some proclaim that they would not allow Odia to be used in offices of administration. It is our misfortune that they are all intellectuals who speak Odia as their mother tongue. Time is running out complaining about the lack of typewriters, shorthand facility, and lack of this and that. But people who are aware of the situation would say that the problem would not be sorted out even after obtaining the typewriter or shorthand facility. Rather, we need the preliminary planning for years together and a huge amount of financial support in that respect. Details of these plans are being published in newspapers and submitted before the government but yield no results. There is no board of language and linguistics instituted at the state level, and local governments therefore cannot determine the future of their own language. It's like the beating of drums that are not accompanied by a ritual *bedi*,[xxxix] for marriage to take place without a brahman in sight. Of course, no marriage shall stop for the want of a brahman or bedi nowadays. One can marry through registration. But language could not be managed without proper infrastructure. It was for that reason that, after making a law for the use of the Bangla language, it was stalled abruptly.

There have been scattered student protests in classrooms around Odisha. In some cases, they have boycotted examinations, perhaps in an effort to convey their

---

[xxxix] Bedi is a citadel where the marriage rituals are performed in Odisha.

> vulnerability. The movement for independent language has a clear objective. Your language must be used in your own state, and every member of that state must learn said language. Students have been trying to defend this since equal opportunities should be given to both categories of people: those who speak the mother tongue and those who don't. However, this could have a grave impact on the state of affairs and would undermine the state language policy negatively.

If the people who do not know the state language occupy influential positions, it may create a problem in the language policy. Besides, if we get overwhelmed broadly for the sake of great Indianness, they may discard the mandatory provision of learning our language before getting the job. Laws are made in the secretariat. If there is an increase in the number of people who subscribe to the larger idea of Indianness, there is a possibility of the said provision being rendered defunct. Probably for this reason, the love for one's own language, exhibited elsewhere, has not sprouted here.

But it makes us wonder to see what provisions other people create for themselves in their own states. Sri Ambika Prasad Singh, finance minister of Bihar, unsuccessfully tabled a state audit report on 9 December 1965. But the report was in English instead of Hindi language, and when tabled, the speaker of the house, Laxminarayan Sudhansu, returned it asking for it to be submitted in Hindi. That is the state the neighbours are in.

It would not be out of place here to speak about the well-known ICS officer, K.P.S. Menon. While serving in Madras, as per the office rule, he had to learn two South Indian languages, Tamil and Malayalam. After appearing in the exam, he passed the Tamil language test. Since his mother tongue was Malayalam and he had sufficient knowledge about the language, he did not sit for the test. As a result, the accountant general held back the payment of his salary.

Menon complained before his higher authority that considering Malalayam was his mother tongue, he knew the language much better than his examiner. So, he should not be forced to take the test. Reacting to this situation, his higher authority narrated a story which is irrelevant to mention here, but this is indicative of the manner in which senior officers functioned. This situation has not yet changed much. He said: 'The accountant general is debarred by virtue of his office from exercising his common sense.' It means the accountant general had no scope to exercise his common sense because of his senior position in the official hierarchy. At least, we have to take note of the fact that the ICS officers were compelled at that time to take the test for their mother tongue even though they were well-versed in it.

In today's context, when the policy of one's language in one's own state has taken a definite shape, there is no necessity to employ people who do not speak the mother tongue or have no knowledge of the state language. But if he does acquire adequate knowledge about the language of the region of his employment, he shall be more interested in learning about the people, language and culture of the said region and develop an affinity towards the said language. If he fails the exam, no one can deprive him of the benefit of acquiring knowledge of another language other than the mother tongue. On the other hand, this would help in promoting the policy of all Indian languages to a great extent. Besides the language, a test on the cultural awareness of the said people is also not undesirable. Unless you know the culture of the said people, it would be difficult to understand the heart of the people you want to serve.

There is another angle to this argument. Is it not disadvantageous to implement such conditions here when there are no such language obstacles in other provinces? But are we equal in every aspect with the other states of India? We have to take note of that aspect. Moreover, our position in the field of education and employment is much lower in comparison to other states. With the fourth five-year plan at our threshold, we have only one university (of course, the agriculture university is a technical university) for such a large state. Eight years ago, I observed that the number of students passing out in matriculation exams is nearer to the number of MA and MSc students passing out from Agra University. It is quite difficult for master's students to teach at primary schools in Odisha, and it cannot be denied that our students would not be able to match the competition, particularly from states with multiple universities.

* * *

Bidhubhushan Das (1922–99)

'Literature and Wisdom'

(Translated 'Sahitya O Prajna' from the Odia by Purabi Das)

What is the true nature of literature and what is its value? The qualities of literature that are being discussed will show that literature is unlike any other branch of knowledge nor is it representative of any. However, there exists a deep relationship between literature and other kinds of knowledge. Due to this, the writer is justifiably, the intellectual central point of his age. We arrive at this truth by a review of the top writers of any age. Since literature considers the whole of life as its subject matter, it would not be right to align it with any one subject.

Literature should be considered the subject of deep study. In ancient times, when literature was not differentiated from religion, it was more akin to philosophy. Even in this secular age, literature has elements of philosophy in it. Aristotle judged literature to be the same as philosophy while discussing the benefits of poetry, whereas the literary critics of our country have described it as righteous knowledge leading to emancipation (*Dharmartha Kama Mokhyesu*). However, our previous discussion will establish that the nature of literature is established by the path it chooses.

If we study these qualities of literature for debate, then what first attracts us to literature is the pleasure it arouses. This pleasure occurs due to a number of reasons and can be judged mainly on two points, form and content. The pleasure derived from form or expression is inseparable from the content. If we accept the distinction of expression and content for the purpose of discussion, by inference, literature establishes its power over the naked truth or the fruitless, corrupt, modern life of today, and by its mastery and control, converts the ugly and the commonplace into the beautiful and the rare.

What is included in literary form, is *style*. The writer's skill, imagination and dexterity are evident in his style. That is why Aristotle gave metaphor the highest rank and considered it to be the best reflection of the writer's talent. The works of Shakespeare and Kalidas provide ample evidence of such talent and the pleasure that is derived from the metaphors reveals the poet's imagination. The charm of this can be described as '*ksane ksane yan navataam upaiti tad eva rupam ramaniyataayaah* [Whatever renews itself from moment to moment happens to be the form beauty]' and if this novelty creates wonder in the case of Shakespeare, in Kalidas, it can be termed as glorious.

Content, too, gives rise to pleasure. This pleasure may come from 'feeling into' and 'feeling with' the literature or due to catharsis. Antigone, Lear, Dimitri Karamazov, Prince Audi, Sukru Jani, Baraja Padhana—all these characters are examples of this. If literature is accepted as mimesis, it is due to the imitation of the characters and their actions. Such imitation can be high, low or commonplace, and the value of the literature is altered accordingly. If we consider the actions of the characters in literature, we generally see the reflection of all of_human life, and that is why it has been said that the ultimate effect of literature is to obtain truth and beauty or the knowledge to understand it.

If we study the nature of this knowledge, it can be divided into two categories, namely, comic and tragic. Both these universal experiences are part of the daily human existence. This universal knowledge is derived from the 'literature of power' described by Thomas De Quincey.[1] The literary man's life is endowed with feeling and experience and ultimately, after sifting through these, he establishes his personal world view or divine vision. This divine vision begins from the ordinary, sensory and worldly experience, and ends in that extrasensory and unearthly realm that is only attainable through the highest literature and philosophy. For the critical review of this life, the writer takes the help of all other disciplines and thus comes into contact with political science, economics, sociology, science, etc. André Gide has called this 'the fruit of life'.[2] But ultimately after weighing all knowledge, the writer determines its significance, and transcends its limits to stand at the doors of tragedy or comedy.

It has normally been agreed that tragedy is the highest form of literature because the chaos of creation and the conflict between evil and good reveal the depths of human experience as reflected in tragedy. That is why W.B. Yeats said,[3]

> The tree of life and the knowledge of right and wrong that is associated with it, is man's natural experience. But if our vision clings merely to the tree, then we remain entangled in its limbs and branches, and fail to obtain the tragic experience. Tragic art overcomes every limit, resistance and experience, and throws us into the world of dreams and the depth of consciousness. But when the writer ascends the tree of life with contemplation and compassion, what he sees at its top cannot be defined merely as the divine vision of tragedy.

The meaning of Yeats' 'Starlit Dome' can be understood if one studies the best of world literature. Human life starts from the gross, physical depth and spreads to the exquisite, extrasensory level. To portray this life is the writer's dharma. If he limits life within the bonds of comedy or tragedy, hedonism or pessimism, he will not be able to depict the full reality and truth of life. John Keats has said that the only real poet is perhaps not a poet in the true sense. This is because he has no identity of his own and is dedicated day and night to breathing life into another form.[xl]

That is why Keats considered Shakespeare as his ideal. The writer who could give equal importance in his imagination to Iago, Iachimo and Imogen, had great generosity and humanity. While defining the poet, Keats says, 'He is nothing, he has no one, he is all and yet none, he has no character. He experiences both light and darkness. He lives in an abundance of fulfilment.' Though the writer accepts a comic or tragic mode to depict life, generally, the depth and gravity of tragedy is more than that of comedy. From this point of view, great tragedies, the Bhagabata, the Mahabharata or even *Paradise Lost*, are of the same religion. However, whatever the writer's own views, his writing gains value according to the depth and range of his life experience.

According to Keats, the peak of any art is defined by its depth and intensity. Due to these qualities, art overcomes all disparities and displays the greatest truth and beauty. Keats, however, had not experienced this truth in its entirety. That is why he called himself only a seeker and an investigator.[xli] He also said, 'We cannot see the equilibrium of good and evil. It is as if we are living in a fog.'[xlii] Other writers have overcome this fog and found light. But Keats embraced a primary ideal of literature, and that is gusto or passion. He tried to experience every aspect of life and find its value. If

---

[xl] John Keats' account of the poetical character comes in a letter to his friend Woodhouse on 27 October 1818.

[xli] An excerpt from Keats' letter on 21 December 1817 to his brothers on negative capability.

[xlii] An excerpt from John Keats' letter to his friend John Hamilton Reynolds on 3 May 1818.

we compare Keats and John Milton, two paths of literature are perceptible. Keats has collected his experience from this worldly life and finally arrived at a humanitarian life view. He made human life the centre of his writing and found the universal truth in the depth of the soul. Milton, on the other hand, has accepted this material world as his subject matter. His experience is not this 'beautiful earth'. His aim is to study the relationship of man with God and fate. His knowledge is philosophical.

'Of Providence, Foreknowledge, Will and Fate, Fixed fate, free will, foreknowledge and absolute.'[xliii]

* * *

[xliii] An excerpt from John Milton's 'Paradise Lost', Book 2, 1667.

Chittaranjan Das (1923–2011)

'Revolution'

(Translated 'Biplab' from the Odia by Krishna C. Goudo)

Everyone is saying that we need a revolution in our country now. In other words, people in their respective fields are squarely unhappy with the conditions they are in. They want change in the status quo, which they call revolution. Everyone from the ministers to the laymen, agree that we badly need a revolution in our country. Some say this out of annoyance, others from anxiety. The other day, a high government official—an engineer by profession—someone totally oblivious of the world beyond his office subordinates and tour itinerary, was seen suddenly breaking the quietude by pouring out from the uncertain depths of his heart before a police officer, that this country needs a revolution sooner rather than later. He was aghast at Indian society's capacity for toleration. Probably, he was indirectly surprised at his own capacity for tolerance.

Everyone wants a revolution. And reasonably or unreasonably, everyone wants to initiate his or her own revolution. Everyone wants to shake the foundations of our old life anchors.[xliv] Everything is an omen or a prediction, even cattle eating away thatched roofs is seen as a prophecy of an upcoming revolution. We love being labelled as revolutionaries, unlike traditional labels of 'a good son' or 'a good citizen'.

[xliv] Conventional support-systems of life.

We used to anoint our children with names that stood for attributes like discipline, peacefulness, softness and beauty. Now the preferred attributes for naming children are revolutionary and valorous. Our children naturally feel a sense of elation and pride, and we see nothing but revolution all around us. Some are creating revolution even in the mundane day-to-day life. There is a revolution in films created by actors, textile factories in Gwalior or Gorakhpur are stirring a revolution in the textures of shirts, and publishers are adding to the revolution through their books.

The word 'revolution' earlier used to remind us of a few epoch-making events like the Russian Revolution, the French Revolution or the Industrial Revolution. Revolution was rare and no more than one revolution took place in an age. Today, revolutions are a dime a dozen; at every step and in every conversation, there is a duststorm of ideas, and the air is thick with the name of revolution. Whether we want it or not, a silent revolution is engulfing us inevitably. It is like a stove silently burning or a jet engine flying without sound—revolution is happening quietly but relentlessly. Old edifices are collapsing like dead wood. There is no time for merriment and no occasion to say 'my time is coming'. In our collective day-to-day life's firmament, there are artificial fireworks of revolutions hovering like satellites over our heads in ever-new orbits, changing and controlling our lives without so much as intimating us and without our knowledge.

Leaders of the reigning party talk of revolution, and so do the members of the opposition. The working class talks of revolution against the owners, and the factory owners talk of revolution as they protest against the government. The lowly government employees protest against measly allowances and the *babudom*[xlv] calls out against the government for pay hikes in parity with their English and American counterparts.

[xlv] Bureaucracy.

Students stop trains and protest against education officers while teachers boycott examinations. The teaching community too, to match the other over-enthusiastic revolutionaries, brings all its negotiating skills to the table where they can work less and be paid more. Earlier, the teachers would expel students from the examination hall if necessary. Now, the students are expelling teachers from the examination hall if they deem fit. The modern literary man does everything possible to demean and vilify the old and acknowledged master of literature to establish his own revolutionary credentials. Perhaps he wanted to be a revolutionary first and became a writer by default—driven to writing by some amorous goddess, he is inclined to recognize revolutionary tendencies more than literary craftsmanship, which he considers his bound duty.

Twenty years post-independence, there were multiple revolutions with multiple names. There were clarion calls for revolution both from official and non-official quarters with drumbeats of revolution being sounded from both platforms. Highly placed babudom running the country from Delhi and the ministers led by the wise counsel of these officers have spoken about government schemes to alleviate the condition of a section of the populace, through a so-called revolution. There was neither silence nor revolution in this, since there was nothing but a cacophonous noise from Delhi, down to the block level, sans any revolutionary element. That cacophony too, it seems, has diminished considerably. The newest buzzword for revolution is now family planning schemes. They are blaring more from podiums and spending more paper on publicity. And by doing so, they consider themselves as proud initiators of and participants in the revolution. Ironically, their actions have only circumscribed the scope and delayed the onset of any real revolution.

Language could be a cause for revolution in our country, and the god-men and high priests of our monasteries indulge in revolution while chanting the name of God. There are instances which stand testimony to this in the context of the events witnessed over the last few years. Revolution can also happen on the subject of caste; it means that a country which dreams of transforming into one people and one nation, and despite efforts made in that direction, we are eminently capable of setting one sub-caste against another sub-caste even as we raise the flag of revolution. These are not simply imaginary things and in the realm of possibility—the truth is, these things are happening under various names and under various pretexts in various places, in Odisha and outside. In every revolution, be it government-led or otherwise, whatever be the driving motto behind these, it is the political class that helped everywhere. Revolutions have happened in the name of religion and also in the name of the cow-mother, *gaumata*—all of them, invariably, are driven by the political class. Those in power, use all their persuasive skills to buy our support to their idea of revolution and those who are out of power, do everything to coax and cajole us to dethrone those in power, so that they can occupy the throne themselves. Once they achieve their goal, they call it a revolution. The leadership has changed in our country as well as the slogans. The raison d'être of our grievances and dissatisfactions have changed, true, but after achieving political freedom, the things that should have changed first and changes that could have been labelled as true revolution, have till now remained unchanged.

There are varieties of revolutions as there are varieties of revolutionaries. It is men who create revolutions, it is they who dream of it and give shape and content to them. The other day, a minister of the government of India, while speaking to a group of students, declared that slogans do not make revolution in society. He also resorted to a lie, saying that the driving factors behind revolutions are science and technology. But science and technology can be instruments of revolution only when human beings are taken care of. Besides, there are uncouth people who can, if they want, hoodwink unsuspecting people with the help of modern technology. It would not be necessary to explain this to observers of our country and society in the last twenty years. Repeating what has already been said, we can say that there are varieties of revolutions since there are varieties of revolutionaries. Slogans do not make revolution, nor does ideology—it is the vision of the revolutionary that makes for genuine revolutions. The wider the vision of the revolutionary, the wider the idea of revolution. When the revolutionary's vision is circumscribed, the revolution fails. During the struggle for political freedom and after independence, our leaders always had a holistic and appropriate vision regarding the developmental trajectory of this country. With independence achieved, we will slip into inertia; in other words, there is nothing more to be done as a nation and as a people—this was not what the leadership of the time thought. We have accepted independence as the necessary step towards our efforts at giving direction and structure to the development of our society. Providing opportunities for every citizen to develop his potential, a society based on merit will be put in place; and the general social, economic, and political condition that fetter the body, mind and spirit will go. Replacing one form of slavery under foreign rule with another kind of slavery masked as an indigenous rule will not do; all our efforts will be undertaken to instil a sense of human freedom, progressiveness and responsibility in every citizen; the education edifice in the country will be transformed, so will be our ways of thinking and doing. We strived for independence to transform our country and Gandhi called this a constructive programme. Even before the end of foreign rule, the soil was being prepared to conceive the garden of a new India. Led by such a constructive vision, Gandhi considered this essential in the struggle for political independence. This is because he used to think that economic, social and educational revolution, along with the political one, if achieved, will converge in the revolution to construct man as man. In Odisha, Pandit Gopabandhu Das was a proponent of this belief. He wrote substantially on political independence but not more substantially than what he passionately wrote and spoke on the subject of developing human personality in all its possible splendour in this free country of ours, which he believes, has become conducive for growth. Whether it is Gandhi or Gopabandhu, creating a handful of ideal citizens was not their principal concern. The meaning and value of the word 'citizen' is limited by its very political overtones. It is the primary duty of the nation and the state to create necessary conditions and provide incentives to every citizen to achieve fullness as human beings. Humanity is larger than citizenship. There were many wrongful attempts, as exemplified in our history, of coaxing people into herds of disciplined citizens and these attempts were called revolution. That the state is favourably disposed towards the citizens is a revolutionary idea. That the citizen would be under the control of the state is an outdated philosophy.

Our country is free, the English have left our shores and the brave who fought for independence have become rulers, but what has become of the imagined revolution? The promise they made before the leadership of the time for complete revolution, was left half-baked—why? From one point of view, the history of the last twenty years is the history of the obstruction of a necessary and spontaneous onset of revolution and the history of related and unnatural shenanigans. Many critics, after examining revolutions from a sociological angle, opine that people who aspire to achieve certain things through revolution, generally fail to achieve those things. Revolutionaries who set out with the flag of revolution, today, after the revolution, find it hard to provide effective leadership to the revolutions of tomorrow, probably due to a creeping indolence or inability. Flaunting his revolutionary credentials, he snatches power from the old rulers, but after the revolution, once he safely enthrones himself, conveniently forgets the name of revolution; now his only preoccupation is to ensconce himself in power. Caught up in this vicious cycle, yesterday's revolutionary becomes today's reactionary. One kind of autocracy is replaced by another kind and revolution grinds to a halt. He wants to stay where he is and muzzle the voice of his followers. Another group of revolutionaries set out to unseat him from power, but at a later stage, they too turn into reactionaries. History stands as testimony to this vicious musical chair in many countries. It happened in Russia—the propounder of a revolutionary idea, Karl Marx, succumbs to the reactionary tendencies leading to the dilution of his revolutionary fervour. Probably from this perspective, the American critic Arnold Toynbee calls America a country of failed revolutions. After attaining political freedom, such disasters and deplorable events have occurred in India too. Yesterday's revolutionary leadership, who made the most amount of noise, turned reactionary after assuming power and considered it their primary duty to shut out all just and rightful ways to revolutions. It has accepted political freedom as the be-all and end-all of human aspiration. This is not led by conscientious consideration but out of greed for power. We may hang our heads in shame or grit our teeth in anger at this, but this is exactly what is happening in our country; otherwise, the history of this country would have been written differently in the long interregnum of the last twenty years. Here, a different set of values would have been worshipped and our enthusiasm would have been channeled in a different direction. With zeal and perseverance, the whole country could have been turned into a land of great opportunities and aspirations to help human life bloom and turn the barren land into a fertile one. But instead ever new fences are created, ever new walls and half walls are erected insidiously, just to keep the people of this country divided. There are so many disjointed little revolutions and cataclysms raising their heads to surround us, sending ominous signals that genuine revolution is prevented here. There is seemingly much emphasis on human beings in the last twenty years probably because genuine citizens are prevented from achieving their potential. Things that should not happen are happening with definitive regularity in this country. There is an ascending cacophony outside, elaborate lectures are blared from podiums about revolution, but in truth, people of contrasting ideologies fight with each other only to perpetuate their hold on power. What is required to start a real revolution? Cleverness and deceit are now seen as the same as intelligence, hence the opportunities for a just revolution are deferred indefinitely.

During the national movement, the struggle largely remained political. Politics at that time meant expulsion of foreign rule; but after independence, if our country had welcomed all necessary revolutions, then politics would have remained secondary, and revolution would have been the primary focus. People elected to run the country would have helped, mainly, to advance the cause of revolution. They would not have thought of holding on to power. What a plethora of opportunities there were for revolutions in this country after independence! 5 lakh villages of the country waited for it; crores of illiterates awaited illumination of their lives with bated breath, the children of the country looked towards education, the working class waited expectantly. But after independence, people in power proved to be ineffective and ignored the challenges before them! They did everything but their duties. They sat in ministers' meetings, ran to public gatherings to be feted, went on lecturing sprees to be called enlightened and always displayed an eagerness to sit at the high table. They dabbed in literature, sat among saints and *sanyasins*,[xlvi] indulged in music and drama, formed academies, but did not do their duties. As representatives of people, they could have been instruments of revolution but instead, they became instrumental in deflecting the mind of the people away from it with crafty words. This ingenuity has expanded geometrically over time, in other words, bigwigs occupying high places in various fields also gradually veered to doing other things and leaving aside their primary duties. University professors and vice chancellors neglected education by deserting their campuses and set out to showcase their virtuosity in other fields. They had time and energy to go everywhere—from literary meets to sports arenas—but no time for teaching and scholastic endeavours. They censored each other in the self-conscious race for success, and for accolades, dug holes for each other. Above everything, they worked assiduously and eagerly to strengthen their respective positions. The engineer probably earned five times more than his due but did only a quarter of what is expected of him. The doctor wrote prescriptions and fattened his own coffers. The qualities and dispositions that would make him a skillful doctor, he left in the medical books of yore as old-fashioned and obsolete. From the highest officer in the education department to the humble village schoolteacher—all declared in one voice that the method of teaching and the system examination should change but showed no moral compunction in reaping pecuniary benefits from the roaring business related to education and examination, carried out in connivance and with the collusion of everybody concerned. Only the elimination of this unholy nexus could have brought about a change in the system of education and examination.

[xlvi] Ascetics.

Where is the time or inclination for these people to start a revolution?

The literary men in our country are no less accountable for deferring the onset of the revolution. In the last twenty years, their passion for literature has been far outweighed by their eagerness to bring politics and politicians into literary meets. Howsoever incompetent the men of politics may have been as appreciators of literary taste, our literary men felt that they had achieved salvation when the politician accepted an invitation to sit at the high table of successful literary conclaves in independent India. Now it is easily understandable why the aspirations of our literary men in this country have, to a considerable extent, been confined to barricaded nationalism like that of an embanked, quiet, standing pond. After independence, there could have been a revolutionary redefinition of nationalism and the literary men could have been vanguards of this change, but sadly that did not happen. Our litterateurs were weak and consequently, our nationalism failed to touch human life, anchored as it were to an era of rootless romanticism.

In ancient times, Odias were said to have established a kingdom called *Champa Rajya* in far East Asia, in present-day Vietnam. It can then be argued that the blood in the Vietnam War had some Odia blood too.

In our world, there are people who set out as revolutionaries but not all of them want revolution—most want power. They want to occupy the seat of political power after removing those who are already there and in this, they find a great sense of joy. In the new dispensation, there is as much darkness as was in the previous one. The same injustices and the same chaotic conditions prevail, but they shut their eyes to the prevailing reality and with arrogance, attempt to cement their hold on power. These machinations they then call revolution.

I am not at all suggesting that power is undesirable or even unnecessary. To make a real revolution possible, power is required, political power is required, harnessing of the power of science is required, and the power of the scepter too, is required. Understandably therefore, all those who exhort for revolution, want people to endow them with political power before starting a revolution. Trusting their words, people hand over power to them and all paraphernalia related to it and then inevitably they forget the idea of revolution because all they want now is to remain immersed in power. In this temporal fleeting world of ours instead of revolution, they give themselves up to political power permanently. Power is required for revolution, power is needed for the transformation of society, establishment of justice and for installing an administration fit for human beings; but that does not ensure the coming of a revolution automatically. Power cannot automatically ensure the establishment of truth and the welfare of the masses. For this, there must be a strong desire for revolution, a craving for truth and the welfare of the people. A craving for political power often makes the empowered oblivious to other such essential desires. He indulges in numerous untruths and injustices but finds no moral courage to acknowledge untruths and injustices for what they are. He cannot call a spade a spade. He cannot call a drum a drum. Whatever suits his position of power he considers them truthful and good. He seeks the light of opportunity. The extreme craving for power kills his desire for revolution, and revolution remains barred. The writ of monarchs in power runs everywhere. At this point in time, the ideals of nationalism come in handy as a potent unfailing weapon. There is great talk of national income, national culture and national literature. While celebrating our past and our heritage, the disaffection with the present is put on the backburner. Led by the conspiracy of making human dignity and humanity shabby and weak, they exhort people to make the nation look large. Like the ministers, the common citizens too sing paeans to the nation forgetting their hunger and in the process they only fuel the ruling elite's hunger for power.

By and large, this is the condition that prevails in our country. Our former revolutionaries have cocooned themselves in their respective shells of power. New entrants look more inclined towards power than revolution. Every other day, new political outfits are formed—party frogs change their masks often and roll every new political rosary beads. After tasting power, they keep hopping from one fish trap of political ideology to another. What they think about our countrymen is a moot point, but the people have come to realize that nothing good will come out of these leaders. Nobody visits these leaders except those who want their personal issues to be settled. Nobody meets these leaders to listen to political discourse. They use sycophancy to get their work done. Nobody invites professors or the minister of education to village schools. Administrators in the department of education are addressed as educationists. People addicted to power are too feeble to bring any meaningful change or a revolution. Who knows? They may perhaps fear both development and revolution. They remain passive and make others remain submissive.

Neither by belching revolutionary words nor by shouting slogans can one become a revolutionary. Only a free man can aspire to be a revolutionary. He must be free from all sorts of narrowness of locality and region, and must not box himself in his lineage and his cultural roots. He must not hide himself in holes like nation, caste, political affiliation or religious attachments. The true revolutionary is a humanist who can feel the throb of an entire humanity in himself, he is someone with joie de vivre, who is in love with life. Having accepted human psychology as his lodestar (the guiding light), he should have unwavering faith in life, though he will not accept anything blindly and emotionally. A humanist of this era has defined a revolutionary in this fashion.

Revolution does not refer to acts of dismantling and destruction of old edifices. There is more positive rather than negative implications in this. It does not mean only some exciting programmes in the heat of the moment. In both the personal and collective life, it refers to a holistic perspective, which has been called a way of life in English and *welt ansehaung* in German. A revolutionary is not satisfied with minor things; he wants to achieve more. He wants to recast life in a new way and only by doing so, does he feel a sense of completion. One may bring about revolution in the domain of justice, in social policy and politics as well as in the field of literature. There is no conflict between the personal good and public good in the life of the revolutionary. There was no such contradiction in the life of Gandhi, nor in that of Gopabandhu. They were great men, their way of life was great and their lives were typically moulded for great contribution to social upliftment. They provided strong leadership to make society more beautiful. In the same way, a revolutionary has the capacity to shape an entire era. They can wake up entire nations from deep slumber and shake the foundation of empires. When devotees visit a shrine, they convert that into a holy place. Likewise, these great men can inspire new dreams, new motivations and new confidence. They are ever ready to adapt themselves. Their words are easily understood by everybody, everybody trusts them and stands behind them. This would suggest that only a revolutionary can set a revolution in motion. Revolutions do not happen on their own, even when the need for revolution becomes sharp and intense in the collective consciousness. Public discontent does not explode into revolution automatically like boiled water turning into steam. So many dissatisfactions have clouded our collective life in this country in the last twenty years, but then, is there any trace of revolution? Is it happening anywhere? Like much ado about nothing, so many revolutions in the country have lapsed into mundane things like smashing street lamps and throwing stones at trains. Numerous mental disaffections regarding language, province, religion (and the sacred cow) have burst to the brim. The true revolution is still awaited, but there are no revolutionaries. There are merely people hungry for power and position. There are rebels, of course, who indulge in destructive behaviour and get vicarious pleasure out of it, true, but where are the genuine revolutionaries? Who is taking the leadership mantle in this country to give the clarion call to transform entire life, the whole of humanity and society at large?

The writer of the book mentioned earlier has further remarked:

'In this sick world of ours, the man who wants to lead a healthy life, the man who wants to live a full and vibrant life even in this infirm and debilitated world, the man who wants to remain vigilant even as people around him are half asleep—he is the true revolutionary, his attitude is the attitude of the revolutionary.'

While thinking about this statement, I am reminded of George Orwell's novel, *1984*. The rampant and wanton way with which the present civilization is hurtling this world ahead, by the time we reach the year 1984, the dance of fury and cruel enactment of control so fearfully envisioned in the novel is surely going to be a reality. Big Brother, the all-powerful authority, will have complete control over human life, and new technology will enable this to happen. The powerful, controlling mechanisms of Big Brother will come to know of anybody who wishes to think independently immediately and to prevent man from such transgression, the state's machinery will move swiftly towards him with great force. Using psychological tools like classic conditioning, man will be kept in total control, he will love and hate when asked to do so, and his mind, heart, and thinking process will be accordingly conditioned to make him remain sheep-like. Man will not seek truth and remain under the total control of the tyrant. The 'Department of Truth' will define what truth is and people will have to follow that enlarged idea of truth. There will be another powerful department to keep track of matters of the heart and it will keep an eye on love and affection, and its presence or absence among citizens. This dispensation will be a pure dispensation without exception. Total control will be the only rule in place. Man will surrender all powers to Big Brother and will lead a life of bliss and obedience like an automaton without the power to think and feel. There will be absolutely no possibility of him going out of the orbit. This all looks as ideal a condition from the yardstick of absolute control as it is dreadful from the point of view of natural human creative propensity. The writer of the novel cited above also tried to indicate a way out of this quagmire.

In the narrative of the said novel, a man tries to live and love like a human being. For this, he is subjected to terrible atrocities—to crucify his humanity, he is subjected to excruciating scientific experiments, and while he cries out loud due to extreme physical pain and loses consciousness often, his steely resolve refuses to let go of his humanity. When everyone shouts 'Long Live Big Brother' like programmed automatons, he is the only one who holds aloft the flag of human faith while shouting defiantly: 'Down with Big Brother'. He announces a revolution in front of the powerful and is shot dead by gun-toting appointees of the rulers. But his heroic act of defiance lives on as an exceptional example. Orwell exemplified the larger vision of his literary craft by citing this exemplary courage in the face of insurmountable odds. He would not have inspired the humanity in all of us if he ended the novel in a sinister fashion. Perhaps, the courage to envision exceptions happening in life springs from a love of humanity, and it probably is the moment when the revolutionary in man finds ascendancy. A combination of love of life and the desire to ascend to a higher plane is what Mahatma Gandhi called *Satyagraha*.[xlvii] One who equates opportunism with realism and refuses to stand up to the challenges of life cannot be a *satyagrahi*;[xlviii] nor can he be a revolutionary. Both the satyagrahi and the revolutionary have the moral courage to say 'no'. The wheeler dealers of power cannot say 'no'. Neither the opportunist nor the so-called realist has this power. These people lose steam before they can achieve maturity.

Gopabandhu was a revolutionary, but we have confined him to the soil of Odisha. He wanted to mould us in his fashion; we, on the other hand, cared only to cast him in an iron frame. We probably feel a sense of elation dragging him into our midst. Gopabandhu was a thinker, an astute organizer, an *Acharya*[xlix] and a founder, and now we have started worshipping him—as if conspiring to cast a living human being in stone!

* * *

[xlvii] The policy of non-violent resistance adopted by Mahatma Gandhi to oppose British rule.

[xlviii] Person following Satyagraha.

[xlix] A Hindu or Buddhist spiritual teacher or leader, a mentor.

Kishori Charan Das (1924–2004)

'Realism'

(Translated 'Bastabata' from the Odia by Krishna C. Goudo)

I have been saying and will keep saying that I am an adorer of realism. If asked, 'Sir, what is this object called realism?' I would be compelled to retort, 'Gentleman, your question, in the first place, is not to the point. The reason being, my reality is different from your reality.' But if insisted upon to explain the difference, I would get a bit annoyed, and be compelled to say (even though that would expose my audacity) that whatever the author has read out to you, if that is to your liking, then that is the reality. Even if Brahma, the creator of the Vedas mutters inaudibly in slumber, that assumes the form and sanctity of eternal truth. (So is the utterances of the writer, who, in his creative capacity, is like Brahma).

Sir, don't laugh it away. This is the familiar and accepted bragging of the top writers and litterateurs. How do I climb down from this lofty tradition? Take, for example, Virginia Woolf, who said that one would realize that reality is amorphous, and its status and stability cannot be relied upon.[1] One might come across reality in the scum and dust of the earth, in a piece of newspaper or in the sun-drenched flower. But the fact is that whatever it touches, it transforms into everlasting truth. Since, then it attaches itself to time, and becomes eternal.'

[1] It is a long quotation on truth taken from *A Room of One's Own.*

It is the obligation of the writer to seek out that and show it to others. And for this, he is uniquely placed and has the opportunity to do that. At least, that is what I think after reading *Lear* and *Emma*. After that, one has the feeling that the mask of the world has fallen off and its life has become more lively and vivid. On the whole, her comment indicates that the effulgence, the so-called exuberance of life, is actually a form of reality, which only an artist can bring forth. A distinguished writer, C.N.O. Faolerie, also could say with some certainty, that literature embodies reality.[li] He did not, of course, say more but added that, every writer tries to bring some sort of verisimilitude to his or her art; the more successful the writer is in this effort, the sharper will be the realism of his art. J.P.M. Stern has asserted that asking metaphysical questions like 'What is reality?' is beside the point. We only expect this: a writer will face up to all available facts within his purview in a given situation and portray that in his art for the reader. In other words, the allegiance of the writer to his art and the reality of things are strung together in the same thread. The greater the truthfulness of the writer, the greater will be the chance for realism to shine through his literary realm. You see how the definition of realism has gradually become so uncomplicated for us!

But in reality, I am unable to accept this definition of literary realism. Although a stakeholder myself, I have become judge and jury to pronounce judgment in my own favour. This is what I am sorry about. I am sure that every honest writer would have gone through the same pain once the garlands faded. How high can I go on the scale of reality? Here there are two aspects—one, though competent, how far can I go; and two, how far am I competent? Let us assume that I want

[li] In the original essay, the Odia expression 'Kahi Parile' is used which corresponds to 'could say'.

to narrate to you, in the minutest detail, whatever I have seen, whatever I have heard and whatever I have thought. Would you be able to absorb everything I have narrated? Summoning courage, if I direct the searchlight into the inner recesses of myself and through that, into the people of my ilk, would you be able to bear that kind of spectacle and bear those words? You will not be able to endure, you will shut your eyes, you will hurl abuses at me, you will call me sick and deviant—I am not blaming you. Which intelligent man would call himself uncouth in this beautiful world of God? The quarrel between truth and beauty is quite serious. Violence, cruelty or forbiddingly extreme sensuality can somehow be condoned. Citing the afterlife, it can be said that God works for the good of man. But I do not know why it is impossible to condone the loathsome beasts lurking inside the inner recesses of man. As soon as one discovers them, one feels like leaving them in the unfathomable depths they are in. Most stubborn is the romance with aesthetics. What do you say, Sir? We may brag about fearlessness in art, but we will lose the bet, you and I. We are bound by a *laxman rekha*,[lii] an outer boundary, because we live in the same society.

Eliot's little bird did not tell a lie to the dark cloud. It said, go, go, go away. The joy and cackle of children lies hidden in the green foliage of nature. The society of men does not tolerate reality—stark reality—don't you know that?

* * *

[lii] The Laxman Rekha is a figurative expression taken from the Indian epic Ramayana. It is a line drawn by Laxman to protect Sita from external danger. Hence, it refers to a boundary or a limit.

Chandrasekhar Rath (1929–2018)

'Darkness'

(Translated 'Andhara' from the Odia by Tyagraj Thakur)

Even if we get old, our unknown fear does not leave us. When we close our eyes in the darkness and cover ourselves up head to toe, fear is an inviolable habit of ours. We are not nocturnal and cannot walk in darkness. We fear darkness, hate it and invoke the luminaries from the solar constellation to destroy it. We all are the children of light, and conquering darkness and driving it away is our fraternal duty.

However, even if one clings to the light, considering it one's own, it certainly sets in the west, and darkness steps in. Both of them, from time immemorial, have been chasing each other but have not been able to touch or succeed each other. It is not true that we would wish and stop the darkness. The way light is true and indispensable as long as the spherical earth keeps revolving around its axis and the sun keeps shining, darkness is equally true and indispensable.

The birth of light is perhaps from a primordial, tranquil darkness. It is a revolt, a rising. Thus, to take it back to its impenetrable military, darkness has been chasing it. The fugitive light is laughing out loud like an untamable child and scattering. Eventually, this child will merge in the lap of that primordial mother. Innumerable dots of light in the endless sky will be extinguished. The tranquil darkness will again doze off and sleep till eternity.

Despite not knowing all of this, we fear darkness since childhood, because everything is possible inside that. The way, at the beginning of the creation there were particles, but not any matter, there was only the possibility of matter; the uncertainty of the night is just like that. That could be a human instead of a pillar, could be a wagon instead of a horse. The witches, spirits, ghosts of dead people, demigods, demons, vampires etc. are freed at that time. While imagining them, they come and stand before us. But we do not want such straightforward talks. Hence, maybe we sleep without thinking about it. Fear is our very primaeval and fundamental nature.

It is true that we fear darkness, but it is also true that we fear truth as well. We keep it covered with many kinds of veils and masks. In this great stage, the lamp of the sun keeps burning. We act splendidly in its light. Many attires, decorations and arrangements, different gestures and styles of acting officers, bureaucrats, ministers and guards. Some get tired of acting in multiple roles. Crores of actors go on performing on this stage in different acts of music, literature, meetings, art and science. The lamp of the sun also gets tired, its unblinking eye gets shut. Hereafter comes darkness, a cover that, as if it conceals all, hides all from one another. This is theatre. Here, all the actors unmask themselves leaving their shyness. Someone wipes off the sweat, someone smokes bidi and the Hanuman of Ramleela takes off the tail.

All come back to their original state in darkness. There does not remain the need to hide or cover anything. Without acting, human beings live very intimately in this darkness. One feels light and natural, and laughs at how one used to cover these hard truths in the crowd of a social light by calling them vulgar. These uncovered genuine moments are rich with the original elements of life, filled with the truth of living till the end. Darkness is truer than light, denser and closer. Maybe we do not fear darkness. We love it. Keep longing for it within. We keep seeking darkness amid the cut and thrust of acting out life's assigned roles. Darkness is not as cruel as light. It does not show by rummaging through everything. It covers and gives a chance to experience intimately. If some colonies of light are seen within us, then those are nomadic establishments. All its new settlers are white rulers. But those attached to the ancestral soil, silently swimming like a dirty shadow, cannot be counted or identified. All the ones as old as that soil, are ours. If light enters us, we hide under trees in the bushes. Once it leaves, we come closer, smelling one another. We are the children of the primordial darkness. Darkness is our wife and mother, and fearing it is a superstition.

Undoubtedly, each one of us is a biped animal inside darkness. We feel the warmth of our innumerable furry ancestors around us there. Maybe nothing becomes visible to us, but everything is felt. Everything under the skin is darkness. Inside that cover, innumerable vessels of ours pulsate, food gets digested and oxygen travels. Hence, only in darkness, we feel the heartbeat of our chest and the intimate heat within our belly.

With light, returns the sight, but also returns a gap. Distance is indispensable for sight, but there is neither a gap nor a distance in touch. There is no possibility of a third being. Touch is another kind of sight. In every pore of the skin, the heat can be drunk like *Sahashraksha*[liii] and the thrill can be sucked. It is true that the eyes get lost once the light is put out, but the rest four sense organs go wild in sync. Humming is more musical in darkness; taste and smell become much more intoxicating. Darkness accumulates everything, concentrates, pulls into the depth; light dissipates, diffuses and descends. In comparison to light, darkness is livelier, it is more real.

[liii] One with a thousand eyes.

It is not a matter of shame to be real. Whatever one is, accepting it openly with ease is not a lie either. Deserting it by calling it a lie is also not a matter of joke. As Plato says, we all are imprisoned in a cave in darkness. One among us gets freed and searches for light. Similarly, no one is disagreeing with Prometheus because no one is fundamentally disagreeing with light.[liv] But when those seekers of light come to start a revolution in the kingdom of darkness, it makes us laugh a little. After spending four months in the tea gardens of Assam, the Odia leader of coolies comes back home and speaks in Hindi, pretends that he is no more an Odia and that he does not remember the language of this place. Even if light is invoked multiple times through morning, fire and the Sun, the Vedas are not silent about the cardinal truth of humans. Even after several austerities, when Vishwamitra from the mythologies faces Menaka, he accepts being in his unconcealed state hidden under many covers.

According to them, being in this state is our tradition by birth and we should be ashamed of it. We do not have any objection to be ashamed, but why, and before whom? If this animal is the indispensable truth everywhere, where is the need to be ashamed of it? Attire has no meaning in a nude kingdom, and there is no meaning in any such acting. There are innumerable hungers in an animal's life, and those are quite natural. Those cannot be wiped off and probably cannot be satiated as well. But covering them with a blanket and showing off cleanliness on the surface is hypocrisy. The tree does not die even if one cuts umpteen palm leaves, its naked roots dipping their face deep inside the darkness of the soil, keep sucking the juice for life. Again, the branch spreads out, and the leaves and buds come out. If it is uprooted and

[liv] Plato saw darkness as ignorance in his *Allegory of the Cave*, while Prometheus, in Greek mythology, symbolizes enlightenment through the gift of fire to humanity.

thrown out along with the patch of land that it had held tightly with 1000 coils of its roots, it will fall helplessly. If all the hungers of life are done away with, then only the pulseless ashes will be left out. If the act of burning itself becomes life, then it is not possible to live without hunger. For one to live, the animal itself lives. As many colourants are applied to it or masks are put on it, it remains unmistakably the same animal.

Darkness loosens this primordial animal. The chain with which it was tied up in the daylight, gets freed at night, and because it gets freed, it gets saved. Unveiled women and men accept each other. The primordial edict of creation continues. Or else, life would end in acting and a false game. There is immeasurable darkness in old age, and the darkness of death is limitless. Human's fickleness between these two boundaries gets over in the hide and seek of light and darkness. Coming from darkness, we enter into darkness again. On both sides of the stage, there is darkness. One just must go from this side to that side.

Light itself is the procession of a revolt. Likewise, chasing light is also an insane revolt. Getting overwhelmed by seeing light has become a kind of habit in us. The morning is beautiful, the sun is beautiful, plants, humans, flowers, buds, and the human child, all these are beautiful. As much the flower garden of motherly love grows and spreads during the day, we become that much encouraged and feel happy. There is plenty of advocacy within us for light, but darkness is inevitable. Compared to other animals, we observe more and understand more. The gate of our intellect is too widespread. Hence, an ample quantity of light enters us and many colonies are set up. We become divided into two. We have no objection if we are divided into a hundred parts instead of two. But that amount of fraudulence enters us. Also enters dilemma and skepticism. A suspicion emerges on whether we are actually from light or from darkness. It is said that once a philosopher dreamt that he was a butterfly. Thereafter, he had a problem knowing whether he was dreaming of becoming a human while being a butterfly or dreaming of becoming a butterfly while being a human. In search of the solution, maybe he would have passed away. We have almost the same problem. Whose are we in this dichotomous country? Of darkness or of light? One group of people says that we are of both. Another group, being perturbed, says that we are of none. However, in this tug of war, we have to accept that what we are in light is not what we are in darkness, and what we are in darkness is not what we are in light. We live in one and act in another. But we become so absorbed and focused in the acting, that it seems as if this acting is true and the living is acting.

Darkness is a state like a still sea—immeasurable, calm and antique. Light is an explosion—indomitable, rhythmic, and moving, and hence, new. The undisturbed darkness itself is the embodiment of nature, the destructive night. From its motionless womb the planets, the moon and the stars take birth, like seeds sprout. Similarly, the plants, animals, birds and humans take birth from it. She is the eternal mother, the bearer of the world. Creators pulsate in her lap, life pulsates and grows, and organisms multiply. She is the only mother of the whole universe, the sun sets in her cool lap, the creation is absorbed in it, motion comes to halt, and the sparks of consciousness dissolve. That fateful night is the cold resting womb of the universe.

Light is a point, a line, a flow. It divides one into many. It is not seen, but it shows everyone. Darkness is a state, a state of trance. All the things merge into it and become one. That only brings the conviction that 'there is only one principle, in which there is no diversity.' It hides everyone and makes everyone lonely. All the planets, moon, stars and earth come inside the mental universe. We hold the universe in darkness and hence hold the light as well. But there is one hole inside us that does not let us live alone. We search for another person. The whole creation drowns in darkness and feels happy being drowned because its element itself is darkness. But this only cunning point revolts inside us and builds waves of restlessness, and that point is perhaps the foremost entry point and centre of the light. We become anxious and desire to be divided into many and be connected, and this division is possible only in light. Hence, in loving the multifaceted entirety, we fall in love with the background of light; just like one while loving an individual goes on loving the individual's house, backyard, orchard etc. Perhaps because of this love, the individual gets reflected while broadening oneself. The things nearby also having received its magnetic field, pull others. So is light. We see the world in it, love the world and in that sequence, we also fall in love with light.

We are not the descendants of the sun, and light is not our fundamental element. We are only darkness ninety-nine out of a hundred. The remaining 'one' which we are unable to understand, naming that as light is also not easy. Our movement from womb to womb is inevitable, and eventually, the inseparable darkness of loneliness is the only truth.

* * *

Kishen Pattnaik (1930–2004)

'Crisis of the Indian Intellectual'

(Translated 'Bharatiya Budhijibira Sankat' from the Odia by Tyagraj Thakur)

Intellectuals in society can be broadly categorized into two classes. First are the artists, litterateurs, scientists and philosophers who provide the creative support that forms social structure; second are the teachers, technicians, doctors, engineers or clerks who work towards the day-to-day operation of society. It is not intended now to enter the sociological definition or analysis of these two classes. Going with the formula of 'actions are judged by results', it ought to be proven by the fertility, originality, impact, and attainment of the first class, and the health and continuity of the second class, especially in a society like India, where the rules of the contemporary society can never be everlasting. Indian society has continually witnessed a gradual upsurge in its moral and material deterioration.

If one depends on the progress report of the five-year plans to justify the fact that the Indian society is passing through a state of degradation and not through the path to excellence, it is natural for one to be suspicious of them. However, the unfailing yardstick for any humanitarian social development is the daily life of an ordinary member of society, one's internal experiences as well as one's continuous and keen efforts to connect to the outer surroundings. Considering it on such terms makes it simple and achievable within one's lifetime. In this realization, excepting a few kinds of technicians, every day we come in contact with the second category of intellectuals—the teachers, clerks, doctors, shopkeepers, lawyers, magistrates, journalists etc. In fact, good and bad, the happiness and sorrow of everyday life are woven with the demeanour, nature and behaviour of these people. What is the name of this realization in contemporary society? Onerous life! Decayed morality! Despair of the Soul! Extreme meaninglessness of life (and hence of human values)!

Behind the bribery and lies, flattery and fear, suicide and despair, are hiding a lack of courage, disbelief in truth, the non-confidence in humanity, and above all, the aversion to taking pain for social development. These cannot coexist with progress. A society that is on its way to a higher civilization cannot suffer from such ailments in their day-to-day lives.

It needs to be inspired by hope and enthusiasm, and the warm waves of courage to run down the arteries of its citizens, and narrowness and smallness to be washed away. Our progress reports have gross errors in them—on one hand, the common man's tasteless life is filled with despair, and on the other hand, the extreme smallness and turbidity in the second category of intellectuals of society are living examples of the national downfall. The common man has already decided that honesty is not possible in the fields of court affairs, politics and business. It is necessary to mention and analyse how there is no sign of humanity in professions that are considered sacred, charitable, and humanitarian such as medicine, teaching, land-donation, and works by the red-cross. With respect to power and money, there is not much of a difference between public prosecutors in courts and doctors in hospitals, or millionaire rice traders and vice chancellors in the business of education or revenue patwari and college lecturer. However, though these mentions and analyses are necessary to awaken the dormant conscience, it is not the motif here.

Our subject of discussion is only the causes of the contemporary social and regional downfall and the responsibilities of the first category of intellectuals towards these. To revive and bring a new lease of life to the people of a nation that has lagged far behind in matters of economic and cultural development, there are only two ways—political and cultural. The first one is revolution, and the second one is popularly known as new consciousness or renaissance. Through political revolution, the economic, social and other material welfare of the people is expected, and with new consciousness or renaissance, there occurs a new rise of intellectual, moral and spiritual values. These two methods are complementary to each other; and if the physical revolution does not have the background of an intellectual renaissance; in other words, if the intellectual revolution, instead of becoming a pathfinder to the political revolution, comes out only as a sub-branch of the latter, then it will become a unilateral one and the civilization or social development inspired by this revolution can never blossom in the humanitarian perspective. The communist revolution is an apt example of this. It is primarily an economic movement and cultural reform looks like a sub-branch of it and subsidiary to it. For a holistic revolution, both political as well as cultural revolutions need to equally emerge together and stimulate public opinion. The ones who are imagining a glorious future for India ought to understand the need for both revolutions.

If the activities of the Indian intellectuals are closely observed, it will be noticed that instead of confronting the moral downfall of society and the individual, they have been preyed on by it. After the Indian society was freed from dependence (colonial rule), a huge and new responsibility came to the Indian intellectuals in carrying out the functioning of society. That responsibility is to think and contemplate the diverse problems of Indian society and pave the way to its solution, examine the existing norms and policies, and offer constructive as well as destructive criticism. In the contemporary world and the Indian context, there was a need for originality in doing this work. This is because of the remarkable story of independence that India has. When India was becoming Independent, Western civilization was collapsing. The invention of the nuclear bomb as an offshoot of two world wars, and the division of nations into two power groups during peacetime are perfect examples of the decline and disintegration of Western civilization. On one hand, there was the demonic war and the manifestation of imperialism, and on the other hand, there was violent internal war and the manifestation of inhuman authoritarianism. There was an endless clash and competition of deadly artilleries between the two. Amidst such circumstances, when a people's society like India searched for a way to the surface of world history, there was no clear path before it. For the Eastern brains stunned by the pride of Western civilization, having the aspiration to become an industrially developed nation like England, Russia or America was quite natural. Japan and China have taken up the model of following the West in two different ways, and they want to achieve it at any cost. The aspiration is grossly this—'We are a backward nation. England, America and Russia are advanced nations. We must emulate them to become civilized and powerful. We can achieve it with the help of their industry and science.' The Indian brain has not been able to accept this. This is not because of the old tradition of the Upanishads. Even China had the Confucian tradition. Once a civilization changes, the courage to quit the old tradition comes with it. However, fortunately or unfortunately, this old tradition revived itself with a new soul and moved the Indian mind space. As a result of this, the Indian mind and heart lost the nature and ease of accepting the prevalent value system of the world.

In the language of sociology, this can be called the problem of intellectual orthodoxy. It is evident from the example of China that after a civilization becomes obsolete, the impact of its tradition weakens, and the attraction toward a new civilization wins over it.

It could have happened in India as well. But Gandhiji's movement has already created problems in the continuity of following the West. Whether it is only a transitory one or an epoch-making one, future history will talk about it, but it is certain that the intellectual history of the East has changed. Gandhi was not a carrier/advocate of antiquity. Displeased with the prevalent value system and to find a new path, Gandhi took recourse to the Gita and Buddha, and to validate his method, he banked on Thoreau, Ruskin and Tolstoy from modern times. Scantily knowledgeable Indian intellectuals have already ill-defined it. In their opinion, Gandhi was only a great soul and a typical idealist. He was not an intellectual like Nehru, M.N. Roy or Jayaprakash Narayan, who had come back from Europe and America after learning socialism, Marxism, materialism etc. One of the Indian intellectuals analysing the life of Gandhi from this perspective has written that when others had accepted science, industry, politics etc. while gaining experience from the West, Gandhi was writing columns on vegetarian food in the newspapers of England. Though the writer of this sarcastic statement is a communist, on the subject matter of Gandhi's life, this is a common opinion of intellectuals from all categories. They do not understand that the strong and original intellect of Gandhi while considering even the Western civilization to be old and non-functional, was imagining new values. To realize this, instead of concentrating on British politics and culture like Nehru did, or being swayed by materialism like M.N. Roy was or by the American pragmatism ideals like Jayaprakash Narayan, Gandhi sought the inspiration for his ideal from the world like Tolstoy, Thoreau or Ruskin, and carried out the first application of his belief in South Africa, and not in India. How the intellectuals educated from Western books are inferior and small as compared to the pervasiveness and farsightedness of his intellect is something to be keenly observed. Frankly speaking, Gandhi was so sure-footed in the establishment of a new universalism while defying contemporary universalism that, despite living the first phase of his youth in England and South Africa, he was not swayed away by the glitters of Western civilization.

Gandhiji's philosophy influenced the Indian mind but his successors did not have his farsightedness or were opposed to it. Nehru and Deshmukh can be taken as symbols of these two categories. The ones who called themselves Gandhian took only the outer shape of some of the activities by Gandhi as a convention and became so narrow and weak that they did not retain much of their social importance; subsequently, in the name of *Sarvodaya* or *Khadi*[lv] through the departments of public welfare and community project, they sought shelter under the government machinery. The general thought process and perspectives of admirers of the Western civilization like Nehru and I.C.S officers like Chintamani Deshmukh are being employed for the political, economic and social development of India today.

If we travel back further in history, two different kinds of reactions were seen in Indian society in response to the establishment of British rule—one, countering the foreign insolence with national pride while reviving ancient knowledge and civilization, and two, being proactive to win against the foreigners with the help of foreign artilleries while obtaining Western knowledge. Subsequently, the common intellectual

[lv] Mahatma Gandhi's philosophy of Sarvodaya and his promotion of Khadi were closely intertwined and formed integral parts of his vision for social and economic transformation in India.

of India wanted a fusion of these two, and in this context, Ram Mohan Roy is perhaps the father of this category. Upon closer inspection, one might discern a subtle undercurrent of inferiority complex at its core. Actually, the inclination toward the West is the crux of the matter in this mindset. The Indian spirituality is exaggerated in order to hide one's own inferiority. Attempts are made to explain Indian religion and philosophy in the framework of European thoughts. It is impossible to have a fusion of a thousands of years old, dead civilization with a prevalent and powerful civilization—it's only pretence. The real question is about the fondness toward foreign civilization, culture and language. In this context, it will be apt to narrate another historical example. An almost contemporary of Ram Mohan, Ishwar Chandra Vidyasagar has also been neglected like Gandhi by the Indian intellectuals. Despite being a stronger character than Ram Mohan, a more original and independent personality, his place in the revival of Indian or Bengali culture is too gloomy, and he is unknown outside Bengal. This is not accidental, because many individuals born in Bengal with lesser talent than him have become famous in India; and in matters of promoting the talents of their own state all around, the Bengali intellectuals are the most capable. Much before Gandhiji's movement on Khadi, the national language and *Harijans*,[lvi] Ishwar Chandra, though not in details and comprehensiveness like Gandhi, had created a revolution for social equality in symbolic form with an indomitable spirit through the shoes-struggle, the widow remarriage movement and the demand for Bengali medium of instruction till university education. Along with this, he

[lvi] Gandhi's movement on Harijans, or 'children of God', was a profound expression of his commitment to social justice and equality. It was a crusade against the entrenched caste system, which relegated certain communities to the margins of society, subjecting them to discrimination and oppression for generations.

also revolted against the old social values as well as protested straightforwardly against the inclination towards Western civilization. This is why it has been difficult to understand his historical significance and very few people know Vidyasagar as someone much more than a charitable pundit. However, our historians consider the ones who had been overwhelmed by welcoming Western culture and English education as the fathers of the Indian Renaissance. In that sense, Vidyasagar's opposition to English medium and English attire perhaps became a bottleneck to his fame.

The source that Vidyasagar and Gandhi represent attacks the value system of the old civilization and at the same time, it has not been carried away by the prevalent civilization. A special outcome of such a mindset could be progressing toward a new culture while striving to resolve all the existing problems. It is our misfortune that the Indian intellectuals have kept this source of originality obstructed due to negligence. They have been flowing on an easy stream of tradition, of which Ram Mohan Roy, Motilal Nehru and Radhakrishnan were the representatives. We must draw attention to this history because it tells us of the futility of modern Indian intellectuals but also analyses its collateral impact.

An intellectual does not apply his intellect in a vacuum. His intellect is applied to the problems of the time and society, and its worth is proved by the impact and the result of this application. Over the past century and a half, Indian society has grappled with multifaceted crises spanning civilization, culture, politics, and economy. At the heart of these challenges lies a profound transformation—a journey from the shadows of poverty, stagnation, and cultural inertia towards a position of prominence and influence in the modern world.

Four types of efforts have been put in to solve this problem: the revival of the ancient culture by the Arya Samaj in the name of Arya culture, imitation of the Western civilization, the fusion of old and new, and vehement opposition to the value system of Western ideology. In our society, there are individuals like Ishwar Chandra or Gandhi, who stand out as strong examples despite being few in number. While there aren't many revivalists like them, and they lack support from mainstream institutions in fields like science, their influence is substantial, especially among Hindus. In times of trouble, many Hindus find themselves drawn to their perspectives. Instead of separating the other two categories, it would be better to merge them, because the ones who want to aggregate ancient Indian culture and Western civilization are attractive in what they say, but their task is almost impossible to achieve. Like Radhakrishnan, while singing the glory of ancient culture, they write books that would be liked by the West; and while accepting a meaningless, luxurious, lavish position of the Vice-President, leave society on the path to imitate the Western civilization in a conventional manner. The followers of the communist ideology have not been excluded here, because despite having a different method of politics, they are part of the Western civilization, just like the fascists, the socialist democrats or the conservatives are. Those Indian intellectuals who have grown up inspired by the communist ideology will be included in this category of Western imitation. The fact that there is nothing wrong with integrating these three categories into one can be known if we take a look at the government machinery and the different institutions of our country. Whatever fiscal, intellectual and cultural schemes have been implemented for the development of India, all these people are their supporters, and in all institutions like the Sahitya Academy etc. that exist, these people are seen in equal numbers. Hence, except for the unreal revivalists, the narrow Gandhians on the verge of extinction, intellectuals in our country are those who want to resolve the problems of Indian society with the model of

Western civilization. These are only the leaders and workers in literary gatherings, scientific laboratories, cultural circles, art exhibitions, political arenas, economic planning forums, and educational institutions. Their opinions are published in newspapers, in the country and abroad, on behalf of India.

Many things have been said about the weakness of the Indian intellectual. For some, he is a rootless personality—he was not brought up in the tradition of this country, and he has not grown up in the soil and air of this country. In another point of view, his personality is dilemmatic, caught in the tug of war between ancient and Western civilization. Again, from another point of view, because he is unprepared to completely accept the prevalent universal culture (meaning Western culture), his progress is stuck. Some say that he lacks admirers, which is why he frequently depends on appreciation from Europe and America. Unless they appreciate it, he is unable to realize his own worth. He is worried because foreign critics are not noticing his work.

From all the above, it is being signified that the condition of the Indian intellectual is not good. But these are not the causes of the predicament, these are the symptoms of it. The two main causes of his weakness are concerned with character and ideology. The 'character' here means only the characteristic of an intellectual. Be it an artist, litterateur or economist, integrity is always considered a given, as he cannot discharge his duty otherwise. If studying society, analysing life, creating values, paving the way to progress, etc. become the work of an intellectual, then he should not accept allegiance to anything other than the truth. His dharma is to be closely associated with his work and stay alert always so that its glory does not diminish. If we measure with this yardstick, the greatest fault of the Indian intellectual lies in his servitude and sycophancy, and his lack of pride in himself.

Whatever exception to this principle was left in pre-independent India, the late Radhakrishnan, while wiping it out completely, created a new tradition of allegiance (his speciality is related to the freedom movement). It is not that a poet, a philosopher or an intellectual would not want political power. If any philosopher or poet, while being faithful to his intellect and belief, climbs to power through the political workflow and behaves according to his ideology, then we should welcome him. But if a highly honourable intellectual, famous as a philosopher in the country and abroad, instead of utilizing his intellect at this crucial moment for the analysis, study and criticism of social progress, sits in the government like an effigy with nothing to offer other than power and pomp, and keeps his intellect and conscience shut, then it would not be wrong to call it an accursed betrayal to the duty of an intellectual. This aspiration of being an intellectual while serving the government which started with high officials has now trickled down to the lower official positions as well. People are trying to be poets or musicians or economists, some in the centre (Delhi Durbar), some in the state level, or if not at these levels, then at least at the block level.

If the activities and aspirations of intellectuals are analysed, one after another at different state, national and Panchayat levels, it will be clear that they are not content with the impact and respect they have among common people, and therefore want to improve their impact and respect through government institutions. A good example of how cowardly the Indian litterateur can be in experiencing self-pride as an intellectual and an artist is found in Odisha. After the Sahitya Akademi award was conferred on an established writer from Odisha, a new edition of the awarded book was released. Three new designs were added to the outer cover of this new edition. These were the photographs taken of the speeches of the prime minister and the vice president that were delivered while conferring the award (which are not the subject matter of this book), and another person receiving the award from the (lotus-like hands of the) prime minister on behalf of the writer. It is true that the book was sold out through the government machinery as a result of this, but what an exhibition of the inferiority of the artist before the government's mercy it is! This is more of a rule than an exception in literary fields now. In 99 per cent of the summits in literature, science, philosophy and history, a minister or any other person with political power is invited as a pathfinder or as part of the jury. This kind of allegiance or lack of self-esteem is rare to be found in any civilized democratic nation; even in authoritarian communist countries, it happens under a limit (because in those countries, the intellectual legitimately accepts the government's ideology as his own). The intellectual in our country has accepted the social objectives of Western civilization but has not accepted the day-to-day qualities. The opposite of this should happen. Rama had not wanted to learn social objectives from Ravana but had sent Laxman to learn from him, the rules of his personal and day-to-day life. It is not the duty of a new nation to accept the social cues of an older, more established civilization. Our intellectuals are eager to accept the social objective of a civilization of motors, air conditioners and televisions, but they take a step back in learning qualities like punctuality, independence in personal and professional life, etc. (Once these lessons are absorbed, it appears one must bid farewell to those aforementioned social goals and embark on a quest for fresh ones.)

When the intellectual does not have self-pride, he is an inferior man. Hence, it is natural for him to not have an impact on people's minds. He is unable to run society because he is not self-guided. Since no one in the country can recognize him, he wants foreign fans. Why is it happening like this? The intellectual might say that the natives are unable to understand him, hence, he is not getting respect, and having no other option, he is taking shelter in the party, group or institution with power. He is giving up his own duty just because he is not getting respect. The two reasons why the common people cannot recognize the intellectual are there in any country and time. Either people are unfit to accept or the intellectual is not doing anything that would touch the core of people's hearts. To make people fit is also a duty of the intellectual.

Whatever it be, the common man is basically a human. He will, of course, be influenced by his relations, and by the art, literature, science, economics and politics that can touch him deeply. That everyone will understand all kinds of artistic excellence and theory is not true, but the thinking, imagination or activity that is done while keeping the deep and intimate experiences of life intact, their meaning penetrates the common mind through different routes with time. There is such a mental attraction in most works that the common wit cannot explain and yet, gets influenced by. If the work, creation and labour of the Indian intellectual are not appreciated by common people, then the main reason behind this is that he (the intellectual) has not been able to uphold a natural and deep relationship with human life.

Be it in any field—economics, sociology, history, science, philosophy, literature or art—the Indian intellectual is doing nothing other than just reinventing the wheel. And the ridiculous thing is that the Indian intellectual wants to do it in a foreign language that not even 1 per cent of the country's people understand. In any country and time, out of the total number of people near whom the intellectual's work reaches, a very small fraction of them accept and help disseminate it. But here, from the very beginning itself, our intellectuals have chosen a way to reach out to an incredibly negligible number of people. Even in developed and educated countries, when an intellectual thinks and imagines in a language understood and spoken by all the people (citizens), it does not get easily accepted. In such circumstances, if the Indian intellectual keeps carrying out every work in English, and expects that it will have its impact and that people will accept and respect it, what could be more unnatural? Who, why and how will this country accept our economists, scientists, historians, social scientists and critics? This is a continuous misfortune in the history of India. Leaving a few exceptions like Buddha and Kabir, the Indian intellectual has worked keeping in view a small fraction of society as his reader, audience and critic. English has become the successor of Sanskrit, Arabic and Persian languages today. The fault of English is more than that of Sanskrit and Persian because, in the earlier days, social unity was not a necessary part like it is today.

The Indian intellectual, instead of looking at this natural social unity, has suddenly moved towards an artificial world unity. Behind this world unity, there is neither the generosity of thought nor the compassion of experience; there exists low self-esteem, the fear of lagging behind and an impatience to quickly become world-renowned. An Indian intellectual does not have historical insight. He thinks that there is nothing in the womb of history beyond the current civilization and that the whole world has become one because of this civilization. He thinks as if there is only one civilization in the world, the Western civilization, and in this civilization there is only one culture, the European culture. Some even do not hesitate to say that there is only one language, and that is English! The consequence of such a macro vision is clear. If the world has already become a place with one civilization, one culture (and one language), a backward country like India will also march ahead and reach there. The country's economy will grow and become like that of Russia or America, its literature will grow and become like that of the English or French. Therefore, to achieve excellence in literature, art or philosophy, their interest, method, principle and yardstick will be the appropriate touchstone. The indigenous people are so backward that if we keep waiting for their needs and cognitive abilities, we will not be counted among the best litterateurs or intellectuals of the world, hence this impatience. The way in which problems in Europe and America are being discussed should be discussed in a similar way here also. If existentialism, surrealism and cubism are prevalent there, then we cannot participate in world culture unless we have these here. Since they are encountering the problems of Angry Young men and the Beat Generation in their society and literature, these need to be born in our society as well.[lvii] An indistinct pain of the war-torn society and disintegrated personality is oozing out in their poetry, hence if our poetry does not carry the thoughts and images of this ravaged society, we will miss the trend of the time. So we will also write poems in that fashion, on such contexts with similar thoughts and images, and receive accolades from world literature. Meanwhile, there is another issue worth noting. If the yardstick of excellence remains there, the things that could not be appreciated by the critics of those countries, even if they are appreciated in our country, the writers and thinkers will not be content. Again, in turn, if one wants to be appreciated by them, one has to take recourse to the word structures, contextual relevance, subject matter and references that are understood by them. It is a polluted recurrence. The Indian litterateur and thinker is so impatient to reach out to the Western reader and critic that the reader and critic in his own country is his subsidiary objective, and writing in English is his primary aim. Even if one writes in an indigenous language, one is worried from the very beginning whether it will be translated into the Western language or not. Even if it is translated, it will not feel like an English or Russian book. Whether it will be compared with Baudelaire, Camus and Russell or not? What is the urgency with the foreigner that

[lvii] The 'Angry Young Men' movement of post-war Britain and the rebellious spirit of the 'Beat Generation' in America were parallel forces of dissent, each challenging societal norms with their raw energy and unfiltered voices.

he would break his head reading the Indian intellectuals? If he wants to know the thoughts and art of Eliot, Baudelaire, Camus or Russell, why would he try to know all these from the second-hand brain of the Indian intellectual? He might read Indian books only to find out about Indian originality, Indian contexts and idiosyncrasies. How do the people of one country become curious about the literature and thoughts of another country? Despite being in one civilization, the readers and critics of England try to understand only those in the fields of literature and intellect, even from America that are speaking a similar language or from the close neighbourhood of France, who get recognized by their native readers and critics. The way the Indian intellectual spends time running after the second-rate and third-rate English writers and wastes energy considering them world intellectuals, the intellectual from England and France instead discusses the authentic and established individuals or work of other countries.

Behind this, there is a deep and important truth related to history and human society from which the Indian intellectual should get ample hope and inspiration. It hasn't emerged from genuine experience, much like the concept of world unity has never been a reality. No such world civilization, world culture or world language has been born yet. Even the Indian social unity could not reach many topographies until now. Language, literature or culture is created keeping in the centre the day-to-day wants, wishes, problems, and experiences of humans and society. Until and unless there is a uniformity of all these across the world, there cannot be one culture, one literature and one language. We are far away from this ideology today, where the colour of the skin has stood as a wall between humans. The way Indian, Egyptian, Greek, Roman civilizations, etc. in the past became the greatest civilizations of the world for others to follow within a short span of time, the European civilization has become something similar in the current time. And after a few days, this will subside and new civilizations will emerge from new regions. One after another, with new experiences and perspectives, many regional civilizations will emerge out of these. A world culture could also be constituted, which could unite all the people socially, economically and spiritually. Until it happens, there is a historical significance of the undeveloped society, undeveloped culture and undeveloped language. A developed lifestyle, developed language and developed culture could be the achievements of a certain civilizational stream, but it is impossible to have new historical experimentation through these again. For the new golden harvest of a civilization, a new area of newly fertile land, new people and a new language are required. Those who say that our indigenous language is unfit to become a medium for the prevailing civilization and culture, while they are at least speaking a partial truth, they are forgetting that the direction to a new civilization may open through our language and through our people, air and experience, which is not possible through English or any other developed language. The Westerners have already said that Western civilization has started declining, but from the prime minister of India to the litterateurs, artists and village touts, everyone is saying that we have to learn Western civilization. How would we quit English then?

Along with this, we must remember another truth. A great philosophy, literature or art takes birth only from deep experience. As long as the soul, brain and heart remain stuck in the cover of blood, flesh and bones, man's deep experiences will come only from tiny people, animals, insects, trees and plants, wants and wishes, virtues and vices, and the climate of a limited environment. The human mind can neither reach the highest peak nor the lowest depth with an implanted experience. The greatest art and literature are created out of deep and local experiences. The climate, trees and plants, animals and humans around have a lasting impact on philosophers, scientists, poets and artists, and with the depth of such experiences, can create world art and world literature. On the other hand, the result of an artificially implanted experience is too short and transitory. Hence, Laxness's stories on the underdeveloped people of Iceland, Pearl Buck's *The Good Earth* and the subject matter of Gopinath Mohanty's *Paraja*, despite being local and parochial, have become carriers of the world experience. Only the local experience can become the carrier of the world experience. The local language has a peculiar and mysterious relationship with this.

From the aforementioned criticism, one should not misunderstand our intent to separate or contract the experience or intellect of the nation or society from the general experience of the current era. Even if society and environment are different, art has a neurological circumference, and the unity of time keeps it bound. Especially in the era of aeroplanes and rockets, it is quite natural that different societies would be bound by the unity of time. In the conscientiousness of the intellectual, both time and society draw their circles from different centres, and the common integral arc of both circumferences will be different for different societies. This common integration is the appropriate ground of experience for the intellectual. Here the experience of time is synthesized with the social experience. Here the experience of time gets life through the experience of the environment, and the social experience gets refined with the experience of time. For example, the Indian intellectual is not being asked to consider only the special experiences of the Indian society and environment; and quit the common experiences of this era, such as a rocket, a nuclear bomb or the Cold War. If one does so, the experience of time will be left out and the experience of place will be limited. There will not be any age consciousness in this. The assimilation of social consciousness and age consciousness should be the ideology of a true artist. If the place is left alone, the experience of time will become hollow and unreal. Hence, when the Indian intellectual here talks about class division and class conflict while keeping silent on caste discrimination, writes poetry on rockets and electric filters instead of thinking about the smoke from the hearth and the burning eyes of housewives, or without ever thinking about the poverty and disease of the country, ignites his brain with cigarette or alcohol to find a solution on how to save the world from nuclear war, it will be apt to call his experience imitative and implanted instead of calling it natural or a healthy world consciousness.

Forgetting all these is the ideological weakness of the Indian intellectual. He has forgotten his historical problems. Treading the path directed by outsiders he cannot realise his true self, he can neither be adored in the country nor can he get recognition abroad. If he works while taking the help of local experiences, local problems and local language then it is certain that he will have recognition in and impact on the country, and that recognition and impact can become symbolic of the rise of a new era and the people abroad will be automatically attracted to him. However, it requires patience and courage. He will have to bear this much of trouble. Ideological weakness does not mean that he would embrace any specific ideology. What his idealism should be, and by which philosophy, politics and economy he would function; the complete answer to these may not be available, but it is not necessary either. He will begin with the pleasure and pain, wants and wishes, problems and solutions of day-to-day life in his surroundings. Wherever something wrong is happening, wherever there is corruption, wherever dirt and darkness are spreading, if one becomes conscious there, the strings within will chime and with the successive pervasiveness of this chime, the local experience will gradually become world experience. If efforts are made to solve sample problems, experimenting with the sample wishes and aspirations; if a remedy towards its fulfilment is searched for, then a comprehensive ideology and vision will emerge out of it. If the Indian intellectual becomes aware of the natural experiences and problems while quitting the implanted ones then the rainbow of a new ideology will be transmitted in the sky of his mind. It will not be out of context to give the example of one of the best modern Bengali poets and litterateurs in this regard. When he was asked why works of high quality are not being created in Indian literature, he replied that the people of our country have not undergone any great suffering. The great novels of Europe have been written out of their war, dictatorship and extreme persecution. Instead of getting suddenly angry with a famous intellectual who speaks like this, one should rather think how such a surprising stupidity could be possible. If India does not have any suffering, if there was no dictatorship in the last hundred and fifty years of the history of India, then what is the meaning of these words? Did the writers forget the atrocities, persecution and aspirations during the freedom struggle so early? When the world war was ongoing, lakhs of people in India, especially in Bengal, died of starvation. Once their war ended, crores of people, children and the old ones, became homeless and destitute in our Hindu–Muslim conflict, and lakhs of people lost their lives in the atrocities and knives of their neighbours. Apart from all these, the unbearable pain of an individual's daily life which a European cannot imagine, is the fate of 90 per cent of people here. Nevertheless, thinking like this can have two types of causes, and both of these are applicable here. The Indian intellectual is so fond of imitation that in order to write great literature, he wants to see the same kind of suffering and pain that have been depicted in European literature. How can there be literature of high quality from the experiences of suffering and pain of other people? Secondly, the experience of the crores of people of India is neither his own experience nor does he have empathy for it. The pain that he feels when a White man dies, is not as acute as what he feels when a Harijan or a tribal man is persecuted or killed. The Indian caste system has stood as such an unparalleled obstacle among humans that the experience of crores of people is not able to become the experience of the intellectuals of society. Their problems and needs are not the problems and needs of the intellectuals. In case of famine or violence, these lakhs of people suffer together, with whom the intellectual does not have any occasion to stay together as a neighbour or a relative. For hundreds of years their blood and flesh have been disconnected from that of the intellectual class, hence there is the famine of experience and empathy. This poverty of experience and the dearth of empathy are to be broken through mental strength. Embracing their experiences through empathy, one has to be associated with their problems. Otherwise, the experience of the original source for an unprecedented creation that the Bengali litterateur spoke about will not come in the fate of our intellectuals.

To amplify the fragmentation of experiences, various artificial amenities are being extended to the intellectual class through governmental initiatives and schemes. These schemes, though imitative in nature, emulate the Western lifestyle, enabling a segment of society to attain similar standards of living. The nation's science, education, industry or literature has not reached the level of the West by adopting the formula of borrowing huge a amount of wealth and spending it. However, many such islands are being set up where Western luxury-inspired buildings, gardens, cars and hotels are coming up. Colossal buildings in the name of scientific laboratories are being constructed, though there is no invention. Huge temples of research in the name of Kalidas are being built by spending lakhs of rupees, though listening to the English speeches from Indian litterateurs in seminars on Kalidas, the well-read scholars of Kalidas literature from Soviet Russia are quitting the seminar out of disgust. When the indigenous language is not being accepted as the medium of instruction in schools and colleges, new jobs with fat salaries are being opened in the name of encyclopaedias with a view to accumulating world knowledge in the indigenous languages. Indulging in all these, the Indian intellectual's energy to experience is further deteriorating. Living in an air-conditioned silver tower, he forgets the summer and winter of the whole country. To stop the experience from further fragmentation, honest courage is required, and sacrifice and rebellion are needed.

Stopping this fragmentation instead of feeling lesser before the prestige of Western civilization and being ashamed of the illiterate people, backward economy and undeveloped language of their own country, if the Indian intellectual gets closely attached to the surroundings, then a new world will be seen to him immediately. He will know that it is not his fate to become inferior by implanting the yardstick, context and problems of the established Western civilization onto the self and by searching for appreciation out of this, rather his fate is to establish a new culture taking into account new contexts. Here, the problems of politics are new, and the problems of economics are new because while writing the political science and economic science of the Western world, the problems have been taken from the local perspectives. There is a need to write it from the world perspective now, or else it will at least have to be written keeping in view the maximum population of the world, meaning Asia, Africa and South America. Similarly, in the questions of philosophy or form and style of literature, new standards need to be created. The manner and form of literature, the style of novels and poetry that seem appropriate in Western society, do not completely apply in our society. Many things are getting restricted within specialist groups. There is a scope for new experiments in these matters. Whatever such new experiments will be carried out taking into consideration the Indian environment these will not be indicative of regionalism, rather there is ample hope of these becoming the yardstick of the future world. Thus, although it is true that the Indian intellectual is basically rootless, dilemmatic, and dependent on others, it is due to the lack of honest courage and ideology that he has remained so inferior and unproductive. He does not have any long-sustained aspirations for new creation. He has an impatience to be equal with others on aspirations created by others. Which one will come first, ideology or character? In a way, he himself can create an ideology from his own experiences. Hence the need for character is primary. If he asserts his rights while being honest to his profession, and vehemently reacts against all the wrongs and darkness of society, his creation will automatically become robust and natural in the new light of his ideology. In doing so, if he stays away from the surroundings, climate and language of his own society, then it will not work. Until he understands this destitution, he is blind, he cannot see anything.

It is not the historical fate of the Indian intellectual to be the recipient of ordinary respect, ordinary development and ordinary impact. In the delusion of ordinary comfort and respect, he might exclude himself from a historical responsibility and be crushed under the juggernaut of history and merge with the dust; or being the charioteer of history, he will be the convenor of a new era. He will have to choose between these two. For new civilizations and cultures to come into the world, there is an acute need for experimentation. The huge ambition to fulfil this need is the only way to the upliftment of the Indian intellectual.

* * *

Sarat Kumar Mohanty (1938–2006)

'Legions of Vulgarity'

(Translated 'Apasanskrutira Senabahini' from the Odia by Krishna C. Goudo)

The opportunities and dignity that the man on the street is getting in the modern era were beyond the limit of his wildest dreams in any era in the past. In every country—be it democratic or communist, the common citizen's rights and opportunities have increased. The poor unlettered common man can travel in the same train that the rich and respectable travel in. One may be travelling in an air-conditioned compartment, the other in second class. The system of third class has been done away with in our country. In many countries, trains do not have different classes. The facilities are the same in the entire train. Our country too will adopt the same system gradually. With common people agitating across the world for their dignity and rights, with the unprecedented contribution of science and for various other reasons, the world is moving towards a more equitable society.

How many would have had the opportunity to listen to Tansen's music during his time? Besides the courtiers of the emperor and a few fortunate famous people, Tansen's voice was a fantasy for the common man. Today, an average person is able to listen to Lata Mangeshkar's songs on the radio from the cosy comfort of his home. He can keep song records of any big singer at home. Like music, classical literature too is within his reach. Before the invention of the printing press and its widespread usage across the world, high-quality writing was an impossibility for a great majority of people. Except for the wisest and the wealthy aficionados, no one could lay their hands on a valuable book or a manuscript. Our poetry and sacred literature remained the property of a few families for generations.

Easy access to philosophy, literature, music and art has had an unprecedented developmental impact on man, which was not the case in the past. This is true but there is more to the entire truth. We will take the example of music to elaborate our argument. Music has a limitless capacity to fill man with celestial joy and soften his heart with finer feelings. Great music has the power to bring the listener momentarily face-to-face with God. But does modern music possess that divine aura? Are we keeping music on the pedestal it used to be on? The day the electric microphone became an inevitable part of music, it transformed greatly. The deafening sound of the microphone kills the mellifluousness of the music. What could be the sensitivity of the ears to musical notes which have, in the first place, been introduced to music through the disagreeable jarring sound of the microphone? Even as music becomes cheaply available to the general public, good taste and the capacity to appreciate good music, breathe their last. A genius like Lata Mangeshkar is a rarity anywhere in the world and in any era. What inane fare she is made to dish out while singing for heroines who dance around the bush, to gratify our taste! There was a huge gap between great singers and the general public in the past. Today, people listen to the incomparable Lata Mangeshkar even as they sip tea and indulge in small talk sitting in a restaurant. This is the way we listen to music. Whilst a good song is being played in the background, someone bursts into loud gossip or hot political chatter. We bother neither to switch off the song nor listen to it with interest but pay all our attention to the loose talk, which we absorb lock stock and barrel. In every conceivable situation and grossly distasteful situation, good music is mixed with tawdry songs, making good music lose its sheen and appeal. What happened to music befell religion, literature, and philosophy as well, in terms of degradation of our aesthetic sense and other finer sensibilities. It seems as if it is the age of miniaturized emotions and sentiments! We are so used to seeing the emperor in a jester's outfit that we fail to imagine how the emperor would look in the royal ensemble. In a democracy, everyone has his own way and inclination to dress the emperor. The marketplace is not bad and supreme knowledge is hard to come by but seeking supreme knowledge in the marketplace is difficult. But in this age, the marketplace has become the foremost forum to get familiarized with supreme knowledge. Getting a speck of supreme knowledge is a matter of providence and dedicated practice. This truism is an insurmountable challenge for people who accept the marketplace to be the one to receive the supreme knowledge.

Whichever direction we may glance, there is this spectacle of the lotus scattered in the dust. When Arjuna, the middle Pandav, shoots his *pashupat*[lviii] arrow from his bow—*Gandiv*, even the conqueror of the three worlds bites the dust. But when the little boy shoots his bamboo arrow from his bamboo bow, even the little bird does not feel the need to fly away. Our greatest words of wisdom are used as the bamboo arrow and the bow in the hands of the little boy. Let us consider one example. In many of our gatherings, especially in religious gatherings, the peace chant (*shanti mantra)—Sarve bhabantu sukhinah* (May there be happiness, peace, harmony and prosperity) is uttered at the end of the meeting. One speaker, after speaking nonstop for three hours, ended his speech with the peace mantra—*'sarve bhavantu sukhinah . . . ma kaschit dukhabhag bhabet'*. It was past

---

[lviii] Name of Arjuna's arrow.

11 p.m. and the organizers were going through the pain of restlessness. One of the invited speakers was yet to get his turn. They were in a fix as to whether they should continue the meeting or end it then and there. The audience was anxious to return home, but they could not just show their backs to a discussion on religious matters. The people of the neighbourhood too had been suffering the blaring of the microphone since the afternoon. After working all day long, the office returnee found it hard to have some quiet time with the day's newspaper. The condition of students preparing for the examination at hand was even more worrisome. A microphone was not a necessity for an assembly of about a hundred people—at least using the device in full volume was not necessary—but such expectations are futile both from the speakers and the organizers. The neighbourhood suffered through sound pollution, the audience made to sit up till midnight suffered, and the speaker who spoke for one hour before the one who spoke for three hours also suffered. To see the suffering of people, one does not need to have a deep insight. They cannot see the suffering that is so obvious and in fact, they become the source of suffering. And from these people, we hear the chanting—let no one suffer (*ma kaschit dukha bhag bhabet*). It is our lot that there are none other than these people to chant the peace mantra to us. The peace mantra was the spontaneous outcome of a great soul's experience of seeing the pain and suffering of humanity and the resultant empathy, and the same *shloka*[lix] in the mouth of people insensitive to the suffering of others would no doubt sound hollow. As a result, there is a disconnect between the *shloka* and its source in human sympathy. Many such wise chants have proved to be the guiding light for humanity, and many such great thoughts tossed around indiscriminately,

---

[lix] Song.

have turned inane and lost their capacity to inspire people. By tossing around the shloka '*yada yadahi dharmasya*'[lx] in every conceivable place, we have made the shloka lose its aura. Failing to procure a cinema ticket even after standing in the queue for two hours, the film aficionado thinks that the time for the annihilation of the wicked has arrived. God will appear shortly to slay the film buff rogue who jumps the queue and the hoodlum involved in cinema ticket black marketing. If He does not, then He is no God. Those who utter the shloka '*sambhavami yuge yuge*'[lxi] fail to show us the decline of righteousness (*dharmasya glanirbhabat*). In fact, looking at these people, we get to understand that the decline of righteousness lies in the acts of the cinema ticket black marketer and the vegetable vendor who cheats with weights.

The condition of fine arts, classical music, and great thoughts in the hands of the hoi polloi is pitiable, to say the least. The wise have looked at this issue from various angles. Art, literature, and philosophy raise man to a higher plane. But instead of climbing higher, the layperson drags these higher things down to the ground. This is a typical modern malady but not entirely unknown in the past. Plato was acutely aware of this about 2500 years ago. Mass mediums like radio, recording technology or the printing press were not there to corrupt public taste. But the theatre had made its appearance. And music flowed through theatrical performances. That probably explains why Plato was drawn to the idea of the impact of music on the human mind. According to him, music has a direct impact on the inner self of man. As such, inferior music will formulate man in an inferior way. This, of course, is an overstatement. Modern music has descended to the level it has and yet, despite this, man has not evolved backward into

---

[lx] Whenever there is a decline of righteousness in Bharata.

[lxi] I appear on this earth, age after age.

ape. Is this not enough to prove Plato's opinion as delusional? Of course, those who think that there is more to monkeys than their tails—and here, one does not know what these people think of today's humans—concur with him. Though there were no popular mass mediums like radio, cinema and television during that time, Plato felt quite disturbed at the adulteration of music and its misuse. During his time there was no printing machine, but the script and writing system had already been invented. They were aware of the recently invented printing machine as a great technological marvel, but the system of writing was even greater and more amazing an achievement, though understandably, it was not acknowledged as such in the distant past. A man like Plato could see the darker aspects of great art and technology, which opened up great new vistas before mankind.

* * *

John V. Boulton (1934–early 1990s)[lxii]

'How and Why Sarala Dasa Translated the Mahabharata'

(An excerpt from *Essays on Oriya literature* by John V. Boulton)[1]

Another thing that has amused me about the criticism levelled at Sarala Dasa is the profusion of detail in discussing how he failed faithfully to translate from the Sanskrit original. His failure in this respect is attributable neither to ignorance nor to the inadequacies of the Oriya language. Sarala Dasa was not, as some allege, an ignorant ploughman. He may have sympathized with ploughmen, but he was not one himself. On the contrary, he was an extremely cultivated author. He may or may not have been well-versed in Sanskrit. That question is irrelevant. He obviously had a fantastically retentive memory and had he wanted to, could have reproduced the Mahabharata faithfully. The Oriya language would have been adequate to the task; since a language is always as developed as it needs to be. Had there been a need for a faithful translation, Oriya could have coped.

No, the common sense answer is that Sarala Dasa had no desire for a faithful translation of the Sanskrit the Mahabharata. Nor did his audience, the Oriya public. Sarala Dasa had the intelligence to see what his critics have failed to—namely that Sanskrit was a foreign language, and

---

[lxii] John V Boulton passed away in the early nineties in a mental asylum in London; no specific information is available about the year.

faithful translation is desirable only when the culture in the foreign language and in the indigenous language is virtually the same. Just ask yourselves why it is so easy and desirable to translate Premchand into Oriya and why it is virtually impossible and useless to translate, say, Tennessee Williams. The difference between present-day Hindi and Oriya culture is slight, whereas the difference between the American and Oriya culture is great. Faithful translations from American English into Oriya are academically possible but unlikely to appeal to the Oriya general public, to whom they will seem both alien and irrelevant.

I realize, of course, that it will be painful to admit that in the days of Sarala Dasa, Hindu–Aryan Sanskrit culture was largely alien to the Oriya masses, but it must have been so. Otherwise, the allegedly distorted inaccurate translation of Sarala Dasa would not have become so popular. So there existed in Orissa in Sarala's day, as in yours, two cultures—one alien and the other indigenous. The alien culture was then Sanskritic, it is now English. The only difference is Oriya culture has over the centuries become more and more Sanskritic. This is what has confused modern critics. But there must have been, in Sarala's day, a cultural gap between the Sanskrit-educated elite and the Oriya masses, similar to the difference between the English-educated elite and the Oriya masses today.

This gap would have made a literal translation from Sanskrit into Oriya largely meaningless and irrelevant for Sarala Dasa's audience, and thus, when translating from the alien Sanskrit into the indigenous Oriya, he did what in such circumstances all intelligent authors do—he did not so much translate as adapt; and he did so with astonishing skill. He was, for example, a far more skilful adapter than Radhanatha Ray. Radhanatha Rays's self-imposed task in adapting Greek myths to Oriya circumstances was no greater than Sarala Dasa's in adapting Sanskrit ones. Yet, Radhanatha failed, except with a very limited audience; whereas Sarala Dasa succeeded with almost the entire Oriya nation. Obviously, Sarala understood the temper of his audience far better than Radhanatha. Yet, critics generally say that Sarala Dasa was a ploughman and Radhanatha Ray, a distinguished man of letters!

Let us forget about the alleged inaccuracies and turn to a much more important question: Why did Sarala Dasa attempt to translate, or adapt, the Sanskrit the Mahabharata? He did so, for the same reasons people always do—because the original contained elements that excited him and applied to the situation of himself and his audience. For example, a friend of mine, Syed Shamsul Haque, at the BBC in London, after the struggle for an independent Bangladesh, translated and broadcast serially a Bengali dramatization of the Greek *Odyssey*. He did so not because he wanted to translate from ancient Greek into modern Bengali, but because the basic theme of the *Odyssey* applied to himself and his audience. A hero separated from the native land he had known and loved in days of peace and afterwards left, and to which he was now determined to return, so as to live in peace once more. That was the basic theme which excited him. The basic theme of the Mahabharata excited Sarala Dasa because it seemed to him to apply so neatly to the situation of himself and the Oriya masses.

The basic theme of the Mahabharata as Sarala Dasa saw it, was the futility of civil war and the need to avoid it through compromise for the sake of the country. Thus, Sarala's point of view of the Mahabharata differed immediately and entirely from that of Vyasa, because Sarala saw it from the viewpoint of war-torn Orissa in the reign of Kapilendra Deva, who had come to power by rebellion and was himself forced to put down further rebellions amongst his feudatories. This was the civil war that Sarala Dasa obviously condemned because of the futility of such bloodshed. No one can read Sarala's description of Duryodhana's swim through the river of blood and not be convinced of the futility of such a civil war. Yet Sarala did not condemn *all* war. It is clear, for example, that the Bharata Sarala saw in the Mahabharata was not *Bharatavarsa*,[lxiii] but Orissa, and that Bharata in Sarala's view was clearly *maha* (great), sacred and worth fighting to the last breath for. It is also clear that Sarala Dasa did not condemn the Savaras for fighting to protect their god from King Gala Madhava.[lxiv] On the contrary, he clearly sided with them because what they were fighting for was very much like the *Saktism*[lxv] Sarala himself believed in. And at that time, Sarala and the Oriyas would have fought to the death for that. So what Sarala saw in the Mahabharata were certain elements that excited him—the futility of civil war, the need to avoid it through compromise for the sake of patriotism, but, nevertheless, the need to fight to the death for what you believed in, even if in the end, it involved civil war, i.e. he saw in the Mahabharata a vehicle for expressing a dire warning about a possible clash between the adherents of two cultures; the alien Sanskritic and the indigenous Oriya, and about the need to avoid that clash through compromise. This is what I believe he was trying to say through the theme and countertheme, which I shall now attempt to describe.

[lxiii] Bharatvarsha is a translation of the Vedic word Bharata, which signifies Bharata's homeland. The phrase had its beginnings in the Vedic era. It later developed during the Epic and Puranic ages. Eventually, the same geographic area was referred to as Hindustan.

[lxiv] Sarala Dasa has also narrated a few episodes that are not available in the original Sanskrit the Mahabharata.

[lxv] Saktism established itself as a separate cult in the early part of Orissa's history with the emergence of famous brahman and non-brahman worshippers.

Ganeswar Mishra (1942–2015)

'My Mother'

(Translated 'Bou' from the Odia by Jatindra Kumar Nayak)

Covered in a reed mat, a corpse lay on the earthen floor. Crying inconsolably, 'O my Gauri, O my Gauri', an old woman rolled on the ground as a few women tried to comfort her. But their words brought no solace to her, and she kept rolling on the ground.

I watched the scene unfold, standing a little distance away from all this and not crying. A little later, a few men came in and carried the corpse away. I don't remember what happened after this. I went and sat in a room in the rear end of the house. A woman from the neighbouring house brought me some food in a small bowl.

I was about four at the time. The woman lying dead on the floor was my mother and the old woman wailing bitterly was my maternal grandmother. This incident took place about forty years ago in Sri Purushottampur in Puri district.

I was born in that village. When the time to deliver a baby drew near, women usually came to their maternal homes and that is how I was born, in my maternal uncle's house. On a wall of the room in which my mother breathed her last, was drawn a holy rectangle. A few cowry shells were stuck into it. This was the abode of goddess Satthi. This house has now crumbled and been reduced to an empty lot and the abode of goddess Satthi is mingled with the dust.

True, I did not cry when my mother passed away; but as I grow older, tears rise to my eyes whenever I think of her. But I have never let anyone see me break down and cry.

I cannot remember my mother's face. Only a few blurred images wrapped in mist would rise before my eyes: my mother sweeping the floor with a broom while holding me in her arms; I, my mother and her mother sitting beside a fire pot on the verandah on a winter evening. It was dark outside and the sound of jackals howling far away filled me with dread and the boil on my hip hurt.

I vividly recall throwing some puffed rice on my mother, for I was angry with her for some reason and even screaming at her, 'You die!'

I do not remember how old she was when she died. I never asked my father about her. It has been eighteen years since my father died too, and now I have turned fifty. My mother's elder sister, my aunt, is still alive. She is over eighty now but is good at remembering dates and years. But even she cannot tell me how old my mother was when she died.

I don't have my mother's photograph or her horoscope. The box my mother had brought to her in-laws' house was lying on a shelf in Pathuriasahi in Puri, but it is no longer to be found. My father had kept a pair of silver bangles my mother used to wear for a long time in a wooden almirah. These, too, are gone.

One day, I came across a yellowed piece of paper in a rubbish heap. On it was written—Annotation copy; Gauri Devi; Student of class III; Sri Purushottampur Upper Primary School, 1935, and the picture of a boat adorned the bottom of the page.

I wondered how this piece of paper had found its way to our house! It seems my mother had brought her school textbooks and notebooks to her in-laws' place after her marriage. From this piece of paper, which had somehow survived, I learned that my mother had studied up to class III. If she were eight to nine years old when she was a class III student, she must have been born around 1927. I once chanced upon a slim book titled *Odisha Naibadhi Kahani* (The Tale of a Flood in Odisha) in our house. The book was published in 1937. That means my mother may have read the book. Why else should she have brought the book with her to her in-laws' house?

Others have told me that my father was away in a far-off village to attend a fair when my mother passed away. My mother died of cholera soon after giving birth to my younger sister. On receiving the news, my father reached Sri Purushottampur two or three days after his wife's death. He returned to his two-room thatched house in Pathuriasahi in Puri, bringing me and my younger sister with him. My father had married rather late in life and lost his wife only six years after his marriage. Now in the house were left my father, my grandmother, myself and my little sister. My grandfather's sister took upon herself the responsibility of raising my younger sister, who went to live with her until she got married. Our family now comprised three members: me, my father and my grandmother.

My father stayed with me till I went to England for the first time at the age of thirty-two. In all the time that I spent studying, finding a job, getting married or having children, my father was with me. But I wondered why he never mentioned my mother. Now that I am writing about my mother, if he were alive, I could have asked him to furnish a few details about her.

I have heard others say that my father cried uncontrollably sitting on a stone verandah after my mother died. It is impossible for me to imagine my father breaking down and shedding tears, for he was someone who was given to laugh heartily but could never cry. He visited my maternal uncle's house several times after my mother's death. I have seen him share jokes with the people of that village and burst into joyous laughter. He would never express his grief and sense of loss to anyone.

Every year, the death anniversary of my mother would be observed on the twelfth day of the bright fortnight of the month of *Chaitra*[lxvi]. In those days, my father would ask me to take a bath early in the morning and he would invite to our house a brahman and offer him rice flakes and bananas. Now that he is no more, my mother's death anniversary is not observed any longer.

It is true that he often used to visit my mother's village, but after her death, he never liked me paying a visit to that place. Of course, he was scared of the village where his wife had met an untimely death and always feared that if I went there, I might contract the same disease. On my part, I was extremely fond of my mother's village, Sri Purushottampur. The thought of making a trip to that village during my school holidays filled me with excitement. No matter how many times my father discouraged and stopped me from visiting that village, I went there many times during my childhood. I have a lot of fun memories of that place.

I do not find it easy to say how my mother's death affected me and shaped my life. A strange feeling of emptiness and an aching loneliness has been haunting me since my childhood. I was deprived of the courage to face the world that mothers are able to instil in their children. I may have become self-sufficient, but the price I paid for this was loneliness. As I had lost my mother very early in my life, I always felt scared of losing someone near and dear. This fear has impacted my life and personality to a great extent.

One night after I had recently married, my wife woke me up and asked, 'What happened? Why are you crying?'

[lxvi] Months of March–April.

I had dreamt that my wife had died and started crying inconsolably. I recounted the dream to her, and she reassured me, 'Don't worry, I am not going to die so soon.' She consoled me, smiling.

It could be that the untimely death of my mother must be the reason why I saw such dreams.

* * *

About the Contributors

Authors

Akhila Naik (1970–2021) was a poet and academic. His published poetry collections are *Gadhuabela* (1993), *Gulikhati* (1996), *Dhobapharaphara* (2001) and *Dhin* (2008). His novel, *Bheda*, dealt with caste hegemony, cultural subjugation and social discrimination, and was translated into Indian languages including English.

Akhil Mohan Patnaik (1927–87) was an influential short-story writer and editor in Odia. A lawyer by profession, he was involved in many literary activities.

Akshaya Bahibala (b. 1980) is a poet and writer. His book *Bhang Journeys* was published in March 2024. He is the co-founder of the iconic independent bookstore, Walking BookFairs, and lives with his cats and partner in Bhubaneswar.

Ananta Patnaik (1912–87) was a poet and leading Marxist leader. He was co-founder of the literary organization Nabayuga Sahitya Sansad (New Age Literary Society).

Anuja Mohan Pradhan (b. 1969) speaks and writes in the Kui language. He has published three books of poems, one short story book, a learning handbook, and more than fifteen papers on Kui culture, language and orthography in different journals and magazines. Pradhan is currently working as the controller of finance and accounts at CSIR-National Environmental Engineering Research Institute (NEERI), Nagpur.

Arjun Charan Hembram (b. 1952) worked as a branch head with the State Bank of India. He has written Santali books like *Lade Sarjom* (1984) and *Chiki Gaban* (1984), and is also associated with various literary organizations like All India Santali Writers' Association and Adivasi Socio-Educational and Cultural Association.

Balarama Dasa 1472–1556 was educated, well-versed in Sanskrit and grew to be proficient in both Odia and Sanskrit. He wrote the *Jagamohana Ramayana*, which is also known as *Dandi Ramayana*. There were five saint poets we call *panchasakha* (five friends) and Balarama Dasa was the eldest among them.

Banamali Dasa (1720–93), considered the foremost poet of the medieval Odia bhakti literature, is known for such lyrics/poems like 'Dinabandhu daitari', 'Kete chhanda jane lo sahi' and 'Manima he etiki maguni mora'. His songs are popularly sung in festivals, public gatherings and in Odissi dance. He spent most of his life in Puri.

Banshidhar Sarangi (b. 1940) has published eleven collections of poems. For over thirty years, he taught Odia language and literature in various colleges. He also published *Selected Poems* in English translation and *Swarodaya* in Hindi translation. He received the Odisha Sahitya Akademi Award in 1991 and an award from India's National Academy of Letters in 2006.

Bepin Vehari Roy (1887–1975) was an acclaimed essayist in Odia literature.

Bhagabati Charan Panigrahi (1908–43) was an Odia writer and the founding secretary of the Communist Party of India in Odisha. He wrote around a dozen short stories before he was mysteriously murdered while under arrest by British India Police in 1943. He was a close associate of Netaji Subhas Chandra Bose. His story, 'Shikar', was made in a film called *Mrigaya* by Mrinal Sen.

Bhanuji Rao (1926–2001) was a well-known poet. The grandson of the eminent poet Bhaktakavi Madhusudan

Rao, he was one of the poets who brought new poetry into Odia literature. He was also awarded the Sahitya Akademi Award (1989) for his poetry collection *Nai Arapari* (Across the River).

Bharat Majhi (b. 1972) is a poet, editor and translator. He works in a media house in Bhubaneswar and has nine poetry collections to his credit.

Bhima Bhoi (1850–95) was a saint, poet, mystic and social reformer from Odisha. He was a follower of Mahima Swami, and his teachings and poetry were deeply influenced by Mahima Dharma, a monotheistic religious movement in Odisha.

Bibek Jena (1937–85) was a poet with two anthologies to his name. He played cricket for Odisha and was in the Indian Audit and Accounts service (1960–85).

Bidhubhushan Das (1922–99) was a public intellectual, educator, professor and senior government official. He was the vice chancellor of Utkal University for a brief period in 1977. Das received his education from Columbia University, Oxford University and Patna University.

Bijay Prasad Mahapatra (1938–2013) was a linguist, academic and acclaimed fiction writer.

Binapani Mohanty (1936–2022) was a short-story writer who taught economics in various colleges. She won the Sahitya Akademi Award (1990) for *Patadei* and the Sarala Award (2010). She was honoured with the Atibadi Jagannath Das Samman (2019) by Odisha Sahitya Akademi and the Padma Shri (2020).

King Birakishore (1737–93) was a prominent lyrical poet of the medieval period, known for his hymns and prayers to Lord Jagannath that arrest the attention of the reader for their devotion, lyrical flow and cadence.

Biswajit Das (1936–2004) was an Odia playwright, short-story writer, film and play director, and scriptwriter. An experimental and contemporary Odia dramatist, he was one of the pioneers of the New Theatre Movement (1960–80). Das wrote more than sixty one-act plays, which include *Chhadmabeshi*, *Tandra*, *Dahini*, *Show*, *Chief Guest*, *Probesh-Prasthan* and *Kitta*. His play *Nalipana Rani Kalapana Tika* was staged by Rupakar Theatre Group in 1968 and received the Odisha Sangeet Natak Akademi Awards in four out of five categories: best play, best director, best actor (Ajit Kar) and best actress (Sandhya Mohapatra). *Mrugaya* was his most acclaimed play.

Biswanath Kar (1864–1934) was a teacher, eminent essayist and the author of *Vividha Prabandha*, a compilation of his timeless essays in Odia. 'Swadhina Chinta', 'Asha', 'Mahasrota', 'Swadhinata', 'Rakshyasalila', 'Stri Sikshya', 'Annanta Prema' were his outstanding gifts to Odia literature. He was the editor of *Utkal Sahitya* for about four decades.

Chandramohan Maharana (1870–1929) was an acclaimed essayist in Odia literature.

Chandrasekhar Rath (1929–2018) was a prolific author who wrote fourteen short story collections, fifteen essay books, devotional essays and three novels that fetched him the Odisha Sahitya Akademi Award (1973), Sahitya Akademi Award (1997), Hutch Crossword Book Award (2004) and the Atibadi Jagannath Das Samman (2010). He was honoured with the Padma Shri but could not receive it as he passed away. Rath was an academic and served as the secretary of the Test Book Bureau before retiring as the deputy director of public instruction.

Chittaranjan Das (1923–2011) was an essayist, critic, public intellectual, globetrotter and a staunch follower of Aurobindo ideology. Among more than the 100 books he has written,

Jatire Mu Jaban and *Biswaku Gabakshya* (for which he got the Sahitya Akademi Award in 1998), are treated as milestones.

Damayanti Beshra (b. 1962) has served in the Department of Higher Education, Government of Odisha in various colleges and retired as the principal of Maharaja Purna Chandra Autonomous College, Baripada, in 2023. She has contributed to both Santali and Odia literature, and was honoured with the Padma Shri in 2020.

Dash Benhur, nee Jitendra Narayan Dash (b. 1953), is a well-known author in Odia. Several of his works have been translated into English, Hindi and Bengali. He is the recipient of the Odisha Sahitya Akademi Award (1987), NCERT Prize for Children's Literature (1989), Odisha Vigyan Academy Popular Science-Writer Award (1999) and Sahitya Akademi Bal Sahitya Puraskar (2014).

Dinakrushna Dasa (1650–1710) was a poet and ardent devotee of Lord Jagannath, known for his fearlessness, courage, and moral conviction. He is well-known for his remarkably long poem 'Rasakallola', which describes the divine leela of Lord Krishna in thirty-four melodious cantos, each line of the cantos beginning with the initial sound 'Ka', the first consonant in the Sanskrit and Odia languages.

Dipti Ranjan Pattanaik (b. 1961) is a prolific writer of fiction, essays and literary criticism. He did his research on children's literature at Ohio State University, USA, on a Fulbright fellowship (1996–97), participated in Cambridge University Young Authors' seminar (2000) on a Charles Wallace-British Council fellowship, and received the Indo-Shastri Canadian fellowship (2009) in the field of translation studies. He received the Erikson Scholar in Residence (2011), the Katha Award (1994) and the Odisha State Sahitya Akademi Award (2013). He teaches at Banaras Hindu University.

Fakir Mohan Senapati (1843–1918), often referred to as Utkala Byasa Kabi (Odisha's Vyasa), was a poet, fiction writer, philosopher and social reformer. His 'Rebati' is considered to be the first story in Odia and his novel, *Chha Man Ataha Guntha (Six and a Third Acres)* is a milestone. Senapati played a leading role in establishing the distinct identity of Odia and is regarded as the father of Odia nationalism and modern Odia literature.

Ganeswar Mishra (1942–2015) was a well-known author, academic, translator and editor. He wrote fiction and non-fiction, and edited about sixty academic and creative books in Odia and English. He won several awards, including the Odisha Sahitya Akademi Award, and distinctions for his literary and academic achievements. Mishra was educated at Utkal (MA), Kent (PhD) and London (post-doc) universities and taught English literature at Utkal for decades, where he was a professor from 1986 till his retirement in 2002. He was president of Odisha Sahitya Akademi, managing editor of *The Samaja* and founding editor of *Prameya* (both leading Odia dailies).

Gangadhar Meher (1862–1924) was a prominent Odia poet of the nineteenth century. Though poor in wealth and education, he remained one of the most prolific and original contributors to Odia literature.

Gayatribala Panda (b. 1977) is an Odia poet, fiction writer, literary critic, essayist, academician and editor. The author of twenty-eight books, she is the recipient of the Kendra Sahitya Akademi Puraskar in Odia for her poetry collection *Dayanadi* (River Daya) in 2022, the first Kendra Sahitya Akademi Yuva Puraskar in Odia for her poetry collection *Gaan* (The Village) in 2011 among other awards.

Girija Sankar Ray (1886–1967) was a critic of eminence in Odia. His works, 'Sahitya Sadarbha' (1933), 'Sarala Bhasatattwa' (1942) and 'Odia Natyakala' (1943) are milestones in literary criticism of Odia literature.

Gobinda Tripathy (1899–1962) was an administrator and author of a few essays in Odia literature. His most readable piece was 'Batua' (Cloth Wallet), in which he criticized foreign influence and advocated for rootedness.

Godabarish Mohapatra (1898–1965) was a story writer, poet and journalist. He was best known as the editor of *Niankhunta*, a monthly magazine of criticism, humour and politics. His books include *Kalama* (1951), *Handishalare Biplaba* (1952), *Kenta O Phula* (1958), and *Banka O Sidha* (1958). He was honoured with the Odisha Sahitya Akademi Award in 1959 and 1962, and posthumously with the Sahitya Akademi Award (1965) for *Banka O Sidha*.

Golok Behari Dhall (1921–74) was an author, academic, translator, essayist, linguist, travelogue and children's litterateur. He is known for his books, *Manishara Bhasa*, *Dhani Bigyan*, *Odia Kebe*, *Ramarajya O Ramayan*, *Godan* (tr.), *Landan Chithi* and *Amerika Anubhuti*.

Gopabandhu Das (1877–1928), popularly known as Utkalamani Gopabandhu Das (Jewel of Odisha) was a social worker, reformer, political activist, journalist, poet and essayist. He was the founder and editor of *The Samaja*, the oldest and most highly circulated newspaper in Odia, and the architect of modern Odisha.

Gopalakrusna Pattanayaka (1784–1862) was an Odia poet and composer of Odissi music. His Odissi songs in various traditional ragas and talas are widely sung across the state as well as other allied traditional art forms of Odisha, such as pala.

Gopalchandra Praharaj (1872–1945) was a lexicographer and a lawyer under the training of Madhusudan Das. He is remembered as the illustrious compiler of *Purnachandra Odia Bhasakosh*, which is a seminal contribution to the development of the Odia language and is a potential marker of the Odia identity.

Gopinath Mohanty (1914–1991) was a prolific Odia writer of the mid-twentieth century. He was the recipient of the Sahitya Akademi Award (1955) and several other prestigious awards, including the Soviet Land Nehru Award (1970), the Jnanapith Award (1973) and the Padma Bhushan (1981). His works include twenty-four novels, ten collections of short stories, one book of poetry, two collections of essays, a couple of plays, three biographical works, five works on tribal culture and his incomplete autobiography.

Gourahari Das (b. 1960) is a popular author, translator and editor. He has published over seventy-five books, including novels, short stories, plays and vignettes. Many of his major works have been translated into other Indian languages. The feature film *Pratiksha* made based on his story has won a national award (2021). He works for *Sambad*, a premier daily in Odisha, and has the distinction of having received two awards from Sahitya Akademi.

Gourishankar Roy (1838–1917) was born in a Bengali family but received informal education in Oriya, Urdu and Persian. He worked in the commissioner's office, Cuttack. He also set up the Cuttack Printing Company and started editing *Utkal Deepika*, a weekly newspaper, for the people of Odisha.

Guruprasad Mohanty (1924–2004) was a member of the Odisha Education Service and retired from service as the principal of B.J.B. College, Bhubaneswar. Regarded as the T.S. Eliot of modern Odia literature, he wrote sixty-eight poems during his lifetime.

Monhanty authored 'Nutan Kavita' (1955), 'Samudra Snana' (1970), 'Ascharya Abhisara' (1988) and 'Kavita Samagra' (1995). He received the Sahitya Akademi Award (1973) for his 'Samudra Snana'.

Haldhar Nag (b. 1950) is a prolific poet with several volumes in the Sambalpuri-Kosali language to his name. His works have been translated into English, Hindi, Nepali, Bengali, Kannada, Punjabi and Tamil languages. He was conferred with the Padma Shri in 2016 and holds an honorary doctorate from Sambalpur University.

Hrushikesh Mallick (b. 1955) is an acclaimed poet, critic, editor and academic in the Odia language. He received the Sarala Puraskar (2016) and Sahitya Akademi Award (2021) for his poetry collection *Sarijaithiba Apera*. He was the president of the Odisha Sahitya Akademi from 2021–24.

Jadumani Beshra (1964–2022) was a prominent Santali poet and received the Sahitya Akademi Award (2005). He worked as an accountant under the Kharagpur railway division. His books include *Bhabna, Onarhe Mohok, Jiyon Gada* and *Onol Mala* (edited).

Jagadish Mohanty (1951–2013) was a trendsetter in Odia short fiction. He published thirteen collections of short stories out of which two, *South-Facing House* and *Album*, are available in English. He also wrote five novels, including *Nija Nija Panipatha*, which has been published as *Battles of Our Own* (2022).

Jagan Mohan Lal (1838–1913) was an actor, playwright, administrator and social reformer. He is regarded as the first playwright in Odia. His works include *Babaji, Brahma Bhajana* and *Bruddha Bibaha.*

Jagannatha Dasa (1491–1550) was a saint poet and great Sanskrit scholar. His standalone *Bhagabata*, written in *nabakshari* (nine alphabets) style is considered the most revered epic in Odisha till today.

Jagannath Prasad Das (b. 1936) is an eminent Odia poet, playwright, essayist and fiction writer. Based on his extensive research into Odishan art, he has published three works on the pictorial arts of the state. His writings have been widely translated into Hindi, English and other Indian languages. He has also translated literary works from different languages into Odia and English. He has been the recipient of many awards including the Odisha Sahitya Akademi Award (1981), Sahitya Akademi Award (1990) and the Saraswati Samman (2006) for the poetry collection *Parikrama*.

Sri Jayadeva (twelfth century) was the prominent poet of the epic poem 'Gita Govinda [Song of the Cowherd (Krishna)]' in Sanskrit. He was born in the village Kenduli by river Prachi in present-day Odisha and married to Padmavati. His songs were performed regularly in the temple of Jagannath in Puri.

Jayanta Mahapatra (1928–2023) was a celebrated poet in the English and Odia languages. Extensively published around the world, Mahapatra has more than thirty books to his credit and received the Sahitya Akademi Award in 1981 for his poetry collection, *Relationship*.

John V. Boulton (1934–*) was the author of *Essays on Oriya Literature* and an academic in the School of Oriental and African Studies of the University of London. He was admitted to a mental asylum and is believed to have passed away there.

* Year of death unknown.

Kalindi Charan Panigrahi (1901–91) was a noted Odia poet, novelist, story writer, dramatist and essayist. Famous for his magnum opus *Matira Manisha*, he has been awarded the Padma Bhushan (1971) for his contribution to Odia literature.

Kamadev Moharana (b. 1979) is a poet and author with three poetry collections: *Kabi* (2015), *Chhai Saha Sabudina* (2016) and *Coffee Bagicha* (2018). A literary activist, he is involved with the editing of *Anam* magazine and curating of the Puri Literature Festival.

Kanheilal Das (1947–75) was a prolific short-story writer who created a sensation during the eighties in Odia literature and died untimely at the age of twenty-eight.

Kanhupa (tenth century CE) is a mystic poet of *Charyapada*, a tantric Buddhist period who wrote poems in code languages. He was also a prominent *siddhacharya* (who achieved a high degree of perfection of the intellect and liberation or enlightenment) to Nath Sampradaya after Matsyendranatha and Gorakhnath.

Kishen Pattnaik (1930–2004) was an Indian social leader, public intellectual, socialist thinker, author and activist. As a member of parliament for the third Lok Sabha, he represented the Praja Socialist Party for the Sambalpur Constituency. Pattnaik also founded and edited a Hindi monthly periodical called *Samayik Varta*.

Kishori Charan Das (1924–2004) was a leading author in Odia, who received the Sahitya Akademi Award (1976) for a short-story collection, *Thakura Ghara*. He was also the president of the Odisha Sahitya Akademi from 1994 to 1997.

Krushna Chandra Panigrahi (1909–87) was a research scholar specializing in pottery at the Archaeological Survey of India (ASI) and a lecturer of history until 1947. He then switched careers to become the curator of the Orissa Museum between 1947 and 1951, before returning to teaching again. He retired as a professor of history (1968). He received the Padma Shri (1976) and Odisha Sahitya Akademi Award (1983) for his autobiography, *Mo Samaya ra Odisha.*

Kumar Mohanty (1941–95) was an anti-establishment poet, editor and police officer who initiated and led *Anam Kabya Andolan* (Anam Poetry Movement) in 1969 in Puri. During the Emergency in India, he wrote poems criticizing the government and was placed under suspension. *Anam Bayara Geeta* and *Anam Chhanda* are two of his poetry collections.

Kuntala Kumari Sabat (1901–38) was a doctor proficient in four languages i.e. Odia, Hindi, Bengali and English. She was a poet, novelist and social reformer who was published in reputed literary magazines like *Utkala Sahitya, Sahakara* and *Mukura.* She came under the influence of Mahatma Gandhi and wrote against child marriage, inequality, caste discrimination, and purdah, as well as for widow remarriage, emancipation of women, equality and social justice.

Laxmikanta Mohapatra (1888–1953) was a poet, writer, performance artist and freedom fighter. He was a leading campaigner of the Odisha State unification movement and an eminent member of Utkala Sammilani. 'Bande Utkal Janani', a poem he wrote, was chosen as the state anthem by the Government of Odisha. He has ten books to his credit.

Madhusudan Das (1848–1934) was the first graduate and advocate of Orissa, and a social reformer who founded Utkal Sammilani in 1903 to campaign for the unification of Odisha along with its social and industrial development. He was one of the prominent figures who helped in the creation of modern Odisha.

Madhusudan Rao (1853–1912) was a well-known poet and author of the popular book, *Chhabila Madhu Barnabodha.*

He was a prominent Odia poet and essayist, who published two volumes, one each in 1873 and 1874, of collections of poems entitled *Kavitabali* in collaboration with Radhanath Ray. Apart from writing essays, he translated a few works from Sanskrit and English into Odia. They were published in *Utkal Darpan,* a literary journal.

Mangalucharan Biswal (1935–2022) had written plays, poems, stories, novels, essays and children's literature in Odia and Sambalpuri-Kosali languages. His play *Bhukha*, made into a Koshli Sambalpuri film, was the first to get an international jury award at the Gijon International Film Festival in 1990. He was a teacher by profession and was conferred with an honorary DLitt degree from Sambalpur University for his contribution to literature.

Manoj Das (1934–2021) was one of the finest and most prolific authors of fiction in Odia and English. A recipient of the Sahitya Akademi Award (1972) and Saraswati Samman (2000), Das was a follower of Sri Aurobindo ideology. His stories are widely read and translated.

Mayadhar Mansinha (1905–73) was a romantic poet, academic, critic and scholar of eminence. Some of his major works include *Dhupa, Hemasashya, Konarka*, *Ei Sahakar, Tale and Saga of the Land of Lord Jagannath*.

Mohini Mohan Senapati (1881–1945) was a well-known critic, academic, essayist, thinker and admirer of Western thinker Nietzsche. He was the son of Fakir Mohan Senapati. Under the influence of illustrious authors like Nandakishore Bal, Radhanath Ray and Madhusudan Rao, he turned into an atheist and iconoclast.

Nandakishore Bal (1875–1928) was a poet of the era of initial modernity in Odia poetry. He is popularly known as *Palli Kabi* (the poet of rural life) for his tender lyrics, celebrating the beauty of rural Odisha in his poems. His popular lyrics for children,

'Nana Baya Gita' are sung to the accompaniment of music as lullabies. His other works include 'Nirjharini' (The Stream), 'Palli Chitra' (The Picture of Countryside) and 'Sarmishtha'.

Natabar Samantaray (1918–2000) was an acclaimed writer, literary critic and academic. Some of his known literary-historical works are *Odia Sahityara Itihasa*, *Adhunika Odia Sahityara Bhittibhumi* and *Vyasakabi Fakirmohan*. His critical review included works of many noted Odia authors like Fakir Mohan Senapati and Radhanath Ray.

Nikhilesh Mishra (b. 1996) is a poet, writer, translator and filmmaker. His books, *Kehi Jane Kejani Kouthi* (2018) and *Kabitie Marigala Pare* (2021) have been shortlisted for the Sahitya Akademi Yuva Puraskar four times in the last three years. An alumnus of Ravenshaw University and JNU, he currently studies at the Satyajit Ray Film and Television Institute, Kolkata.

Niranjan Mohanty (1953–2008) was an academic in Visva Bharati, Santiniketan, a translator and an Indian poet writing in English. His works include *Life Lines, A House of Rains* and *White Whispers*.

Nirmala Devi (1907–89) was a poet and author known for three poetry collections, *Deenantay, Seemantay* and *Barnaraag*. Nirmala Devi was awarded the Odisha State Sahitya Akademi Award for *Barnaraag* in 1985.

Paresh Kumar Patnaik (b. 1960) is a well-known and prolific author with twenty-two story collections and three novels to his credit. He received the Odisha Sahitya Akademi Award in 2009.

Prabhat Mukherjee (1914–84) retired as a reader at the Department of History, Utkal University, Bhubaneswar. He wrote books primarily on the history of the Orissan region, notably, *History of Medieval Vaishnavism in Orissa* (1940), *History of the Gajpati Kings of Orissa* (1953), *History of the*

Freedom Movement in Orissa Vol. II (1957), *The Buddhist Remains in Orissa* (1961), *History of Orissa in the 19th Century* (1964) and *The History of the Jagannath Temple in the 19th Century* (1977).

Prafulla Kumar Tripathy (b. 1945) is a prolific poet and short-story writer in Odia and Sambalpuri-Kosali. Involved in designing the spellchecker and predictive lexicon for the Odia and Sambalpuri-Kosali languages, he was the recipient of the Odisha Sahitya Akademi Award (1980).

Pranabandhu Kar (1914–98) was a playwright and short-story writer. An author of thirty-five plays and fifty-one short stories, he was a champion of women's emancipation. He was the recipient of the Odisha Sahitya Akademi Award (1980) and the Sangeet Natak Akademi Award (1968).

Pratibha Ray (b. 1944) is an eminent fiction writer in Odia with more than seventy-two books to her credit. Her novel *Yagyaseni* has been widely translated into English, Bengali, Hindi, Telugu, Tamil, Malayalam, Assamese, etc. She received the Sahitya Akademi Award (2000) for her short story collection, *Ullanghana*, and is a recipient of the prestigious Jnanpith Award (2011). Ray was honoured with the Padma Shri (2007) and Padma Bhushan (2022) by the government of India.

Pratibha Satpathy (b. 1945) is a poet and author of *Asta Janhara Elegy* (1969), *Grasta Samaya* (1974), *Sahada Sundari* (1978), *Niyata Vasudha* (1980), *Nimishe Akshara* (1985), *Kahi Na Hele* (2006). She has received the Sahitya Akademi Award (2001), Sarala Award (1992) and N. N. Thirumalambha Award (1999).

Purna Chandra Hembram (b. 1964) is a Santali poet. He has published two Santali books, holds a master of technology degree and is presently working in a *Maharatna* company[i] based in New Delhi.

Rabi Patnaik (1935–91) was an acclaimed author of *Andhagalira Andhakara*, *Ragatodi*, *Hiranya Garbha*, *Amarilata* and *Asamajikara Dairy*. He received the Sahitya Akademi Award for *Bichitrabarna* in 1992.

Rabi Singh (1931–2020) was a firebrand poet and writer. An author of more than fifty books, he was a journalist and known as Nazrul of Odisha. He was also the vice president of Odisha Sahitya Akademi (1997–99).

Radhamohan Gadanayak (1911–2000) was a poet known for his ballads and poetic creations. A recipient of the Sahitya Akademi Award (1975) for *Surya O Andhakar*, he was honoured with the Padma Shri in 1990.

Radhanath Ray (1848–1908) was an eminent poet of the initial modernity era in Odia poetry during the later part of the nineteenth century. He was born in a zamindar family in Baleshwar (Bengal Presidency), now in Odisha. In his early life, he wrote in both Odia and Bengali languages but later shifted his writings to Odia only. He contributed verses and epics for Odia literature in the nineteenth century.

Pandit Raghunath Murmu (1905–82) was a Santali writer and educator. Until the nineteenth century, Santali people had no written language and knowledge was transmitted orally from one generation to another. It was he who developed the Ol Chiki script for the Santali language.

[i] Maharatna companies are major companies in India granted substantial autonomy and authority by the government of India. The term *maharatna*, meaning 'a great jewel', highlights the immense value these companies hold for both the nation and on a global scale.

Rajkishore Patnaik (1917–97) earned his BSc from Ravenshaw College (1938) and LLM from Banaras Hindu University (1944), and started his legal practice. He also taught at the Law College, Cuttack, for about five years. His works include *Sindura Gara* (1943), *Ashranti* (1944), *Smritiramanasi* (1944), *Panjuri Pakhi* (1945) *Hrudayara Bandhan* (1945), *Pathuki* (1948), *Salagrama* (1955), *Kalpnarafula* (1958), *Patharadhima* (1963) and *Hata Bahuda* (1974).

Ramakanta Rath (b. 1934) is a renowned poet who experiments greatly with form and style. He received the Sahitya Akademi Award (1977) for 'Saptam Ritu', Saraswati Samman (1992) and the Padma Bhushan (2006). He was the vice president of the Sahitya Akademi from 1993 to 1998 and the president from 1998 to 2003. He also served in the Indian Administrative Service (1957–92).

Ratnamala Swain (b. 1967) is an architect, entrepreneur, Odia poet, translator and editor. The former editor of the literary magazine *Chitra* for over two decades, she has translated the works of playwrights such as Badal Circar, Girish Karnad, Mohan Rakesh, Utpal Dutt, Indira Parthasarathy, Krishna Sobti and Sushma Deshpande.

Reba Ray (1876–1957) was the first woman short-story writer in Odia, a poet, educationist and administrator. She was also the founder of the Model Girls' School, Cuttack. Her short story 'Sanyasi' is considered the earliest modern Odia short story by a woman. Ray founded a woman's magazine *Asha* in 1892.

Sachidananda Routray (1916–2004) was a prolific poet, novelist and short-story writer in Odia, and is regarded as the father of modernism in Odia poetic canon. A recipient of the Sahitya Akademi Award for *Kabita 1962* and Jnanpith Award, the highest literary award of India, in 1986, RoutRay is known for his long poem 'Baji Rout'. He has published as many as twenty anthologies.

Salabega (early seventeenth century–1608) was a saint poet. Muslim by birth but a staunch devotee of Jagannatha, he wrote *bhajans*[ii] in praise of the Lord. 'Ahe Nila Saila' is the most popular among them.

Santanu Kumar Acharya (b. 1933) is a well-known author, academic and public speaker. He is the author of a brilliant novel, *Nara Kinnar*, and received the Sahitya Akademi Award for *Chalanti Thakura* in 1993.

Sadananda Kabirsurya Brahma (1720–90) was a medieval Odia poet. An erudite Sanskrit scholar, he renounced worldly life on initiation into the Vaishnava faith of the Suddha Bhakti school and travelled widely as a preacher of the faith.

Sahadev Sahoo (b. 1959) is a writer and columnist. His books are *Kasatandira Swapna* (2003), *Lata Pramoda O Anyamane* (2007), *Head Office* (2021) and *Anicchuk Prashasaka* (2021). He has been honoured with the Bishub Jhankar Galpa Samman (2009), Fakir Mohan Upanyas Samman (2019) and Akhil Mohan Katha Samman (2021).

Sarat Kumar Mohanty (1938–2006) is a leading essayist, academic and a publisher. *Gandhi Manisha* is one of his major works.

Sarala Dasa, nee Siddheswara Parida (fifteenth century AD) was known as the *adi kabi* (first poet) of Odia literature. He was an author of magnum opuses in Odia like the Mahabharata, the Vilanka Ramayana and the Chandi Purana. There are

---

[ii] Poems set to music in praise of god.

several indications in his Mahabharata that he served as a soldier in the army of the Gajapati King of Odisha.

Sarangadhar Pradhan (1922–2012) was born in the village Jhimangia in Kandhmal district. The first MLA of G. Udayagiri constituency, he is the author of *Kai Bhakta Gitika*, *Jyada Yahar* and *Tribhasi Kai Bayakaran*, a book on Kui grammar in the Kui language. He was also instrumental in bringing out the Kui workbook by the Academy of Tribal Language and Culture, Bhubaneswar, and assisted several researchers in Kui language and culture.

Satya Dash (b. 1991) is a recipient of the Srinivas Rayaprol Poetry Prize and a finalist for the Broken River Prize. His poems appear in *Ninth Letter*, *Denver Quarterly*, *Poet Lore*, *Prairie Schooner*, *Cincinnati Review* and Diagram, among others. Apart from having a degree in electronics from BITS Pilani-Goa, Dash has been a cricket commentator. He grew up in Cuttack and now lives in Bengaluru.

Satya Misra (b. 1952) has authored four volumes of Odia short stories and contributed a few stories to various English magazines. He was awarded the Bishuba Award for short stories in 2016 and lives in Bhubaneswar.

Satya Mohanty (b. 1957) is a poet, playwright, novelist and prose writer in English. A former union secretary of education and a regular columnist in a wide range of national newspapers, he has published two volumes of poetry and a book of plays.

Satyanarayan Bohidar (1913–80) was a high-school teacher and prolific poet in the Sambalpuri-Kosali language. *SriPanchami* (1953), *Ghubukudu* (1964), *Ghabghabo* (1969) and *Tikchahanra* (1986) are among his notable books of poems. He was honoured by Odisha Sahitya Akademi (1971).

Sitakant Mahapatra (b. 1937) is a prolific and leading postmodern poet in Odia literature. Widely translated into Indian and foreign languages, Mahapatra has received several prestigious awards, including the Sahitya Akademi Award (1974) for *Sabdara Akash*, Jnanpith Award (1993), Padma Vibhushan (2010) and Atibadi Jagannath Das Samman (2022).

Soubhagya Kumar Misra (b. 1941) is a poet who retired as a professor of English from Berhampur University in 2001. Misra has published twenty books of poems and one short fiction. He is a recipient of the Odisha Sahitya Akademi Award for *Andha Mahumachhi* (1979) and *Dwa Suparna* (1986), Gangadhar Meher National Award (2011), and Odisha Governor's Plaque of Honor.

Sourindra Barik (1938–2016) was an academic and well-known poet who received the Sahitya Akademi Award for his poetry collection, *Akash Pari Nibida*, in 1988.

Suniti Kumar Chatterji (1890–1977) was an Indian linguist, educationist and litterateur. A distinguished scholar, he was the recipient of the second-highest Indian civilian honour, the Padma Vibhushan in 1955. He taught English in the postgraduate department of the University of Calcutta (1914–19).

Surendra Mohanty (1922–90) was an author, critic, columnist, editor and politician. He received the Sarala Samman for *Kulabruddha* and the Sahitya Akademi Award for his novel, *Nila Saila*.

Tarun Kanti Mishra (b. 1950) is the author of two novels and over 300 short stories. He received the Sahitya Akademi Award (2019) for *Bhaswati*, a collection of short stories, and lives in Bhubaneswar.

Umacharan Digal (1942–2013) was an accomplished poet in the Kui language.

Upendra Bhanja (1670–1740) hailed from a dynasty family and was known as Kabisamrat. A widely respected poet-composer of classical Odissi music, he is most known for his Odissi songs and epics like *Baidehisa Bilasa, Labanyabati* and *Koti Brahmanda Sundari.*

Translators

Aditya Nayak (b. 1997) translates works from the Odia to English and vice-versa. He has four publications to his credit. His English translations of two critical essays were published in a volume by Routledge titled *Critical Discourse in Odia.* His English translation of Gopinath Mohanty's *Utkalamani* has been published by Odisha Sahitya Akademi.

Ajit Kumar Kullu (b. 1985) is a poet, editor and translator. He is the translator of *Dawn Rhapsodies,* a collection of poems, and *Preetilagna and Other Stories*, a book of stories. His areas of interest are translation studies, cultural studies and tribal literature. He is an assistant professor of English at Sambalpur University and lives in Jyoti Vihar, Burla.

Animesh Mohapatra (b. 1982) teaches English literature at Delhi College of Arts and Commerce, University of Delhi. His research interests include literary history, translation and print culture. He has co-edited *Critical Discourse in Odia* (2022), a volume comprising twenty-five Odia essays in English translation, which forms a part of the series titled *Critical Discourses in South Asia.* At present, he is translating and editing *Madala Panji,* a pre-colonial chronicle of the Jagannath Temple written in Odia.

Anita Resma Guria (b. 1987) is a teacher at the Government High School, Kacharu, Kuarmunda. A resident of Dahijira, Kutra, she belongs to the Munda tribe and is a literary enthusiast. She speaks Munda, Sadri, Odia, Hindi and English.

Anpa Marndi (b. 1981) is an assistant professor at Utkal University. He writes poems in Santali, his mother tongue, and is the recipient of Sahitya Akademi's Yuva Puraskar (2014).

Asima Ranjan Parhi (b. 1971) is an acclaimed academic, critic, translator and poet. His book *Indian English through Newspapers* is a path-breaking venture in the description and standardization of Indian English. He is the editor of *The Man and His Creations*, an anthology of essays on Gopinath Mohanty, and *Makers of Modern Indian Literature: Rajkishore Pattnaik*, a monograph, published by Sahitya Akademi, New Delhi. His poetry collection, *Of Sons and Fathers*, has been reviewed and taught widely. A professor of English at Utkal University, Asima lives in Bhubaneswar.

Bhagirathi Mishra (b. 1958), a poet and translator from Odisha, he has published four collections of Odia poems: *Jatipata* (1987), *Akasha Khoja* (2000), *Bhababhaunri* (2008) and *Mane Achhi Na Abakash* (2015). He has translated many poets of national and international repute into Odia and has been published in different Odia literary journals.

Bidyut Bhusan Jena (b. 1984) is a poet and writer. He has two poetry collections—*Pages* (2019) and *A Letterbox across Time* (2020)—to his credit. He teaches literature and philosophy at Christ (Deemed to be) University, Bengaluru, India.

Bikram K. Das (b. 1935), a former professor of English at the Central Institute of English and Foreign Languages, Hyderabad, is a linguist, lexicographer, editor of textbooks, and translator of Odia fiction and poetry. He was the recipient of the Sahitya Akademi Translation Prize in English in 1989 for *Paraja*. His English translations of a few Odia classics include the works of Gopinath Mohanty, Sitakant Mahapatra and Pratibha Ray, all winners of the Jnanapith Award.

Birendra Kujur (b. 1978) from the Kishan[iii] tribe is an independent scholar. A PhD in Odia from Sambalpur University, he specializes in tribal literature and culture. He speaks Kishan, Sadri, Odia, Hindi and English.

Chandrahas Choudhury (b. 1980) is a novelist and literary critic. He is also the author of the novels, *Arzee the Dwarf*, *Clouds* and *Days of My China Dragon.*

Chinmoy Jena (b. 1951) is a poet and translator. His poetry collection *White Addition Black Total* was published in 2019. Along with literature, his passion is cricket, which he played for Odisha. He is currently serving as a member of the Cricket Advisory Board of the Odisha Cricket Association.

Chittaranjan Misra (b. 1959) is a bilingual poet, critic and translator. He has translated Albert Camus' novel *The Outsider* and four plays by Harold Pinter into Odia. An author of seventeen books, including his research-based work, *Harold Pinter: The Dramatist*, Chittaranjan's poems and papers have been published in national and international journals.

Chonhen Ekka (b. 1960) from the Oraon tribe is a farmer by profession and loves her culture. She resides at Kesramal Badkatoli, Rajgangpur, Sundargarh, and is conversant in Kudukh, Sadri, Odia and Hindi.

Gopa Ranjan Mishra (b. 1954) is a poet, translator and academic associated with many educational institutions as an adviser. His latest English translation was *Birds of Water* (2023), a collection of Odia poems by Jayanta Mahapatra.

[iii] Kishan is one of the sixty-two tribes of tribal people residing in Odisha. They prefer to call themselves a branch of the Oraon tribe and mostly live in western Odisha. Though originally hunters and gatherers, they have been, as their name suggests, primarily cultivators.

Himansu S. Mohapatra (b. 1958) is a critic, translator and former professor of English. He has translated, with Paul St-Pierre, the Odia novel collective *Basanti* (2019), Jagadish Mohanty's *Battles of Our Own* (2022), and J.M. Joardar's *Following My Heart* (2023). His latest rendering is *The Life and Times of Banka Harichandan* (2023), a composite novel by Dipti Ranjan Pattanaik.

Jatindra Kumar Nayak (b. 1956) is a former professor of English at Utkal University. He is a recipient of the Hutch-Crossword Book Award (2004) and the Katha Translation Awards (1997). He is a member of the English Advisory Board of Sahitya Akademi. His English translations of classic Odia novels include Chandrasekhar Rath's *Yantrarudha* (Astride the Wheel, 2003), Fakir Mohan Senapatis's *Mamu* (The Maternal Uncle, 2007) and J.P. Das's *Desh Kal Patra* (A Time Elsewhere, 2009). He has co-edited *Reminiscences: Excerpts from Oriya and Bangla Autobiographies* (2004) and *Memory, Images, Imagination: An Anthology of Bangla and Odia Writings on Colonial Burma* (2010).

Kalidas Misra (b. 1955) taught at the Department of English, Sambalpur University in October 2015. His doctoral dissertation titled 'The War Novel in America: A Study of Changing Response' received the Best Dissertation Award from the American Studies Research Centre (ASRC), Hyderabad, in 1989. He was a post-doctoral Fulbright Fellow in 1992 at La Salle University, Philadelphia, and Colorado State University, Ft. Collins, USA, and a Shastri Indo-Canadian Faculty Research Fellow in 1996 at the University of Manitoba, Canada. He has been published in *Indian Literature*, *New Quest*, *Chandrabhaga*, *Skylark*, *Four Quarters* (Philadelphia), *Indian Journal of American Studies* and *Journal of Contemporary Thought*.

Krishna C. Goudo (b. 1962) is a critic, translator and polyglot. He has three books to his credit. He was awarded the Shiksha Ratna Puraskar (2013) and Best Educationist Award (2015) for his contribution to teaching.

Madhusudan Pati (b. 1941) is an eminent professor, bilingual critic, translator and poet. He has translated Gangadhar Meher's *Tapaswini* into English and Tennyson's *In Memoriam* into Odia. An author of twenty-one books, he was awarded the Atibadi Jagannath Das Award (for 2015) of Odisha Sahitya Akademi. *Sanskrit Drama: A Critical Reappraisal* and *Bhagabat Gita: A Literary Elucidation* are two of his important publications.

Mani Rao (b. 1965) is the author of eleven poetry books, three books in translation including *Bhagavad Gita*, *Kalidasa* and *Saundarya Lahari*, and an academic book *Living Mantra: Mantra, Deities and Visionary Experience*. She has an MFA in creative writing and a PhD in Religious Studies. She lives in Bengaluru.

Manu Dash (b. 1956) is a bilingual poet (*Kala Harina, A Brief History of Silence*), editor (*Rebati: Speaking in Tongues, Anam Kabya Andolan* and), translator (*Bagha, Shakuntala, Mohan Das*), publisher (Dhauli Books) and director (Odisha Art & Literature Festival). An author of almost thirty books, Dash joined the Anam Writers Movement—an anti-establishment movement in Odia literature—shortly before the imposition of Emergency in India in 1975. He is the founder of Dhauli Books, which won the prestigious Publishing Next Industry Award for the Best Printed Book of the Year (Indian Languages) in 2018. Currently, he is editing *anām*, an international journal for literature.

Mousumi Patra (b. 1984) teaches English at Shaheed Bhagat Singh Evening College, University of Delhi.

Naku Hansdah (b. 1969), a bilingual author, also teaches Santali at Sambalpur University. Hansdah has written a few books in Santali and Odia, and is currently translating the Odia novel *Paraja* for Sahitya Akademi into Santali (Olchiki).

Panchami Manoo Ukil (b. 1967) is a birdwatcher, educator, wildlife photographer, conservationist, writer and translator. She lives in Bhubaneswar.

Purabi Das (b. 1967) is a writer, poet and translator. She has published several books including four volumes of poetry, two coffee table books, and a novel and two short stories in translation. Her latest work is a translation of a collection of Odia poems, *Claiming the Sky* (2023).

Samanjasa Das (b. 1965) has translated Odia plays *Mrugaya* and *Nalipan Rani Kalapan Tika* into English as *The Hunt* (2023) and *Queen of Hearts and Ace of Spades* (2024), written by Biswajit Das. He joined the Indian Revenue Service (Customs & Indirect Taxes) in 1990. He was awarded the Presidential Certificate of Appreciation for a distinguished record of service in 2006. He is currently posted as the chief commissioner of the Delhi Customs Zone.

Sandeep Sahu (b. 1960) is a senior Bhubaneswar-based journalist with thirty-seven years of work behind him. He has worked for a host of top media houses at the local and national levels, including BBC and *Outlook*. He writes two popular columns, 'Scandeep' and 'Dhinkishalaru Dhenkanal', in a news channel and Odia Daily. His book *Madam President: A Biography of President Droupadi Murmu* was published in 2023.

Sanskruti Pujari (b. 1999) is a content writer, poet, editor and translator. She is currently pursuing a career in academics in the field of English literature. She indulges in the theatrical arts and has a keen interest in collecting and reading books.

Siddharth Satpathy (b. 1978) is presently a fellow at the Indian Institute of Advanced Study, Rashtrapati Niwas, Shimla. He has edited a special issue titled *Between History and Literature: Essays for Dipesh Chakrabarty* for the journal *South Asian History and Culture* (2023). He has also co-edited a special issue, *Vernacular Victoria: The Queen in South Asian Languages* for the journal, *Victorian Literature and Culture*. He teaches in the Department of English, University of Hyderabad.

Snehaprava Das (b. 1956) is an author and prolific translator. She has been felicitated by various organizations for her contribution to the field of translation.

Sunanda Mishra (b. 1957) is a translator and homemaker. She divides her time between Bhubaneswar and the USA.

Sudeshna Mohanty (b. 1957) an alumnus of Miranda House, Delhi University, taught English in an affiliated college of Bangalore University. She has extensively translated the short stories of Gopinath Mohanty, a doyen of Odia literature. Her translated works include *Hidden Ganga and Other Stories* (2019) and a short story titled 'And the Tide Turned'. She co-translated *Oblivion and Other Stories* (2023).

Surendra Nath (b. 1958) is a translator, novelist and short fiction writer. He translates into and writes in English. He has translated the works of Haldhar Nag and other Sambalpuri-Kosali authors into English and compiled them into six volumes, under the series title of *Kavyanjali*. He has two novels to his credit—*Karna's Alter Ego* and *Kavach of Surya*. He lives with his family in Cuttack.

Tyagraj Thakur (b. 1986) is a teacher, researcher, editor, creative writer and translator. He has published research articles in journals and books of national and international repute. He has co-edited a book titled *The Unbilled Hour:*

Essays on Literature, Culture and Theory. His reviews of books like *Basanti: Writing the New Woman* and *Translating Odisha* have received a global readership.

Urmishree Bedamatta (b. 1975) teaches at the Department of English at Ravenshaw University. She is working on a research project that aims to produce a digital edition of the Odia Sarala Mahabharata and natural language processing tools for the Odia language trained on the Sarala corpus.

***

Acknowledgements

I express my deep sense of gratitude to all the translators for their enduring support for the project, which they displayed through their spontaneous generosity and readiness. Without their hard work and commitment, this volume would not have seen the light of day.

The copyright holders of original works were very kind to accord permission and I thank each of them for their unflinching cooperation. The website odiabibhaba.in, hosted by Srujanika, often proved to be a great help in accessing the Odia texts. Additionally, I am grateful to Prafulla Publications, Odisha, for permitting me to publish the essay of John V. Boulton and the Sri Aurobindo Ashram Trust, Puducherry, for granting the permission to publish the story, 'The Bridge in the Moonlit Night' by Manoj Das.

Though every effort was made to trace the copyright holders, a few of them could not be traced. Their consent will be duly taken at the time of reprint of the anthology.

I record my sincere indebtedness to the late Jayanta Mahapatra, Bikram K. Das, Dash Benhur, Jatindra Kumar Nayak, Kalidas Misra, Gopa Ranjan Mishra, Prof. Radha Madhab Dash, Asima Ranjan Parhi, Krushna Chandra Pradhan, Krishna C. Goudo, Santosh Kumar Ratha and Tyagraj Thakur, who have made immense efforts to make this project a success.

I would like to give thanks to Himansu S. Mohapatra exclusively for imparting his valuable thoughts during the preparation of this anthology.

I am indebted to Milee Ashwarya, Moutushi Mukherjee, Aparna Abhijit and Premanka Goswami of Penguin Random House India for making this book happen.

A big shout-out to my family—my wife Jayashree Dash, children Mrinal Madhubrata, Mukul Mantosh and Manisha Manideepa—who were my rock while I was preparing this anthology day in and day out.

***

Notes

Editor's Note

1. Sachidananda Mishra, *Bhasatattwa Samikhya* (Cuttack: Lona, 1970), p. 64.
2. Bijaylaxmi Mohanty, *Bhasa O Lipi* (Bhubaneswar: Vidya, 2017), p. 10.
3. Pandit Binayak Mishra, *Odia Bhasara Itihasa, Barnamala O Dhwanitattwa* (Cuttack: Utkal Sahitya Press, 1927), p. 46.
4. Bansidhar Mohanty, *Odia Bhasara Utpati O Kramabikash* (Cuttack: Friends Publishers, 1970), p. 23.
5. Debi *Prasanna* Pattanayak, *Odia Bhasa O Bhasa Bigyan* (Cuttack: Grantha Mandir, 2007), p. 15.
6. Khageswar Mohapatra, *Odia Lipi O Bhasa* (Cuttack: Grantha Mandir, 1993), pp. 159–60.
7. Satyanarayan Rajguru, *Odia Bhasara Upabhasa* (Bhubaneswar: Odisha Sahitya Akademi, 2004), p. 73.
8. Bijoy Prasad Mohapatra, 'Agami Satabdi Payin Odia Bhasa', *Odia Bhasa Prasanga* (Cuttack: Grantha Mandir, 2006), p. 181.
9. Khageswar Mohapatra, *Charyagitika* (Cuttack: Friends Publishers, 1976), p. 43.
10. Bijaychandra Mazumdar, *History of Bengali Language* (Calcutta University, 1920), Lecture XIII.
11. Khageswar Mohapatra, *Charyagitika* (Cuttack: Friends Publishers, 1976), p. 43.

12. Surendra Mohanty, *Upodghata, Prachina Odia Kabita* (Bhubaneswar: Odisha Sahitya Akademi, 1984)
13. Pathani Patnaik, *Mahakabi Sarala Dasa* (Bhubaneswar: Odisha Sahitya Akademi, 1995), p. 3.
14. Jatindra Mohan Mohanty, *Sarala Dasa Rachana Sambhar* (Bhubaneswar: Vidya, 2010), p. 12.
15. Chittaranjan Das, *Balaram Das: Makers of Indian Literature* (New Delhi: Sahitya Akademi, 1982), p. 84.
16. Surendra Mohanty, *The Ornate Age in Oriya Literature and Dinakrushna* (New Delhi: Sahitya Akademi, 1985), p. 26.
17. Mayadhar Mansinha, *History of Oriya Literature* (New Delhi: Sahitya Akademi, 1962), p. 118.
18. Mayadhar Mansinha, *History of Oriya Literature* (New Delhi: Sahitya Akademi, 1962), p. 136.
19. Ibid, p. 140.
20. Ibid, p. 200.
21. Ibid, p. 150.
22. Dasarathi Das, *Kabya Bitana: Sabujaru Sampratika* (Cuttack: Biswabani, 1978), pp. *ka* and *kha*.
23. Annada Shankar Ray, *Sabuja Akshara* (Cuttack: Das Brothers, 1966), p. 2.
24. Nityananda Satapathy, *Sabujaru Sampratika* (Cuttack: Grantha Mandir, 1985), pp. 51–52.
25. Himansu S. Mohapatra and Debendra Kumar Dash, Foreword in *Rebati: Speaking in Tongues*, Manu Dash, ed. (Bhubaneswar: Dhauli Books, 2021), p. 25.
26. Manu Dash, 'Editor's Note', *Rebati: Speaking in Tongues* (Bhubaneswar: Dhauli Books, 2021), p. 11.
27. Himansu S. Mohapatra and Debendra Kumar Dash, Foreword in *Rebati: Speaking in Tongues*, Manu Dash, ed. (Bhubaneswar: Dhauli Books, 2021), pp. 36–37.

28. Mayadhar Mansinha, *History of Oriya Literature, Plays and Theatres in Orissa* (New Delhi: Sahitya Akademi, 1962), p. 220.
29. Mayadhar Mansingh, *Odia Sahityara Itihas* (Cuttack: Grantha Mandir, 1967), p. 337.
30. The Sahitya Akademi brochure on Manoranjan Das for the 'Meet the Author' programme on 26 November 1991.
31. Sharmila Chhotaray, 'Narratives of Regional Identity: Revisiting Modern Oriya Theatre from 1880-1980', Archives and Research Centre for Ethnomusicology, American Institute of Indian Studies, Gurugram.

'The Oriya Character'

1. *The People, Language and Culture of Orissa*, Artavallabha Mahanti Memorial Lectures (Bhubaneswar: Orissa Sahitya Akademi, 1966).
2. Narasingha P. Sil, 'Vivekānanda's Rāmakṛṣṇa: An Untold Story of Mythmaking and Propaganda', *Numen* 40 (1), 1993, pp. 38–62.

'Chaitanya in Oriya Literature'

1. Prabhat Mukherjee, *History of Chaitanya Faith in Orissa* (New Delhi: Manohar Publishers & Distributors, 2023), pp. 11–18.

'Literature and Wisdom'

1. 'The Literature of Knowledge and the Literature of Power', *North British Review* (August 1848). This was first published as part of a critical essay on Alexander Pope.

2. 'The Fruits of the Earth [French: Les nourritures terrestres]' is a prose-poem by André Gide, published in France in 1897.
3. 'The Two Trees' by William Butler Yeats, 1913.

'How and Why Sarala Dasa Translated the Mahabharata'

1. John V. Boulton, *Essays On Oriya Literature* (Odisha: Prafulla Publication, 2003), pp. 10–14.